"I've kept this library safe for hundreds of years. How can you think I'd shirk my duties now?"

Without preamble, an earthquake tremor shivered through the room. Baylee braced himself, amazed at how the books didn't fall from the shelves.

A cloud of smoke erupted from the top of the desk, taking the shape of a huge, naked humanoid. The smoke kept coiling and climbing. In less than a moment, the desk was gone, reshaped into a stone golem that stepped ponderously toward Baylee.

The golem stood nine and a half feet tall and was as broad as any two men. The stone flesh marbled, turning white under the ranger's lantern light. It opened its mouth in a soundless scream.

"In moments, this library will shift to the astral plane," the lich said. "There's nothing you can do to stop it. And once we get there, you won't escape this labyrinth alive."

Lost Empires

The Lost Library of Cormanthyr
Mel Odom

Faces of Deception
Troy Denning
(November, 1998)

FORGOTTEN REALMS ®

FANTASY ADVENTURE

Lost Empires
Book One

The Lost Library
of Cormanthyr

Mel Odom

Dear Matt Lane Odom,
Thanks for being part of my life, and bringing with it the understanding of what being a first born son is like from a different perspective. I appreciate your conversations and candor, and the thought you put into things as you seek understanding. I'll always remember that night in Ada when you were pitching a near-no-hitter. And thanks for lunch!
Love,
Dad

THE LOST LIBRARY OF CORMANTHYR
©1998 TSR, Inc.
All Rights Reserved.

Distributed to the book trade in the United States by Random House, Inc. and in Canada by Random House of Canada, Ltd.

Distributed to the hobby, toy, and comic trade in the United States and Canada by regional distributors.

Distributed worldwide by Wizards of the Coast, Inc. and regional distributors.

FORGOTTEN REALMS and the TSR logo are registered trademarks owned by TSR, Inc.

All TSR characters, character names, and the distinctive likenesses thereof are trademarks owned by TSR, Inc.

TSR, Inc., a subsidiary of Wizards of the Coast, Inc.
Made in the U.S.A.

Cover art by Alan Pollack
First Printing: March 1998
Library of Congress Catalog Card Number: 96-60823
9 8 7 6 5 4 3 2 1
ISBN: 0-7869-0735-5
8579XXX1501

U.S., CANADA,
ASIA, PACIFIC, & LATIN AMERICA
Wizards of the Coast, Inc.
P.O. Box 707
Renton, WA 98057-0707
+1-206-624-0933

EUROPEAN HEADQUARTERS
Wizards of the Coast, Belgium
P.B. 34
2300 Turnhout
Belgium
+32-14-44-30-44

Visit our web site at **www.tsr.com**

Prologue

North of Mintarn in the Trackless Sea
600 Years Ago

"May Lloth take your soul into her evil embrace, woman, as penance for killing us all!"

Her beautiful elven face drenched by the torrents pouring from the unbridled sea around them, Gyynyth Skyreach turned to face the speaker. Dark moonlight spearing through the black clouds overhead sparked fire from her pale green eyes. "On the contrary, Captain Rinnah, I ordered us into the only chance we had. If we'd tried to sail around the storm front, we'd have been caught by the pirates that pursue us."

The captain held on to the ship's rigging as his body swayed instinctively with the rolling pitch and yaw of his vessel. "Putting a dagger blade across the throat of every person on this ship would have been a cleaner death than the one you've ordained," Rinnah roared back at her over the crash of thunder and the horrendous splash of twenty-foot waves falling across the ship's deck.

"You should be directing your crew," Skyreach yelled.

"Those men hardly need any direction going to their deaths as they are!" Rinnah staggered as the ship wallowed between waves, tossed like a child's toy. Gallons of brine splashed across the deck, gathering into a force that swept men from their feet, broken only by the railing and the masts. A harsh, ragged yell started up somewhere behind the captain, then echoed down the side of the ship before it ended abruptly.

Skyreach steeled herself, pushing away the fear that threatened to consume her. The devotion to the quest she'd been given by her great-grandfather would see her clear. She wore her copper colored hair tied up and was dressed in a warrior's leathers. The metal breast plate she'd ordered readied before the sea

1

drank down the sun hours ago banged against the side of the ship, held by the braided leather thong she'd used to tie it into place.

Barely half the captain's size even though he was Tel'Quessir as well, she'd be washed over the side in a heartbeat if one of the treacherous waves caught her in the open. One of her leather gloved hands was twined in the ship's rigging. She held her long sword bared in the other, the runes etched dark in the metal. She was not used to having her decisions questioned, much less challenged. Her temperament would not allow it, nor would the station her great-grandfather had bequeathed her.

"I was told you were a brave man, Captain Rinnah," she said in acidic accusation. The tips of her pointed ears and parts of her face had gone numb from the cold that had descended with the storm over *Chalice of the Crowns*. Yet, still her anger burned hot within her.

Men scattered in all directions around them. The ship's crew tried to handle the lines of rigging. The sails had been dropped when the worst of the storm swept over them, but so many of the booms had broken loose the ship itself had become a danger.

The warriors that she'd led sought to maintain their positions along the railing, staying ready for the battle that she expected might yet come. Before the storm had arrived so quickly in all its gale and fury, one of the trio of pirate ships that had pursued them from the Sword Coast for the last few days had been closing in rapidly, finally cutting down on their lead.

"I am a brave man," Rinnah yelled. "But I have to admit, I am far, far too greedy. I should never have taken on this fool's quest no matter how much gold was involved. If we had jettisoned the cargo as I suggested—"

"That would never have been allowed," Skyreach promised.

The captain took advantage of a roll of the waves, managing a couple steps down the deck toward her. "You purchase my services, woman, you don't own me," he said.

Skyreach lifted her long sword in an eye blink, her arm bringing the weapon into line as natural as breathing. Her great-grandfather had seen to her tutelage himself, graced her with his motivations, and turned her relentless in the pursuit of his goal. She knew she'd kill the captain for his impudence alone, not even allowing the man the offense of laying his hands on her. But, perhaps, she still had need of his skill. That was the only thing that stayed her hand.

The long sword's point stopped bare inches from the man's face. She froze the ship's captain into place with the steel of her blade and the iron in her gaze. "Another step, Captain, and we'll both get a look at whatever guts you profess to have."

Rinnah started to say something, but he was interrupted by a squall from one of his mates.

"Caaaaptaaain!"

Skyreach kept her weapon ready.

Rinnah swiveled his head around. Big and burly, his hair a twist of wet knots and his finery all undone by hours spent in the inclement weather trying to find safe passage through the storm, he looked to be a ferocious opponent. A brace of throwing knives went around his waist on a weathered belt made of lizard skin. The scarred and worn handles of the knives showed much use and a certain . . . familiarity. He stared up at the crow's nest.

Skyreach looked as well, her arm aching with the strain of hanging on to the rigging. She peered through the sheets of needle-sharp rain whipped by the frenzy of the storm. She barely made out the crewman's pointing arm.

Aft of *Chalice of the Crowns*, a ship with full sails burst through the storm's darkness and gained rapidly. Its spinnaker was out before it, dancing wildly in the ripping winds. A trident of living lightning seared across the bruised sky, running almost horizontally at what seemed only a hand's span above the writhing black water. In the afterglow of the lightning, Skyreach spotted the flag snapping out from the main mast. The skull and crossbones looked stark, white on a field of black.

"Pirates!" someone screamed.

The cry echoed along the deck of *Chalice of the Crowns*, picked up by sailors and the men Skyreach led. She eyed her enemy grimly. She didn't know who had pursued them with such tenacity. The horde of darkness that had gathered to tear Cormanthyr down had drawn forces from everywhere. She did not know if the

City of Songs still stood, and that uncertainty had weighed so heavily in her heart these days that she had been gone from it.

Skyreach lifted her voice, bellowing above the swell of the waves and the thunder to the knot of men along the rail. "Scaif!"

A tall elven warrior turned to face her. He wore simple leather, but Scaif had been one of the most trusted men in her great-grandfather's courts. "Aye, milady."

"Get Verys to my side," Skyreach commanded.

"At once, milady." Scaif saluted, then tapped one of the warriors at his side on the shoulder. The warrior took off immediately but was overtaken by a roil of dark seawater. Miraculously, the man grabbed the railing around the central hold as he was washed across the deck, saving himself. He staggered to his feet as *Chalice of the Crowns* twisted again, then seemed to drop into a bottomless pit.

"Captain Rinnah." Skyreach made her voice unforgiving, pulling much of her great-grandfather's wrath into it.

The captain spun toward her.

When the ship bottomed out against the sea again, Skyreach thought for a moment that her legs weren't going to be strong enough to hold her. The railing abraded her palm even inside the leather glove, promising blisters on the morrow. She ignored the pain. She had never failed her great-grandfather while he was alive, nor would she allow herself to fail Faimcir Glitterwing's memory. She pointed her long sword at the approaching vessel and said, "Would you see your ship taken as a pirate's prize?"

The captain bared his teeth in a grimace of disgust. "Haven't you been listening to me, woman? We're all dead. The men in that ship are only fooling themselves to even pretend to think otherwise."

"We're not dead until I say we're dead," Skyreach yelled back in a harsh voice. Lightning cascaded across the dark heavens again, underscoring the terrible possibilities of her words. No one knew the capability she had—or was prepared to use. "Now, do you captain this ship, or do I give your first mate a field promotion?"

Chalice of the Crowns bucked again, surging up the next swell of the Trackless Sea. Water crashed onto the decks, spilling over the prow this time. Then she was clear again for the moment, plunging deep into another valley of waves.

Rinnah cast a hate-filled glance in Skyreach's direction, then turned and stalked off. He bellowed orders between his cupped hands, managing the water-slick deck with effort. In response to his orders, sailors clambered the rigging like monkeys. Sails were run up and let down. Cloth filled the rigging in broad expanses of sheet, eclipsing the dark sky. The fabric cracked in the irresolute grip of the storm winds.

Skyreach braced herself as the sails took hold. The ship surged into the wind. Before, *Chalice of the Crowns* had been a piece of flotsam trying to wait out the fury of the storm until calm returned. With the sails filled out, the vessel was a live thing fighting to free itself from the trap it was in, running mad as it was driven before the storm.

Rinnah scrambled up the stairs leading to the helm. He took the large wheel himself. Almost immediately, Skyreach could feel the difference the man's hand made upon the tiller. *Chalice of the Crowns* came about slowly, fighting the sea as it cut through the waves and gained speed. Gradually, her prow came around, putting the wind behind her sails. The ship suddenly dropped again as the sea slipped out from beneath her.

A wave, fully as tall as any sea giant Skyreach had ever heard of in any tale, whipped across the deck. The elven warrior lost her footing for a moment. Only her tight grip on the rigging kept her from being swept overboard.

Her hand burning like she was holding live coals, Skyreach pulled herself back to her feet. Out across the sea, the pirate ship drew even with them. White foam broke across the vessel's prow. Lightning split the sky, igniting the metallic scale and cut glass encrusted visage of the Eye of the Deep that had been worked into the prow. The beholder-kin lived only at great depths in the sea. The artist who had rendered the reproduction had worked masterfully, making the obscene round body as large as a man, including the ten eye-stalks, the great, staring, central eye above a slash filled with razor-sharp teeth.

Then the terrible sight was extinguished as the quick burst of illumination from the lightning disappeared. Skyreach tightened the grip on her long sword. Squinting against the drumming rain that came as hard as barbed darts, the elven warrior estimated the distance separating the two ships to be less than twenty paces.

The pirate vessel closed, coming up alongside *Chalice of the Crowns*.

"Milady, I am here." Verys came to an uncertain stop at the railing beside Skyreach. Thin and nervous, the old man looked bedraggled in his sopping clothes. Still, he carried his signal flags at his side.

"Is your group in place?" Skyreach asked.

"Yes, milady." Verys had marched as a boy with her great-grandfather, quickly rising to captain of one of Faimcir Glitter-wing's signal corps.

Skyreach didn't insult the man by looking around for his group. If Verys said they were there, then they were there. She watched the pirate ship cutting through the crashing waves of the sea. The prow of the other vessel cleared the water and hung for a moment, like it had suddenly taken wing from the gusting winds. Then it slapped back down, almost burying the prow under the sea. *Chalice of the Crowns* behaved in the same manner.

More men yelled in fear and anger. A man tumbled from the rigging above Skyreach. The sailor slammed against the main deck with a sickening thud and remained still. His neck was at an unnatural angle. The corpse stayed there only the space of a drawn breath, then the hungry waves came slavering across the deck. When the foamy sea water recessed as *Chalice of the Crowns* crested the next wave, the body had disappeared.

Skyreach murmured a quick prayer to Rillifane Rallathil, god of the wilderness that she found herself so far from now. Corman-thyr had been the only home she'd ever known. Evermeet was only a place her great-grandfather had bade her visit a few times, not home at all. And it lay days in her future. Provided she had a future. She swallowed hard and remembered her great-grandfather's words and the importance of the duty she was doing.

"Ready the mages," she told the signalman.

"Yes, milady." Verys chose his flags, one scarlet and one white, then waved them in prescribed patterns. "They are ready."

Peering across the roiling waves, Skyreach saw the humans lining the side of the pirate ship. Lightning flickered, burning reflections from the burnished pieces of the crew's armor and their bared weapons. She knew none of them, but she had no doubt that they knew her. Faimcir Glitterwing had acquired a number of enemies over his long life span. Her great-grandfather's stand against allowing humans into Cormanthyr despite Elminster's arguments that had swayed Coronal Eltargrim and the Elven Court had never wavered.

She didn't hate the humans. At least, she didn't hate all of them. There were many who'd been brave, and had died defending Cormanthyr against the Army of Darkness that had gathered to bring the city down. But there'd also been many who'd tried to ransack the city and the homes of the inhabitants on their way out of town. Some of those had died on her sword. What *Chalice of the Crowns* carried was only a fraction of what remained to be taken out of the doomed city. It represented her great-grandfather's legacy. She would not let it be taken.

The rustle and snap of fabric as well as the sudden movement to her right drew Skyreach's attention forward to the prow. The ship's spinnaker shot into the air, catching the rush of air as it blossomed from its storage area. The circle of cloth reached out like a giant fist and gripped the wind. *Chalice of the Crowns* pulled free of the sea, suddenly more sprightly.

"We're outrunning them!" Verys crowed.

"Not for long," Skyreach said. Though the woods were her home of choice, her great-grandfather had seen to her education even in boating. Sailcraft had been one of the old man's loves, an interest he'd carried with him since childhood. If they'd lived nearer the ocean, had more business there, Skyreach had no doubt that they would have owned a ship instead of her having to lease one for this voyage. "If the captain of that vessel has come this far, through storm and all to pursue us, I think he has a trick or two up his sleeve as well."

Captain Rinnah fought the wheel, his voice belaboring his men in hoarse shouts. They moved the sails, making the most of the wind.

Skyreach moved toward the knot of her warriors. Naked steel gleamed in their hands, desperation lighting dark fires in their hollowed faces.

"Milady," Scaif greeted. "The archers want to launch a few shafts at the enemy."

"Wait," Skyreach said. "The waves and the wind will only make their shafts too uncertain. Exposure to this rain will loosen the strings in short order, then they'll be worthless. We'll have need of them later."

Scaif nodded. "As you wish."

Abruptly, the pirate vessel dropped back as *Chalice of the Crowns* jerked forward with renewed speed. A ragged cheer started up among the ship's crew. Skyreach's men took up the cry, banging the flats of their swords against the railing. The elven warrior didn't give in to the emotion of the moment. Even if they managed to escape the pirates, the storm remained to threaten them.

She glanced forward, seeing *Chalice of the Crowns*'s own spinnaker suddenly exploding forward as it continued the seize the wind. The cloth hollowed and filled, becoming an alabaster full moon against the dark sky.

Rinnah squalled orders to his men amid curses at them and promises to his god. In that moment, seeing the man at the wheel, Skyreach knew he was right about her. She *had* led them to their doom.

She hardened her heart and her thinking. There had been no other choice, no other way. And the cargo the ship carried was much too precious to let fall into the hands of humans. So much of Faimcir Glitterwing's life's work was wrapped up in that cargo. Yet so little of it had they been able to carry. The other journeys that would be required to claim the rest of her great-grandfather's legacy would require even more cunning to complete. Only certain knowledge that his legacy would be well guarded until her return had given her the strength to leave it.

The humans deserved whatever hells they wrought for themselves. And if there was a way, Skyreach would send Coronal Eltargrim there among them.

"Verys," she called.

"Aye, milady."

"Signal the warriors to assemble properly. I want them in diamond formation if we have to close with the other ship." Skyreach scanned the other ship through the darkness, her eyes burning with the effort and the blowing brine picked up in the gale.

Verys gave his signal.

Chalice of the Crowns bucked through the waves again, twisting before it came down into the water again. The ship tilted sickeningly hard to port, and Skyreach was suddenly facing a wall of writhing water that seemed about to suck her into it. Then the ship straightened itself again, cresting another wave.

A ragged cheer started along the ship's crew and Skyreach's own men. It was quickly extinguished when they spotted the pirate vessel cutting through the brine less than ten paces off the starboard. Lined up along the port side of *Chalice of the Crowns*, Skyreach's men were out of place to defend the ship.

"Order them to the other side," Skyreach snapped.

Verys hurriedly did as she bade, his flags snapping code in short arcs.

Skyreach released her hold on the rigging and plunged across the deck. The wooden deck raged across the wallows of the cruel sea, making footing treacherous. The slick scum left by the lapping brine contributed to the danger.

Even as trained as they were, Skyreach saw a handful of her men go down in twisting heaps as they lost their footing across the deck. The careful formations they'd arranged themselves into were suddenly confused and broken.

The elven warrior stumbled across more than ran across the deck. She fell, caught herself on her hands, and forced herself back to her feet. A curling wave caught her, rising almost to her knees, and the spitting spume splashed across her, drenching her even more. She felt clothed in liquid, only the harsh bite of the leather breaking that illusion. Verys struggled at her side. She reached out and helped the man to his feet.

"Thank you, milady."

Reaching the other side of the deck, Skyreach saw the grappling hooks launched from the pirate vessel claw for *Chalice of the Crowns.*

"Cut the ropes!" she yelled. Lifting the long sword, she brought the keen edge down against a grappling hook's trailing rope. The hemp was tightly wound, and it took two more blows to completely sever it. The grappling hook, a trident of curved metal, dropped at Skyreach's feet. She kicked it away, then it vanished in a new coil of waves that slapped across the deck.

A long, feathered shaft embedded in the railing before her. The barbed head sank through the decorative gingerbread of the railing, stopping only inches from Skyreach's abdomen. More arrows from the pirate ship suddenly thudded into *Chalice of the Crowns.*

A jagged lightning bolt seared through the dark sky. The illumination temporarily washed away the shadows clinging to the pirate ship. Humans were there, but among their ranks Skyreach also noted dwarves and kobolds. She did not doubt that the crew knew exactly what they were after. Faimcir Glitterwing's legacy would draw many hunters.

"Signal the archers," Skyreach ordered Verys.

The man flagged rapidly.

Skyreach moved along the railing as her men regrouped themselves. The archers drew their bows and strung them with difficulty.

A number of grappling hooks had found the side of the elven ship. Axemen from among Skyreach's warriors brought their weapons thudding down against the ropes. But they were left open to counter-attack. Arrows from the pirate ship cut down the number of axemen, as well as the other elven warriors.

The sea floor dropped away unexpectedly. Skyreach grabbed for the railing, maintaining her precarious balance. Water rushed in over and through the railing, drenching her. Salt stung her eyes and she blinked them clear.

The pirates gathered along the railing. Knots of men hauled on the grappling ropes, securing them around spars. Sections of the railing splintered and pulled free, but others held. The pirate ship created a staggering amount of drag on *Chalice of the Crowns*, but the other ship suffered as well. Much as it tried, it couldn't hold against the elven cargo vessel's heavier weight. Skyreach had seen to it that the holds were a full as they could be.

Chalice of the Crowns jerked like a fish at the end of a line as it fought with the water and tugged at the grappling lines. Chunks of railing floated on the sea, riding out rolling waves. Those loose timbers became dangerous weapons as well when the ocean shoved them back aboard the ship.

The elven warriors struggled to hold their formation, but the combined elements of the storm, sea, and pirates kept them off balance. At home in the woods around Cormanthyr, their foes would never have stood a chance.

"Signal the archers," Skyreach ordered, "to fire at will."

Verys complied.

Even over the rolling thunder of the storm and the protests of the lines and masts aboard *Chalice of the Crowns* Skyreach heard the thrum of the elven longbows. The shafts pierced the flesh of their enemies at once, breaking the spine of the first attack as men fell back and cursed their shield mates to stand forward.

Skyreach couldn't count the dozens of foes spread across the other ship's railing, but their sheer numbers told her that she had been betrayed. Someone with in her great-grandfather's courts had told the raiders what the prize aboard *Chalice of the Crowns* was. Or someone had paid dearly for the ship's capture.

She didn't try to fathom who the traitor might have been. There were many in Faimcir Glitterwing's House who felt she should not have received custodial responsibility for the wealth he had amassed. She had even agreed. But it had been her great-grandfather's bequest, announced by the law-reader after his death.

The problem was, there was no one she trusted more then herself.

The archers fired freely, and the shafts vied with the falling rain to fill the air. Human, dwarf, and kobold fell backward or over the side of the pitching railing as the arrows took them. But more men stepped forward. In the next few heartbeats, more and more of the elven arrows shattered against the leather and iron shields held up in defense.

Chalice of the Crowns squirmed at the end of the lines binding her to the pirate ship. Then the pirates began to take up slack, hauling irresolutely on the ropes, gaining speed and strength in their endeavors with each handhold of success.

"They're going to close with us, milady," Verys announced. His flags dripped water, but their bold colors stood out in the storm's lightning bursts.

Skyreach knew it was true. She swung her long sword and hacked at another grappling line. "Signal the mages."

Verys popped his flags at his team.

Almost immediately, Skyreach could feel the mystic forces that sparked around her. She was very sensitive to any actions conducted through the Arts, even had some of the talent herself and had a modest list of spells she could perform. Besides the sword, she'd been schooled in spellcraft as well, learning of it even if not possessing the means.

She swung her sword once more and saw the reinforced rope's last remaining strands part. The grappling hook spilled into the churning sea.

"Verys, signal the axemen to follow me," she said as she started forward toward the prow of the ship. Nearly a dozen axemen trailed after her before she'd gone ten paces. They looked questioningly at her as she turned to face them.

"Free the prow," she ordered, pointing at the grappling hooks holding fast the ship's nose. "Free the prow and maybe we can yank away from the pirates."

The axemen fell to at once, hacking with enthusiasm inspired by desperation.

Skyreach looked back at the cargo ship's bow. Captain Rinnah stood at the great wheel, his shoulders hunkered against it to show the strain he was physically under while manhandling his vessel. "Verys, send a runner back to the captain. Let him know we're trying to free the prow."

Verys signaled quickly.

Skyreach didn't check to see the effect. Gazing across the

harsh spume of the sea trapped between the two ships, she saw a group of pirates reacting to her own attempt to hack the forward grappling lines free. Archers fell into position, covered by shield carriers. Arrows descended like carrion birds, ripping into the unprotected flesh of the axemen.

One of the axemen went down at Skyreach's side, a cloth yard shaft through his neck. The elven warrior didn't hesitate, sheathing her sword and taking up the double-headed axe from the man drowning in his own blood. She stepped forward, dropping the weapon over her shoulder, then swinging it over her head and down. The blade cleaved cleanly through the grappling line, thunking solidly into the wooden railing. She ripped the axe free and moved toward the next grappling line. When she'd sheared it as well, only two remained. They were both cut before she freed the axe again.

"Milady!"

Skyreach started to turn, but Verys collided into her, knocking her to the side. She reached for the man, believing he had only lost his balance. Then she heard the meaty smack of flesh being struck. The barbed point of an arrow sliced into the elven warrior's shoulder.

But it came through her signalman to reach her. He'd sacrificed himself to save her.

"Verys!" Skyreach held the old man to her, knowing the arrow's barb offered her no real threat and only a small discomfort. At the same time, it was taking Verys's life.

"Milady," the old man gasped, blood leaking from the corner of his mouth, "it was the least I could do. Your great-grandfather was my fr—" His eyes rolled up into his head as his body relaxed.

Two other arrows sank deep into the old man's corpse before Skyreach could take them to safety. Reluctantly, she laid Verys beside the railing. Water sluiced around him. She forced herself to her feet and looked back into the bow. "Rinnah!" she screamed, though she knew it was futile. The captain would never hear her over the thunder of the storm, the yelling of the men, and the sound of the dying.

Still, across the distance, the captain's eyes met hers, his gaze dark and seething despite the frenzy of cold rain between them. Rinnah bawled orders to his crew. The lines of sail changed. The big man hauled hard on the wheel, controlling the tiller.

Chalice of the Crowns came about slowly, fighting time and tide and ties to the pirate ship, thrashing amid the crashing waves. With the grappling hooks on her prow cut asunder, though, she began to turn away from her tormentor.

Skyreach fisted her sword, letting go the axe. It was too late to cut any more. The pirates were closing even more quickly than before. Their only hope lay in the other grappling hooks not being strong enough to hold the elven cargo freighter.

Chalice of the Crowns's spinnaker had emptied when she found herself crossways in the wind. Under Rinnah's skillful hand, the ship came about to port. In the next gale, the spinnaker filled once more, cracking loud enough to be heard over the storm.

A renewed cheer came from the throats of her men and the cargo ship's crew.

Glancing back, Skyreach saw sections of the railing come loose and drop into the sea. Scaif tossed her a salute, his proud face creased in a smile despite the blood streaming down from his forehead. His axemen had been busy as well, chopping away the supports that held the railing.

For a moment, Skyreach made herself believe they would make it if the storm did not take them.

Then her sensitivity to magic spells tingled again, becoming an almost painful itch. The smell of ozone pervaded the air. A sudden crash dimmed the noise of the thunder. Fire clouds suddenly wreathed the elven ship's sails. Timbers split from the horrendous impacts of the spell that reduced the ship's rigging to char. The impact knocked Skyreach from her feet.

The elven warrior scrambled at once, her hands struggling to find a grip anywhere on the slick timbers of the deck. She forced herself up, staying crouched to keep her balance as the ship reared again. Harsh light from the burning sailcloth above her limned *Chalice of the Crowns*, turning her decks into target areas. Arrows from the pirate archers took their toll, dropping men in their tracks for the sea to claim with the next wave.

The swarm of fireballs cast by a mage or collection of mages aboard the pirate vessel took away all of the cargo ship's drive. Instantly, *Chalice of the Crowns* was reduced to a prisoner of the sea, a plaything that would be discarded and swallowed whole once she turned wrong.

The pirates hauled on the grappling lines again. The distance between the ships lessened. Any of Scaif's warriors who dared attempt to cut the ropes died before they got close enough to sever a single strand of the hemp. The archers among the pirates evidenced their skill without flaw.

Only one man made it to the remaining railing. He raised his axe. Then a curling flare of lightning spanned the distance between the ships and caught him full in the chest. His blackened husk hit the deck. The corpse rolled for only a moment as the deck rose and fell, then a swell of water washed it away, leaving nothing behind.

Skyreach had failed. She gathered herself, one hand grasping the long sword as the pirate ship came alongside. Swiftly laid planks bridged the gap between the ships and pirates flooded onto the deck of the elven ship Scaif rallied his men, urging them into the fray. But Skyreach knew it would only delay the inevitable. They would be taken, and the cargo would be stolen.

A grim smile twisted her lips as she staggered toward the cabins in the bow. She stumbled down the steps, finally giving up and letting herself fall from halfway down. Pain wracked her body, but she channeled it as she'd been taught, turning it into further energy to keep her moving. Hate and hurt, her great-grandfather had instructed her, were two things that could be attained through force of will, nourished, and used to get more from one's self than any other emotion save love. And love was far too costly and too narrow to be of use.

Rising at the bottom of the drenched steps, trapped water in this section of the ship already coiling around her ankles, Skyreach staggered down the line of cabins. The uncontrolled rocking of the ship threw her back and forth across the passageway. It wouldn't be long before the sea broke her, scattering all the treasures in the hold across the bottom of the Trackless Sea.

She stopped at the fifth door and rapped on it with the long sword's pommel. "Cylthik!" she called.

"Milady?" The voice on the other side of the wooden barrier sounded old, quavering and almost lost amid the plaintive creaks and groans of the battered ship.

"Open the door," Skyreach commanded, leaning heavily against the wood. Her elf vision helped her see through the natural dark. The water rolling through the passageway look black. A drowned rat slithered loosely across her boots, animated by the motion racking the ship. She turned away from the tiny corpse as the door beside her opened.

Cylthik stood before her, huddled in robes. His ever-present mage's cap rested askew on his head. Blood spotted the iron-gray cloak he wore. He was back-lit by a lantern hanging from the ceiling and sending twisted shadows spiraling across the walls.

"It's time," Skyreach said.

The old mage's eyes looked rheumy and unfocused. The gnarled staff in his hands possessed a clawed foot that it hadn't had before, and the talons were sunk deep into the hardwood deck. The old mage held onto it with both hands. "You are sure, milady?"

Skyreach was surprised when she found she had to release a tight breath before she could answer. "Yes."

"Would it not have come to this," the mage said, shaking his head.

"You have the strength?"

A new light flared within the old mage's eyes. "Milady, my magicks were something your great-grandfather counted on. I *never* let him down."

"Then don't let me down either."

His eyes locked with hers and held. "I will not."

An ache pierced Skyreach's heart, surprising her. She had always kept her distance from men and women she commanded, especially those like Cylthik who had known her as a child. Command was never easy, and familiarity—she'd been told—only bred contempt. She pushed the emotion away. "Thank you, Cylthik. Now see that it is done."

"And where will you be?"

"Up on the deck," Skyreach answered simply. "I have men dying there, to fulfill this mission that I undertook. There can be no other place for me."

"You great-grandfather would be proud."

"No," Skyreach said as she turned her back and started back along the passageway. "Faimcir Glitterwing would expect no less." Before she reached the top of the stairs coming up out of the passenger hold, she felt Cylthik's magicks cascading around her.

Above decks, the fires incinerating the sails had almost died out, but the light was replaced by lanterns held by the attacking pirates. The humans among them wouldn't have the excellent night vision of the elves. The expanding circle of lanterns marked the outer perimeters of the pirates' encroachment.

Reacting instantly, taking the pitch and yaw of the ship into account, the elven warrior parried the slashing thrust at her head, then riposted and shoved the point of her long sword deep into the man's throat. She yanked it out of flesh forcibly, lifting a foot and kicking the dying man in the face.

Gazing across the deck, she saw Scaif battling three men. The warrior's long sword and dagger seemed to be everywhere, and his footing was sure in spite of the wet deck. The dagger licked out suddenly, sending a pirate spinning away. Even as the man fell, his throat cut, two more pirates took his place.

Further down, Captain Rinnah held off a group of pirates with a belaying pin and a cutlass. The burly man roared with savage glee, almost sounding as if he was enjoying the fight despite the fact that his ship was coming apart around him.

Over half her warriors were dead. Skyreach figured that from the numbers she could count that were alive. Only a few of the bodies remained aboard the cargo ship. The sea had claimed the rest.

However, Skyreach knew that Cylthik's magicks would make the sea give up those dead. Their souls were already claimed by a service that they would not be released from. She moved out of the hold as two more pirates came at her.

Putting her back to the wall, she dropped into a defensive position.

"A woman!" one of the men roared. "I claim first rights!" He was middle-aged and gap-toothed, tattoos scoring the flesh of his cheeks.

"First, second, or thirtieth," the second pirate bellowed back, "it matters not to me. The feel of a woman's flesh is something I've been missing for too long now."

Skyreach didn't hesitate. Her left hand closed about the dagger at her hip, ripping it free. She parried the first man's thrust, taking advantage of their efforts to take her alive. The second man stepped in closer, thinking to be too quick for her. Skyreach swirled back around and opened a gash in the pirate's thigh near his crotch with the long sword. Only his quick reflexes powered by fear kept him from being unmanned.

"Damn her!" the pirate screamed, stepping back, his palm pressed to his wound. "Kill her and be done with it!"

Feinting, Skyreach whirled again, stepping into the other man's hasty lunge. The elven warrior lifted her dagger, holding it point downward from her fist. She whipped her arm back and sheathed the dagger into the man's gapped teeth. The point slid home easily, then became lodged in the spinal column at the back of the neck.

The wounded pirate lunged forward again, his cutlass hacking at Skyreach's face. She ducked below the blow and twisted away. As the pirate readied himself for another swing, she brought her long sword up and shoved it through the man's armor, through his breastbone, and into the heart beyond.

The pirate gasped and stiffened in surprise, gazing down at the enchanted rune blade that had run through his leather armor as if it were so much paper. He died and toppled over, sliding from the long sword.

Skyreach glanced out over the darkening waves. The moon retreated behind a bank of clouds as if afraid to see what would happen next. The deck of *Chalice of the Crowns* was lit only by the lanterns carried by the pirates and the few that hadn't been washed out along the cargo ship itself.

"Gyynyth Skyreach!"

The elven warrior turned at the sound of her name, tracking the voice through the crash and boom of the sea slapping at the cargo ship, and the pirate vessel pounding up against its prey. She spotted the man coming up the stairway from a lower deck, then recognized him by his movements and dress.

"Hagris!" The name ripped from her lips like an oath of the foulest nature.

Markiln Hagris gained the deck with acrobatic ease. Broad-shouldered and narrow-hipped, the man was Tel'Quessir, a Gold elf. He'd held a high station on the Council of Twelve. His armor would have prevented such physical alacrity had it not been mystical in nature and wrought from the best metalsmiths in the City of Songs. His face was lean as a wolf's, his nose as pointed. Long red hair was tied back in braids, trimmed to lend him an aristocracy that his features failed to give him.

He gave her a courtly bow, stooping low, but never taking his eyes from her. "At your service." His long sword gleamed in the lantern light.

"Betrayer!" Skyreach shifted on the deck, keeping her own long sword between them. "It was you who set these yapping dogs at my heels!"

Other pirates gathered along the outer edge of the deck, snarling foul oaths and making rude comments. Thankfully, the roar of the sea carried most of them away.

"Yes," Hagris replied. "Unlike many in Myth Drannor's courts, I believed in what Faimcir Glitterwing was doing. Preserving knowledge from the masses. There are things to be known only among the Tel'Quessir, and only a handful of them are to know it all."

"And you think yourself to be one of them?"

Hagris smiled. "Perhaps the *only* one if this does work out to your benefit." He raised his sword meaningfully.

"Yet you allay yourself with humans and kobolds, and social malcontents. No wonder my great-grandfather never allowed you into our home."

"His mistake," Hagris assured her, "and he paid his life for making it."

A chill ran through Skyreach at the confirmation. Rumors still circulated concerning the how of Faimcir Glitterwing's murder. She felt it change to anger, and held onto it. Cylthik's magicks rose stronger around her. The mage had prepared long for this day, all of them hoping against it.

"You've signed your death warrant," Skyreach said.

"Milady Skyreach, I seem to hold the view that I am in the position of signing *your* death warrant."

Behind the pirate leader, Skyreach saw the rest of her men being killed and cornered. They couldn't last but a few moments more.

"You can make this hard on yourself," Hagris said, "or you can submit. Either way, I shall claim what is mine. Your great-grandfather's collections are far more valuable than many were willing to believe. I'll have this ship, then I'll have the location of where the rest of it was hidden."

Skyreach shook her head. "You've laid down your life for nothing. You'll never have any of it."

"I beg to disagree." Hagris brandished his sword. "I have this ship. I have you. Soon, I'll know where the rest of it is."

Suddenly, the itchy feel of the magicks being worked around Skyreach gave way to a feeling of lassitude. "No," she replied calmly, "you won't ever have any of those things."

As if sensing the subtle change in the ephemeral himself, Hagris craned his head to glance out at the roiling sea. The waves were coming more huge now, buoying the two ships up higher, washing over the decks in increased rage. Masts gave way on both ships, timbers tangling in the sailcloth.

"What have you done?" Hagris demanded, shifting his attention to the restless ocean.

"My duty to my great-grandfather," Skyreach answered. "Having the cargo aboard this ship fall into the hands of others is unacceptable. I will not allow it."

A jagged streak of white-hot lightning seared the sky, showing two giant tentacles emerging from the ivory-capped foam. Both tentacles latched securely onto *Chalice of the Crowns*.

"*Squid!*" one of the pirates bellowed in terror.

The cargo ship suddenly jumped, then dropped abruptly, tugged deeper into the crashing waves. Water filled the holds, but Skyreach knew the cargo would be protected by Cylthik's spells and wards. The mage had bound powerful forces to his bidding, including the giant squid that was pulling the cargo ship under.

Hagris turned to Skyreach. "You selfish wench, you've undone us all!"

Skyreach eyed him coldly. "You're the second man tonight to accuse me of that. No one will have my great-grandfather's legacy. No one who is not deserving and worthy, and not until Toril is ready for it once again."

With an inarticulate cry of rage, Hagris threw himself at her.

Skyreach met his challenge with steel, sparks flaring from their blades. His fellow pirates had fled, running across the decks toward the dubious safety of their own ship. Maybe they would have time to cut loose before the squid pulled *Chalice of the Crowns* to the briny deep, but Skyreach doubted it. Her arm moved her long sword, countering Hagris's blows but finding herself unable to land any as well. They were too evenly matched.

Then the sea rose from their knees to their chests.

Hagris tried to turn and flee, but couldn't. "My feet are stuck to the deck!" he blurted in horror.

Skyreach tried to move her own feet, and found that Hagris's predicament was hers as well. She glanced at the rest of the ship, finding pirates and elven warriors and ship's crew likewise adhered to the deck. Everyone aboard was doomed, held like flies in amber.

Fear swelled within her, but she kept it at bay, accepting the fate that lay before her. It was all part of keeping her duty to her great-grandfather. Then the sea closed over her head, at first cold to the touch and leeching the warmth from her body. Instinctively, she struggled against it, fought against drawing the briny liquid into her lungs.

The time came when she could no longer fight the impulse to breathe. She drew in great draughts of the salt water, filling her veins with ice.

And she began to change, to become something both stronger and weaker, something that would hide her great-grandfather's legacy forever.

1

We've been followed.

Resting his shovel in the dark, fresh-turned earth of the tree-covered hillside, Baylee Arnvold gazed up at his companion. *We weren't followed.*

I told you back at Waymoot that I thought it was a possibility.

Yes, you did, Xuxa, Baylee replied calmly in the telepathic communication that his companion excelled in, *and the candle maker that you believed to be following us had the scare of his life when I jumped him in the alley behind Beruintar's Bone Warmer. If I hadn't been worn out from doing without sleep over the past days, I would never have fallen for your paranoia.*

Have you ever noticed that you never call it my paranoia when I'm right? Xuxa sounded put out. She was an azmyth bat and had been with him for a handful of years, taking part in a number of excavations and explorations. She was three feet tall, twin-tailed, and her body colored emerald green, her wings only slightly lighter in color, like the beard at her throat. Her intelligence was high, but her telepathic communications with him usually interpreted themselves with his words to ease in understanding. Still, a few strictly bat-thoughts occasionally intruded into their conversations. She was his companion by choice, in no way a possession. Blessed with a life span of over a hundred years, she was decades older than Baylee and sometimes grew irritated that he did not give that more credence when they disagreed. Like now.

Baylee didn't reply. His companion was right, but he'd be damned if he gave Xuxa the satisfaction of admitting it. At least, not right away.

He was following us. Xuxa sniffed in disdain, a delicate snuffling sound that hardly carried beyond their current site.

He was going to the back door of the inn to sell a tenday's supply of candles.

The man got you to believe that. I am not so gullible. And here we are, out in the open on this hillock with no place to turn.

Baylee knew his companion was right about being alone. Seventeen miles north of Waymoot, six miles west of Ranger's Way (the trail they'd followed into the city) there was no one around save a few hunters they'd passed hours ago. They'd taken pains to see that the hunters never saw them, even though he still didn't believe they'd been followed. Still, there were many who would have killed for the piece of lore he hoped to uncover tonight.

He gazed at the surrounding forest, the setting sun adding a red and purple haze to the darkening sky. He felt at home here, though he'd only visited this part of Cormyr rarely. His true home in his heart was the Sword Coast, filled with all the old histories and wars that had left scars still to be found on the earth.

And there were the various treasures left to be uncovered as well. Those provided a siren call Baylee found irresistible. No matter how often he followed a barely tangible lead to a dead-end, every success, regardless how small, served to drive him on.

The wind shifted, blowing more toward Baylee. His sensitive nostrils picked up the faint scent that did not mix in well with the fragrance of the surrounding foliage.

You smell it too, Xuxa said.

Yes. Baylee admitted it readily. Mixed in with the scent of trees and blossoms and grasses, with the musk of wild deer going into season, he smelled human sweat. A few moments more, with the wind just right, and he would have known whether there was one or more, whether it was male or female.

Then it was gone.

The way the scent disappeared, with nothing visible on the horizon, let him know the disappearance was deliberate. The knowledge raised the hackles at the back of his neck. Even if he hadn't admitted being wrong, Xuxa would sense his reaction and know. He cursed and turned his attention back to the shovel and the excavation he'd worked so diligently on for hours. His leather gloves and armor chafed at his sweat-drenched skin, and his muscles ached from days of hard travel and the effort of digging deep into the hillside.

He picked up the shovel and wiped his brow, as if he was reluctant to contemplate returning to his task. The whiff of the scent returned to his nostrils. This time he was sure: it was definitely feminine. A faint waft of Arabellan herb soap traveled with it, letting him know the stalker was no stranger to good, and expensive, hygiene. It was a solid clue to the stalker's identity. Local brigands didn't care much for cleanliness.

He took his waterskin from his pack on the ground and drank deeply, using the movement to mask his gaze roving over the surrounding tree line. Forests provided much in the way of natural hiding spots to someone who knew how to use them. And evidently the person or persons stalking him knew the wind changed and took steps to prevent being found out.

Have you seen anyone? he asked his companion.

No.

Have they seen you?

I don't think so.

Good. Then let's keep it that way. Baylee dropped the waterskin back to the pack.

The hole he'd dug was precious little more than broad enough to accommodate his shoulders. He'd hauled the loose soil and rock out in a bucket he kept in a bag of holding in his pack. Determined effort allowed him to reach a depth of nine feet. By his own estimates, he could scarcely be more than inches away from his goal. The arrival of the stalker could not have been more ill-timed.

He made as if to climb back into the hole, hoping the slope of the hill and the mounded earth blocked him from view. He let go the shovel and slithered forward on his belly, taking care not to make noise. He marked time by counting heartbeats. Only a few minutes remained open to him to move before the watcher realized no sound of shovel blade cutting into the earth issued from the tunnel area.

He got to his feet behind a pine tree, hidden from the watcher's point of view by the broad limbs. *Anything?* he asked.

No, Xuxa replied. *Be patient. Be quiet.*

Baylee gazed up at the tree where his companion held watch. Xuxa remained hidden even to his trained eye. But he knew the azmyth bat was sheltered in the tall cedar overlooking the dig.

Baylee moved lithely through the forest, relying on his ranger's skills. Something short of six feet in height, and slender despite his broad shoulders, he wore his mane of black hair loose, tied back now by a rawhide headband stained deepest blue. Clad of the forest, he wore deerskin breeches, a sleeveless deerskin shirt, and knee-high moccasins crafted of jaculi skins. The particular tree snakes used in his boots were from poisonous boomslangs. The hides were supple, carefully crafted together, waterproof, and maintained some of their ability through magic to blend in with their surroundings from the lightest greens to the darkest black.

Bronze skin, kissed by tropical suns as well as the Sword Coast where he'd grown up, marked him as an outdoorsman. A handful of scars tracked his arms and face, leftover reminders of brushes with fang and claw, and weapons. His eyes gleamed harsh jade like a cat's, captured in them the intensity of the wild.

He worked his way around the area he held suspect in his mind. Xuxa's telepathic ability only extended sixty feet or so. In a few more strides, he would be out of the azmyth bat's range, having only his own senses to depend on. The only weapon he carried was the dagger he used for meals, and to clean and skin wild game. He'd been trained by his mentor to rely on his wits, not the weapons most men carried about.

The lack of weapons, Fannt Golsway had often reiterated, made a man use his head. And it made him make certain his needs and wants were attended to by something more than a mere moment's passion or a passing fancy. Of course, Golsway was also a mage. Baylee would have relished having some of the old man's abilities at the moment rather than the meager few spells known to him through his ranger studies.

Xuxa's telepathic voice interrupted Baylee's thoughts, sending the ranger to ground. *Someone else is there.*

Baylee peered through the thick cover of forest, still counting his heartbeats. The woman had to know by now that he was taking much too long. She would be getting nervous. He pricked his ears up as the wind washed gently around him, hoping to pick up a fragment of conversation if she spoke to anyone with her. *Who?*

A small group. I have not seen them, but I have seen their passage.

Turning his attention to the forest, Baylee noticed a raven take wing over a hundred yards away. Other birds rippled in an unsettled manner along a trail to the south, and the silence followed behind. The thick forest prevented view of the small party there, but Baylee believed that it had to be a group rather than an individual from the size of the disturbance. *Separate from the first?*

Yes.

Maybe we should consider discretion. Baylee froze behind a lightning-blasted ash that had maintained growth in the lower branches.

That would be my advice, Xuxa replied. *Though you've seldom heeded it.*

We'd be leaving the dig site open for them, clearly marked. Even from his position now, Baylee saw the dig site easily.

Perhaps nothing lies at the bottom of that abandoned well.

Neither of us believes that.

The bat gave a grudging reply. *No.*

Then there is no choice, Baylee said.

Maybe in your afterlife, you'll be granted the ability to know if the leads you followed this time did indeed bear fruit. Even for a highly intelligent azmyth bat, Xuxa exhibited a disturbingly acidic sarcasm.

I can't leave it.

I know. I'll be with you, friend Baylee. Whatever you should need.

The bond between Baylee and Xuxa was something more than mere ties between a ranger and a companion. Past companions had never been as close or gotten to know him as well. But then, Xuxa was the first that had the ability to really get to know Baylee. He knew Xuxa would never willingly leave him. In the past five years, they'd never been separated despite all the hardships endured.

Choosing an aggressive stance in light of the things that faced him wouldn't endanger only himself. Baylee would be risking Xuxa's life as well because the bat would not leave him.

The ranger glanced back at the pit he'd dug into the hillside. He was so close; he felt it. And it had been so long since he'd had a find of any real significance—intolerable months. The chance at this one had been hard-earned, and now it would be hard won.

He couldn't give it up.

Silently, he shifted, choosing to go for the woman first. *If you can, keep me informed.*

Yes.

Baylee moved silently through the forest. He was as at home in the verdant green as he was on the unforgiving sea or on the highest mountain or in the crypts, tombs, and burial sites he'd prowled through. He'd seen them all in his twenty-seven winters.

He followed the land, gliding over it with sure-footed grace. He passed by squirrels and a lark in trees and brush, never startling any of the animals with his presence. The woman stayed within the forest. He wondered if she was aware of the other party as well. If she was who he thought she was, he was certain she'd have noted the other group. And if they were not with her, he knew she'd have been busy trying to figure out what to do.

He rounded a final copse of trees, down in a gully that was awash with dying leaves and broken branches.

He pushed all stray thoughts out of his mind, concentrating on one problem at a time. From his earliest youth, Golsway had chided him constantly about taking on more than he could handle. But the eagerness in him was something that he had trouble containing. That same eagerness was what had prompted the old mage to invest so much time in an orphaned youth begging scraps on the streets, and what had ultimately driven them apart when Baylee had been a young man come into his own vision of his career.

If he did find what he was seeking in the abandoned well, Baylee had promised himself to return to Waterdeep after the ranger forgathering at the Glass Eye Concourse and show Golsway the item he hoped to recover. Maybe it wouldn't bring them together again as they had been, but there'd been almost three years between visits as well. They'd grown; he had, at least, and maybe Golsway had softened with the years. How much remained to be seen.

The scent of soap and woman strengthened in Baylee's nostrils. This time, the wind also carried a hint of lavender blossoms. His heart quickened in spite of the situation. He was sure his instincts were correct.

Stepping over broken branches and bits of forest debris, the ranger made his way to the bottom of the gully. Footing was made more treacherous by the rocks exposed due to run-off and the waves of twisted dead grass trapping branches. A single snap of dry wood would carry for several paces in all directions.

He paused at a blackberry bush, staying well out of reach of the brambles. Even though they couldn't bite into his leather clothing, the thorns would catch and jerk as he moved away, possibly alerting the others in the area.

The woodcraft of the small group to the south was lacking. Their feet clumped through the forest, loud to the trained ear. Baylee smelled them as well, breathed in the foul odor of the long-unwashed and the sulfurous taint of fear. They weren't sure of themselves, and that was good.

Whether they trailed him or the woman remained to be seen. There were those who had placed prize money on Baylee's head for past transgressions, and there was the possibility that he'd been recognized in Waymoot despite his precautions.

Baylee pressed on, moving slowly, parting the branches and brush ahead of him and making sure he didn't move too fast as he slipped through them. The incline ahead of him grew steeper, broken by trees stubbornly growing out from the gully sides. Darkness continued descending over the forest.

A soft rustle of leathery wings sounded behind Baylee.

Xuxa's telepathic voice tingled into his mind to reassure him. *No one saw me.*

Have you seen them?

No.

Baylee scanned the forest briefly, but the azmyth bat remained out of sight. He turned his attention forward, scanning up the gully wall before him. Shadows twisted and writhed ahead and to his left. Squinting, he made out the figure lounging there.

The woman crouched in the gathering gloom. Something edged gleamed in her hand.

She holds a hand crossbow, Xuxa said.

The announcement confirmed again Baylee's guess as to the woman's identity. He smiled in spite of the situation he found himself in. Jaeleen always added the spice of danger to any meeting between them.

Yes, Xuxa said, reading his thoughts. *And that has never been a good thing.*

I believe I asked you to stay out of my mind when you weren't invited, Baylee retorted.

Thoughts like that are hard to avoid. I am quite sensitive, after all.

And a busybody.

Were we not in such dire straits, Xuxa threatened, *we would discuss that accusation at length.*

The azmyth bat never discussed anything that wasn't at length. Baylee made a mental note to apologize some time before their eveningfeast to avoid the discussion. Hopefully they would be more occupied with their find.

He breathed shallowly, waiting as the woman turned her attention from the dig site to the approaching company of men. The smell of their pack animals lingered in the air, mute testimony to the fact they'd been ill-treated over whatever distance they'd covered. Easing a branch aside, the ranger peered at the woman.

He kept his eyes from directly resting on her. Most people had the ability to know when they were being stared at. Jaeleen was a warrior herself, trained in frontier woodcraft, though certainly not of ranger caliber.

She hunkered down next to a thick-boled oak tree. Early in spring, the oak seeds still fell to the earth in waves, twirling endlessly with each new breeze. Already the seeds clung to her homespun clothing, taking away some of the alienness of her that didn't fit in the forest.

Her face was as he remembered it, triangular, with a short nose and a generous mouth. Her yellow-gold hair blazed under the hooded brown cloak. The homespun clothing masked some of the generous curves of her body, but couldn't hide the fact that she was all female.

She held the hand crossbow in her gloved right hand and glanced back along the trail she must have made in her journey through the forest. Only a few bent grasses remained to mark her passage. She'd been careful. Most people would never have been able to trail her. Someone among the pursuing group must have known woodcraft.

I could go scout them and report back, Xuxa offered.

No, Baylee replied. *You could be seen. That's a risk we don't need to take yet. Jaeleen may know who they are.*

She may not be inclined to share that information.

Baylee grinned, feeling his spirits soar as he contemplated the coming confrontation. Fighting in the forest was something he was very familiar with. He dropped a hand to the ground and gingerly lifted small rocks from the gully side. He discarded them patiently, searching for ones that were about the size of a robin's egg, as round as he could manage, and worn smooth as churned butter to the touch. By the time he had a dozen of them located and pocketed, the first noises of the approaching party reached him.

The scrape of steel against leather sounded totally out of place in the forest. Horses blew their breath out in tired nickers.

Jaeleen shifted, laying her hand crossbow over a tree limb in front of her, a fletched bolt locked into place. Nestled into the side of the gully as she was, chances were small that she'd be spotted right away, and her position was defensible. Even with numbers on their side, the approaching group was certain to lose a couple members or more. Jaeleen was deadly with her little crossbow, and even more deadly when a man came within embrace of any of the small knives she kept secreted on her person.

Still, Baylee knew the woman would be overrun. He reached for his belt and loosened the strip of heavily worked deerskin hiding inside it. Holding the ends between his fingers, he took a rock from his pocket and placed it in the end. The pocket formed around the stone instantly, turning the simple piece of leather into a sling.

He clasped the sling in his hand, then moved forward into the open, gliding between the leaves and the branches. Jaeleen had her back to him. He made no noise that she could hear.

Coming up behind her, he reached forward and clapped a hand over her mouth. She struggled immediately, becoming a hellion in his grasp. Baylee used his body weight to subdue her, managing it with difficulty because he didn't want to hurt her.

She waved the vicious little hand crossbow and tried to bring it to bear.

Baylee kept his hand over her mouth. She bit him, and her teeth penetrated the rough leather of his gloves with enough force to hurt but not break the skin. "Jaeleen!" he hissed into her ear. "Be quiet, or you'll have them down on us!"

She stopped struggling, but her body remained tense. He released his hold on her lower face. She turned her head to look at him.

"Baylee?"

He met her gaze. "Yes."

Without warning, she kicked him betwixt wind and water.

I warned you about her, Xuxa said. *She knows no allegiance except what she gives willingly. You do not mean as much to her as you think.*

Baylee rolled away to deflect part of the kick. But he crashed through the dead leaves and branches scattered across the ground, causing a great deal of noise. As he got to his feet, he heard orders bellowed in the distance. Then the sound of running feet echoed through the forest, approaching quickly.

Jaeleen leveled her hand crossbow at Baylee's chest. Her finger whitened on the trigger.

2

"Baylee!" Recognition dawned in Jaeleen's eyes over the edged bolt of the hand crossbow.

"Yes." Baylee took a tentative breath, really surprised when it didn't hurt too badly.

"What are you doing here?" Jaeleen remained behind cover, her attention divided between the ranger and the approaching group bashing their way through the forest.

"Camping," Baylee replied. He turned his own attention to the crashing noises coming through the brush. The group no longer worried about remaining quiet. He pointed at the hand crossbow. "Would you mind aiming that somewhere else?"

Jaeleen shifted the crossbow, but not far. She reached up and knocked leaves from her hair. Oak seeds whirled around and descended to the ground. "You expect me to believe you were camping?"

"Not since you've been spying on me."

Dark anger coasted across the shadowed planes of the woman warrior's face. "Spying is kind of a harsh term, don't you think?"

Baylee let some of his own anger sound in his voice. "What exactly would you call it?"

Jaeleen's mouth made an O of surprise. "You think I followed you here!"

"I've been here for hours," Baylee retorted, "and you've only just arrived. What would *you* think?"

The crashing through the forest neared, sounding remarkably like hounds taking to the brush. The bellowed commands became clearer, and this time Baylee was able to recognize the language being used.

An orc raiding party, Xuxa said. *They must have cut your trail, or the woman's.*

"How dare you think I would follow you! I swear by the fair hair

32

of Tymora, my chosen goddess, that I had no idea you were here until I saw you on that hillside!" Jaeleen looked indignant.

Her words rang true, but Baylee knew the woman had the gift of making any implausibility sound like the truth. He'd had experience. "Then what are you doing here?" he demanded.

She hesitated. "Traveling."

Baylee snorted his disbelief, an obscene sound that Xuxa instantly rebuked him for through their silent communication. "Ranger's Way is six miles to the east. You're out in the rough."

"I was hoping to shave a few days off my journey to Plunge-pool."

"What business have you in Plungepool?"

"I went to see the falls, if it's any business of yours," Jaeleen snapped. "Which, of course, it isn't. I've heard a lot about the area."

"You've never been there?"

"No."

Baylee struggled to believe that. Still, most of the times he'd occasioned to meet Jaeleen had been along the Sword Coast. Though there had been that time in Mulhorand when he and Golsway had recovered the Orb of Aurus, which had contained a codex that had given scholars clues into one of the dead languages contained in that country.

It had been the third meeting with Jaeleen, and the first time they'd been intimate with each other, giving in to the impulses both had. However, Jaeleen had taken advantage of that tryst to steal the Orb of Aurus. Golsway had been incensed, and it had taken them six days to track her down and steal it back only moments after she'd sold it to a rival collector. She got to keep her money, and Baylee and Golsway had barely escaped with their lives. The Orb was now part of a collection in Candlekeep where scholars still worked on divining the languages detailed in its codex.

"Why are you on your way now?" the ranger asked.

"I was responding to an invitation."

"From whom?"

"Tarig Phylsnan."

"Who is that?"

"I don't owe you any explanations," Jaeleen retorted angrily.

"You're here," Baylee replied, "and you've brought a war party of orcs down on us."

"Me?"

"You!" The ranger was surprised at the feelings of jealousy that assailed him. After all, Jaeleen was most likely the last person he'd ever want to trust again. Memory of the wine of her lips and the smoothness of her skin haunted him at times, up in the stillness of the mountains or the deep of the forest. Golsway had always assured him that those feelings would someday be followed by the kiss of edged steel. Baylee didn't doubt his old mentor's words, but the temptation blew fire through his veins at times.

"I didn't bring any orcs with me."

Baylee!

The ranger turned in response to the telepathic warning screamed into his mind. His gaze swept the tree line to the south as the first of the orcs burst into view.

The creature screamed at once when it realized it had been seen, an ululating wail of presumed triumph. The orc wore a mustard yellow tunic that showed days of accumulated wear, and months of hard usage. Tears revealed the rusty chain mail beneath. An open-faced iron helm covered its head, baring the brutish snout and close-set eyes. The mottled gray-green skin showed lighter against the onset of night.

Baylee turned instinctively to protect Jaeleen. He flipped his hand, dropping the length of sling and seating the round stone. He whipped it around his head and took a step forward. He released the stone before the orc had covered another three paces.

Moonlight glinted off the upraised axe in the orc's hand. Then it disappeared as the stone struck home, shattering the creature's low forehead between its eyes. The orc dropped to a suddenly silent heap on the forest floor.

Baylee seated another stone as two more orcs crashed through the wilderness and came at him. He glanced over his shoulder to check on Jaeleen, finding her in full flight a half-dozen paces away.

And you risk your life for someone such as that, Xuxa rebuked.

It wasn't like I thought about it, Baylee responded, falling into cover beside the oak tree. *It was a reflex.*

Faugh! You humans would do better off going into season once a year and having done with it. At least there would be an end to such foolishness and it would not insist on being a constant part of your everyday life.

Baylee snapped another stone toward the approaching enemy. The stone bounced from one of the orcs' chests with a metallic thud.

The orc stumbled and almost fell. Hoarse gasps exploded into the clearing as it fought to recapture its breath. The creature's companion ducked into cover, drawing back the string of its bow. At least eight others moved through the forest around Baylee.

The ranger turned and ran after Jaeleen. His longer legs gave him the edge over the orcs for the moment. As he ran, his mind raced, laying out the terrain for the coming battle. Giving up the dig before he'd fathomed the truth of it was not an option. His muscles responded somewhat sluggishly, his body already taxed by the days of traveling through the brush and the day spent working his way deep into the earth.

Leathery wings beat the air above him.

Xuxa, he called.

I am here, Baylee.

Stay with the girl. Protect her if she needs it. Baylee saw her again, still fleeing through the forest, instinctively reading the terrain herself and making for a defensible position. Her rapid departure from the area bothered him somewhat. Together, they could have made a stronger stance against the orcs. And Jaeleen had weapons.

We owe her nothing.

No, but I mean to see her protected. Still in full flight, Baylee sprang for a thick limb overhead. Skillfully, he transferred his forward momentum into climbing as he scampered up the tree as easily as most men might scale a ladder. The leather work gloves protected his hands from the rough bark. He carried the sling in his mouth as he took care not to disturb the branches with his climb.

My place is with you.

Xuxa, please don't argue now.

The azmyth bat made a sound of displeasure.

Glancing upward through the tree, the sky limned by the quarter moon and looking a dark sapphire color now that the sun had dropped below the rim, Baylee saw the angular bat's body suddenly flip in mid-flap and alter course. *Thank you.*

Be safe, Baylee. Until we are together again. The bat streaked after the woman.

Baylee felt Xuxa's presence fade from his mind as the limits of the bat's telepathic abilities were exceeded. Being separated from Xuxa seemed unnatural after all these years. Even when he dropped off to sleep, Xuxa's mind-voice was generally the last thing he heard of an evening.

Jaeleen reached the high ground near the dig site, choosing an area that was ringed by high rock and dense brush. Her chances of holding the position looked good. But the probability remained that the orcs would choose to starve her out.

Baylee didn't intend for that to happen. He smiled grimly as he scouted the terrain and spotted the advancing line of orcs. Apparently none of them saw him take to the trees. They concentrated their efforts on closing on Jaeleen, calling to each other in their rough tongue. Baylee could only make out snatches of conversation. Even his prodigious knowledge of languages, both spoken and written, was taxed to figure out the orcish communications. Despite having common roots, few of the orcs held a common tongue.

The ranger moved through the trees with hardly a rustle. Exploring the elven environs of Cormanthor, in particular those in the Tangled Trees after Fannt Golsway had been invited by one of the elven families to pursue a lost cache of heirlooms thought destroyed when Myth Drannor fell, had schooled him in the ways of woodcraft. His mentor had only been partially successful in recovering the lost items, but in the months that Baylee had lived among the elves, he'd learned how to pass through the trees as if born there.

He swung from the branches, and landed with sure-footed balance on chosen limbs, closing in on his target. The orcs had the advantage of being able to see in the night, but Baylee's own abilities had been sharpened by long living in the wild. He hunted as easily by night as by day, moved as quietly. Catacombs often held no light either, save for torches carried along for that purpose. And those had to be used sparingly. He hadn't always made it back out with benefit of light. So he'd learned to trust his other senses and his intuition.

He hurled himself through the air again, landing on a thick-boled limb thirty feet above the ground. A pair of orcs ran through the brush, their path taking them beneath the tree he'd chosen.

The ranger released a tense breath and focused all his attention on the orcs. Both of them neared the base of the tree. Baylee let himself down through the limbs hurriedly, avoiding dead branches that could break off and fall below to warn the orcs. He dropped the final six feet, having no choice if he wanted to arrive in time.

He hooked his legs around one of the lower branches, then fell so he hung upside down. Both orcs heard him and tried to figure out where the sound came from.

"Cat!" one of them yelled out in warning.

The forest held a number of feline predators, including leopards. Baylee had witnessed them in his travels since leaving Ranger's Way. He reached down and grabbed the second orc's head. Hanging by his legs, making any use of his upper body strength was difficult. Still, he managed to cup the orc's skull tightly and twist.

The orc's spine splintered.

Baylee released the corpse and it collapsed to the ground. Evidently enough noise had been made to warn the orc's companion. The creature turned around in surprise and nocked an arrow to the short bow it held.

Hanging upside down from the tree branch, Baylee stared death in the eye. The shifting of the orc's shoulder told him when the arrow was about to be released. The ranger threw himself to the side. The arrow fletchings slipped along the side of his face, letting him know just how close it had been.

On his way to the ground, he flipped in midair and landed on his feet. The orc screamed out a warning to the others of its party. The sound of running feet started immediately toward Baylee.

Seeing the human still alive sent the orc into a panic. The creature drew back to the shelter of a nearby tree as it tried to nock a new arrow.

Baylee sprang forward, reaching for the orc. He seized the creature's head and slammed it into the tree hard enough to smash its skull. The orc let out a long breath, shivered, and died in the tangle of roots thrusting up from the ground.

The ranger gathered the short bow and the quiver of arrows. A quick count showed him fourteen arrows in the quiver. He took five of them out, fitting one to the string and taking four more up in his left fist, holding them with the bow, managing the handful with ease.

Though Golsway had been reluctant to allow Baylee to carry weapons, he had seen his apprentice trained in their usage.

Happily better armed, Baylee faded into the darkness of the forest. It was time for the hunted to become the hunter.

* * * * *

"Detestable creature," Jaeleen said aloud. Her words dripped spite and venom.

Roosting upside down high overhead in the tree the woman hid under, Xuxa regally chose to ignore the woman and sent her senses ranging far out, seeking Baylee. She touched the minds of two of the orcs and retreated instantly by choice.

Orcs had such narrow, closed minds filled with horrific dreams fueled by the smell of blood. Xuxa shuddered, re-closing her leathery wings about herself. She still could not sense Baylee, and she was beginning to feel somewhat anxious.

"I know you can hear me," Jaeleen called out from below, "and I know you're up there."

Then do us both a favor, Xuxa flashed at the human woman, *and shut up.* She intentionally made her telepathic voice loud enough to hurt.

Jaeleen loosed an oath, summoning up a colorful, but wholly inaccurate family history for azmyth bats in general, and Xuxa in particular.

Xuxa ignored the outburst. Seated in the upper branches of the tree, she had a good field of view. Her night sight stripped away the dark shadows twisting across the land. One of the orcs had closed the distance between itself and Jaeleen to sixteen paces. Feeling disgusted, Xuxa also noted that the human female still did not register the orc.

Baylee would never make such a mistake, the azmyth bat knew. She had trained the human ranger to be alert to everything going on around him, and she took pride in Baylee's skills, which were well beyond those of most humans.

The orc continued creeping up on Jaeleen.

Xuxa briefly considered sending a warning to the human female and letting her fend for herself, but decided not to. In the ensuing fight, Jaeleen might manage to get injured, and Xuxa didn't intend to listen to Baylee berate her for it. And there was a certain amount of territorial pride involved since Baylee had made the woman her charge.

Unfurling her wings, Xuxa let herself fall from the branch. She dropped like a stone, emitting her high-pitched squeak too high for either humans or orcs to hear. The sound bounced back up at her from the forest sward, instantly letting her know how near she was to her quarry.

She broke her fall at the last possible moment. Her leather wings stretched out and caught the wind, straining her muscles and the tendons of the joints. She rode the breeze, arrowing at her target.

In the last moment of its life, the orc noticed the azmyth bat coming at it silently. The orc shifted defensively against the movement, raising its club.

Xuxa knew the orc probably hadn't even identified what she was at the time she struck. Not wanting to take a chance on the opportunity presented her, Xuxa screamed again. The sound waves bounced back at her, bringing the orc into clearest focus for her bat senses.

She twisted in the air violently, bringing her twin tails stabbing into flesh while her fangs sank deeply into the orc's throat. In a flicker, she unleashed the lightning charge bottled up inside her.

Overcome by the onslaught, the orc tumbled to the ground, smoke rising from its twitching body, unable to even manage its own death throes.

Xuxa frantically beat against the wind to gain altitude quickly. She swooped around, circling the tree where she had left Jaeleen. Her keen eyes picked the woman out of the darkness.

Jaeleen leveled the hand crossbow. Her hard eyes projected anticipation.

Miss, Xuxa promised in a whispering voice in the woman's mind, *and I won't.*

Jaeleen snarled an oath and lifted the weapon clear. "Have I ever told you how much I hate flying rodents?"

Xuxa flew to the top of the tree and took up her search for Baylee again. She remained aware of Jaeleen below. The woman scurried for Baylee's shovel and dropped into the hole the ranger had dug. The shovel's blade bit cleanly into the dark earth.

Xuxa shifted along the branch. She could neither sense nor see Baylee, though she was aware of the orcs as they pursued something through the forest.

Then her attention was divided as the shovel Jaeleen wielded so vigorously broke through into hollow space. The azmyth bat peered down.

Jaeleen dropped to her hands and knees, tossing the shovel to one side. She dug frantically into the earth, enlarging the hole she'd made.

Xuxa felt anxious. Baylee had been so close to the prize he had sought. Now it appeared he was to lose not only that prize, but perhaps his life as well because of the treacherous woman below.

And even as she thought it, Xuxa knew that Baylee would probably never see it that way. She threw herself into the air.

3

Baylee ran along a thick-boled branch twenty feet above the forest floor. Moonlight splintered through the leaves and limbs in brief flashes.

"There!" an orc yelled in one of the few words the ranger recognized. Harsh clucking followed as other orcs took up renewed pursuit.

A spear slashed through the trees, burying itself in a tree trunk in front of Baylee. He slapped it away with his free arm and kept moving.

Measuring his stride, Baylee hit the last bit of safe footing he guessed that he had on the rapidly thinning branch. He flexed his knees, riding out the spring of the limb as it bent, then threw himself forward. Graceful as he'd become over the years since his teaching in the Tangled Trees, he knew he only grasped a fraction of the woodland elves' skills in their chosen terrain.

The branch had little spring to give, so he didn't gain height, but it did allow him to leap toward the branch on the next tree he'd selected. His boots hit the rough bark and skidded. For a moment he thought he might slip and fall, then his feet found the friction point. He stood, swayed on bent legs, then turned to face his foes.

Four orcs twenty paces away searched the trees for him. Their rheumy eyes glistened sickly in the dark.

Changing his stance to properly bring his target into view, Baylee drew the arrow he had ready on the string, braced into place by his finger. The shaft felt surprisingly true and straight for an orcish weapon. The grain of the wood slid along his skin, speaking volumes of skill of the arrow's making. The fletchings brushed feather light against his cheek and remained stiff and aligned. He guessed that the bow and arrows were stolen, and not long ago at that.

Both eyes on his target, Baylee released half a breath, held it, then released his shaft. The arrow leaped from the bow as fast, straight, and deadly as a falcon cutting air after a dove. Before his first arrow took the rearmost orc in the throat, the ranger had another arrow on the bowstring. He released again at his second target.

The first orc seized the arrow that suddenly feathered its throat and made choking noises. The creature took a few halting steps, pulling weakly at the shaft. The second arrow slid into the face of another orc, burying itself to the fletching in an eye socket as the arrowhead crashed through the back of its skull.

The remaining orcs howled in fright as they saw the one in front of them fall dead, its head snapping cruelly as the spent force of the arrow turned it. Both of the unwounded creatures turned to be confronted by the one drowning in its own blood behind them.

The hesitation gave Baylee time to get off two more shafts. The first sped true, snapping into place beneath the helm of one orc and cleaving the creature's backbone. The second shaft buried itself in the side of the last orc but did not slow the creature's frightened run back into the forest.

Keeping an arrow nocked, Baylee took four more arrows from the quiver and fisted them with the bow. He moved instantly into the shadows in case he had been spotted.

He stayed with the trees, moving silent and quick. His mind searched for Xuxa, thinking he might be within range of the azmyth bat's telepathic range. *Xuxa.*

I am here, Baylee. Her mental voice sounded distant and anxious.

Baylee took a final look around. Only two orcs appeared to have survived the encounter and were hastily making tracks out of the forest, pausing only long enough to gather the horses tied beneath a copse of trees a hundred paces distant. *What's wrong?*

Jaeleen has found the sacrificial well of the trollkin you sought.

A smile tweaked Baylee's lips in spite of the fact that Jaeleen was so close to the prize he'd come seeking. *Surely you didn't think she just happened along out here.*

No.

Baylee turned his steps toward her, following the lay of the land.

42

Never once had he not known where he was during the course of the battle. *I killed six of the orcs.*

I have killed one.

Baylee dropped to the forest floor. Another few paces and he crested a hill that overlooked the dig. He peered through the shadows and spotted Xuxa only through practiced effort near the top of the tree. Jaeleen was nowhere to be seen. However, the meaty smack of the shovel blade biting into the earth echoed to Baylee's ears.

Keep watch, Xuxa, he said as he moved for the dig.

Baylee crept up on the hole and looked down into it. Jaeleen was on her hands and knees, digging with grim determination. Seeing the hole widening before the woman fired Baylee's blood. A wide grin filled his face. He had known the well couldn't be much farther down.

Jaeleen looked back over her shoulder as she took a broad-bladed knife from her trail kit. "Are the orcs gone?"

"Yes," Baylee replied. "The ones that aren't dead."

"Tymora willing, there are more dead than alive."

He gave her a tight nod, slightly put off by her apparent blood-thirstiness. Though they were orcs and would have spilled his life's blood, the ranger felt that all life was precious. He culled stories from the ages, walked the paths of men and women, humans, dwarves, and elves, learned how they'd lived and how they died. In that pursuit, he had learned to revere much about many people.

"You always were good in a fight," Jaeleen acknowledged. She snapped a glance at him, her face showing thinly disguised impatience. "Those orcs will be back soon, you know."

"I know."

"Then help me! By Tymora's grace, we will be long gone from here by the time the survivors are able to find us, and interest another group of orcs in attacking us."

If she didn't need your help, Xuxa announced, *she'd have been praying that you'd be as dead as those orcs out in the forest.*

You're wrong. She's not like that. Baylee stepped into the pit he'd been working on. There was barely room for them both. Their bodies brushed together, and he was too well aware of her scent, thinly disguised beneath the lingering trace of Arabellan herb soap. *Not all the time.*

Dragons, Xuxa assured him, *are less greedy by nature. You live in the wild, friend Baylee, and you should know these things. My nature and yours . . . there are things we would never do. She is too civilized to trust.*

Keep watch. The azmyth bat's silence rebuked Baylee. He picked up the shovel. "Move aside. We'll be here all night while you pick at those stones with that toy."

Reluctantly, Jaeleen slid aside. "Dare we risk a light?"

"The orcs already know we're here. A light can do no real harm." Baylee rammed the shovel home. "How did you find out about the well?"

Jaeleen rummaged in her trail kit and brought out a compact oil lamp hardly bigger than her palm. It had six sides and seemed to be constructed more of glass than of worked metal. The glass sides held tiny etched figures of silhouette dancers. She spoke a quiet word Baylee could not catch. Obediently, the lamp's wick ignited. A warm glow grew from the lamp, bathing the dig site.

"You still have Yarik's lamp, I see." Baylee slammed the shovel against the stonework of the well. A chunk of mortar and rock broke free. He saw it fall and heard it echo as it scraped the sides on the way down.

Jaeleen pushed the lamp toward the opening. The darkness within retreated slightly, becoming an ellipse trapped in the mouth of the well that went down ten feet. "I didn't hear it hit."

"No," Baylee said with conviction, "it's supposed to be bottomless."

The woman glanced up at him, her eyes widening slightly. "You're joking."

He kept his face serious with effort. Jaeleen had always lorded it over him that she knew more than he did when he'd been Golsway's pupil. That hadn't stopped in the days since Baylee had been on his own, even though they both knew it wasn't true. "What have you been told about the well?"

Jaeleen shrugged. "Not much. I only just found out about it." She paused, looking deep into his eyes in that way that she had that Baylee found so damned irresistible. "Probably not nearly as much as you have."

"Probably not," Baylee agreed. "May I have the lamp?"

She handed it over somewhat reluctantly.

"I heard the tale in Jester's Green two tendays ago. You know where Jester's Green is?"

"North of Suzail." Baylee was intrigued. He had heard of the legend himself in Dhedluk while searching for another treasure altogether. Mention of the sacrificial well of Vaprak had been contained in a history of herbalist's lore the ranger had borrowed from a private library in the town to conduct research. The writer had been a native of Waymoot back in the days when the trollkin ruled the hills around that city, attacking caravans and travelers at their leisure. "Who told you the tale?"

"They have a number of soldiers garrisoned there." Jaeleen peered over Baylee's shoulder.

From the periphery of his vision, Baylee saw the smooth, rounded curves of the woman's breasts pressing from the top of her bodice as if they were going to fall out. He reminded himself to breathe.

"Those soldiers were all too willing to try to impress a woman with a nice smile and seeming innocence with their stories. Most of them were twice-told tales as stale as a fishmonger's love life. But, as you know, every now and then, there is that kernel of truth."

Baylee knew. He shifted, sending the lamp further down into the yawning mouth of the cursed pit.

"One of the stories told was by a retired sergeant of the Purple Dragons," Jaeleen went on. "As a boy, he'd lived in Waymoot. Most of the stories he told were of course about Lord Filfar Woodbrand, the local legend." The woman leaned in closer and her cheek brushed against Baylee's bare shoulder. The touch of perspiration covered skin was electric. "He told the story of how Woodbrand killed all the marauding trollkin in the area five or six times before he ever mentioned the well. In their day, the trollkin were very successful. A number of caravans as well as private individuals were murdered by the trolls. Thrown into this very well."

"That's not all of the story," Baylee said. "This well was used as a sacrificial altar for Vaprak. He put a permanent spell of silence over the well to mask the screams of the dying from any passers-by. That's why you didn't hear the rock hit."

"Then there is a bottom."

"Yes."

"What are we waiting for?"

"Because the spell of silence may not be the only magic Vaprak put over the well."

"The faint of heart never gets white meat at a family banquet," Jaeleen said.

"And the daring adventurous who leap before they look end up in unmarked graves," Baylee growled. It was the first rule Golsway had given him as a boy.

"Baylee," the woman urged, reaching out to turn his face toward hers with a soft hand. The lamplight made her blond hair glisten like spun gold. "Do you know what riches might be waiting down there to claim? For *us* to claim?"

"Wealth is a burden only weak men choose to carry," Baylee said. "I'd rather not have more than I can pack into a good travel kit, and what I can put into my head."

"That's only Golsway talking to you," Jaeleen said irritably. "I'd hoped by now that you'd learned to think for yourself."

The words stung Baylee, surprising him. He turned his attention back to the well and the lamp.

"I've offended you," Jaeleen said. "Tymora's sweet kiss, I'd not meant to do that, Baylee, truly."

Baylee wanted to believe her so badly. Too often in most of his travels, he encountered only those who measured life and the worth of a man in gold pieces. The friends that he could trust could be counted on the fingers of both hands. The ones he felt comfortable with asking for something that he could not get for himself could be counted on one hand with fingers left over. "I've got a climbing rope in my kit. Get it."

Jaeleen disappeared instantly from his side. She rummaged in his travel kit and brought the rope back. The ranger tied the string to the lamp through his belt, then took the rope.

I could go first, Xuxa offered.

No, Baylee replied. *I need you here in case something goes wrong.*

You need someone to watch your back if you're going to turn it on that woman.

And the orcs could come back and bury us all.

Go, Xuxa said. *If we are fortunate, you won't be out of my reach by mindcall.*

Baylee secured the grappling hook around a tree bole, then shook out the length of rope. Knots were already tied into it. He kicked the coil of rope into the well. The hemp slithered audibly for the first few yards, then became totally silent.

"What was the spell of silence for?" Jaeleen asked.

"Not all of the sacrifices were dead when they went into the well," Baylee answered.

Sobriety dulled the excitement in Jaeleen's features. She peered down into the well. "You've never said what you were here for."

"Before Woodbrand ended the trollkin raids, the well had been in existence for decades." Baylee said, testing the rope and finding that it held. He eased his feet over the well's edge, then put his weight on the rope. Satisfied it continue to hold, he started down, going knot by knot. Dust and rock debris tumbled down around him. He glanced up where the rope hung over the edge of stone above. Bracing his feet against the walls of the well, he took his weight off the rope long enough to slide a worked bit of leather under the rope to prevent the rough rock from sawing easily through. "I'm here to see what bits of the past might yet remain."

"You're talking about the dead Obarskyr kings that are purported to sleep somewhere beneath Waymoot." Jaeleen climbed onto the rope as Baylee made his way down.

Baylee went slowly, noting the scratches and old stains on the ragged walls of the well. The deep smell of must filled his nostrils with carrion and rot. He didn't bother to correct the woman's thinking about the Legend of the Sleeping Kings. If the day truly came that the Obarskyr kings were needed and did return from the dead, he felt certain they would return from some other place than Vaprak's sacrificial well. The power of the well hadn't been enough to conquer Woodbrand, or prevent the man from sealing it once he'd killed the trolls.

"What do you hope to f—" Jaeleen's voice suddenly stopped in mid sentence.

Baylee halted his descent and looked up at the woman. Her face was barely visible from the lamp burning below. Her mouth was still moving, but no sound was coming out. The ranger tried his own voice, but discovered he was also forced into silence by the spell.

The well bottomed out at nearly forty feet, opening into a final, wide chamber. Baylee stopped ten feet above the rough stone floor and peered around. He had left the bow above, feeling little room would exist to use the weapon. Instead, he was not able to see the sides of the chamber below.

Jaeleen impatiently kicked him in the head.

Baylee reached up and swatted her foot away. Grabbing the string attached to the lamp, he moved it around in a slowly widening circle. The lamplight burned evenly, trapped inside the glass walls.

The dark stone floor seemed to absorb the light except for tiny patches that appeared luminescent. Baylee recognized the green glowing patches as lichens. Presence of the lichens confirmed the occasional presence of water in the well.

The lamp swung nearly fifteen feet across in an elliptical arc. Broken bones and smashed skulls showed yellowed white in the lamplight. Estimating from the number of skulls he was able to see, Baylee knew dozens of people had been thrown into the well over the years. Jaeleen kicked him in the head again.

Wishing he had a third hand so he could strike back, Baylee continued swinging the lamp.

She's worried that you might break her trinket, Xuxa said inside his mind.

Baylee grimaced ruefully, remembering that the azmyth bat's powers provided her a means of communication, even inside the spell of silence.

She won't kick again, Xuxa promised. *I told her that you would smash the lamp if she didn't mind her manners.*

Thank you. I see nothing moving in here. Can you sense anything?

Nothing living. But that doesn't mean there are no traps.

I know.

The ranger climbed further down the rope, taking up the slack in the string that held the lamp. Nothing appeared to be moving in the chamber. He put his feet on solid rock, then let go the rope.

Jaeleen dropped beside him and reached out to snatch the lamp from Baylee's hand. She turned away from him, casting the light before her and scattering dancing shadows that twisted over the rough surface of the chamber.

The chamber was at least ten feet tall, Baylee decided, and easily three times that in diameter. He took a small torch from his belt pouch and lit it with the flint and steel he had. The sparks ignited the torch and he breathed on it to encourage the flame. The thin, gray smoke curled up toward the open well above.

Holding his torch aloft and spotting the haphazard mound of bones and rotting clothing against the east wall, Baylee thought his companion might be right. Water could have carried the remains against the wall. Jaeleen's lamplight also set fire to the smooth, warm texture of gold within the tangle of ivory limbs.

She reached out and seized a skeletal arm. A worked gold bracelet with inlaid gemstones circled the wrist, loose now that the flesh had been stripped away.

Curious indentations in the bone as Jaeleen moved the limb attracted Baylee's attention. He moved closer, using his own torch. Upon closer inspection, he realized the indentations were teeth marks.

Trollkin are known for their appetites, Xuxa put in. *Human flesh is thought of as a delicacy by some.*

Baylee knew that was true. He drew back as Jaeleen slipped her captured prize free and dropped it into the pouch at her side. She quickly started shifting the bones, searching for more.

She is a grave-robber, not an explorer, Xuxa sneered.

Baylee moved around the chamber, exploring the perimeters. His breathing was easier as he grew accustomed to the hint of foul stench that clung to the well. *Jewelry is often taken,* he defended. *An historian can tell much about the craft of metal-smithing from the way the piece is crafted. And the inscriptions—*

Faugh! The things that woman gathers will see only the inside of a merchant's case.

Baylee moved along the chamber. In a few places, faded messages were scratched on the walls with the points of daggers or sharp rocks. Nearly all of the writings were pleas for help, or hopes that others would bury them decently. Some of them were prayers to a handful of deities. Apparently none of them had been answered. It was almost enough to make a man give up religion.

Gifted as he was by native imagination, trained as he had been under Golsway's critical eye and demanding mien, Baylee slipped easily into an understanding of what the poor wreches' last few hours must have been like. Trapped in the throat of the well, some of them perhaps trying to stay afloat, yelling hoarsely till fatigue or their injuries finally took them, despair had undoubtedly filled them.

The feeling was leaden in his mind, making him aware of the thick, still air around him. Dust coated his exposed skin now, and perspiration cut rivulets through it. With effort, he pushed the feelings from him. His affinity for getting the sense of places and things had always stood him well. But it was a two-edged sword because those feelings could overwhelm him if he wasn't careful.

Without warning, the sound of rattling bones came to the ranger's ears. He turned back toward Jaeleen, in the direction the sound had come from. She was prying a pouch from under a tangle of bodies. The skin it had been crafted of had split in two areas, revealing a few silver pieces.

Baylee's senses came on full alert. Something had broken the spell of silence. Jaeleen halted her efforts to get the bag, though she did not relinquish it. Crouched down, she turned her head to look at the ranger over her shoulder. "Baylee?"

Before he could think to frame an answer, movement exploded from the pile of skeletons in front of the woman, hurling bones whirling madly in all directions. A predator's wail of triumph filled the chamber.

4

Baylee caught Jaeleen's shoulder and yanked her back as the shaggy creature rose from the pile of skeletons. The ranger pulled the woman with him as he retreated across the chamber. His torch and Jaeleen's lamp threw uncertain light across the thing that pursued them.

It stood over six feet tall and had been a big man in life. It was emaciated now, even for one of its kind. The grayish skin stretched tight over the bone structure, making the face appear blocky and misshapen. Wild hair alternately curled tight to the scalp and jutted out in unruly tufts. Dark circles shuttered the narrow eyes fired by unreasoning hunger. A long, thick tongue flicked out from between crooked, elongated teeth. The dry mouth cracked as it opened, and the sound of the tongue passing over the thirst-bloated lips rasped through the chamber. Clothing hung from the creature in shreds, scarcely covering the pallid body.

What is it? Xuxa called. Her telepathic ability didn't allow her to see through his eyes.

A ghoul, Baylee replied as he looked around the scattered bones for a weapon he could use. Ghouls were very dangerous, and fighting one in such close quarters was not a good plan.

The creature moved slowly, its joints and sinews snapping and popping with the effort. Evidently it had been in the well for a long time, probably drawn by the scent of decay. Once in, it had been unable to scale the walls and get back out.

Jaeleen brought her hand crossbow up and fired a bolt into the ghoul's face.

The bolt thudded into the ghoul's cheek with the sound of a knife splitting into an over-ripe melon. Stuck there, the bolt shoved its way between the creature's jaw, wedging it open and exposing the sharp teeth inside through the gaping flap of skin. There was little blood. Baylee guessed that the creature had been near the end of its unnatural life at the time they had entered the well.

The wound also unleashed a noxious odor.

The ghoul roared with rage, struggling to get the cry out of its parched lips and past the embedded bolt. Pausing, swaying uncertainly, it reached up and ripped the feathered shaft free. It threw the bolt aside and charged.

Jaeleen worked to reload her weapon.

Baylee breathed a quick prayer to Mielikki, the Lady of the Forest, and tossed his torch to the ground. The Lady must have been smiling, because the torch remained lit, adding to the uncertain illumination Jaeleen provided as she jerked her lamp around in her efforts to reload the hand crossbow.

Drawing into a defensive stance, Baylee reached into his boot for his dagger. The blade came free in his hand. Despite the warring perspectives offered by the two light sources in the dark chamber, he concentrated on the weaker illumination provided by the torch. At least it was steady. Torch light flickered across the ghoul as it lunged at him.

The blackened talons jutting from its fingers ripped at Baylee's midsection. Dodging, the ranger almost got away. The talons sliced through his deerskin shirt. Baylee stepped quickly to one side, intending to kick the ghoul's exposed leg and hopefully smash the joint to cripple the creature. Instead, his support foot slid across a pile of bones, throwing him off-balance. Before he could recover, the ghoul smashed him with a backhand blow.

Baylee flew across the room, throbbing waves of pain filling his head. His vision blurred as he slid across the rough-hewn chamber floor in a crumpled heap. A brief paralysis touched his limbs, numbing them, but it quickly retreated. Blood salted his mouth, and the warm ooze of liquid trickled down his chin.

Get up, Baylee! Xuxa yelled, swooping gracefully down the shaft.

The ranger shook his head, trying to clear his double vision. The ghoul roared with savage glee and threw its head back to take a deep whiff. The scent of fresh blood sent it into a frenzy.

Shoving himself to his feet, Baylee narrowly avoided the creature's lunge. He bounced off a wall, too far away for the torch to show his surroundings. Bones clattered beneath his feet.

The ghoul struggled as well. The bones and loose rocks provided treacherous footing. It's baleful gaze lingered on Baylee, hot eyes boring into the ranger's. The narrow tongue flicked out of its mouth again, and drool flecked its lower face. It took a step toward him.

Suddenly, a heartbeat of activity shot across the ghoul's face, snapping its head back. Xuxa expertly skimmed away from the nearby wall, heeling with a lot of trouble in the still air trapped in the chamber.

Baylee! Get moving! The azmyth bat wheeled around, taking another dive at the ghoul.

This time the creature was ready for her. The black taloned nails scraped through the air scant inches behind Xuxa. It snuffled in anticipation, tracking the rapid wing beats.

Baylee spotted the dropped knife resting beside the smashed remains of what appeared to be an elven woman, judging from the dress and the shape of the broken skull. Ignoring the pain in his head, he crossed the floor and picked the knife up.

Instantly the ghoul turned and was on him.

Baylee ducked beneath the outstretched hands. Keeping his feet planted, he rocked a shoulder into the creature's thighs. With the ghoul's emaciated skin worn so thin from hunger, his shoulder felt like it had collided with solid bone. He shoved with all his strength, putting his back into the effort.

The ghoul left its feet and slammed back against the chamber wall. Baylee set himself barely in time to avoid the slashing nails as the ghoul bounded back from the wall. He looped out his empty hand and caught the loose fabric of the tunic the creature wore. Yanking and using the ghoul's momentum as well as leverage, the ranger brought his opponent slamming into the ground.

Placing a knee in the creature's back and pinning it, Baylee slammed home the point of his dagger into the base of the ghoul's skull. The blade grated against bone and undead flesh. The ranger twisted, severing the creature's spinal column. All the limbs went dead at once, though the ghoul continued to cry out in rage.

Baylee stood on trembling legs. He wiped his mouth and blood streaked his arm. He glanced at the azmyth bat hanging from the ceiling. *Thank you, Xuxa.*

The bat chuckled warmly, then dropped and flapped its wings, flying back up out of the well.

Jaeleen looked pale as she walked toward the ranger. She held her lamp high. "Is it dead?"

"Dead or dying," Baylee growled. Every shadow stubbornly clinging to the inside of the chamber looked suspicious now. He picked his torch up from the ground. "Help me gather some of the clothing that still covers these hapless souls."

In a few moments, with Baylee doing the bulk of the work because Jaeleen was busily stripping whatever jewelry and coin purses she found among the dead, they had a pile of clothing in the center of the chamber. The ranger tossed the stub of his small torch into the clothing, then lit another.

The clothing burned quickly, throwing out heat that made the chamber suddenly sweltering and filling the air with eye-burning and throat-searing smoke. They worked quickly, without talking.

Baylee tried to keep track of what prizes the woman gathered, but found himself unable to. Her hands moved as quickly and skillfully as any thief's. And the items she procured disappeared, he noticed, not only into the bag she carried, but into her clothing as well. Baylee soon saw that her clothing was littered with concealed pockets he'd never known about.

The ranger's own searchings were more limited. The object he sought wasn't jewelry or made of gold or silver or precious gems. In truth, he was surprised at how much remained to be claimed among the victims.

It was a sacrificial well, Xuxa intruded into his thoughts from above, *and Vaprak is a jealous and vicious god. He would have known if the trollkin stripped their victims of their wealth and claimed it as their own. It probably only took Vaprak killing a semi-loyal follower or two before his displeasure was made clear and the others fell in line with his demands.*

Going through the accumulated bones took more time than Baylee had at first guessed. From the mention in the herbalist's book, he had come expecting to find a number of victims. The section in the book had been written before Lord Woodbrand had broken the hold the trollkin had on the land. The ranger had figured some families of the deceased would have exhumed the bodies for proper burial.

Perhaps there were other magicks at work, Xuxa said. *It is possible that not even Lord Woodbrand knew of the well. Not all of the trollkin were as devout as the ones who built and maintained the well.*

True. When we get back to Waymoot, I'm going to mention the location of this well to some of the town criers, and to Woodbrand himself. Finished with the current pile of bodies, Baylee started back among the ones Jaeleen had gone through.

The woman straightened, rubbing her back as if it ached. Dust stained her face, but Baylee found even that alluring.

"I've already gone through those," Jaeleen stated. Her eyes covetously roved over the bodies Baylee had examined. "You won't find anything of worth there."

"I look for different things than you," Baylee replied.

"What? A scroll with a treatise on philosophy? A map concerning trade routes that have long been discarded for one reason or another? The pathetic scribblings of some farmer who learned to compose his thoughts and put them down in ink?" Jaeleen snorted her disbelief. "Treasure are items you can trade. Gold, silver, gems, maybe an occasional magic item that you don't have a use for yourself, those are treasures."

It hurt Baylee to hear the woman speak so. When he had been younger, still protectively under Fannt Golsway's wing, to listen to her talk of the places she'd been, the things she'd seen, had seemed the pinnacle of achievement any young man with adventuring on his mind could hope for. He'd heard the tales of others, men with the same drive as Jaeleen, but Jaeleen had been hardly more than a girl then. Already in those days she'd seen more than he thought he ever would, and she'd done so many incredible things. Her education was self-made and very thorough. Golsway himself had said she could teach archeology at any of a number of universities. Except that Jaeleen never got past the greed that so tainted the profession.

"There are many lessons to be learned that are contained in the objects you ridicule so easily," he said.

You are wasting your breath, Baylee. She has only deaf ears for the perspective you offer.

Jaeleen pounced on a silver necklace with a trio of very nice emeralds Baylee had passed up. He'd only taken a few coins, some coppers and some silvers to tide him over on his journey to the Glass Eye Concourse in the coming tendays, in case he wanted to lie in a bed for a change and eat something another person had prepared.

"By Tymora's bountiful breast," Jaeleen exclaimed, "how could you have missed this?"

"I didn't," Baylee assured her. His heart beat rapidly as he spied an embossed leather pouch. He pulled it up from the tangle of bones and opened it.

"You left this here?"

"Yes."

"Fool." The necklace disappeared into one of Jaeleen's hidden pockets. "Do you know how much Algan One-Thumb will give you for something like this down in Suzail?"

Baylee looked into the pouch and found a thick sheaf of papers inside. He glanced swiftly through them, finding they were only a collection of letters. Evidently one of the victims of the trollkin had been a mail carrier. He stuffed the parchments back into the pouch and slung it over his shoulder. "Do you remember how Algan became known as 'One-Thumb?' He was a butcher who always tilted the scales in his own favor when no one was looking. Till someone did look, and removed that thumb for him."

"He has a fat purse."

"And a way of keeping it that way," Baylee agreed. Algan was known among the explorers and adventurers who brought back whatever booty they could from their expeditions. The moneylender was even good for an occasional loan to some who were willing to ferret out the truth of a rumor he'd chanced upon.

"I know how to deal with him," Jaeleen replied. "He doesn't

dare short-change me. I always bring him quality merchandise, and there are others I could deal with."

Though none with a faster *purse,* Xuxa said. *That's why Jaeleen will always deal with Algan's kind, and take quick money over good money.*

Jaeleen continued her searching, crying out in small, surprised yelps that Baylee knew were designed to needle him. He ignored them, concentrating on the prizes he turned up. The elven quill and ink pot looked more like refuse than treasure, but the style to his trained eye identified it as being little more than a hundred years or so past the fall of Myth Drannor. He put it into his bag of holding. With luck and a proper diviner, he could get a sense of who had owned it and perhaps fit another piece of the historical tapestry of the area together.

He added a gray coral mariner's good luck charm that looked like a hunk of broken rock no bigger than his thumb. It took closer inspection to see the symbol of Selûne, the circle of seven stars surrounding two feminine eyes, carved into the coral. It was a delicate piece of work, worn by time and by rubbing so that the carving was barely visible. He judged it to be of Turmish origin, and a few characters—probably a prayer—on the back of the rock confirmed that it was from the Vilhon Reach, off the Sea of Fallen Stars. There was no apparent reason why a mariner would be in the area. The mystery intrigued him, and perhaps a historian would be able to place the time period by the writing on the back.

Only a little while later, he found what he came looking for.

The book was small, hardly bigger than his unfolded hand, surely no wider, not even as thick as his forefinger. Baylee took it from the waterproof pack strapped to the back of a skeleton. The foodstuffs in the pack had long since ruined, though pots with wax seals somehow remained miraculously intact amid the packed clothing. He took them from the pack and set them gingerly aside. Probably they contained wines or mendicants, but all of them would have long ago gone bad. Accidentally breaking them open in the enclosed space of the chamber would have been a foul experience.

Baylee rocked back on his haunches, put his torch aside, and held the book in both hands. He ran a finger down the straight spine, noting that the title was inked there, not put there in gilt or stitched. In its day, even though books were prizes, it would not have caused most people to take a second look.

Which was exactly its purpose, Xuxa said.

Yes, Baylee responded. He turned so that the torch light fell better across the pages when he opened the book. The smell of the parchment pages and the ink was strong, letting him know the book had never seen much use and had been well protected in the pack. The other items were not so well kept by comparison.

It was warded, Xuxa confirmed. *You have found the prize you came seeking.*

Maybe, Baylee said. *If there is a secret page spell placed upon this volume as the old herbalist's book recorded. And if that magicked page really contains the agreement by two Cormyrean nobles with the Zhentarim to arrange King Azoun's assassination in Waymoot, there could be some political upheaval when the news is released.*

Jaeleen crossed the room, her pouch bulging. "What have you got?" With the excessive heat in the chamber, her hair had become damp and stringy.

"A book." Baylee held it up to her, surrendering it easily so she wouldn't assign any real worth to it.

She took the book and read the title from the spine. "*Seeds, Cuttings, and Transplants: A Gardener's Tome for All Seasons.*" She passed the book back. "This is worth something?"

"To an herbalist," he said, "yes." Or to a ranger or druid, and Jaeleen was neither. Baylee wrapped the book in protective leathers, then shoved it into the bag of holding.

"I've never even heard of the author."

Baylee knew that despite her greedy nature, Jaeleen was well-read. That had been the only chance he'd taken in letting her see the book. "You've never read any of Iwann's herbologies?"

"Why would I read something like that?"

Baylee had only read the single volume he'd found that mentioned the book in the sacrificial well, but there had been a monograph on the man. "To learn."

"About plants? I've got more discriminating tastes than that. Are you done here?"

Baylee stood and nodded.

"Then let's be off," Jaeleen said, "before those damned orcs decide to gather again." She looked around the chamber. "And staying down among the dead when they no longer have anything of worth is more than I can stand." She grabbed the rope and started up with sinewy grace.

The words stung, but as Baylee watched Jaeleen climb the rope above him, watched how the fabric of her breeches tightened over her hips, he minded less. Jaeleen had a good side; a person just needed to know where to look for it. He smiled, and started up the rope. He'd found his prize, and the night was still young.

5

"As your friend, Fannt, you know I have only your best interests at heart."

"You, my dear Keraqt, only have my best interests at heart when it is good for your purse." Fannt Golsway chuckled at the embarrassed look he saw in the other man's face. They sat at a circular table out on the balcony of Golsway's home. The balcony was festooned with a dozen different flowering boxes. The sweet aroma of the moon blossoms circumvented the wind blowing over the Sea Ward of Waterdeep from the Dock Ward. "But, of course, that very predictability about you is what makes you so endearing. I've always found a man should know what motivates those he keeps company with. Would you care for some more wine?"

Thonsyl Keraqt shifted uncomfortably in the plush chair on the other side of the crystal table. He was a broad man gone to fat with his successes. His robe appeared voluminous, cut of lightweight blue and white silks. His round face beaded with perspiration in spite of the cooling breeze. Long red hair striped with gray hung to his shoulders, echoed in the short beard. He motioned to his nearly empty wine glass.

Golsway poured. He knew Keraqt was only there visiting to find out what he could regarding the old mage's recent renewed interests. It was amazing that Keraqt's lackeys within Waterdeep had discovered the new venture so quickly.

"I'll not bother to respond to your taunts," Keraqt announced, lifting his glass in a silent toast. "Not when it is the only price I have to pay for imbibing of such an excellent vintage."

"You like the wine?"

"Most definitely. I've never had this at your home before."

"No. It is new."

"A new vintner?" Unbidden, Keraqt leaned forward with

considerable effort and grabbed the wine bottle's neck to check for a label or a wax seal bearing the bottler's crest.

"Actually, yes." Golsway said nothing about the other man's ill manners. Those who knew the merchant ignored his failings if they intended to use his skills or his resources. What was sad to think for the old mage, was that a merchant who could be as churlish as Keraqt came close to being his best friend in all of Waterdeep.

That was of Golsway's own choosing, however. With his home base of operations in Waterdeep, he had never allowed many into his home. He neither needed their pandering or their questions. Usually there were too many maps and books and little-known documents scattered throughout every room and on every conceivable surface to permit anyone to come visiting. As a result, usually the old mage went calling, or a meeting took place in an agreed-upon tavern or inn.

Despite his years, Golsway remained a lean, tall man. Age had not stooped his back yet, nor robbed him of his vigor. His silver hair lay forward on his scalp, coming down to a widow's peak, cropped close in a military-styled cut. He wore a goatee that scarcely covered his chin, then tucked neatly under to come to a point. His ears lay back against the sides of his head, though the right one had a notch bitten out of it. He had never had the wound properly tended to in order that it might be made to look more presentable. He chose to wear it to remind him that he was not infallible. His hooded eyes and narrow face made him resemble a hunting falcon to a degree that he could never deny. He wore a brilliant red robe with a field of stars that announced his fealty to Mystra.

"And who is this new vintner?" Keraqt asked.

Golsway cocked an eyebrow, a move that was known to send those who knew of him into conniption fits. "Do you press me on this matter?"

Keraqt shook his head then laughed. "Press you about a vintner, you say? You have always had the tongue for pretty thoughts, haven't you?"

Golsway turned a hand over. "The new vintner is myself."

"You jest."

"Should I show you the basement where I have casks fermenting now?"

"No. I believe you. What I find hard to believe is that boisterous Fannt Golsway, self-appointed re-discoverer of Toril, should spend his days raising and pressing grapes."

"You admit that the wine is good?"

"Readily."

"Then my efforts are not met with failure."

"But to be squashing grapes when you should be putting expeditions together, my friend?"

"Things have changed. I no longer run willy-nilly through the forests and deserts and mountains seeking the truth in some frivolous tale of wonder or drunkenness. There are books that must be written, and I have put them off far too long if I hope to inspire another generation to seek out the mysteries of the ancients." Golsway shook his head. "Too many of them are only grave robbers, destroying priceless relics for the gemstones and beaten gold before they know what they hold in their hands."

"It is the times," Keraqt lamented. "You remember the brand of fleeting youth. How it drove us to do things that we should never have done."

"But my agenda was always clear," Golsway replied. "Never did I destroy anything that would advance our knowledge of the past."

Keraqt kept silent.

Golsway knew the other man could not make that claim. Though in recent years, the merchant's tastes had changed. He had enough money and riches now to be more discerning about what he did with objects that came within his grasp. Many times Golsway had learned that Keraqt had taken less of a profit from some items to place them in the proper hands rather than break them up. It was one of the things that had convinced the old mage to open up his friendship more than it had been.

"Getting back to the wine," Keraqt said. "Do you have any flasks ready for sale? I'll send a boy around in the morning. With a fair price only, mind you, and not one copper more."

"It's not for sale."

Keraqt spluttered in denial. "Everything is for sale. It's only a matter of finding the proper time to buy."

"Send a boy around in the morning," Golsway invited with a smile. "I'll send him back with a few flasks I can spare."

The merchant sipped his wine again and smacked his lips in appreciation. "What an evening this is turning out to be. First you invite me over for one of the best meals I've had in five tendays or more, then you promise me free wine, *and* offer to send it to my door." He linked his fingers in front of him, his elbows resting on the table. The candlelight from the sconces in the corners of the balcony splintered from the jeweled rings on his fingers.

"I am glad you accepted my invitation to share eveningfeast."

"Bah! I invited myself and you were gracious enough to accept me into your home. We both know that."

It was true, but Golsway didn't acknowledge the statement. He took his pipe pouch from a pocket of his robe and worked the dottle out in anticipation of using it. Keraqt was a talker; the mage doubted the man would be gone before the morning cock crowed.

"Put your bag away," the merchant said, producing a pipe bag of his own. "I've only this tenday found a new blend I fancy. A trade ship I had owned part of a cargo in brought this from Beregost and I've found it quite pleasing."

Golsway took the bag and performed a quick spell to detect magic. If Keraqt noticed, he gave no sign. Finding the pipeweed free of any spells or wards, the mage quickly filled his pipe from the bag, packing the bowl tight.

"Allow me." Keraqt offered a light from one of the nearby candles. When both pipes were going, curling streamers of smoke about their heads that vanished into the night stretching out over Waterdeep, the merchant replaced the candle. "So tell me about the latest venture you are planning."

"What do you not yet know?" Golsway asked.

Keraqt grinned. "I know that you received a man in your home only four days ago. He carried a package for you that was nearly the size of a bread loaf, but was heavily wrapped and warded, so that may not be its real dimensions. I know, too, that the man spent the night and left early the next morning. You are not wont to allow overnight guests. I myself have spent a night here, but generally at this table or the one in your dining room, never as an overnight guest."

"Your spies are very good."

Keraqt shrugged. "They are paid generously."

"Do you have someone in my house?"

"No. I would never do something like that."

"You would," Golsway argued, "if you thought you could get away with it. But go on."

"I also know that your interest of late has been in Myth Drannor. I have people among the sages and book shops who say you've again been searching the histories and legends of the place."

Golsway released a deep lungful of smoke. In truth, he found the pipeweed quite pleasing. "My interest in Myth Drannor is no secret; nor do I stand alone in that interest."

"No, but I've not heard of you wasting research time in idle curiosity. It would take away time from the books you are writing. I am guessing you have turned up a new lead to follow."

"One that no one else has followed after all these years? Do you think such a thing could exist?"

The merchant nodded his big head deliberately. "It is the only kind of clue you would follow. Probably only one that you could turn up. Remember, I've known you for years."

"There are all kinds of new legends and rumors springing up about Myth Drannor. More now than at the time the city fell. You can pick and choose your illusions." Golsway made his voice deliberately demeaning.

"I've heard a name," the merchant whispered conspiratorially.

"You needn't whisper in my home," Golsway said. "It is well warded against those who would seek to invade my privacy."

Keraqt held up a plump hand. "I know, my friend, but this name is not to be bandied with."

"Tell me."

Keraqt leaned forward, covering his wine glass in case any would use the liquid in the goblet as a scrying vessel. Golsway recognized the action immediately for what it was. He quickly checked the wards around his home and found them all intact.

"Faimcir Glitterwing," the merchant said in an even lower whisper than before.

Golsway covered his surprise by sipping his wine. "How did you come by this name?"

Keraqt raised his eyebrows and widened his eyes. "Then it *is* true!"

"Answer my question," the mage snapped irritably.

"Please, my friend, there is no reason to take your wrath out on me." Keraqt did his best to look humble and slightly afraid, but Golsway saw only the glitter of greed in the other man's muddy brown gaze. "Remember, the messenger should not be killed." He paused, pushing his control of the conversation.

Golsway's patience was near to an end. The crystal table suddenly shook between them, holding an inner vibration like a bard's tuning fork.

"There was a man down in the Dock Ward this morning," Keraqt said quickly.

"What man?"

"I did not know him."

"What did he look like?" Despite all the wards on his home, despite the magical powers he had access to on demand, a thin worm of fear crawled inside the mage's stomach and twisted. Faimcir Glitterwing's legacy was worth an empire's ransom, but the sheer impact it would have on education and thinking about so many fields was beyond the pale. For the first time in many months, he wished that Baylee was home with him, that the harsh words that had passed between them had never been spoken.

"A tall man, and thick of neck and shoulder." Keraqt touched his brow with his fingers. "There was a livid red scar, bright as fresh spilled blood here. I don't know what kind of weapon would have made a mark such as that."

"Where is this man?"

"I don't know. I sent two of my best men after him when I heard mention that he was seeking you. They were dead by noon, and no one has seen this man since."

"Why was this man in the Dock Ward?"

65

"Asking after you, my friend."

"Did he say what he wanted with me?"

"No."

Golsway considered the answer. No more than a handful of people knew about the package he'd received. Only two knew the name of Faimcir Glitterwing. "And did someone direct him my way?" The mage knew there was a slim chance that the man could not have found the way to his home. He was well known in Waterdeep, but not many knew where he lived. His closest friends were ones he'd made in other lands, on other adventures. None of those would have come without an invitation.

"I could not tell you," Keraqt answered. "But I can tell you the man is no longer on the streets of this city. I can't even find his shadow."

"Maybe he left."

"After killing two of my best sellswords?" Keraqt shook his head. "You are not fool enough to believe that even for the time it takes to say it."

"No." Golsway stood and paced the balcony. He looked out over the city, out over Gulzindar Street where he lived in lower Sea Ward. His house was not so grand as it was carefully placed. To the north, the spire of the temple of Mystra burned like a star as moonlight caressed the beaten silver. He also spotted the lights from Piergeiron's Palace and the Field of Triumph.

Suddenly, for the first time since he'd inherited the house almost forty years ago, Golsway felt vulnerable there. He wanted to laugh at his fears, but he knew they were legitimate.

"Fannt?" Keraqt said. "Are you all right?"

The mage steeled himself, making his face neutral. "I am fine. Perhaps we should take our pipes and the port inside. I find the night air a bit chill."

Keraqt only hesitated a moment. "Of course." He gathered his glass and followed Golsway through the twin doors of the drawing room.

Golsway closed the doors, taking a moment to secure the double locks. Well above the ground and warded defensively, the balcony generally presented no opportunity for thieves.

The drawing room held several trophies the old mage had gathered during his adventures. Shelves filled the walls, and small tables set up miniature exhibitions of discoveries he'd made. The room wasn't for bragging purposes, for few had ever seen it. It held only touchstones of his life, memories that soothed him when he grew troubled with other problems or lacked a myth to track down.

"What do you know of Glitterwing?" Golsway asked as he indicated Keraqt should sit in one of the two stuffed couches.

"He was one of the best and brightest of the wood elves," the merchant said. "A warrior at heart, with an eye always toward the future."

Despite the tension that had arisen in the last few minutes, Golsway smiled. "You've been talking to Vlumir."

Keraqt nodded. "Easily the best historian that can be had for a gallon of cheap wine."

"He has fallen off the wagon again?" Golsway felt bad about that. Vlumir at one time had been among the most learned men in the Heartlands, maybe in all of Toril. But he had lost the use of his legs on an expedition while still a young man. Over a handful of years he'd fallen into drinking heavily, telling stories culled from legends and literature for a few coppers to keep himself drunk.

"Has Vlumir ever been on the wagon?" Keraqt shook his head. "Never in the time I have known him."

"There were other times."

"One supposes." The merchant didn't appear convinced.

"The stories you got about Faimcir Glitterwing from Vlumir were all tainted. He weaves truth with legend, never bothering to separate the twain. All of his elven history bears checking."

"He's a half-elf. I guess he's prideful about what he almost is and what he once almost was."

"What did he tell you of Glitterwing?"

"That the man amassed a fortune before Myth Drannor fell, and that it still lies hidden somewhere in the ruins of the city."

Golsway shook his head. "Go into any tavern, into any inn, any gathering where there are three men who want more out of life than the jobs they're currently working at, and you'll find as many tales like that as you'd care to listen to. In fact, you'll hear more."

"Then what is it that you have?"

The question, so simply put, threw Golsway off for a moment. It was silent testimony to the fact of how much time he'd spent working on the current problem. His gift for magic had never been more taxed. His need for a diversion was part of why he'd let Keraqt force an invitation into his home. "A foothold," he answered at last. "A foothold on a path to what may prove to be the greatest find since the fall of the City of Songs."

Keraqt leaned back on the couch, his eyes fixed on the old mage.

Golsway knew the man was carefully considering how to frame his next question. When it came to bartering, none was more shrewd than Keraqt. The merchant would take into consideration that they had shared a large meal together, had a considerable amount of wine, and the fact that Golsway himself had evidently not talked to anyone about his find.

And the fact that Baylee had not been around in months. If the ranger had visited of late, Keraqt would figure that Golsway had vented his excitement somewhere already, perhaps even sent Baylee out to look for another piece of the conundrum the old mage was working on.

Truth to tell, Golsway did feel himself weakening. There was only so much excitement that he could contain, even after a lifetime spent being close-mouthed about everything he saw fit to involve himself in. Even he could not have answered how the evening would have gone.

"Fannt Golsway."

The old mage turned at the sound of his name, as cold and piercing as a winter wind sweeping through the Storm Horns.

A man stood on the balcony. He was tall and broad, and bore the scarlet scar Keraqt had spoken of. His dress was rough but the leather armor was serviceable. Cold gray eyes blazed under square-cut bangs.

Golsway turned to face the man, readying the spells he had at his command. "Who are you who dares invade my home?"

"My name doesn't matter," the man said in his cold voice. "I only bring a message." He kicked open the balcony doors, then raised an arm. Ruby pinpoints of light in his fist refracted from the candle sconces behind him.

Golsway unleashed a magic missile at the man and watched as he staggered back, obviously in pain.

Still, the man managed to bring his hand down. The old mage had only a brief glimpse of the ruby helix that tumbled from the invader's hand before it shattered against the stone floor. "*Villayetaix!*"

Golsway's senses detected the presence of powerful magic even before the secondary explosion filled the room with curling red fog. The scent of crushed violet fungus filled the air. A figure formed in the fog, brought into sharper relief as the open balcony blew away the obscuring mist.

The old mage knew the ruby helix had been part of a succor spell even as he faced the new arrival. His eyes widened in surprise as he recognized the lissome form of a drow elf walking toward him.

6

The drow walked toward Golsway, a spiked morning star naked in her fist. A mocking smile played on her lips. She wore a *piwafwi*, a magical shielding cloak, and wore a white sheer silk half-shirt and matching girdle that stood out sharply against her ebony skin. A holstered hand crossbow hung at her left hip in a cross draw, leaving her right side free for the morning star. Her white hair was cropped close enough to leave no curl at all. The iris of her eyes were so pale as to possess no color at all.

"Fannt?" Keraqt called from the couch. The merchant shoved himself back, trying to get clear of the confrontation without drawing attention to himself.

"Silence!" Golsway ordered. None of the business he currently dealt in had anything to do with the drow. He had stayed clear of the Underdark for most of his career. The dark elves had more lies than truth, and absolutely no honor. To enter the Underdark was to walk with death itself.

The drow elf kept advancing. "You have something that does not belong to you, old man." Her voice was rough, as though it wasn't used often.

Knowing the drow communicated by silent hand code when in bureaucratic environs, Golsway guessed that this was no ordinary drow. If there was such a thing. He'd rarely heard stories of any of the creatures being encountered above the surface. "I don't know what you're referring to," the old mage said, buying time to organize the spells he carried in his head.

The drow elf gestured with her free hand.

Hastily, Golsway erected a shield in front of himself, expecting her attack to come directly at him. He felt the crackle of magic in the air and knew he faced someone of considerable talent and power.

A flaming sphere a yard across formed on the stone floor in

70

front of the female drow. Her thin lips pulled back in a smile as she directed the fiery ball's progress. The sphere smashed into Golsway's shield, wrapping spongily around it for a moment, then ricocheting off with amazing speed.

Keraqt never had a prayer. The flaming sphere rolled over him and engulfed him. He screamed in agony, his voice ripping through what had been the quiet halls of Golsway's home. The fat merchant struggled across the couch as the flames sizzled the meat from his bones. Every place his hands or face touched started new fires.

Even hardened as he was by everything he'd seen in his adventures, Golsway could not stand to see a man die in such pain. He chanted quickly, sending energy to dispel the flaming sphere.

The fiery ball cooled somewhat, turning blood red just as Keraqt's struggles ceased. The merchant's burned and blackened body spilled to the floor, knocking aside a low table containing memorabilia from a dig site in Shadowdale. Tiny ceramic statutes shattered against the flagstones.

"Mercy," the female drow said in her rusty voice, "is something shared only by the weak to end their miseries." She renewed her attack, abandoning the flaming sphere as it collapsed in on itself. Her hands moved again.

Golsway prepared spells of his own, choosing them in order. The female drow was a strong opponent, one he'd not want to do combat with at anything less than his best. His staff was in his study on the third floor. Had he been outside, he would not have been without it.

Bilious yellow-green vapors formed in front of the drow and began filling the room. The gentle breeze blowing in from the broken balcony doors pushed the vapors toward Golsway.

The old mage backed away, recognizing the cloudkill spell. One whiff of the toxic vapor and he would be dead or defenseless. The spell let him know the woman didn't intend to let him live.

Staying behind his shield, he summoned his magic, focused, said the words, and drew the tiny feathered fan from his sleeves.

He waved the fan in the direction of the coiling vapors. Immediately, a huge updraft of wind surged from the floor to the ceiling high overhead. The vapor rushed up with it.

The drow took a step back as her own spell threatened to backfire on her.

While she was off-balance, Golsway reached into a hidden pocket for the vial containing a piece of squid tentacle. He dispelled the wind wall and smashed the vial against the floor, mouthing the words of the new spell. He felt the drain of energy from his body as the spell formed long black tentacles that writhed up from the floor.

The spell for Evard's Black Tentacles was a potent one against most foes. Golsway hated using it because getting rid of the tentacles was dangerous and time consuming, and there was no real control over them. They were just as dangerous to him as they were to the drow.

She gave ground before the tentacles. Setting herself, she lashed out expertly with the morning star, slashing hunks of the blubbery black flesh from one of the ten-foot long tentacles. It coiled away from her.

Golsway had to duck himself as he pulled a piece of gauze from his pocket and seized a fistful of smoke from Keraqt's smoldering corpse. The sickly sweet smell of the dead man filled his nostrils as he said the words that activated the spell.

Instantly, his corporeal body became insubstantial and the weight of his flesh dropped away. He activated the ring on his right hand and rose into the air, flying quickly. He didn't try for the door. Even though the tentacles could no longer touch him, such a move would expose him longer than necessary to the female drow's magic.

He rose to the ceiling and focused on one of the holes he'd deliberately had installed in the house. It only took a moment for his wraith form to pass through the hole. He continued rising through the next floor, passing through one of the spare bedrooms.

In a moment, he was in his study, surrounded by his things. The staff was in its case against the wall. He returned to solid form and dropped to the floor. Crossing the room quickly, grateful that he'd arranged all the tables against the walls and left none of them in the center of the room, he spoke the word of release. The case opened, revealing his collection of higher magic; some he understood and some whose natures he had yet to divine.

The staff was seven feet long, of thick gnarled pecan that held a dark luster. Iron caps covered either end of it. He turned, feeling more confident. The staff was one of thunder and lightning and surely held enough power to handle the drow.

"You run well, old man," the drow said as she floated up through the floor in wraithform herself. She carried a large hunk of tentacle that she was pulling from around her midsection. She threw the tentacle to one side and resumed physical form. The tentacle smacked against the floor wetly when it landed. "But I grow tired of the chase."

"Who sent you?" Golsway demanded. He held the staff before him. Power radiated in the wood. The woman had to be able to see it if she was the kind of mage he thought she was. Still, she gave no pause to the threat that he offered.

"One whom you would steal from." The drow glanced around the room, spotting the table where Golsway's latest interest lay. "You've been prying into affairs that are none of your concern."

"You've not told me who—"

"Nor will I." Ignoring the staff pointed in her direction, the drow crossed to the table.

"Stay away from that."

"You've no right to this." The drow lifted the box the artifact was packed in. She lifted it from its case, turning it in the light.

For the woman to know so precisely what it was that he had, Golsway knew that a scrying spell had been used on the object. But the caster must have been very good, otherwise the wards the old mage had up would have notified him of the scryer.

She turned back to him, locking her colorless gaze with his. "Now, old man, the chase is over, the prize won, and it is time for you to die for daring trespass." She lifted a hand clad in a snakeskin glove.

Even as Golsway activated the thunder and lightning spell from his staff, a giant disembodied hand formed in the air. Each of the fingers was as thick around as his waist. The palm spanned the distance of two axe handles laid end to end.

The hand struck as quickly as a spark snake. The long fingers wrapped around Golsway with crushing strength, covering the staff as well. The thunder and lightning charge erupted against the giant palm. By some miracle, the hand absorbed most of the damage, but too much reflected back into the old mage.

Blackened and maimed, the sorcerous hand fell away in a lifeless heap. It disappeared before it hit the ground.

Golsway dropped, unable to make his limbs find the strength to hold him. Death hovered around him and he knew it. His vision narrowed. Gasping for breath to feed lungs too seared to use it, he tried to cast one last enchantment. But there was nothing left in him to give.

His last sight was of the drow as a golden aperture opened behind her. Smiling, she stepped through. The aperture closed to a tiny yellow dot that fragmented and vanished.

Golsway closed his eyes, surrounded by mysteries he'd yet to solve, truths he'd yet to find. He'd always known there would never be a proper time for leaving. Then he died.

* * * * *

It's all right, Baylee.

The ranger came awake in the night, gasping for air and shuddering with the force of the nightmare. For a moment, he couldn't remember where he was. His chest heaved and perspiration filmed his skin.

It was only a bad dream, Xuxa soothed. *You are safe here with me.*

Baylee ran a hand through his wet hair. Only then did he realize he was alone in the hammock stretched between two limbs thirty feet above the ground. *Jaeleen?*

Gone.

The loss hit Baylee harder than he'd have thought even though he'd been expecting it. His body groaned with the aches and bruises he'd gotten from the fight with the ghoul. *She didn't wake me.*

No.

Baylee made himself relax back into the hammock. He stared up at the dying moon and the handful of stars dusting the remains of the night. He wondered if anyone could feel more alone than he did at that moment. *Did she try to wake me?*

Xuxa hesitated.

No lies, Xuxa. We could never have lies between us.

She didn't, Baylee.

The ranger glanced further up into the tree, folding his arms behind his head, and tried to pretend the leaden lump in his breast wasn't his heart. He forced a smile. Xuxa hung upside down, barely a yard above him, her leather wings folded tightly around herself. *Did she talk to you?* he asked.

No.

Did you talk to her?

I saw no point. We have nothing to discuss.

Did she take much this time?

The azmyth bat stretched her wings. Her small mouth opened in an almost human yawn. *She took some of what you found in the chamber last evening. I do believe that you haven't got a single silver piece left to your name.*

It's a good thing you and I don't take much to get by in this life.

Yes, but then what better life can there be than living out in the open as we do. Neither of us were born for the cities of Man.

No, Baylee agreed. *I love the openness of this world. A room at an inn is a nice thing to experience once in a while, but I'd get bored looking at the same land all the time.*

Then why get so attached to Jaeleen?

Baylee looked the azmyth bat in the eyes. *I can't explain it even to myself.*

Let me help. Have you ever heard of the word aberration?

Baylee ignored the comment. He knew it wasn't the bat's word, but he also knew her telepathic link always hit closely to what she was thinking. But he wanted to talk, not argue. *There is so much she is good at.*

I could tell you thought so from the way that hammock was jerking around earlier. I was actually fearful the two of you were going to break your necks before you exhausted yourselves.

Baylee smiled at the memory in spite of the pain that went with it. *There was something missing. Wine. Some wine and some cheese, maybe some chilled fruit. That would have been nice.*

That reminds me, Xuxa said. *Jaeleen also stole the last of our journeycake.*

'Stole' is too harsh a word. 'Borrowed' is better.

The azmyth bat sniffed in disdain, choosing deliberately to throw the artifice response at him. She'd learned the habit from a previous human she'd traveled with. Azmyth bats lived to be well in excess of one hundred years. Baylee had never gotten Xuxa to admit how old she really was.

Either term, Xuxa replied, *it will be berries and spring water for breakfast.*

I'll make it up to you at the Glass Eye Concourse, Baylee promised. *You know there will be more than enough to eat once we arrive there.*

And we'll stay the duration?

Xuxa, this is a forgathering. Not only that, it's one of the biggest forgatherings of rangers in the year. Once it starts, it may not end for months.

The azmyth bat gave a happy chuckle of expected contentment.

We'll stay a tenday, Baylee promised.

I'll hold you to that.

In the silence, the ranger's thoughts wandered again to Jaeleen. He felt drawn to her in a way that moths winged to flame. Though he was loathe to admit it, there was not much to like about Jaeleen. She was self-centered, arrogant, and petty. But during the times he shared with her, contested against her own nature to try to get her to see a wider view of the world, he was convinced he'd never meet another woman like her who set his heart thrumming in quite the same fashion. When there was no sarcastic remark forthcoming from Xuxa, he was grateful. He knew he was allowed to have private thoughts in the azmyth bat's presence in spite of her telepathic powers, but he remained suspicious of how much Xuxa monitored him.

After the forgathering, Xuxa asked, *are you still planning on returning to Waterdeep?*

Baylee hesitated.

Remember, Xuxa said, *no lies.*

I don't know.

Well, at least that's honest, if not definitive.

It's not that easy, the ranger protested. *Too many things were said between Golsway and me. Some of them I now realize I had no place to say.*

And some of them Fannt Golsway had no place to say, Xuxa said gently. *I am sure he realizes that by now as well. You are not the only one who can see the error of your ways.*

Baylee looked deep into the azmyth bat's milk-white eyes. *Golsway is a hard man. He's been my teacher. He can make no mistakes in his eyes.*

He was much more than your teacher, and I think he's had time to realize that. Baylee, you would be better served to spend your time in Waterdeep repairing that relationship than in haring off after Jaeleen.

How did you know I was thinking about that?

Because being around that—that woman—locks up your thoughts. I expect you to be pining away after her for a tenday or more. I am looking forward to very depressing times, I'm afraid. I hate it when you mope.

You're no walk in an elvenglen yourself.

Baylee, why do you think Jaeleen left without saying good-bye?

She didn't want me to try to convince her to spend a longer time with me.

Xuxa chirped in frustration. *That's only half the truth. The other part is that she has feelings for you and she knows she will never be the woman you need in your life.*

What kind of feelings?

Xuxa spread her wings and shook them. *Listen to all that I say, not half of it. As much as I find to dislike about that female, I sense that in her own strange way she loves you and would spare you the trouble that she would undoubtedly bring.*

Baylee couldn't help but think that somehow sounded romantic.

Ill-fated lovers was a theme that played to most audiences, and all the legends and histories he'd ever read had been full of such stories.

You can't change her, Xuxa said, *and I fear a bad end for her.*

She can take care of herself. Baylee turned cautiously in the hammock and stared off into the darkened forest. To the east, the sun was starting to taint the sky a rosy gray. It would be so easy to trail her through the forest. She was good at her woodcraft, but he was better. He could find her before noon.

But he knew he wouldn't. In a few minutes more, he fell back asleep. There was no hurry.

* * * * *

Tirdan Closl surveyed the wreckage inside Fannt Golsway's study, seeking to understand everything that had happened inside the house. He was a tall man, and broad, slower now in his mid-fifties than he had been as a younger man. His dark hair and beard were well kept by his wife, but he had a habit of pulling at it while he thought.

The carnage inside the home gave him plenty to think about.

"Sir," a young guard said behind him.

Closl turned. He was a senior civilar of the watch in Waterdeep, his leather armor strengthened with chain bearing the green, black, and gold that marked his station. He fisted the pommel of his short sword as he regarded the junior officer. "Yes, Daike?"

"I located the cook, sir." Daike looked around the room with wide eyes.

Closl didn't blame the boy. Despite all the fights and bar brawls that happened in Waterdeep that the watch took care of, nothing could prepare a man for the sight of his first wizard's battle. "Where is she?" the senior civilar asked in a gentle voice.

"Outside, sir. Her name is Qhyst. She asked that she not have to come in."

"Of course." Closl took another look at the ruined corpse of Fannt Golsway. The old mage was a crumpled shell of himself, lightning blasted so that his flesh had lost all its color, yet charred in places where the magicks trapped inside him had vented themselves. The early morning sunlight only made the horrific death seem even more evil. The watch senior civilar had been born a farm lad, brought to Waterdeep for a time to sail with the trading ships and see bits and pieces of the world, and had been with the watch for his last twelve years. He had seen such sights before, but not often.

Two men worked on Golsway's corpse. One was Hazra, a watch member trained as a physician. The other was Mintrivn, who was wise in the ways of magic. Both of them were there to determine exactly how Golsway had died. If possible.

"Daike," Closl said.

"Sir." The young man whipped his attention toward the senior civilar and straightened his carriage. Closl ran a tight shift.

"Help Oryan question the neighbors. She will need every man she can get to do it all properly."

Daike snapped a salute and led the way out of the room.

Closl sighed heavily and followed the younger man out. With a murder like this, all the weak members of the watch would be culled by the end of the week. Especially when Piergeiron, Warden of the Guard, Commander of the Watch, Overmaster of the Guilds, and Open Lord of Waterdeep announced that they were intent on bringing the person or persons responsible to justice.

He stepped into the hallway and found the cook. Surprisingly, besides the drawing room below and the study on the top floor of the house, little damage had been done. Whoever had done the killing had known exactly what they wanted and took no chances about getting it.

"Dame Qhyst," he said.

The cook turned to face him. She was a short woman, surprisingly comely for one who chose to work out of sight of most people in a wizard's home. Her dress was homespun, a pale green that set off her dark good looks. Her hands were weathered and red, the hands of a farmer's wife.

She curtsied, bowing her head. "Milord."

"No, Dame Qhyst, senior civilar will do nicely. Or Closl, if you feel so inclined. I am a working man, no lord." He bowed and gave her a smile, thinking of his mother when she'd been much younger.

"Senior civilar," she agreed.

"You understand what has happened?"

"Yes. Are you sure that Fannt Golsway is dead?" Tears glittered unshed in her eyes.

"There can be no mistake, dame. Two of his neighbors have identified his body just this morning."

She raised a hand to her mouth. "Who would do such a terrible thing? He was such a good man."

"I don't know," Closl said. "All that I am sure of is that Lord Piergeiron is going to want answers when I see him later this morning. He takes the protection of this city very seriously."

"I am well aware of Lord Piergeiron's interest in this city."

Standing in the hallway, Closl was aware of the smell of burned flesh coming from the study. "Walk with me, dame."

The woman fell into step beside him.

Closl lead the way down the curving steps to the lowest floor, then out beside the house where a small garden contained a number of vegetables, grape vines, and flowers. A stone wall ringed the patch of land, and Mintrivn had confirmed that it had wards of protection placed on it. Care had been taken in the placement of the small stone benches in the garden. He took a deep breath, clearing the smell of death from his nostrils.

"Is this your garden, dame?" he asked.

She looked around, her cheeks wet with tears now. "No. It was the master's. He put it in, saying it was for me, but he spent hours out here when no one was looking. It was a habit of his since he'd quit traveling quite so much."

"Please sit." Closl waved to one of the benches across from an alabaster fountain with birds cut from sapphires sitting on the edge. The water trickled noisily from an artesian well that tapped an underground source, but the sound was soothing.

"Thank you."

"I am told you had the night off last night."

"Yes, sir. It was my routine to set the master's table for him, then go home myself. I have three children, you see. The master was very generous with his time."

"I understand that. I am also told that you were paid even for those days that Golsway was not at home."

The woman nodded. "As I said, Senior Civilar Closl, the master was a very generous man."

Closl almost smiled. In most circles, Golsway had been known as a very hard and demanding man. His research, when presented, was flawless. His lessons, when executed, were poetry.

"Tell me about last night," the senior civilar suggested. "You prepared the eveningfeast before you left. What time did you leave?"

"Just after moonrise," she answered.

"I'm told that was later than usual."

"Yes." She nodded. "I prepared my own eveningfeast for my children earlier, then came back to prepare the master's. He was entertaining, you see."

"I understand that was a rare occasion."

"True."

"Who was he entertaining?" Closl asked. There was still the body in the drawing room burned beyond recognition to be explained, though the senior civilar had some ideas.

"Thonsyl Keraqt, the merchant."

"Do you know what business he had with Golsway?"

"No. The master had his business, and I never pried into it."

Closl talked for a while longer, going over the evening until he was sure he had everything the woman knew. There were no clues, nothing to suggest who had killed the men. After only a little while longer, he released her from his questioning.

She was almost to the door leading back into the house when he called for her attention.

"What can you tell me about Baylee Arnvold, dame?" he asked.

"Only that he would never have anything to do with this," she replied without hesitation. "If that's what you're thinking."

"It's been brought to my attention that there was a falling out between them in the past year."

"Ten months ago," the woman replied, her eyes sparking fire.

"And I would like to know whose tongue has been wagging so loosely."

"I'm afraid I can't reveal that. Those who talk to me have my confidence."

"Then please take a message back to that person for me that they should respectfully find some other way to spend their time than passing on idle gossip."

"I'll consider that, should the information prove false or misleading."

"The falling out you refer to," the woman explained, "was nothing more than a boy growing to manhood, despite his father's best wishes."

Closl studied the woman. "I'd never heard that Baylee was the old mage's son."

"He wasn't, by blood," Dame Qhyst replied, "but in every other way that mattered, that was their relationship. Even the master didn't see it till months after Baylee had left this house. And a sad awakening it was, too, because by then the master had let too much time pass to be comfortable patching the rift between them himself. And Baylee, you can be sure, is on the prideful side himself. Youth can be such a detriment."

"How well do you know this young man?" Closl asked.

"Well enough that you are asking me questions about him, Senior Civilar Closl. If you didn't trust my answers, you should not have asked."

Closl laid an apologetic hand over his heart and bowed his head. "Forgive me, Dame Qhyst, for I meant no offense. Of course you are right."

"If I can be of any further help, please let me know." She turned and nearly ran over the man standing suddenly and quietly in the doorway. "Oh, excuse me, Lord Piergeiron! I didn't know you were there!" She backed away hurriedly and curtsied very low.

Closl straightened his own stance, coming instantly to attention.

"My fault, dame," the Commander of the Watch of Waterdeep said. "I should have spoken up. Please continue on your way and know that no ill favor on my part has been garnered."

The woman curtsied again, excusing herself, and disappeared into the house.

Piergeiron Paladinson strode into the garden, looking striking in his watch armor and colors. He was tall and graceful, much as his father had been. He gazed about the garden, then looked at his senior civilar. "This is a right and proper muddle of affairs."

"Yes sir," Closl responded, feeling like the whole arrangement had suddenly gotten many times worse than he thought it was going to be if Piergeiron himself was going to get involved in the murder investigation.

"Do we have any ideas about who did this?"

"Someone quite capable in the field of spell-casting, or someone armed with a magical weapon of some force."

Piergeiron shook his head. "I knew that from the moment I found out it was Golsway who was killed. I knew that man as one of my teachers, as hard a taskmaster as a man would ever want to meet."

"There's not much else, sir," Closl said. "Golsway didn't have much in the way of friends."

"There was always Keraqt," the warden said. "Though I never knew what Golsway liked about the old pirate."

"Sir, Keraqt was the other victim."

Piergeiron looked surprised. "Well, rest his soul in peace then. If not friends, what of enemies?"

"Someone who could do this?"

"You'll be working from a short list, then."

Closl knew he wasn't being let off the hook. "The people you're suggesting, sir, well, we'll be trampling on some blue blood toes to get the answers we're looking for."

"I know, and you'll ask those questions on my order. If there are any who give you trouble, tell them I'll free up my schedule to question them myself. I will have the answers for this." Piergeiron looked out over the city. "Waterdeep stays with constant rumors and outright lies crossing her from one end to the other every day. I'll not have this help feed the grist for that if I can help it."

Closl said nothing, but he knew even the answers they found would only create more half-truths in their wake. "Yes sir. If I may,

I'd like to suggest another route in this investigation."

Piergeiron looked at his senior civilar.

"Baylee Arnvold," Closl said. "I would send a watch team to find him."

"Would you know where to look? He's been gone from this city for months."

"I think I might. Baylee is a ranger. I've a nephew who is a ranger. Young Varin has regaled us from time to time with tales of forgatherings. Festivals of a sort where rangers meet to discuss their trade and sharpen their skills. In a few days hence, the Glass Eye Concourse, one of the biggest of such meetings, is going to be held. It's possible that Baylee will be there, or at least someone who knows him."

"You want to send a watch team from Waterdeep there?"

"With your permission."

Piergeiron stroked his chin as he considered the option. After a moment, he nodded. "Make it so, senior civilar. Whatever aid you need from me, consider it done."

"Thank you, sir."

"And let me know what your people turn up."

"Of course. You'll be the next man to know after me." Closl watched as the lord walked away, deep in thought. The watch senior civilar sighed heavily, looking back at the house. He knew what Piergeiron's deepest fear was even though the noble had not spoke of it: that Golsway's death really was part of one of the many plots that began every day in Waterdeep instead of a separate act.

The senior civilar shook his head, imagining the power that had run rampant inside the house. And as skilled as the murderer or murderers were, he feared for any man that tried to take them in for the crime.

7

Krystarn Fellhammer stared angrily into the darkness that stretched ahead of her. The underground passage twisted and turned and fell away down into the earth. The smell of decay filled the thick air around her. She kept her morning star in her fist. The battle with Fannt Golsway had left her more drained than she would have liked to admit.

She peered down over the crest of the hill she stepped out onto. She thought she knew where she was, but the chain of caverns was huge. If she was at the location she thought, she had more than an hour's walk ahead of her. The teleport spell on the gem she'd been given had not worked as completely as she'd been told it would, or Shallowsoul had deliberately lied to her about where she would return in the subterranean lairs.

Having been raised in Menzoberranzan for the first forty-three years of her life, where a dozen acts of treachery could be committed before morningfeast—sometimes within her own family—being lied to came as no surprise. It only meant that even with the recent turn of events she hadn't maneuvered herself into the bargaining position she'd planned to with Shallowsoul.

The complete lack of light in the caverns didn't bother her either. The lights back at Golsway's home had hurt her eyes. Drow vision was capable of seeing the heat of a living body, or even the subtle changes in temperature from rock to wall to rodent. She navigated the path through the broken rock with ease. Mice and rats scurried before her, finally packing together enough that they dared try to rush her and bring her down.

She read their predatory thoughts easily, then twisted the silver band on her left ring finger and said the activation phrase. The spell filled her and she directed it at the gathering of rats.

The wall of telekinetic force slammed into the vermin, knocking their bodies back against the cavern wall. The ones that weren't killed outright died when they struck the wall in a series of meaty smacks. Twisted, broken corpses littered the rocks and uneven terrain.

Krystarn smiled to herself. Every death viewed, even the small ones, were worth watching. She would remember Fannt Golsway's passing for a long time with joy. Her only regret was that there had been no time to savor it before being yanked out of the house, no time for the torture that could have been the prelude.

All around her were the dead of Myth Drannor. Some of them had been buried by the cataclysmic forces that had brought the City of Songs down so many years ago. Others had been hauled underground by the remnants of the Army of Darkness that had overwhelmed Myth Drannor. Gnolls and hook horrors and other flesh-eaters had joined up in the forces that had ripped the city to shreds.

Not many knew of the wide-spread system of pocket caverns that existed under the grounds where Myth Drannor and other cities had been. The ones that did know of the subterranean areas were not aware of the connecting tunnels that were often times disguised by corrupted and diseased bits of the mythal that had been laid to protect the city. The left-over magic forces these days were fickle things, choosing when and how to work, and often on whom.

She continued walking for a time, content in the darkness and the old death in a way that she hadn't been settled in the Underdark. She preferred the solitude, even though it lessened the number of potential victims. Each victim she did choose, however, she was able to devote all of her energies to, Lloth willing.

A cacophony of chittering and squeaking and sometimes challenging growls kept her company as she passed through narrow valleys that had been riven in the land, and through the remnants of dungeons and houses that had fallen in the battle. The only things she feared in the subterranean world beneath the corpse of Myth Drannor were the Phaerimm, the Sharn, and the baatezu. Only those stood a true chance against the magic forces she controlled. And those she knew how to avoid.

She walked into a large cavern that she identified immediately.

Turning, she reached into the bag of holding at her waist and took out a pair of climbing claws that would cling to the rock better than her hands would. She put another set on, strapping them on over her boots.

Lean and limber, she scaled the side of the cavern with ease. Her *piwafwi* caused her to blend in with the shadows even as she moved. From a distance, she knew she would only be detected as an occasional ripple of movement, if at all.

At the top of the wall she put her climbing gear away and located the trail she'd been looking for. The path was scarcely two feet wide. She had to turn sideways to ease through the rift splitting solid rock. Sixty feet further on, the rift widened into another cavern.

She knew Shallowsoul couldn't have been hoping to get her lost. In the four years she'd been down in the caverns with Shallowsoul, she'd explored much of the surrounding territory. She knew her way around the areas here. So she wondered what Shallowsoul's intentions might have been. Second-guessing someone skilled in treachery was second nature to the drow, but Shallowsoul's psychology added in the mercurial element of madness and paranoia. It was frustrating that one who had so much of what she wanted also came so powerful.

Voices below her caught Krystarn's attention.

She froze in the opening and listened. They were still too far away for her to hear properly. Taking up her hand crossbow in her free hand, she crept to the ridge in front of her. The tip of the quarrel in the pistol was coated with poison, guaranteeing no human-sized survivors.

From the coloring of the ruby glow in front of her, the drow knew that someone had a fire going below. She peered over the edge.

A group of hobgoblins sat around a cookfire. Krystarn did a quick accounting, finding there were more than forty of them in all. Nearly half of those were male warriors. The rest were divided almost equally between females and children. She shifted, getting ready to creep even closer till she could hear them.

"You're still doing his bidding, aren't you?" a voice said at her side.

Krystarn leaped to her feet, the morning star and the hand crossbow at the ready. Her eyes narrowed when she spotted the figure in front of her. "Shouldn't you be off rattling chains and haunting your crypt like a good little ghost?" she asked sarcastically.

The being drew himself up to his full height. Obviously of elven blood, he wore raiment fit for a king. He looked far too pale to be healthy, even for a Moon Elf. "You know very well I am no ghost," he declared haughtily. "I am a baelnorn, sworn and loyal protector of my family's wealth and power."

"An annoyance by any other name."

The baelnorn pursed his lips, the pride suffusing him coloring even his undead face. "You know that I have no respect for you, drow. Your kind were never welcome in fair Myth Drannor, even when the city opened its arms to the humans and dwarves."

"Then allow me to pass in peace, ghost. I know that you won't offer me any harm as long as I don't try to unlock your family's crypts or the secrets they left hidden behind when they fled before the Army of Darkness. And I have no intention of trying. I have found the treasure I seek."

"Yes," the baelnorn agreed, "and you scurry around Folgrim Shallowsoul's feet like a sniveling lapdog. And you call yourself a warrior of the drow race. Hah!"

Anger threaded through Krystarn. If not for her training to prefer treachery and duplicity over face-to-face confrontation, she would have struck the baelnorn with her morning star. "You talk brave words, ghost. Is this your true form, or do you taunt me from a projection of yourself?"

"I should tell you?" The baelnorn grinned and shook his head. "Better that I should wear at you like the conscience that you do not possess."

"Do not wear too heavily, ghost. If you try my patience too hard, it may be that I find it necessary to track you down to your lair and destroy you." Krystarn gave the baelnorn a harsh look. "Or maybe you've lived so long down here that you no longer remember that it is possible to die a true death?"

"I would never fear a drow." The baelnorn curled his lip at the thought.

"That is your choice, foul creature," Krystarn said. "But in the year and a half that I have known of you, I find it interesting that you have never given me your name. Perhaps this is because I will find out who you are, and where you hide."

"Finding me would only bring you your death, heartless wench."

"I would find death, true, but that would only send me on my way to the Spider Queen. If you were to die, where would you go? You've already turned down the elven afterlife as your people see it."

The baelnorn remained silent.

"And what of the precious treasures of the house you yet guard?" Krystarn taunted. "I have seen you fret and worry because of the wights and skeletons that roam these tunnels who might discover your secrets. Can you imagine the hands of a drow going through those treasures?"

A pained look flashed through the baelnorn's eyes.

"I also promise you this, ghost," Krystarn said, stepping closer to the baelnorn and drawing her remaining magic energies into a tight weave around her, "that any of those treasures that I find lacking, I'll scatter above the ground in the ruins of Myth Drannor for any wandering band of adventurers to find. Each located far enough apart to guarantee that they'll be found by separate groups. Your house, should they ever realize that you have failed in your assigned task to keep their legacy intact for a time when they could return from Evermeet and safely claim it, would take lifetimes tracking them all down again. And it would be *your* fault."

"You have no honor."

"Honor," the drow said, "is merely one of the weaknesses I do not have. Thank you. I had not expected a compliment from someone such as you so early this morning."

"I will relish the day that Folgrim Shallowsoul turns on you, witch." The baelnorn turned and walked into the solid wall of rock beside it, vanishing without a trace.

Krystarn cursed the baelnorn and turned back to watch the hobgoblins below. None of the creatures had heard the exchange between her and the elven crypt guardian. An idea formed as she looked at the hobgoblins. Servants within the confines of the subterranean world were lacking. Especially ones that Shallowsoul did not know of.

Marshaling her strength, she stood up, making herself visible to the hobgoblins fifty feet below.

The females and the children scattered, taking the bedrolls and supplies from the illumination of the cookfire. With her drow vision, Krystarn could still see them all clearly.

"Beware, drow!" a hobgoblin male challenged. The dark gray hair covering the exposed parts of its body bristled. Its blue nose wrinkled in distaste, pulling at a ragged wound along its right temple. The naked length of a short sword reflected firelight in its right hand, and a coiled whip shook loose in its left, black leather slithering across the rock. "This place is claimed by the Sumalich Tribe!"

Krystarn almost laughed at the petty arrogance of the hobgoblin. "Who are you to address me in such a threatening manner?"

The hobgoblin stretched to its full height of nearly seven feet, taking a deep breath to throw out its chest. "I am Chomack, Taker of Dragon's Teeth, chief of the Sumalich!" Another hobgoblin male trotted over to stand beside him, holding the tribe's standard, a hand holding a spear thrust through a skull on a field of red and jet. "Taker of Dragon's Teeth?" Krystarn said in obvious disbelief. "Were the dragons then asleep when you took them? Or were they through with those teeth? Maybe these were truly old dragons who kept them in a pot by their bed."

Chomack howled in rage. He gestured to a pair of his warriors. They nocked arrows to bows and fired without hesitation.

The shafts sped true. Before they covered half the distance, though, Krystarn unleashed her magic. A double-forked lightning bolt licked out and burned the arrows from the air in a blaze of white fire. The bolt continued across the cavern till it struck the other side, then doubled around and came back.

Krystarn stood her ground. With her drow vision, she knew the breadth of the cavern and she'd chosen the effect the rebounding would have. She opened her hand as the lightning bolt traveled back toward her. The gale winds that accompanied the electric energy swept around her, stirring up dust devils that held glinting bits of rock.

The lightning bolt faded to nothing less than five paces from her open palm. The drow looked down at the hobgoblin tribe and appreciated the way they had thrown themselves down to the ground. Only Chomack and a handful of his more seasoned warriors remained standing.

"Sorceress," several of the hobgoblins whispered. The children cried out in fear.

Krystarn stepped forward, over the edge of the sheer ridge, and stood on empty air looking down at the hobgoblin tribe. "Know me, Chomack, and fear me, for I hold your life in my hands!" She made a fist. Allowing herself to descend within the semi-circle of fearful hobgoblins, she touched down lightly in front of the tribal chieftain. "I am Krystarn Fellhammer of the House Ta'Lon't, loyal servant of Lloth, the Spider Queen!"

A snarl rippled across Chomack's face, exposing his yellow teeth. "Kill me if you can, sorceress. I call no one master!" The tribal chieftain leaped at the drow, slashing with his short sword.

Krystarn met his attack with a warrior's skill. She parried the short sword with her morning star. Sparks flared as the weapons crashed together. Chomack dropped back into a crouch, then cracked his whip at her.

Metal glinted at the tip of the leather braid as it flashed at her face.

Whirling, Krystarn avoided the whip. She advanced again, swinging the morning star. The hobgoblin chieftain blocked her blow, then launched a kick at her face. Expecting such a move, the drow caught her opponent's foot and twisted.

Howling in rage and pain, Chomack threw himself up and back, flipping himself over in a show of skill and dexterity. He landed on his feet and prepared to attack yet again.

"Hold, Chieftain of the Sumalich Tribe!" Krystarn commanded. "I would not take your life if I could spare it!"

The hobgoblin chieftain halted, wariness in his eyes. "I have to keep my honor."

"Then keep your honor, Chomack, Taker of Dragon's Teeth."

Krystarn hung her morning star at her side from a leather loop. The hobgoblin chieftain's attack had been fierce and exhausted her still further. She longed to be in bed in the suite of rooms she'd claimed for herself in the underground ruins Shallowsoul managed. "I am here neither to take your life nor your honor. You challenged me justly." That behavior was a fatal character flaw the drow would never allow herself. "Instead, I would seek to make an alliance between us."

"I need no alliance," the tribal chieftain declared.

"You have a small tribe at present, and you are in uncertain lands," Krystarn pointed out.

"We have met foul beasts and ill magic in this place," Chomack said. "We have triumphed with our skill and bravery."

"So far. Yet how many have you lost in your wanderings through these caverns?"

Chomack did not answer, but some of the hobgoblins shifted around him uneasily. The drow's words had struck a chord of concern.

"You are here to seek your fortune," Krystarn said. "You do not have to tell me this because I can see by the packs your women and children carry. You have been busy accumulating wealth."

"I will raise an army," Chomack said. "With the treasure from these dead-elf pits, I will find an outlaw trader and buy more weapons. New weapons that are made of polished steel to fire the heart of any hobgoblin who call himself a warrior. When others hear of what I have, they will flock to my tribe."

"You are ambitious," Krystarn said. "What will you do with this army when you gather it?"

"There is an accounting of vengeance that must be made against the Ulnathr Tribe. They attacked our tribe from behind while we battled a band of troglodytes that had moved into our homeland and started eating us. Caught between the troglodytes and the Ulnathr Tribe, most of us were left for dead. We traveled deeper into these ruins. The coward-chieftain of the Ulnathr will not come here because of the wild magic."

"I can help you," Krystarn said.

The hobgoblin chieftain glanced at her suspiciously. "How?"

The drow opened her bag of holding and reached inside. When she drew out her hand, she opened it to show the jewels inside. "Here."

Hesitantly, Chomack held out his hand. Krystarn dumped the handful of diamonds, sapphires, rubies, and emeralds into the hobgoblin chieftain's palm. "Let this be a token of my interest in your success."

"This is much," Chomack said.

"Only a small fortune," the drow replied, "against the measure of my interests. I have been lucky in my life, Lloth be praised."

The hobgoblin chieftain passed the gems back to a subchieftain, who made them quickly disappear. "Why would you care about my cause?"

"I am not interested in furthering your cause," Krystarn answered honestly. "However, I am investing on a return against my good will."

"Huh?" Chomack asked suspiciously.

"As a down payment for the use of your sword arms at a time when I would need it." Krystarn felt a glow of satisfaction when the hobgoblin chieftain didn't immediately turn her offer down. The tribe was indeed in dire straits if they were delving into the ruins of Myth Drannor. She also knew that agreeing to a bargain with a drow was not something Chomack would want to do under normal circumstances. Shallowsoul did not control everything that happened in the ruins.

"When?"

"When I should so declare it." Having a small, well-equipped army within the caverns might prove beneficial, the drow knew. For the first time in the four years of her sacrifice to Lloth, she felt as if she might soon be freed.

"I will not throw away my life or my tribe," the hobgoblin chieftain warned.

"Nor would I have you do so. I do not fight battles to let the gods decide. If I ask you to fight for me, it will be to win, not to lose."

"And if we do?"

"There will be more gems and treasures for you to add to your coffers. I find vengeance a powerful motivation. I can see in your eyes that nothing less than blood-letting will sate yours. In that, we understand each other."

Chomack took a step back and swung his hard gaze on his tribespeople. None of them had moved any closer to the drow, nor had any of their weapons been lowered. "When I speak my answer to this sorceress, I speak for all of us. I want this to be understood. Any who would oppose me later will oppose me now."

Quiet murmurs and nods of assent spread around the half-circle of hobgoblins.

Chomack turned back to face the drow. "I agree to your terms, Krystarn Fellhammer. We shall give you our sword arms when you need them, and you will give us four gems for every gem you have already given us."

Irritation stung the drow. It wasn't that the amount was so much, she had managed to gather several times that much in gems and coins and other items in the years she had been with Shallowsoul, but the humanoid's greed offended her. Having the hobgoblin push the bargain so hard only meant he believed he had her at a disadvantage. She did not want him thinking that. "You are greedy," she said quietly.

"I thought your Lloth invented greed," Chomack said.

"Careful that your tongue does not commit a sacrilege that I cannot abide," Krystarn warned.

"I meant no offense, sorceress, but I've heard of the Spider Queen. Lloth, it is said, weaves webs of betrayals, treacheries, and deceits, and gives them all power by the driving force of greed."

"You misinterpret," Krystarn said.

"I don't know what that means, but maybe I was lied to once," the hobgoblin said. "I meant only to flatter, and for understanding. After all, I seek a way to achieve my vengeance, not half a way. That is why I must ask for what I ask for."

Krystarn smiled, thinking that Chomack acquitted himself very well in the negotiations. Perhaps the hobgoblin chieftain was destined for better things. "Very well, Taker of Dragon's Teeth. You shall have the amount you ask for, but only upon successful completion of the task you undertake for me."

"I have only one more question to ask, sorceress."

"What?"

"How do you know that you can trust me?"

Krystarn walked toward the hobgoblin chieftain. She felt powerful, the way a drow female was supposed to feel, the way Lloth had bred them to be. "I can trust you, Chomack, because as a hobgoblin you are not quite the antithesis of a human, as is such a wide-spread belief. Many of the same values they have, you and yours try to emulate, to bring you on equal footing with them."

Chomack started to disagree.

"Hold your tongue and hear me out," Krystarn ordered. "You are what you are, but you channel and direct yourself. It is not a bad thing. But you asked a question and I am answering it to the best of my ability. Your people live in a military fashion, and the basis of that lifestyle is order and honor." Neither of which, the drow admitted to herself, did she want in her own life.

"I have been told, sorceress, that honor means nothing to the drow."

"Indeed it does not," Krystarn replied. "But we understand how binding it can be on other species that prize it. I know you will bind yourself because of it."

"But how can you trust something you don't believe in?"

"By asking you to trust in your own trust, Taker of Dragon's Teeth. Hold, this will only hurt for a moment." Krystarn laid her forefinger against a bare spot on the hobgoblin's neck. To Chomack's credit, he flinched only a little when her fingernail laid open his flesh in a furrow almost two inches long. The drow plucked a single silver coin from her bag of holding. Working quickly, she warded it, allowing the designs she drew in the air to show as traces of pale green fire.

Chomack paled, but he did not move.

Finished with the spell to permanently mark the coin, the metal still warm to the touch, the drow shoved it into the cut in the hobgoblin's flesh. Chomack staggered only slightly, then regained his footing. Blood seeped down his neck.

"If you think to disappear, this will ensure that you won't," Krystarn stated. "No matter where you go, this coin will mark you and

I'll find you. If you seek to cut it out of your flesh, the coin will sink further into your body and become poisonous." What she said was a lie, but the drow knew the hobgoblin chieftain would be too afraid of her power to disbelieve. Reaching into the bag of holding, she took out a small vial of healing potion. Pouring carefully, she sprinkled the area she'd opened up on the hobgoblin's neck and along the side of his face. The torn flesh in those areas quickly mended. She stepped back. "Unless you have reconsidered your bargain."

"No, sorceress. My desire for revenge is strong."

"Then may your gods be with you. I will call you when I need you." Krystarn walked from their campsite, listening to the chatter of voices fill the void she left. Only a heartbeat before the light from the cookfire left her entirely, she used her magic to teleport her to another spot along the trail above.

When she arrived on the trail, she glanced back down at the hobgoblin tribe, finding them suitably impressed. The demonstration of her power made her feel good about herself. The last four years spent with Folgrim Shallowsoul had been unsettling to say the least. But her obedience in the matter had been demanded by Lloth. The Spider Queen demanded harsh sacrifices for the rewards that she offered.

Krystarn turned her steps back toward the underground keep Shallowsoul had erected from the ruins. According to Shallowsoul, much remained to be done to undo the damage Golsway had managed.

She only hoped there would be more killing. The business tonight had only whetted the drow's appetite, and she'd been too long without death at her hands.

8

"Baylee Arnvold!"

The young ranger turned his head, trying to track the familiar voice across the noise and imagery that were constants at any ranger forgathering. Long wooden tables hewed by axes from trees felled only two days ago occupied space under leafy awnings around the clearing.

Most of the activity remained around these tables. Stories were told there during all hours of the day. Amid the lies and boasts lounged half-truths that could save a man's life one day. Above all, though, it was entertainment that many of the ranger breed would never have except at a forgathering.

At other tables, bartering and competitions were held amid dozens of crafts. And there was song. Songs of humor, songs of bravery, songs of great sadness, and songs of legend. Some of those songs were quietly strummed, while others were given a boisterous voice.

Xuxa, Baylee prompted.

The azmyth bat darted through the night sky, chasing insects for her eveningfeast. After all the succulent fruits and cakes she had eaten since their arrival early that morning, Baylee did not see how Xuxa could swallow another morsel. He guessed that she used the exercise of chasing after her next meal to work up another appetite.

I am looking, the azmyth bat protested. *I did not hear the call clearly myself.*

Baylee passed through the thronging crowd that made up the forgathering.

"Baylee!" the voice called again.

It was a man's voice, the young ranger knew this time. That knocked out nearly half of the assembly.

West, Xuxa called from above.

97

Baylee turned slightly, getting his directions from the constellations spread across the clear sable sky. The Dragonspine Mountains ranged across the northern horizon, creating craggy gaps against the night since the forgathering was located in the foothills of the broken land.

A tenday and two days had passed since he'd recovered the book from the sacrificial well. He'd traveled to Waymoot and had the spell lifted from the page in the herbalist's book, finding the contract between two noble families of Waterdeep and a Zhentilar house of assassins for the murder of King Azoun. What he was going to do with it remained to be determined. From Waymoot, he'd traveled north again to Hillsfar on the Moonsea, then up to the forgathering area.

His heart had pulled at him in Hillsfar to forget the Glass Eye Concourse and travel on to Waterdeep to show Fannt Golsway his prize. Seeing Jaeleen again had wakened his feelings for seeing the old mage again. But Baylee had decided to wait. The Glass Eye Concourse happened only once a year. At his age, a year seemed like a long time. Looking back on it now, the concept of time passing had been one of the biggest points of contention between himself and Golsway.

"Baylee! Over here!"

The ranger recognized the voice only an instant before he spotted the man it belonged to. Aymric Tailpuller leaned against a tree near one of the wagons the mountain men had provided. Casks of wine and mead loaded the wagons down, and all of them flowed constantly.

"Deaf as you are," Aymric protested, "how is it you've managed to stay alive so long?" Tall and thin, the falconer enjoyed the slim good looks of youth and the vigor of the Moon elven bloodline. He wore his long blue hair in a single braid that ran down to his narrow hips when he let it loose. Deep blue eyes emphasized the paleness of his face and the sharp planes of his features. His leather armor showed the advantages of great care and considerable attention. A well-used bastard sword with a runed handle stuck up over one shoulder.

He has me to watch over him, Xuxa answered from above.

Aymric crowed with laughter as a smile split his face. He turned toward the sky. *Xuxa! How are you?*

Finally being properly cared for after nearly starving to death, the azmyth bat responded. *Thank you for asking.*

A number of rangers, their senses ever alert despite the amount of wine and mead that had been consumed, ducked as Xuxa came winging down in great, leathery flaps that cracked the air. The azmyth bat made a show of her aerial prowess, coming to nearly a dead stop in front of the Moon elf ranger before reaching out with her claws to seize the leather band around Aymric's wrist. She hung upside down, looking at the Moon elf and chuckling her happiness.

Despite his bond with the azmyth bat, Baylee always felt a pang of jealousy to see Aymric with Xuxa. She seemed clearly to favor the Moon elf with her attentions, and never had a cross word to say about him.

With quick hands, Aymric seized a morsel of an apple nut confection from a passerby involved in conversation before the owner knew he was there. The Moon elf held out the tidbit on a forefinger.

I couldn't, Xuxa said.

Of course you can, Aymric replied. *After all, it will be a whole year before another Glass Eye Concourse, and there is no better food at any of the other forgathering. This apple nut confection is a favorite, and you don't get it like this in many places.*

Xuxa accepted the treat in one winged paw and brought it daintily to her mouth.

"Watch out," Baylee warned aloud, abandoning the silent conversation, knowing Xuxa would resent it, "this is the bite that will make her burst."

A handful of people standing nearby who knew Xuxa and her prodigious appetite laughed.

You need to teach your friend manners, Aymric chided.

Xuxa ignored the exchange. She leaped from Aymric's arm and took up roost from a nearby tree branch.

"My friend," the Moon elf said warmly, reaching for Baylee and hugging him close, "how have things been with you?"

"Busy," Baylee admitted.

"Having much luck?"

"Some." Baylee had learned never to tell the first story around the elf, because the elf would surely top it with one of his own.

"How's Golsway?"

"I haven't seen him in some time."

Aymric shook his head. "Are you still insisting on going it alone?"

Baylee kept his emotions cloaked. "I like it that way."

"Of course you do." Aymric took a clay cup from one of the stacks near the wine casks. He filled it with help from a woman who happened to tap the cask at the same time as he needed it. When the cup was filled, he passed it to Baylee.

The young ranger tried to turn it down. "No, really, I've had enough."

"Enough wine?" Aymric looked incredulous. "That could never happen. The gods willing, you'll have a discretionary bladder that keeps everything flowing."

"I remember a forgathering a year or two ago in which I ended up cutting you down from your own hammock one morning because you couldn't even stand up by yourself."

"This is a party," Aymric protested. "A man can be forgiven his occasional indulgences."

Baylee is in no position to throw stones at anyone over indulgences, Xuxa spoke up. *Little more than a tenday ago, he ran into Jaeleen again. . . .*

Aymric shook his head. "I tell you, Baylee, that woman is worse than any bad habit you could pick up. You should stay away from her."

"It was a chance meeting," Baylee stated.

"Ill fortune, you mean." The Moon elf shook his head.

"Jaeleen is not my problem," Baylee replied.

Aymric clapped him on the shoulder. "And you would do well to make sure she never becomes your problem, my friend." He gestured toward the central area of the forgathering. "Come, let us enjoy what festivities lay before us."

Baylee followed his friend, moving from table to table and

speaking with those rangers he knew. They watched arm wrestling competitions and dart slinging championships, and listened to a few of the lies the mountain men spun with such silver-tongued ease, and even joined in with a chorus or two here and there when favorite songs were being sung.

"Aymric, Baylee," a young lad called from behind a tree. "Filston sent me to gather you if I could." He was tall and slender limbed, his hair springing about his freckled face.

"What is it?" Aymric asked.

"He said you would want to hear Vaggit's re-telling of the rise and fall of Myth Drannor," the young boy said. "Hurry. Vaggit is only now starting."

Aymric glanced at Baylee. "Shall we?"

Baylee grinned in anticipation. "How could we not?" He filched a slice of plum and pear pie from a heavily laden table and cupped it in his hand.

They followed the boy, taking a meandering path around the central campfire that blazed taller than a man. Spits hung with roasting venison and fowl still turned as volunteer cooks manned them, dripping honey glazes and pepper seasons across them.

Vaggit sat on a limb ten feet above the ground, resting on the soles of his bare feet with his arms wrapped around his knees. An audience of forty and more men and women, young and old, had already gathered for the telling. Baylee knew the forest runner had only just begun the lengthy telling because Vaggit wasn't yet pacing along the thick branch like a stage orator from a house of arts in Waterdeep or other civilized areas.

Short and scrawny, looking near to flesh leaned out over bone, the forest runner wore gray and green splashed garments that blended in with the night and his chosen environment. His leather armor stayed supple and loose, moving without a sound. In his profession as heckler of the aristocratic greedy in and around Zhentil Keep, moving quietly was a necessity. His gray hair and long gray beard testified to the experience he had, and the scars and way he carried himself spoke of the skills he'd learned. A long bow occupied a space beside him on the branch, an arrow resting at the ready on the bowstring.

Baylee took up a position against a gnarled elm with low sweeping branches. Winged animal companions and some possessing climbing skills sat in the trees surrounding the small pocket clearing of the forgathering. Occasional cries or cawing as they shifted chased through the cool breezes coming down from the Dragonspine Mountains.

"And lo," Vaggit said in his deep basso voice that was so surprising from so little a man, "wise and mighty Eltargrim, himself a warrior and experienced in many battles, looked out over this city that had become known as the Towers of Song, and he listened to the counsel of Elminster even though it cost him the support of the Starym and other families who left the Elven Court."

A young girl of no more than five or six summers walked forward and held up a stone cup of mead. Her blond hair whipped in the breeze, almost touching the ground when the wind died down.

Amazingly, a section of the branch above Vaggit's head shifted liquidly. The color changed as Baylee watched, becoming the red-brown skin of a pseudodragon that fell from the branch in a loose sprawl.

For a moment, the pseudodragon looked certain to smash against the child. Then it opened its wings and deftly took the cup from the little girl's hands. She laughed gaily, then turned and ran back to her mother.

Vaggit held out a hand, never bothering to check for the cup. The pseudodragon put the cup gently in his hand.

"The old scoundrel has had a good year from all accounts I've heard," Aymric whispered at Baylee's side. "He's emptied the purses of several Zhentil nobles in his pursuit of justice in his woods, then spread the wealth back among the people those nobles robbed under the statutes of the law. Though why he didn't keep enough for a good set of clothes to wear to the concourse this year is beyond me."

Baylee smiled. He respected and admired the old forest runner. "If Vaggit cared about material possessions, he'd never be the man he is. Should he have wanted a new suit of clothes, I'm sure one of the lonely ladies around Zhentil Keep who think so highly of him would have made a set for him just for the asking."

"To hear him tell it, mayhap."

"I've been in Zhentil Keep," Baylee said. "The people there who struggle against the tyrants talk well of Vaggit."

Aymric waved the comment away. "I meant no disparaging remark, old friend. In truth, the matter I was referring to was how many of the children in those homes that Vaggit himself might have fathered during his adventures. You forget, I'm older than you are. I remember Vaggit when he was your age."

Baylee smiled at the thought. Of all the rangers gathered at the concourse, old Vaggit indeed did have the least problem finding someone to care for his tent and precious few belongings.

"There you are," a feminine voice said. "I've been looking for you everywhere."

Aymric and Baylee turned together. "Serellia," Baylee said with a smile, opening his arms. "And how are you?"

The woman came into Baylee's arms with a flurry of leather. She was as tall as he, her garments crafted of purple-dyed leather, and her raven's-wing black hair cut short around her face. The one-piece skirt/tunic allowed a view of generous cleavage and an expanse of toned, healthy thigh. A short sword hung upside down from her back in a quick release sheath.

The hug lasted long enough to make Baylee feel uncomfortable in the presence of so many other people. He politely broke the hold and stepped back, his hands resting on Serellia's shoulders.

"I am fine," Serellia said.

"The last I saw of you," Baylee said, "there was the matter of a certain Red Wizard of Thay who'd sent a dozen or so sellswords after you to return a bauble you stole from him."

Serellia's eyes widened playfully, and she looked around behind Baylee. "Surely, they're not still in pursuit. It's been months."

"They gave up?" Baylee asked.

Serellia nodded. "After I killed three of them in their sleep, over the course of five days."

"Dear lady," Aymric said, "I can't believe any man would cease to chase after you." He took Serellia's hand and kissed her fingers delicately. "It would take death to still a man's heart after he's looked upon your beauty."

Serellia laughed out loud as she took her hand back from the elf. "What a bag of offal." She looked around the crowd. "Has someone got a camp spade?"

Baylee laughed as well when he saw the pained grimace flicker across Aymric's aristocratic features.

Why couldn't you be more interested in someone like Serellia? Xuxa asked. *Now here's a human female even an azmyth bat can appreciate. Other men think she's beautiful. I've read their thoughts while they've been around you and her. Even Aymric appears smitten.*

It's the wine, Baylee said.

Faugh! Look at her. She is beautiful, and I know she cares about you because I've read her mind on more than one—

Xuxa!

"Who's your friend with the quick compliments?" Serellia asked.

"You two haven't met?" Baylee asked, surprised. Sometimes it seemed that Aymric knew everyone, and everyone knew him.

"No," Aymric answered. "I've never had the . . . pleasure."

"No," Serellia said, "you haven't. Otherwise you'd know not to try to mire me in such an approach."

Baylee managed the introductions. "Aymric, I'd like to introduce Serellia Oparyan, an explorer like myself."

"For profit or play?" Aymric asked.

"For knowledge," Serellia replied without rancor. "And a chance to see all of Toril."

"Ambitious," Aymric said.

"Very," Serellia agreed.

"And this is Aymric Tailpuller," Baylee said. "A falconer without equal."

"I've heard of you," Serellia said. "Your birds are among the best in all of the Heartlands."

A shadow of a smile returned to Aymric's face. "Then I am to assume that you've not traveled much further than there. Otherwise, you would have learned that the birds I have trained are the best in other lands as well."

Baylee noted the disapproving looks they gathered from nearby people who were listening to Vaggit's tale of Myth Drannor's fall. He ushered his two friends out of the group and toward a campfire that had been all but abandoned. A small knot of men surrounded one of the tables, trading goods scattered across folded cloths as they bartered.

"I'll go get some wine," Baylee offered as Aymric and Serellia took up seats at the table. He guessed that would take the edge off for the elf, and Serellia liked wine as well.

Maybe it would be in your interest to try to spend more time with Serellia, Xuxa said.

At the closest wine cask, Baylee took up three clay cups and filled them. *No.*

She could fill those nights when you're lonely for companionship.

There is some concern about the past that is between us. Baylee took his cups back to his friends, finding them deeply engaged in a conversation regarding the care and handling of doves aboard sailing ships.

"They took doves aboard ships because they were far more trainable," Aymric was saying.

"Not according to Dakilinan," Serellia objected.

"And, pray tell, who was this Dakilinan?"

Serellia sipped her wine. "You've heard of Lantan?"

"Dear lady," Aymric stated, "I have lived there."

Serellia looked at Baylee, who only shrugged. Lantan lay a thousand miles south of the Moonshaes and was renowned for the maroon-sailed trading ships that plied the waters in the southern seas.

"It's true." Aymric acted as if he took offense at the doubt and the lack of support. "And during that time, I've not heard of Dakilinan."

"He lived there as well," Serellia announced.

"Nowhere near me," Aymric stated.

"About a thousand years ago," the beautiful ranger went on. "He was an historian of some repute."

"There are some who don't think highly of his work," Baylee supplied.

"Did he ever write of precious metals or gems?" Aymric asked.

"Only in passing," Serellia said. "He was more concerned with peoples and countries. Particularly the sea-faring traders."

"All this has a point, I'm sure," Aymric said, "that has something to do with doves."

"Dakilinan suggested that doves were taken aboard ships only because they were far easier to spot against the emerald expanse of the Trackless Sea and the blue sky. Trainability came in as a secondary reason. Domesticated doves were kept aboard ship and freed during different parts of the day. Wind directions were charted, as were ocean currents, anything that could offer a clue about an unexplored patch of sea."

"Your historian cites the people of Lantan as a race of explorers?" Aymric inquired.

Serellia smiled and shook her head. "Never for a moment. They were a race of traders, always looking for a new trade route, new countries with which to trade. Profit has always spurred every new discovery made in our world. Ask any explorer worth her salt if that isn't so. The first thing she'll tell you about is the difficulty in securing funds for an expedition. You have to meet with such small-minded people, and the things they're willing to search for are extremely limited."

So true, Xuxa added, and chirped woefully.

"That's why," Aymric said with a sarcastic grin, "so many explorers have gone to the trouble in the past to create a treasure map that no one has ever found before."

"Not all explorers are that way," Serellia replied. "Only enough to give the rest of us a bad name. I've never created such a map, nor has Baylee, or Fannt Golsway to name others."

"But treasure maps make such a pretty story," Aymric said.

"There are some out there," the woman answered. "Particularly among people whose treasures are ill-gotten. And many of them are merely bait to bring the avaricious and curious to their doom. I've been on more than a few such expeditions myself. This is a very dangerous business. Make a mistake in one of the crypts and dungeons where all too often these treasures are kept, and you're dead."

"Or undead, as the case may be," Baylee pointed out.

"Remember our trip to the Lonely Moor two years ago?"

"Three years ago." Serellia smiled at the memory. "Even Golsway didn't think we were going to make it out of that one without becoming undead ourselves."

Aymric raised his eyebrows. "Really? Now this sounds like a tale to spend over a wine cup or five. You've not mentioned this before, Baylee."

"That's because I'm generally listening to your stories," the ranger replied.

Aymric placed a hand over his heart. "You've lanced me ignobly."

"It is a good story," Serellia agreed. "Perhaps before the concourse is over, I could tell it."

"I'd be enchanted, dear lady." The elf nodded his head graciously.

"And if you try to touch me, I'll break your arms."

Baylee laughed, knowing that Serellia meant what she said, and seeing that Aymric was realizing that as well.

Baylee . . . Xuxa began.

No.

"Getting back to the doves," Aymric said. "I understand why the sailors used them. Loosing them as they did, the doves circled in all directions, but returned at some point in the day when they grew tired, to be with their mates."

"Exactly," Serellia nodded. "The sailors used them as scouts. When a bird returned well fed and rested hours after it had taken off, they knew they were close to land. But Dakilinan also suggests this is why the early races view doves as a symbol of peace."

"How so?" Aymric asked.

"The early explorers only went to trade," Serellia said. "The conquerors arrived later, after the way had been thoroughly mapped. The traders brought the doves, and they brought goods to trade. The would-be conquerors who went to rape and pillage didn't."

"And this is what Dakilinan bases his theory on?" Aymric asked.

"It is as good as any other reason for why doves are so revered among so many cultures."

Aymric shifted his gaze between Baylee and Serellia. "How is it you two know each other? Through your various adventuring?"

Baylee tried to signal to the elven ranger to stop his question, but Aymric either missed it or paid it no heed.

Serellia sat back in her chair, her demeanor losing some of the cheer she'd possessed. "I was a student of Golsway's before Baylee."

That's why it could never work, Baylee chided Xuxa. In truth, Serellia had been Golsway's first chosen, the best and the brightest of the pupils he sometimes apprenticed in order to ferret out a new associate for his expeditions. In the end, the old mage had selected Baylee over Serellia, but no explanations were offered. The event had left both of them wondering. Though Serellia apparently had no ill will toward either Golsway or Baylee, the ranger recognized that both of them were uncomfortable with the situation.

"I see." Aymric stroked his chin, obviously knowing there was more to the story. "Would you care to see some of the birds I brought for show at the concourse?"

A wave of relief washed through Baylee. He drained the dregs of his wine cup as Serellia asked the elf about the birds.

"Baylee."

The ranger looked up and spotted old Karg the Thunderer approaching.

Karg was a massive man, shoulders a full axe handle and more across. His arms were as thick as most men's thighs, and his thighs were strong enough to lift a table of ten men over his head. Baylee had also seen him crush small rocks in his callused bare hands, dropping nuggets and dust to the ground. The head of a huge, double-bitted dwarven axe poked up over his shoulders, incredibly nearly as wide across as his shoulders.

"Well met, Karg," Baylee called. "And how are you?"

The big man's face split into a grin. "There's a few less stone giants roving these lands than there were last year, thank the Lady. I trust you've had an eventful year."

"I've had better," Baylee replied, curious about why Karg would seek him out. Usually they only talked in groups. Giant killers were notorious boasters, and at best only made good company for a limited time.

"Have you been to Waterdeep lately?" Karg peered back across the concourse.

"Not in months."

"Did you leave trouble there?"

Even more curious now, Baylee asked, "What's wrong, Karg?"

"Interlopers," the giant killer snorted. "We end up getting a few of them every year. Usually give 'em the bum's rush if they start interfering with the festivities. Most of them pretend to be rangers, but they've never really had the calling. Or the talent. But we've a group here now that's downright interesting."

"Why?" Baylee asked.

"You know Tryklyss?" Karg asked.

"Known as the Quick-Handed," Aymric said.

"The very same." Karg nodded without enthusiasm. "Of course, he doesn't do any stealing here, but after some of us got suspicious about this new group, we found Tryklyss and suggested he take a peek in their things."

Baylee was intrigued, wondering how all of this had sent the giant killer looking for him. His limited contact with Waterdeep had been only inquiries about Golsway. The last he'd heard, months ago, the old mage had been well.

"Tryklyss didn't get very far," Karg said. "Their personal belongings are heavily warded. At least one of the group possesses extensive training in magic. What he did find out, though, was that this group is traveling under orders from the Waterdeep Watch."

"What are they doing here?" Serellia asked. "The Watch is concerned only with what goes on inside the walls. They'd have no power out here."

"What they want has yet to be determined," Karg answered. "However, they have been asking questions about young Baylee. It seems they've come all this way to find you."

9

"Baylee Arnvold? Yes, I believe I saw him only a short time ago. He was deep in his cups, wandering, you know, so I don't really know where he might be at this moment. But you might try over at the axe throwing contest. That's always been a favorite of his."

Cordyan Tsald listened to the explanation from the woman ranger with increasing irritation. She and her watch group had been led in circles for the last hour. "Thank you for your time," she said politely.

The ranger, a woman in her late fifties dressed all in forest green and touching the head of the great panther at her side, shook her head. "And why would you be thanking me? This is a party, isn't it? Not some functionary in a noble's court." She turned and walked away. The panther hesitated only a moment, its tail twitching reflexively as it covered the ranger's back. Its deep green eyes regarded Cordyan steadily. Then it turned and padded away.

Cordyan let out a sigh of relief. Personally, she loved animals. But the abundance of them at the concourse was staggering. She glanced around to get her bearings again, and spotted the axe throwing contest. Cinching her sword over her hip more comfortably, she looked to her left and saw the two members of the watch who worked in tandem with her.

Signaling her intent, she indicated where they were going and to remain back away from her. She had already drawn more attention than she wanted to with all of her questions about Baylee Arnvold.

She walked toward the axe throwing competition, guessing that she wouldn't find the ranger there, either. The rangers were hiding Baylee because he was one of their own, she understood that, but if he was somehow responsible for what had happened to Fannt Golsway more than a tenday ago, she didn't think that would be so. Granted, there were outlaws among the rangers, but none who were outright.

As she passed through the concourse grounds, she was aware of the men's heads who turned to watch her pass. Five and a half feet tall and slender, not having seen twenty-five winters yet, she carried herself well. Her chestnut colored hair ended at her shoulders and flipped in toward her neck, a proud mane that caught the firelight and burned copper. Her traveling leathers were worn but serviceable. She wore riding leathers over her breeches, and left her arms bare with the patched leather tunic. Her boots had low-cut heels so she could navigate broken terrain better. Her left hand closed automatically around the long sword at her side to hold it in place. Secreted in a number of pouches throughout all her traveling clothes, she carried a number of leaf-bladed darts. Dagger handles thrust up from her boots.

Find Baylee Arnvold and bring him back to Waterdeep for questioning.

That had been Captain Tirdan Closl's orders to her. Cordyan had been greatly surprised that the Watch was being empowered to go so far to bring someone back. It was no secret that the Watch extended their reach from the city upon occasion, but coming to the forgathering was the farthest she had ever heard of.

Nearly thirty men and women ringed the competition area. Lanterns hung from trees along a path nearly twenty feet long. Competitors stood at one end of the twenty foot distance and threw their favorite axes at the target at the other end, a tree trunk hewn and laying on its side. The target was almost three feet across. Innumerable scars cut into the tree trunk already. A silver piece gleamed in the center of the target, but no one had hit it yet.

The current ranger at the line drew back and let fly with a camp axe. The axe flipped end over end, then smacked into the target with a loud, meaty *thunk*. The handle quivered for a moment from the force.

A ragged cheer went up from a handful of the watchers, while others groaned. It had come closest to the small target.

Approaching one of the cheerers, thinking the man might be more inclined to answer favorably while winning, Cordyan said,

"I'm looking for Baylee Arnvold."

"When you find him," the man said, "tell him Rasnip says 'well met,' and he owes me a drink." He turned back to the competition, clapping as the next contestant stepped to the line.

Cordyan looked up at the trees and curbed her anger. A host of birds and climbing things stared back at her from the branches, their eyes amber, orange, and red from the lantern light. Senior Civilar Closl should have known this would be a fruitless mission. However, after hearing how Golsway's body had been found, she supposed there was no choice. Baylee Arnvold was the only lead the Watch had. She sighed. "What does it take to step to the line and compete?" she asked.

Rasnip looked at her and cocked an eyebrow. "You've evidently got a willing heart. Have you a keen eye and a strong arm to go with it?"

"There's only one way to find out."

The newest contestant made the throw with the axe, further away from the center than the last contestant had been. More cheering and groaning followed.

"Then it will cost you a silver piece," the ranger said.

Cordyan reached into her belt pouch and took out a silver coin. She flipped it at the ranger, who snatched it from the air with practiced ease.

Rasnip moved forward. "Hold up. We have a new contestant." He looked at Cordyan. "What is your name?"

"Cordyan," she answered, moving to the line.

"Cordyan of where?"

"Waterdeep."

"And you are a ranger?" Rasnip asked.

"No." Cordyan knew the group at the forgathering had already guessed that. However, they didn't know her true nature. "I'll have to borrow an axe."

Several rangers laughed at the request. "She doesn't have her own axe?"

"Going to throw with someone else's?"

"I'm willing to make a wager on this," a man cried. "Does anyone want to try to take my money?"

A young man with a feathered cap stepped from the crowd and handed Cordyan a weathered hatchet. "It might not look like much because I've put it to ill use over the years, but it's a trusty weapon."

Cordyan took the hatchet. She ran her fingers along the smooth handle. It didn't have a practiced finish, rather it was probably accomplished by rubbing a rough stone against it till the present finish was achieved. The head had a few nicks that a whetstone hadn't been able to remove.

Some of the rangers guffawed at the condition of the borrowed piece of equipment, believing it to place Cordyan in even more dire straits. The young ranger blushed, evidently embarrassed by his own offering.

"That hatchet didn't do young Turloc any favors," someone said. "He's already had his attempt at the prize."

Cordyan took her stand at the throwing line and concentrated on the target, marking it in her mind. "And what is the prize?"

"What is the purse so far?" Rasnip asked.

"There have been eighty-two misses so far," a woman called out. "It's the ill lighting and the wine."

"That means there's eighty-two silvers to be won," Rasnip answered.

Cordyan let out a breath and shrugged, using the movement to disguise the act of removing two of the leaf-bladed throwing darts from her tunic. Around her, the rangers fell silent. With a smoothness born of long practice, she threw the hatchet.

The weapon flipped exactly three times. True to the young ranger's word, the hatchet was expertly weighted for throwing. On the final revolution, the axe blade came around hard and bisected the silver coin. Partially held by whatever was used to hold the coin in place, the halves dropped to either side.

In an eye blink, Cordyan threw the darts. No one knew they were there until they embedded in the tree trunk. Their feathers jutted from the wood, and the leaf-shaped blades caught the two coin pieces before they could drop to the ground.

Stunned silence followed the display of accuracy.

Cordyan had no doubt that the rangers at the forgathering

would talk afterwards. She crossed the twenty feet, took out her darts, then tugged the hatchet free and returned it to the young ranger she had borrowed it from.

Stopping in front of Rasnip, she said calmly, "There was some mention of prize money."

Rasnip thrust out a hand. A woman dropped a bulging leather coin purse into it. Quietly, he surrendered it to Cordyan. "What was your name again?"

"Cordyan Tsald," she replied as she took the purse. "Junior Civilar Tsald, of the Waterdeep Watch. And I'm here on business to see Baylee Arnvold. Tell him that when you see him." She turned and walked away, leaving a crowd of staring rangers and assembled animals behind.

A tall, thin man with a short, clipped, graying beard fell into step beside her. He kept his hands clasped behind his back. He wore robes and a pointed skullcap that marked him as a wizard before he worked one spell. "Was that really necessary?" he asked in a dry voice.

"Not if you've found Baylee Arnvold," Cordyan answered.

"I haven't."

Cordyan watched the movements of the rangers around them, reading the patterns from long years of practice. "They know who we are."

"Yes." Calebaan Lahjir nodded. He was a watch wizard assigned by Closl to Cordyan's unit. As such, they shared a joint command over the watch team, which irked Cordyan.

"They let us in," the watch lieutenant said, "so they could watch us."

"Precisely." Calebaan smiled slightly. "When you look at it in the right fashion, you can see the humor of the situation."

Cordyan cut her eyes toward the wizard. They'd worked together off and on for years. When she had worked some of her first investigations in Waterdeep that had involved wizardry, Calebaan had tutored her and given her time that he hadn't had to. "They're hiding him."

"Baylee *is* one of their own."

"So I thought I'd let them know we knew what was going on as well." Cordyan stopped at a table burgeoning with food. "The fact of the matter is that we can't just take Baylee from them." She worked to fill a clay plate with foodstuffs, finding herself politely aided by the rangers helping serve out. "All we can do is make ourselves as interesting to Baylee as we can."

"I see. You have always had a direct way about you, Cordyan, that I only sometimes admire." The wizard surveyed the table, finally settling on a few squares of apple nut crunch.

Cordyan signaled to the rest of her troops, having them stand down. They could watch over each other and join in the feast. All fourteen men and women signaled back. The watch lieutenant couldn't see them all, but the signals were relayed. By the time she had two cups of wine for herself and Calebaan, she had all the numbers.

"How much do you know about Baylee Arnvold?" she asked the wizard as they found space at an empty table.

"I have heard of him," Calebaan admitted. "Though I must admit, usually only in conjunction with Fannt Golsway, may the Lady keep him close."

Cordyan said a short prayer to Mystra, asking her to bless the food and her quest. At the end, she touched the Harper pin hidden by her tunic. Lord Piergeiron and the Watch of Waterdeep weren't the only ones interested in what had happened to Golsway. "Baylee's major weakness is his curiosity."

"So you seek to draw him in." Calebaan looked around in distress.

"Like the moth to the candle."

10

Krystarn Fellhammer.

The drow warrior felt the words in her mind as she sat before her altar to Lloth. The rooms around her were immersed in total darkness, but her drow vision brought all the details out clearly. The smell of incense lingered in the room. "Yes," she replied. The telepathic touch of Folgrim Shallowsoul made her cringe inside.

I have found the ranger, Baylee Arnvold. Shallowsoul's voice sounded, thin, raspy, and cold.

"I am on my way." Krystarn closed her prayers to the Spider Queen, asking only for the strength to see her mission through to the end, begging forgiveness for not being able to offer up the heart of an enemy at this time in sacrifice.

She took up her weapons and her traveling clothes. Shallowsoul would not have called had she not been going somewhere. With all her gear strapped about her, she pulled on her *piwafwi* over it all. The last tenday had been filled with boredom awaiting Shallowsoul's attempts at finding the ranger, but she'd pursued her efforts at finding Shallowsoul's real hiding place. None of those efforts had met with success.

The rooms were elegantly furnished with furniture she had recovered from what had been the finest houses around Myth Drannor. It was a pocket-sized palace, but she knew it was only a gilded boil inside a corpse.

She warded the door behind her as she stepped through into a hallway filled with ruin. Two male drow under her command stood watch over her door. They worked in shifts, making sure she was never alone or unprotected in her rooms.

"Malla," they said in unison, using the drow term for an honored one. The title always made Krystarn smirk.

"Go get the others," she ordered one of them. She couldn't remember his name.

The drow male hurried away. The remaining one fell into step with her, holding his spear butt just clear of the ground so it wouldn't make any noise.

Krystarn followed the hallway to the other end. No lights lit the walls, but she didn't need them. A wall blocked the end of the hallway. She put her hand out against it, then discovered it was still solid. She remained facing the wall, listening to the others of her entourage fall into lines behind her.

She didn't need to look to make sure they were all there. Twenty-two drow males had followed her from Menzoberranzan, their lives pledged to her task, accepting that she had been placed upon her quest by Lloth, Queen of the Demonweb Pits, herself.

The wall rippled before Krystarn, then pulsed like a great mouth about to open.

"Come." Shallowsoul's command filled her mind.

"Wait for me," Krystarn ordered the male drow warriors.

"Yes, Malla," Captain V'nk'itn responded. "We shall stand steady."

Krystarn knew that the male drow wouldn't stand there out of loyalty, but out of fear of her vengeance if they failed. When she had taken them, she had tied their blood to hers; if they fled, she could follow.

She wrapped her fingers around the hilt of the morning star and stepped through the door. Immediately, the rush of cold wind wrapped around her and she went blind and deaf. She felt like a leaf trapped in a treacherous whirlpool in the streams that cut through the Underdark. Yet, at the same time, she maintained her sense of equilibrium.

The darkness cleared like cool fog drifting in from one of the streams leading into Menzoberranzan. Cool air obscured her true Drow vision for a moment.

"Enter." Shallowsoul's physical voice sounded even worse than his mental one.

Krystarn took exactly two steps forward. As always, the room she appeared in was not one she had been in before. Her heart stilled in her chest as she gazed around at the shelves of books that occupied all four walls and stood in stacks in the center of the large room.

This was what she lusted for, what she had promised Mother Lloth her direct obedience forever after in exchange for her success. A stack of books stood so close to her that she could reach out and touch them if she but moved her arm. But she didn't, because she knew to do so would mean instant death. Shallowsoul allowed no one to touch the books.

She scanned the titles, finding them in a language she did not comprehend. Shallowsoul played his games with her avarice and she knew it. Deliberately, she was teleported of late into rooms of the vast library where she could not read the titles. Thick and pristine, arranged so neatly on the shelves, the books called out to her.

Shallowsoul laughed, and the noise sounded like bones grating, somewhere on the other side of the stacks. "Even from here I feel your greed, drow." His voice sounded like it was squeezed from a narrowly open crypt, deep but somehow still breathless.

"Be glad of it," Krystarn said. "Else how would you know I would stay in your thrall?" She let him have his laugh. Every time she saw a new volume that she had not seen before, she carefully recorded the symbols and warped languages she remembered. Already in her bag of holding that never left her side, she possessed a book with dozens of inscriptions.

"It would do you good," Shallowsoul said, "to remember who is master in our relationship."

Krystarn bowed her head in humility. She was a drow female, not born to know the yoke of a man even among her own people, much less to subjugate herself to the whims of such a *thing* as Folgrim Shallowsoul. A lesser drow, one less committed to Mother Lloth, would have broken. There were some, she knew, who would have mistakenly believed that the Queen of the Demonweb Pits had deserted them.

Instead, Krystarn knew that Lloth was only molding her anger, tempering it into the greatest weapon the Queen of Spiders would ever have in her arsenal. And when the time came to bare that weapon, edged with all the knowledge she would reap from the library, all of Toril would not be safe from her unleashed hatred.

Folgrim Shallowsoul rounded the stack in front of the drow elf and stopped. Tortured nightmares had given him shape, while fierce magic had given him form. Gaunt and skeletal, his gaze burned with the pinpoints of green light surrounded by the black emptiness nesting inside the eye sockets. A fistful of dead white hair stuck to his head in a long, unkempt mane that trailed down his back. Blue–green dead flesh clung to its skull, stubbornly giving it features in spite of the immutability of nature. The lips had peeled back from its teeth, giving Shallowsoul a permanent sneering grimace.

He wore clothes of nobility, the cloth interwoven with fine strands of gold and silver, spotted with sapphire chips worked in intricate patterns. Over the long decades, the clothing had rotted and become tattered.

He held a volume in one hand. A long taloned finger with skin so thin the bone showed through marked his place. "You remember Baylee Arnvold?" he asked.

"Fannt Golsway's apprentice," Krystarn answered, knowing Shallowsoul should know by now that she never forgot anything.

"Yes. He is at a forgathering. You're aware of what that is?"

"A forgathering is a meeting place of rangers." Krystarn waited, knowing from experience that Shallowsoul would not tell her his news until he was ready.

"This one is called the Glass Eye Concourse," Shallowsoul went on. He walked through the stacks, motioning Krystarn to follow.

The drow elf waited a step before trailing. Shallowsoul was a lich, and as such he radiated an aura of cold and darkness that unsettled even her nerves. Immediately, she felt the wall of freezing despair lift from her, and it seemed as though a thousand pounds had dropped from her shoulders.

"There will be hundreds of rangers at this forgathering." Shallowsoul reached out and meticulously straightened one of the books on a shelf where the corners did not quite overlap.

Krystarn took full opportunity to gaze at all the shelves of books. The room was even more vast than she had imagined. Twenty paces in now, and she still couldn't see the other side of it.

Only one wall was visible to her left. It soared up thirty feet before meeting the ceiling. A wheeled ladder hooked to the shelves ran all the way to the top, allowing a person to climb up to reach the highest volumes.

The two walls visible to her through the gaps in the intricate shelving looked like stone. The drow believed the vast library had been initially buried underground, not sunk there as the magic of the Army of Darkness had stricken the city and the protective mythal had come apart.

The room appeared to conform to no real shape as well, furthering her suspicions that the library had been deliberately designed to confuse any who entered it. Fragments in scrolls that she had found that spoke of the library had mentioned maps being necessary to find a way through.

Without those maps, even the parts of the library that Krystarn had seen would require years to merely catalog, even without getting into the content. Once in, if a searcher allowed himself or herself to be pulled in too far, there would be no return.

"I want you to find Baylee Arnvold and kill him," Shallowsoul ordered.

"When?" Krystarn asked.

"Now." The lich rounded another stack and the way widened, leading to a high desk in front of a tall stool. A large book occupied the center of the desk, the pages still wet with ink. A quill and an ink pot sat to one side.

Krystarn surveyed the writing, finding it like nothing she'd seen before in all her studies. Liches were undead, usually long removed from any vestiges of humanity. Once she'd discovered Shallowsoul's true nature, she'd studied about liches. One of the key points of Su'vann'k'tr of the House Fla'nvm's writings, was that liches often created brand new magic items and spells that no one had heard of before. Removed from the driving needs of the flesh, a lich instead obsessed on harnessing the mystical powers it could never achieve while remaining a living being. That it would create its own language was no surprise.

"You would have me kill this ranger in the midst of hundreds of his own?" Krystarn let her incredulity sound in her voice.

"It is true that I am a harsh taskmaster, Krystarn Fellhammer," Shallowsoul said, "but it would be foolish for me to give such an assignment without giving you the means to see it through. Even while mortal, I was never a foolish man."

Krystarn had some reservations whether the lich could remember back that far to make such a statement.

Shallowsoul sat at the desk. A single candle burned at the desk, but the drow knew it was more for conducting spells that needed heat or fire rather than any need for light. The lich saw as well as the drow in the absence of light, perhaps even better.

Krystarn surveyed the room as her mother had taught her. Her peripheral vision took in the short flights of stairs heading in three different directions less than a stone's throw from the desk area. When she had time, she fully intended to map out the area in her book based on the parts of the library she had seen so far.

"Why not have Baylee killed away from the forgathering?" the drow asked.

"I want a message sent," the lich said, digging in a drawer of the desk. "Fannt Golsway found the bitter dregs of a trail better left uncovered. I will not allow it to come anywhere close to this library. I want no one else to come after Baylee Arnvold or Fannt Golsway with prying eyes. The secret dies with them."

"Are you sure that Baylee knows about the library?" Krystarn asked.

The lich regarded her with his fiery green pinpoint gaze from the hollowed eye sockets. "You ask so that you may add to your own small store of knowledge."

"I ask because I have a vested interest at stake as well." Krystarn forced herself to stare into the lich's dead gaze. Her muscles trembled against the urge to turn and flee from the cold emanating from the foul creature. "You and I have an agreement. For every five years of my servitude to you, I am allowed to make a copy of a book from this library."

The lich waved to the shelves. "A pittance against all that is actually here."

"Yet a fortune to me," Krystarn countered. "I would learn from you, as I have offered."

"I have no need of an apprentice. I do not intend to forsake this unlife."

"As you have made so clear."

Shallowsoul regarded her, and a cold smile curved his tattered lips baring his teeth even more. The drow thought she even heard the flesh crack and split. "I want you to kill the ranger, Baylee Arnvold."

"How?" Krystarn challenged.

The lich brought a bag onto the desk. Four gold bands big enough to go around Krystarn's head encircled the bag. Even as the bag lay on the desk, the cloth jumped and moved. "Do you know what these are?" He tossed one to her.

At her knowing touch, Krystarn could feel the magic within the band. "No."

"You've seen skeleton warriors, I presume?" Shallowsoul asked.

"Yes." Krystarn's stomach tightened at the thought, and the announcement confirmed the suspicion she had about the gold bands.

"These are control bands for the four skeleton warriors in this bag." Shallowsoul tossed the bag across. "Do you know how to use them?"

Krystarn caught the bag of holding. "I've been told once you're wearing a band, you have control over the skeleton warrior."

"Their souls were captured and placed within those bands," Shallowsoul agreed. "Those particular four were once enemies. I killed them, stripped their souls from their dying bodies, and enchanted them within those bands. They've been there for hundreds of years."

The bag shifted in the drow's grip. The gold bands felt chill against her skin.

"Choose three of your men and take them with you." Shallowsoul crossed the room to a stack and took down a weathered wooden staff. "This staff has already been charged with enough magic to take yourself and the three you've chosen to the forgathering. There are two charges. One to open a dimensional door to take you there, and the other to bring you back again."

Krystarn caught the staff, folding it readily into her grip.

"Go now," the lich ordered, "and do not fail me."

Questions filled the drow's mind, but she uttered none of them. She had learned never to question Shallowsoul. The lich brooked no such thing. She inclined her head again, taking one last glance around the room to memorize it, then turned and walked away. She deliberately chose another path, hoping the lich thought she'd merely gotten turned around.

Two steps forward, her eyes hungrily devouring the texts around her, searching for a clue as to what the pages might contain, the air in front of her suddenly rippled. Shallowsoul's grating bone laughter flared to harsh life around her. Then the dimensional door pulled her through.

In one cold, falling eye blink, she stood back in the tunnel. A wave of dizziness overcame her as the last of the lich's laughter faded away.

One of the males reached out to aid her.

Regaining her balance, Krystarn drew one of the short daggers secreted in her corset and raked a cruel line of blood across the male's cheek. Even as he reacted, trying to step away from the blade, Krystarn stepped forward and shoved the dagger up under his nose, hooking the tip into one nostril to freeze the male into place. A trickle of blood ran down his upper lip.

"Do not forget your station," she warned. "I've killed drow *women* for less, much less a member of an imperfect gender."

"Forgive me, Malla. I only forgot—"

"There is no forgetting around me," Krystarn said.

"Yes, Malla."

"Step back." When the drow warrior moved back, Krystarn flipped the dagger slightly, cutting through the male's nostril and creating a slit almost a half-inch long.

To his credit, the warrior said nothing, though his ebony face grayed in pain.

Krystarn put her dagger away, secreting it once more. "Do not ever let me think you see me in a moment of weakness," she told all of the men. "I shall not be weak because that would only encourage the craftiest among you to try to slip a blade between

123

my ribs. And I do not intend to lose any more of you than I have to." So far, only two of her warriors had died in the tunnels surrounding the library's hiding place.

The wounded man stepped back into the military formation, ignoring the blood that streamed down his chin and dripped to his tunic.

"Captain V'nk'itn, we are traveling again. Get your men into a bag of holding."

The captain waved his arm and one of the men produced a large bag of holding from a backpack. He held it open while the man next to him climbed inside and disappeared without a sound.

"Also," Krystarn told her captain, "I want yourself and two other men whose nerve will not fail to stay with me." She grasped the staff Shallowsoul had given her and waited for her orders to be carried out.

It would be good to get back to the business of taking lives. Lloth would be pleased. The ranger was as good as dead.

11

"What would the Waterdhavian Watch want with you, Baylee?"

The ranger shook his head at Serellia's question as he lounged in the shadows by a tree overlooking the table where Cordyan Tsald sat with one of her companions. The female watch lieutenant's name was already being passed rapidly throughout the forgathering after the axe throwing event.

"The only tie I have there is Golsway," Baylee answered. He watched a brief fluttering of leathery wings take to the air from a branch near Cordyan's head. *Xuxa, what have you learned?*

A lot of silly intrigues that are currently in vogue in Waterdeep, the azmyth bat answered. *But nothing regarding you.*

Baylee watched the woman, eating as unconcernedly as if she had a right to be there. He smiled. In a way, he found her behavior curious. And she had chosen the right way to set all the tongues wagging at the forgathering. As well liked as he was by most rangers who knew him, Baylee also knew he had people who disliked him, if they didn't count him as a definite enemy.

Aymric held up an arm. Xuxa landed neatly on it, hanging upside down. "A reward, dear Xuxa, for your daring efforts." He offered her a small piece of apple nut crunch.

Gossip collecting, you mean. Still Xuxa took the offered treat.

"They are deliberately not talking about you," Serellia stated.

"Well," Karg rumbled, standing beside them, "after the display I'm told she put on at the axe throwing contest, everyone else is talking about you."

"They came at you straight-away, my friend," Aymric pointed out. "If they had a fell purpose in mind, they would have waited for you outside the forgathering."

"Even then, that would not have been a wise move," Karg said. "Our sentries spotted them a full two hours before they arrived and had word sent back to Myndhl. He's in charge of security this year, you know."

Baylee did know. Myndhl was a forest runner like Vaggit, and several areas in the Dalelands named Myndhl as an outlaw. His largesse didn't necessarily stem from the coffers of Zhentil Keep as Vaggit's did. Many times over the years, Myndhl's victims had included the wealthier houses around the Dalelands whose only crime was success. As such a wanted person, Myndhl's security systems were elaborate.

"Then I suppose there's nothing to be done for it," Baylee said.

"What do you mean?" Aymric asked, peering through the branches.

"I'll go down there and kill the man sitting with the lieutenant," Baylee replied. "Then she'll talk."

"You're kidding," Karg rumbled.

"Yes." Baylee started out from the tree, aiming straight for the table where Cordyan and her companion sat. Heads turned as he passed by, and he knew that most of the rangers at the forgathering knew what was going on.

"Then what are you going to do?" Serellia demanded, rushing up to walk with him.

"I'm going to introduce myself and ask her what she wants."

"And what if she grabs you and teleports you out of here?" Aymric demanded, coming up on the other side of Baylee.

"That's why I'm here," a voice spoke out of thin air.

"Carceus?" Aymric asked. "Is that you, you old god-seller?"

"And whom else would it be?"

Looking in the direction of the voice, Baylee thought he saw a shadow ripple through the darkness at his side. Carceus Ravnei was a traveling cleric in the service of Gond Wonderbringer. He enjoyed friendships with a number of rangers due to his wandering travels trying to increase the number of followers of Gond in the Dalelands. His invisibility was due to some enchanted item that no one had quite nailed down over the years. The cleric had his secrets.

"Thank you for coming," Baylee said.

"After Xuxa's impassioned plea but a moment or two ago, how could I not come?"

Baylee watched as Cordyan's head came up. Her eyes held the color of newly worked copper still drawing some of the red of a fire into them. He stopped at the head of the table.

Cordyan stood up, her left hand drifting down to her sword hilt.

Baylee spread his hands, showing he was unarmed. "You were looking for me."

Xuxa fluttered through the night overhead, then settled onto a branch over the table. *Her thoughts are closed to me,* the azmyth bat announced. *She has a very disciplined mind, though. And her intentions are definite.*

Whatever they are? Baylee asked sarcastically.

Xuxa chirped in disapproval, almost drawing the lieutenant's gaze.

The man sitting at the table remained on the bench, looking up with no expression. He ate neatly from a small clay plate.

He is a watch wizard, Xuxa announced, *though more than that I cannot fathom.*

"Baylee Arnvold?" Cordyan asked.

"And you are Lieutenant Cordyan Tsald, though I don't know why you would be looking for me." Baylee watched the way the woman moved, noting the symmetry of power and grace. Though young in years, she carried experience wrapped around her. And for one so young, she had gone far in a very challenging arena to make lieutenant.

"First I must inform you I am here in an official capacity."

Baylee inclined his head. "Of course. I hope you've enjoyed the festivities despite that capacity. I hear you're quite good with an axe."

The woman let the compliment roll past her without acknowledgment. "I need to know when the last time was that you spoke with Fannt Golsway."

"I would have to refer to my journal to give you the exact date," Baylee said. Without warning, a leaden feeling filled his stomach.

"An approximation at this point would be adequate."

"Months," Baylee replied.

"What was the nature of that discussion?"

"I'm sure it had something to do with an antiquity or a point of history," Baylee assured the watch lieutenant. "Golsway has little time to talk to anyone about anything other than that."

"Would that be in your journal as well?"

"If it was something I was interested in."

The woman shifted, taking a step closer to Baylee. "I've been told you and your mentor weren't on the best of speaking terms the last time you saw him."

"We had a disagreement," Baylee agreed. "One which I fully intend to redress when I see him at the end of the second tenday from now."

"You have intentions of traveling to Waterdeep?"

Baylee glanced around at the forgathering. The questioning had drawn more than a few spectators. "Yes."

"Why?" Cordyan asked.

"You ask a number of questions without giving me an explanation," Baylee said.

"I'm afraid that is the nature of my business." Cordyan's face remained unreadable even to Baylee's trained eye.

"I'm returning to Waterdeep to see Fannt Golsway," Baylee answered.

Cordyan regarded him silently for a moment. Then she said, "I'm afraid I have some bad news for you. Fannt Golsway is dead."

* * * * *

"Malla, we are ready."

Turning her attention from the staff she held, Krystarn looked over the three men standing in the hallway with her. Only minutes had passed as the men readied themselves for the coming battle. "That is satisfactory, Captain V'nk'itn." She handed him one of the golden bands Shallowsoul had given her. "You understand my instructions on how to use this?"

"Yes, Malla."

Krystarn gave the two remaining bands to the other drow

males. "To flinch or lose your focus will get you killed more surely than a blade in the back."

All three males nodded. None of them appeared happy about being in possession of the bands.

"Those of you who fail to use the bands will die by my hand," she promised. Then she took up the staff the lich had given her. She spoke the activation phrase and tapped the staff against the floor.

A ruby beam spat out from the tip of the staff and splashed against the empty space between the walls of the hallway. The beam formed a thin crescent at first, finally flaring out into a full circle that rapidly expanded and filled with swirling rainbows. In heartbeats, it filled the hallway.

Once the dimensional door was secure, the beam faded away.

"Kill the ranger, Baylee Arnvold," she said. "And kill any who are with him." The drow warrior leaped into the dimensional door in front of her. The familiar chill wrapped around her, then took her away.

* * * * *

"When did Golsway die?"

Cordyan Tsald stared into the jade gaze of Baylee Arnvold. "A tenday and two days ago." Her heart went out to the ranger, and she wasn't used to it doing that so easily. In her trade, she worked with thieves and liars on a continual basis. And men motivated by a need for power or wealth. There were few whom she respected.

Hurt flickered in his eyes, scarcely under control. He had not known about the old mage's death. Cordyan would have wagered anything on that.

No, child, he did not know. Nor did he realize how hurt and confused he would be by such an act.

Cordyan looked at the woman standing beside Baylee who gently put a hand to his shoulder. She was surely too young to have been the one to touch her mind. The voice that she had *heard* carried more age than the young woman beside the ranger.

My name is Xuxa. I am in the tree above you.

Cordyan kept her off hand on her sword pommel as she glanced up. She saw the bat hanging from a branch above her, spreading its wings to further draw her attention.

He must know the rest of it. There will be no easy way to tell him.

"What happened?" Baylee asked.

With practiced neutrality, the watch lieutenant relayed all she had learned of the old mage's murder. She had worked the night patrol in Waterdeep long enough to know there was no proper way to tell anyone a loved one would not be returning home. Each word seemed to weigh the ranger down. The easy, light-hearted and challenging smile had dropped from his face from the beginning, and grimness hammered his features into tight, hard lines.

"Someone sent you out here to tell me about this?" Baylee asked.

The elf at Baylee's side shook his head slowly. "They suspected you of the old mage's death, my friend. Isn't that right, lieutenant?"

Cordyan didn't flinch from the question. Hiding wasn't her way. "There has been some consideration."

The words reached through the confusion and hurt that had surrounded Baylee. The ranger's emotions were immediately apparent to Cordyan, as were the real concerns of his friends around him. As she watched, a portly bald man in priest's robes materialized at his side as well, offering his sympathies.

"I am your only suspect then?" the ranger asked.

"I don't know," Cordyan answered. "I was given only to find you and question you. Then find out if you would be willing to accompany me back to Waterdeep. Even without the matter of the assassination, there remains the estate to be administered."

"The estate?" Baylee looked at her, clearly puzzled.

"Yes. He had his will filed with a law-reader. The house and the surrounding grounds in Waterdeep are all yours. Most of his other belongings as well, except for a few items that are to be disbursed among other friends."

Baylee shook his head. "When will you be ready to leave?"

"As soon as you are."

"I would be willing to start riding tonight."

Calebaan Lahjir shifted at the table. "My sympathies for your loss, Baylee Arnvold, but after morningfeast would be more logical."

"Of course. I shall be ready." Baylee looked into Cordyan's eyes. "If there isn't anything else, I'd like to be alone with my friends now."

Cordyan nodded and watched the ranger walk away. She cursed the luck that she should have to tell him the old mage was dead. It would have almost been better had he been Golsway's killer. That way her own heart wouldn't be filled with sadness. Movement broke away from the branch overhead. She glanced up and watched as the bat flew after the ranger in a flutter of leathery wings. She signaled across the way to two of her best trackers, setting them on Baylee and his party. Even though she believed the ranger, there was a possibility other information could be gleaned from watching him.

Cordyan sat at the table, suddenly overcome from all the fatigue of the travels that had brought them to the Glass Eye Concourse. She had no stomach for the remnants of the meal she'd been enjoying only moments ago. "Some days I hate the employment I have."

"You like him." Calebaan seemed genuinely surprised by the announcement even though he'd uttered it.

"I feel for him," Cordyan said. "His pain is real."

"Yes, and I have the feeling that if we don't leave after morningfeast, we're going to be chasing him all the way home, hoping to catch up."

"Captain Closl and Lord Piergeiron are not going to be happy about Baylee's arrival there," Cordyan prophesied. "When I first heard the stories about him, I thought perhaps they were tall tales, made up because he walked for so long in Golsway's shadow. But now that I get the measure of the man, I don't think that is the case at all." She looked after the ranger, watching him disappear in the darkness between the campfires spread out across the forgathering.

"No," Calebaan agreed. "Baylee will bear watching even after he returns to Waterdeep. I don't think he will let—" Calebaan sat up, suddenly more straight. "Do you feel it?"

Cordyan looked at her friend. "Feel what?"

Calebaan pointed toward the east, in the direction Baylee had walked. "The cold breath of death itself."

Knowing her friend was sometimes given to poetic expression, Cordyan turned her head. Only darkness met her gaze. Then she felt the chill, like a high wind coming across Icewind Dale. The sensation came to her sharply, bringing with it the memory of two tendays the circus had spent playing Ten Towns when she'd been yet a girl, not then allowed to swing from the high wires with her brothers and sister.

But suddenly that dark space seemed to fold in on itself. Ruby light spilled from the corners of those folds in the next moment. Then the center of that fold collapsed, opening onto a hole.

Four figures stepped through that ruby hole into the midst of approaching rangers and a horde of animals.

"Something's wrong." Cordyan said. She stood and loosened her sword in its sheath. The copper and gold Shandaularan coin mounted in the hilt sparked a yellow light and felt warm to the touch. The sword was the watch lieutenant's as a reward from Khelben Arunsun for work she had done as a Harper while she was sixteen years old. The sword, Khelben had assured her, came from the renowned collection of Azoun, King of Cormyr for a bit of business the archmage had performed for the king.

The enchantment on the blade made it move lightly in her grasp, and it cleaved more surely through armor than any edged weapon she had ever owned. But the Shandaularan coin had an even further enchantment laid upon it. In the presence of drow, the coin would spark yellow.

Cordyan knew the enchantment was true because she'd seen it spark twice before. Both times, drow had been around. Once, the sword's warning had been enough to save her from a drow down in the warrens under the Waterdhavian docks.

The Shandaularan sparked again as she studied it. "Drow," she told Calebaan. She looked up at the glowing red hole to see the first of them step through. Her hand covered the Shandaularan coin as she bared her weapon.

12

"Hurry!" Krystarn Fellhammer ordered the three drow males hurtling through the dimension door behind her. She carried the staff in one hand and gestured with the other. Her magic swelled inside her for a moment, then burst out to roll over the line of approaching rangers.

A streak of flame leapt from her forefinger to arc across the sky above the forest. A few of the rangers managed to stop short, evidently having seen the spell before.

Krystarn narrowed her eyes as the fiery sphere took shape in the air, then burst with a low roar that spread flames in all directions. At least a handful of the rangers died in the immediate inferno, and others were dreadfully injured. Fires caught in the grasses and trees, driving the animals back in panic.

The advance of the rangers halted when they realized they faced a truly deadly foe. A number of arrows streaked toward the drow.

Krystarn loosed a second burst of magical energy. Thick strands materialized in the air, spanning the distance between the trees in front of her, becoming a mass of sticky gray webbing that ran twenty feet across, ten feet high, and forty feet deep.

The flying arrows didn't make it through the web, getting caught in the multilayered, sticky strands. Several of the rangers were also ensnared. A moment later and the webbing touched the fires burning in several spots across the ground. Extremely flammable, the webbing caught fire at once.

The rangers trapped within the webbing burned with it. Several of them screamed in agony. Many of them died. None of them were Baylee, Krystarn saw.

She gestured once more, unleashing the third spell she'd prepared for the raid. She felt the calm warmth surround her as the magic threaded into place before her just in time to stop two of the arrows that had managed to get through the webbing. Less than a yard in front of her, the arrows suddenly stopped dead and dropped to the ground.

Behind her, Captain V'nk'itn shook out the bag of holding that held the other drow males. They assembled around her at once, adding to her defense with their weapons. All of them were armed with hand crossbows, quivers tied down along their thighs with extra poisoned quarrels.

"The others," Krystarn ordered.

V'nk'itn emptied the other bag and jumped back as the four figures suddenly rose up from the ground. The drow warriors drew back from their unwelcome allies, swords and axes going up in defense.

Krystarn had seen a skeleton warrior only once before in her life, before it had ripped out the throat of the woman she had been tomb raiding with at the time. She had barely escaped with her life. The experience had left its mark upon her, and she found she had to fight to retain her calm.

Now, seeing four of the skeleton warriors take up their dread two-handed swords and immediately walk toward them, the drow elf barely managed to stand her ground.

They all wore the remnants of finery, but the holes were large enough to spot the yellowed bone through the hunks of dark purple corpse-flesh flushed with congealed blood. None of the clothing or the House markings on them looked familiar. Two of them still had fragments of ears hanging onto their hard planed faces, and the ears held elven points. The elongated hands and feet also gave away the skeleton warriors' mortal beginnings.

They growled in shrieking voices as they closed on the drow.

"Don the circlets!" Krystarn ordered. She watched as V'nk'itn and the other two men put the circlets they held on their heads and immediately lapsed into unconsciousness while remaining on their feet.

Little more than ten feet away, three of the skeleton warriors halted. The fourth continued on toward Krystarn, drawing its sword back to strike.

Krystarn fitted the circlet on her head, having no trouble at all of fitting her mind into the magic built into the band. Her senses swirled as she watched the fourth skeleton warrior suddenly freeze into position. A further mental push put her inside the skeleton warrior's body.

She looked back at herself, noticing the way the firelight flickered over her own ebony skin. Then she tried lifting her sword arm, watching the long two-handed sword come up in the skeleton warrior's grip.

Movement to her right drew her attention. She whirled, finding the skeleton moved slightly slower than she was accustomed to her own body responding. Before she could fully turn around, a young male ran his heavy war spear into her.

Krystarn cursed, not believing she had left herself open to such an attack. Then she was surprised when there was no pain. The spear expertly shoved through her ribs, finding the place where a heart was supposed to be. Rotted meat broke away in chunks, streaming down to the ground in front of her.

Realizing that she was in no danger of dying, Krystarn raised the two-handed sword and smashed the blade against the spear haft. The hardened wood splintered almost effortlessly. Before the ranger could get clear, she swung the blade again, decapitating her opponent.

Krystarn grinned, then reached down and pulled the spearhead from the skeleton warrior's dead flesh. A moment later, she waved to the other three skeleton warriors and headed in search of more victims. Baylee Arnvold was at the forgathering somewhere, and she meant to kill him. No matter how many she had to kill first to do it.

* * * * *

Baylee spotted the skeleton warriors moving among the twisted shadows where the fireball had detonated. He had his sling in his hand, but against the undead, he knew the weapon would be almost useless.

A woman in priest's robes ran toward the undead warriors. She lifted her staff and drove the bottom into the ground. The holy

135

symbol at the top glowed a lambent orange as she stood her ground.

"It's Vithyr!" someone shouted. "She'll turn these undead horrors!"

Baylee wanted to shout a warning to let the cleric know that even her powers wouldn't turn a skeleton warrior. Before the first word tore free of his throat, however, the lead skeleton warrior ran her through with its spear. Then the creature hurled her body away contemptuously.

"Gond protect these people," Carceus the priest said. His round face held intense sorrow as he surveyed the dead and dying.

By then, Baylee was already in motion, heading back toward the undead at a run.

What are you doing? Xuxa demanded.

I'm going to help, Baylee replied.

They're skeleton warriors, the azmyth bat protested. *In order to harm them, you'll need a magic weapon. Even then, there is the skill they still possess to consider as well.*

They're killing people, Xuxa, Baylee said. *People I know . . . friends. I can't sit back and do nothing. And those skeleton warriors are being guided by someone. They didn't come here on their own.*

Aymric, Karg, and Serellia caught up to him, their weapons bared in their fists. "Do you know about the circlets that bind them?" the elf asked.

"Yes," Baylee replied. "Golsway and I have—" The pain hit him again, muffled partly because he couldn't believe everything the watch lieutenant had told him. He'd have to see Golsway's body to believe it. "There was one we faced a few years back in Lathtarl's Lantern."

"You survived," Karg growled, "that means you learned something." He held the dwarven double-bitted axe in his hands. "Me, I'll trust this axe of mine. She's got a bit of magic in her that's stood me in good stead over the years."

"My sword has been blessed by the Lady herself," Serellia said, her weapon in hand.

"And my father gave me my falchion and this dagger." Aymric

brandished the two weapons. "Both had been in his family for generations, and both carry magic. But you are weaponless."

"Slow the skeleton warriors down," Baylee said. "Xuxa and I will see if we can scout up the people controlling them." He mentally contacted the azmyth bat, sending her winging ahead. Many of the animal followers had already fled the immediate vicinity of the attack, driven before the fire and by the fear the undead creatures instilled with their very appearance.

Then they were in the thick of the fighting. Most of the rangers tried to hold their ground, but few of them possessed magical weapons that would do any damage to the skeleton warriors. Conventional weapons shattered against them or had no effect at all. The same held true for magical spells.

Leaping forward, Karg caught one of the skeleton warriors from the side, smashing his great axe down on its left arm. The keen edge of the magical axe slashed deep into the arm bone. Fractures split through the ivory. Amazingly, the arm remained intact.

The skeleton warrior turned immediately, striking out with the two-handed sword.

Karg blocked the blow with the head of his axe, trying to capture the blade between the bits and shatter it. Serellia stepped in as the big giant killer fought for his life. She drew her blade back, then brought it crashing against the undead creature's ribcage. Bits of bone tumbled through the ribcage.

The skeleton warrior whirled back to face her. Both hands locked around the pommel of its weapon. It swung, bringing the sword off its shoulder.

Serellia ducked, moving under the whirling blade. Then Karg chopped down on the weakened arm again, this time cutting it from the skeleton warrior while the woman swung at one of the knee joints. Aymric met a second undead warrior with a flash of steel that quickly echoed with the grate of steel on bone. Then three hawks joined the battle, attacking the pits where the skeleton warrior's dead eyes were. The creature itself would have known there was no hurt that could be taken, but the person controlling it didn't. The skeleton warrior flinched away from the battering wings and tearing talons.

Baylee ran, noting that a third skeleton warrior was being delayed in its attack by the Waterdhavian watch lieutenant. Blue sparks jumped from her blade's edge every time contact was made.

Xuxa! he called.

I have found them! she cried.

Baylee followed her directions, stepping over a man who had been disemboweled by one of the skeleton warriors. Burned bodies, the dead and the soon-to-be, lay scattered across the sward. Knots of fire hung in the trees and grew larger on the ground as more of the brush caught.

He followed the azmyth bat's commands, going to cover when she bade him. Then he saw the drow elves spread out before him. His blood ran hot in his veins. He'd never had a love for spiders. Even during his earliest years when his tolerances were more forgiving, he'd never learned to like the eight-legged creatures. When he'd still been small, a giant spider in a dungeon Golsway had taken him to in Hluthvar had captured Baylee from the party and tied him up in its web before the old mage had found and freed him.

And the drow worshipped Lloth, Queen of the spiders.

The drow spread out in a semi-circle. A few dead surrounded them, but the rangers for the most part had fled before the skeleton warriors. A burning branch from the tree above broke loose and dropped, smashing against the invisible barrier in front of the woman Baylee surmised led the group. The drow society, he knew, was matriarchal rather than patriarchal, led by women rather than men. She would have to be the leader.

Surprise will be your only edge, Xuxa said.

Then we'll have to make the most of it. Baylee reached under his tunic and touched the white star of worked silver and the green leaf that was the older known symbol of Mielikki, his chosen goddess. He prayed to her as he touched the symbol, asking her blessing while he gathered his spell. When he felt it roaring and strong within him, he flung his hand toward the area where the drow hid behind the invisible shield.

The long grasses around the drow shimmered and came to life, suddenly twining around the dark elves. As they yelled hoarsely and started beating at the underbrush with their swords and axes, Baylee gathered himself and stood. Before the drow could react, the trees leaned down and seized some of them in their branches, wrapping them securely. In places, fire still clung to them, and drow screamed as they were burned.

The branches curled around the four stationary figures as well. Two of the drow lost the circlets from their heads, coming back to their senses and immediately fighting for escape.

Baylee looked at the confusion of drow and plants and trees, and knew that his actions must have been blessed by the Lady of the Forest herself. Never had he thrown the spell and had so much success with it.

He ran for the drow. *Xuxa, attack the dark elves with the circlets first.*

The azmyth bat flapped ahead of him, disappearing against the night sky. *Of course.*

A drow male fought free of the entangling underbrush just in time to meet Baylee's rush head-on. The ranger held nothing back, covering himself so he didn't risk serious injury.

The drow's breath exploded out of him as Baylee's shoulder drove deeply into his stomach. They went down in a tangle of limbs. The drow drew his mace back to swing, but Baylee rammed his head into the warrior's mouth. He captured the drow's wrist in one hand and fought for control.

A shrieking growl filled the area, and Baylee knew exactly what it was. With the circlets knocked from the heads of the drow elves, the skeleton warriors were free from their slavery. And the first urge that would hit them would be to destroy whoever had controlled them last, that was part of the sorcery.

The drow tried to bite him, mouth open wide and showing blood between the teeth. Motion to the right drew Baylee's attention. Two other drow warriors sprang free of the underbrush as his spell faded. One of them swung his short sword at Baylee.

Yanking the drow under him, Baylee rolled over and used the man as a shield. He felt the drow's muscles tighten as the short sword sank into his flesh.

Baylee, I'm coming!

Struggling to keep from getting stabbed, the ranger got only a glimpse of leathery reflex as the azmyth bat swooped in. One of the drow staggered and fell, muscles still shuddering and giving evidence of being hit with Xuxa's controlled shock that her system could put off.

Throwing the dead man off him, Baylee pushed to his feet. Perspiration drenched him, but his muscles felt loose and ready. He wrenched the mace from the dead drow's fist and blocked the other drow's sword swipe. Metal clanged, then the ranger stepped away and whirled, coming at the drow again with a backhanded swing.

The blow nearly caught the drow unaware. The top of the weapon caught him on the side of his face, drawing a line of blood. The drow took a step back and raised his wavy dagger as well as the short sword.

"You'll die for that indignity, human."

Spotting one of the small, adamantite bucklers the other drow had lost at the moment of impact, Baylee lunged for it. He scooped it up and took three more strides to set it in his hand. Even then, he almost had the drow's sword in his throat before he managed to deflect the blow with the buckler. The sword clanged across the black metal of the small shield, striking sparks.

Baylee feinted with the mace, drew the drow's sword to block, then stepped in and hammered the man in the face with the buckler. The drow's nose broke, and blood cascaded down his split lips.

The drow female's voice rose in harsh command, speaking the grating elvish language of her kind.

Breathing hard, Baylee pressed his advantage. At first he thought he was about to be overrun by the other drow warriors flanking the one he engaged. But they pulled back unexpectedly. However, when the first skeleton warrior came crashing into the midst of the drow, he understood.

The two-handed sword wielded by the undead creature cleaved a drow in twain, dropping the halves to the ground. Fired by its own supernatural rage, the skeleton warrior didn't hesitate about attacking the next drow. The drow warrior put up a valiant effort to block the creature from his mistress, but the skeleton warrior battered him aside, stretching him out unconscious or dead.

Slipping the sword of his opponent and pushing it away with the small shield, Baylee blocked the drow's dagger thrust with the mace, then slammed the buckler into the man's face again. Robbed of his senses by the blow, the drow collapsed at Baylee's feet.

The female drow growled her order again, gesturing to the ground.

Shifting, Baylee spotted the circlet laying in the grass. Moonlight kissed the silver and glinted against the pure white of diamond. The ranger surged forward, intent on seizing the prize. If he gained control of the circlet but did not choose to exercise control over whichever skeleton warrior whose soul it contained, the undead creature would continue to wreak havoc while trying to reach its previous enslaver.

Baylee managed two steps, then a drow stepped before him. The hand crossbow in the warrior's hand snapped as the missile fired. Baylee twisted in mid-stride, throwing himself off-balance. *Xuxa! Get the circlet!*

The azmyth bat broke into view, swooping low across the ground with her feet lowered. Baylee caught himself on one hand, then pushed up and swung a foot into the drow's crotch. With a high-pitched shriek, the drow went down. Behind him, Xuxa dragged her claws across the circlet and ripped it out of the drow's hands as he was about to take it. Her leather wings beat the air hard, trying to gain height as two other drow warriors scrambled after her.

Baylee locked eyes with the drow woman.

"Baylee Arnvold," she hissed in the human tongue.

Roaring in rage, the skeleton warrior reached the drow it was after. The undead creature's free hand reached out with reflex much too fast to be mortal. It caught the drow's head in its bony grasp, then yanked the drow warrior from his feet.

Even held by his fearsome opponent, the drow did not give up. He flailed at the skeleton warrior with his short sword.

Baylee watched as the skeleton warrior's inexorable strength shoved the drow's head back. The ranger's stomach chilled at the cruel death that was about to happen. It was one thing to kill a man in combat, but this was another. The drow's eyes bulged in fear and resistance. With a snap, the dark elf's neck broke and his body went slack.

The undead creature laughed with foul glee, then tossed the corpse to the side. It turned its empty black gaze toward the sky and spotted Xuxa. Unerringly, it took off in pursuit of the azmyth bat hovering over the area.

Baylee looked back at the drow female. She had frozen in place, the gold circlet once more on her head. She had known his name and his face. The fact that the drow party had invaded the forgathering was no accident. They had come for him.

And seeing the magic the drow female had at her command and remembering the story Cordyan Tsald had related, Baylee guessed the woman had helped in Golsway's murder if she hadn't planned it all herself.

He stepped toward her, intending to take the battle to her.

13

"Baylee!" Serellia's warning cut through the sound of combat.

Looking around, Baylee realized his friends had joined him in the battle with the drow. But so had the skeleton warriors. One of them swung its two-handed sword at Baylee. Leaning backward, the ranger flipped out of the way. The sword nicked his leather armor, slicing through neatly and scoring the flesh underneath.

Baylee prayed the great sword wasn't poisoned. His feet pounded into the ground, bringing him face-to-face with the undead creature again. Maybe it would have had him, but Aymric was suddenly there, his falchion managing to turn his larger opponent's swing. The two-handed sword thudded into the ground, cleaving deeply into the earth.

Seizing the opportunity presented, Baylee stepped forward and smashed the heavy mace against the imprisoned sword. Sparks flared up at once, but the sound of shattering steel rang across the clearing.

The skeleton warrior drew back its broken blade and paused only for a moment. Then it attacked Baylee again. The ranger blocked the blow with the buckler, feeling the impact run down his arm, numbing his hand.

Aymric stepped in, weaving a net of steel before him with his sword and dagger. "Do you know who controls this monster, my friend?" His blades licked out, scoring deep bites in the skeleton warrior's dead flesh.

"I think so," Baylee answered.

"Then break that control." Aymric defended another blow from the broken blade.

Trusting his friend after their years of companionship, Baylee turned and raced toward the female drow. Around him, more rangers had joined the fray, bringing with them their animal followers. It looked as though the forest itself stood aligned against the dark elves, filled with tearing claws and flashing fangs. The drow backed down slowly, but the cost for the rangers was high.

Breathing hard, blood matting his tunic and his leather armor from the wound across his stomach, Baylee sped for the female drow. Before he could get to her, two drow warriors closed in front of him. Their swords forced him back. He went to work with the buckler and mace, trading blow for blow with each of them as he used the terrain itself against them, taking the high ground where he could, and using trees and brush to block them.

He kept them from taking his life with effort. The mace vibrated in his hand, and his other hand hadn't quite recovered from the blow of the skeleton warrior.

"You need to live, Baylee Arnvold," a feminine voice said at his side.

Stepping back to take advantage of a tree that broke up the two drow, Baylee glanced at his side and saw Cordyan Tsald fall into position beside him. "This isn't your fight," he told the watch lieutenant.

"I have questions that you need to answer," she replied, then riposted a low sword thrust. Her return blow drew blood from the drow's shoulder. "If you die tonight, Captain Closl will still be asking them in the morning."

Baylee beat the other drow's attack to pieces, filling the air with the mace and the buckler. He swung the small shield at the end of his arm and slammed the black adamantite against the drow's knee hard enough to break bone. When it came to survival, there were no rules of conduct.

"I have questions of my own I want answered," he growled. "This drow female knew my name. Were there any drow involved in Golsway's death?"

"If we had known there were," the watch lieutenant replied, "I'd have been searching the Underdark, not this forgathering."

Glancing past his opponent, Baylee saw that Xuxa had landed in the top of a tree. She had her wings spread out to hold herself up in a branch while she kept the gold circlet clutched in her clawed feet. Below her, the skeleton warrior pursuing the circlet started climbing the tree.

Without warning, the sky flared into magnificent golden light that drained the shadows and darkness from the immediate area. The drow in front of Baylee drew back, raising his arm in front of his eyes.

Half-blinded himself, Baylee glanced back toward the direction he'd come from and spotted Carceus less than fifty paces distant. The priest held his hands aloft, and the light seemed to pour from them.

The skirmish line the drow had held broke. Arrows flew at them, filling the air as the archers among the rangers tried to find their targets.

Baylee stared hard into the group of drow, seeing that the female among them was once more conscious. Her hot gaze rested on the ranger briefly, then she called to the drow warriors. They flocked to her quickly, having no place to hide under the fierce light of Carceus's creation.

A ruby limned hole opened in the air behind the female drow. Two of the skeleton warriors held the line against the rangers. One of the drow popped open a bag and pulled it over the warrior next to him, swallowing the other man instantly.

"They're escaping!" someone yelled.

"Let them!" yelled another. "There's been enough death tonight, and I've no wish to visit the Underdark before morningfeast."

Baylee raced toward the drow group, but two of the skeleton warriors fronted him. He drew up, frustrated. The hole behind the drow group flared a deeper red as it flashed. Then it was gone. A handful of fletched shafts cut the air where the dimensional door had been.

The skeleton warriors turned from Baylee and ran back toward the area where the dark elves had disappeared. Both of them searched the grass until they found the gold circlets. One touched the circlet immediately to his forehead. Under the clear light of Carceus's spell, Baylee watched as the skeleton warrior and the circlet turned to dust, blowing away in the strong wind left over from the dimensional door.

Then the second skeleton warrior knelt in the grass. Its arms spread out in supplication as its dead face turned toward the sky.

"It looks like it's praying," Cordyan said quietly at Baylee's side.

"Maybe it is," Baylee said. "In the end, those creatures may be capable of great evil, but not all of them had beginnings in evil. Good men have often been bound to the curse of those gold circlets, I am told."

The second skeleton warrior drew the circlet to its forehead and turned into a pile of dust that rapidly blew away in the rising wind.

Baylee glanced anxiously about. Two of the skeleton warriors had been accounted for, and one climbed the tree Xuxa took shelter in. But a fourth remained.

"What are you searching for?" Cordyan asked.

"The fourth skeleton warrior."

"Why?"

"Because it will follow them," Baylee said. "No matter how far they go. The magic they used to control it will bind it to them. If we want to find them, all we have to do is follow the undead creature."

"It looked like they all threw the circlets away," the watch lieutenant stated. "And the other two skeleton warriors didn't try to follow anyone."

Baylee surveyed the bodies of the dead drow in front of him. Seven dark elves lay stretched out near the battleground. "Then the people who controlled them were dead."

"The ones who controlled the skeleton warriors were the most protected of the group," Cordyan pointed out.

"I know." The situation didn't make sense to Baylee either. The people who controlled the skeleton warriors had been deep within the group of drow. He quickly searched the dead, seeking answers.

Two of the drow had died by the sword, their bodies opened up in great gashes. But the third one he checked didn't appear to have a mark on him. Grabbing the corpse by a shoulder, the ranger pulled and rolled it over.

He spotted the black fletchings of the small crossbow bolt that jutted out from the back of the man's neck. The bolt was of dark elf design, matching ones Baylee found in the small quiver on the man's thigh. "This man was killed by his own." He released the corpse and let it fall back to the ground.

"As was this one," Cordyan informed him grimly. She indicated the quarrel sticking out from below the man's left ear.

"They were taking no chances about being followed," Baylee said. "Someone had already taken into account the cost of failure."

Cordyan let go the corpse she'd handled and looked up at Baylee. "They came here for you."

"Perhaps."

The light from Carceus's spell faded from the sky and moonlight returned to highlight the watch lieutenant's features. "There is no 'perhaps' about it," she replied. "Whether there was a drow involved with Fannt Golsway's murder or not, his death exhibited strong magic. Just like this."

Baylee knew it was true. His thoughts had already taken the same fork in the stream. He gazed around at the carnage that had ripped so bluntly into the festive atmosphere of the forgathering. Only moments before, so many of the people around him had been involved in swapping stories, swapping possessions, eating and drinking, competing, and perhaps even flirting at love.

Now, they tended the wounded and dead comrades among them, and sought to tip the scales on the ones they might lose. Thankfully, a number of clerics and druids had attended the forgathering. Those who had healing potions shared willingly among the fallen.

Guilt chafed in Baylee's mind.

You did not know, Xuxa chided him. *If you had, you would not have brought this trouble among your friends.*

Baylee looked at the tree where the azmyth bat held her prize from the clutches of the skeleton warrior. The undead creature swayed unsteadily in the thinner branches near the top of the tree, searching in vain over and over, like some kind of artisan's automaton for safe passage higher.

He turned at the sound of his name and saw Serellia approaching him. Her beautiful face was streaked with blood, and tears ran down her cheeks. Her sword remained naked in her fist.

"It's Aymric," she said.

Baylee felt like a cold fist closed around his heart. "Where?" He knew many people in many places, but so few actually got close to him. The elf was one of the closest.

Serellia guided him to Aymric.

Pale and disheveled, Aymric lay on the ground as Karg and two other men sought to bind the horrible wound across his midsection. The skeleton warrior's sword stroke had laid him open. The elf looked up at Baylee and tried to speak.

Baylee knelt beside his friend, feeling the tears burn his eyes. He took Aymric's hand and closed it tightly in his. "I should not have left you," he whispered in a hoarse voice.

Aymric showed him a small smile and moved his head back and forth.

"Let me through!" a voice urged. "He may not yet be too far gone!"

Baylee shifted and let Carceus through. The priest's face remained blank as he surveyed his patient. "Gond willing," Carceus said, "I'll not suffer him to die." He pulled up his robe sleeves. "Water, please." He held his hands out.

Karg stood nearby and removed the small flask at his hip. "It's spring water, god-speaker, brought from the airy heights, only one step removed from the heavens themselves."

"Even better. Pour." The giant killer sluiced the water over the priest's hands. Prayer spilled from Carceus's lips, coming so rapidly that Baylee understood only a few of the words.

He added his own prayers to the Lady of the Forest to the priest's. Aymric's hand in his was already growing weaker.

A smoky blue aura glowed around Carceus's hands. He kept his fingers wide-spread. Then he placed his palms against the violent wound in Aymric's midsection.

The elf's body jumped in response, bowing up. Aymric's hand closed around Baylee's tight enough to cut off the blood flow. A keening moan escaped the elf ranger's lips, spitting out blood with it.

The smoky blue aura around the priest's hands spread, covering all of Aymric's stomach and lower chest. Miraculously, the flesh knitted itself back together. Muscle reconnected to bone, then to each other. Long moments passed as the healing continued. Perspiration dappled Carceus's forehead, trickling down through his eyebrows. After a time, the blue glow faded. Even after the work was done and he sat back in exhaustion on his haunches, the priest's prayer to Gond Wonderbringer continued unabated.

Baylee stared at Aymric's face. Once the blue glow had faded, the elf's body had gone into total relaxation, his eyes shut. He didn't appear to be breathing. "Aymric," Baylee called gently.

There was no response.

Fear clawed at Baylee's mind, bristly as the spider's leg had been all those years ago when he'd been tied securely in the web before Golsway had shown up to save him. There were stories from time to time of those who had been healed after having severe wounds who only turned out to be well-preserved corpses. Healing could still be done on the body even though the spirit had departed. His hand trembled, surprising him. "Aymric." He spoke louder, but his voice was lost in the myriad moaning and bits of other conversations circling around the group with the elf.

Serellia placed her fingers against Aymric's throat. "It's all right," she said. "He only sleeps. His heart beats strongly."

Baylee.

Heartened by his friend's survival, the ranger turned to look back at the azmyth bat. The skeleton warrior had gotten closer to the circlet in Xuxa's claws. Men and women surrounded the base of the tree. Even over the distance, Baylee heard the group talking about firing the tree. Someone else told them that firing the tree would do no good, that only magic weapons had any effect on the undead creature.

We have to deal with the skeleton warrior, Xuxa urged. *I have but to release the circlet and he will go.*

Not yet. Baylee stood and walked toward the tree with the skeleton warrior in it. He knew that the undead creature wasn't mindless. Far from it, skeleton warriors possessed cunning intelligence far above average. But they were bound by the drive to recover the circlets and become one with their souls again. That obsession weakened them once they were no longer in a controller's thrall.

"What is it you're going to do?" Karg growled, joining Baylee. He carried his axe in one huge hand.

"We have no clue where these skeleton warriors came from," Baylee answered. "But they were elves."

"Aye."

"Where is the skeleton warrior you and Serellia fought?"

"Destroyed," the giant killer replied. "It put up a fierce fight for a time. Of course, it helped when I removed one of its arms. Then it erupted into a frenzy that almost caught me unawares. Serellia saved me with as fancy a piece of sword play as I've seen in a long time. We were hard pressed for a time, but it turned its attention back to the drow. Were it a human foe, I would not have attacked it from behind. The blow cut its spine in two and took its legs from it. Still, it tried to battle. Then, of a sudden, it went limp. I wasted no time in cleaving its skull to pieces, I tell you."

"It's dead?" Baylee asked.

"Oh, and it didn't turn to dust, that's true," Karg said, "but it's deader than it has been in a long time."

How long a time it had been originally dead was only one of the questions on Baylee's mind. He'd noted the clothing the skeleton warriors almost wore. Fashion sometimes was very indicative of time period, and the bits he'd seen of the clothing on the skeleton warriors looked near to ancient.

Xuxa, he called. *Bring me the circlet.*

Are you sure?

Baylee came to a stop forty paces from the tree. He hoped it would be enough. *Yes*. He glanced at one of the nearby rangers, a young boy who trembled as he tried to stand still under a shuddering pitchblende torch. "Could I borrow your torch?"

The boy gave it without answering, then wrapped his arms around himself.

Xuxa hurled herself from the tree, dragging the heavy circlet after her. The skeleton warrior tracked the band instantly, abandoning the tree. It fell through the branches, plummeting toward the ground. When it hit, it sank into the ground nearly to its knees from the weight and the height of the fall. A normal man's legs would have shattered.

Instead, the skeleton warrior put a hand against the ground and levered itself from the impromptu grave. An arrow glanced from its head, leaving a trail of silvery sparks behind to show that the arrowhead had possessed magic properties. Thin cracks blossomed in the undead creature's skull.

That creature will kill you to get this, Xuxa warned.

Baylee reached up as the azmyth bat let the circlet tumble from her claws. Gold flashed as it tumbled through the air, fired by the torches and lanterns the rangers brought with them. He caught the circlet, the metal cold under his fingers.

"It's coming," Karg stated.

14

Studying the circlet even with the skeleton warrior bearing down on him, Baylee felt drawn to it. The piece of jewelry was old, hundreds of years old. Sometimes when he touched something, he just knew. Most instances, when challenged to discover which was an actual artifact and which was a cleverly constructed replica, Baylee had picked the artifact every time. It wasn't just knowledge with him, and the aspect had fascinated even Fannt Golsway enough to attempt to find out how his young apprentice could be so accurate. No answers had presented themselves. It was a knack, Golsway had been forced to concur, just a small gift from Mystra, Lady of Mysteries, in fact as Golsway was wont to declare, maybe a small homage to her own title.

He turned the circlet in his free hand, noting the rune work inscribed in the metal. Only some of the characters looked at all familiar.

Baylee!

The ranger knew Xuxa referred to the growing proximity of the skeleton warrior, but he found himself loathe to let go his prize. The band felt heavy, solid, and so, so old. He had to wonder what stories the runes might tell if he could have time to decipher it.

But there was no time. The skeleton warrior ran at him, its great sword drawn back to strike.

"Tell me, Baylee, are we going to fight?" Karg asked.

You can't ask them for any more blood tonight, Xuxa counseled calmly. *Not when there is an easy way out.*

It's not so easy for me, Xuxa. Everything in my being cries out to hold onto this piece.

I know. But you can't. Not unless you're prepared to ask someone to die for it.

Baylee held the circlet tight in his fist. Karg had already taken a step in front of him, pulling the huge, double-bitted axe into readiness. *There is an inscription here. What stories it could tell.*

Xuxa flapped over and landed on Baylee's shoulder. The ranger knew she didn't like to stay upright. Even her slight weight was too much for her hind legs to maintain her balance. She laid over his shoulders like a cripple. *A trail remains,* Xuxa said. *The female drow. Fannt Golsway's death. Someone here is covering something up. Something that may be awaiting you in Waterdeep. You've not even gone there yet.*

And if there's not something waiting there and the trail ends here?

I have not often been wrong, Xuxa reminded gently. *This trail will not end so quickly.*

Baylee peered at the circlet, drawn deep into the hypnotic glint of it. *But to lose this. . . .*

There have been other lost treasures. Else how would we find these adventures to go on?

Baylee looked up, seeing the skeleton warrior bearing down on him. The rangers nearby started to scatter, so close was the dreadful being. Everything in him screamed to clutch his prize tightly and run for all he was worth. *You need to fly away,* he told her. *I don't want you to be trampled.*

Why should I leave? she asked in that wise voice of hers. *You will make the right decision. I have faith in you.*

Baylee thought briefly about bolting from the skeleton warrior and taking his chances. Xuxa was right in that probably no one would help him while he seduced his own doom by trying to hang onto the circlet. But he knew if he bolted and ran, the azmyth bat might tumble from his shoulder and lose her life. She would be that stubborn.

The skeleton warrior was less than ten paces away and coming hard when Baylee flipped the circlet out to it. The ranger covered Xuxa with one hand, feeling her small, fragile body press against his palm. "We're not going to fight," he told Karg.

For a moment, he thought he had waited too long after all. Then the skeleton warrior stretched out a hand and ripped the tumbling circlet from the air. The yellowed ivory finger bones clicked against the soft gold. With amazing grace and control, the undead creature came to a stop, its legs buckling under itself as it prostrated on the ground.

With a cry of relief and anger, the skeleton warrior dropped the two-handed sword. It turned its face toward the sky and spoke. The words sounded brittle as they echoed in the clearing, but they were filled with the strong emotion of pain.

Seeing the exquisite workmanship of the two-handed sword lying beside the undead creature, Baylee moved forward and picked it up. No one tried to stop him, and no one came forward with him.

The skeleton warrior could have reached him easily, but it remained on its knees, shrilling up at the sky.

The sword pommel was fashioned of the teeth of great cats, each tooth carefully inlaid in the overall pattern to lock precisely with the others to create a smooth hilt. A loop of silvery-gray hair hung from the hilt, carefully braided to be decorative.

Even as Baylee took the weight of the sword into his arms, the skeleton warrior's cries ended. It turned its hollow-eyed gaze on the ranger, then brought the gold circlet to its forehead.

Baylee thought he saw a smile on the undead creature's mockery of a face, twisting up the tattooed flesh of the cheek. At first, the ranger had thought the lines of tattooing were old scars or even dirt, but now he knew them as tattoos.

In the next instant, all that remained of the skeleton warrior was a pile of white, powdery dust. The sword disappeared from Baylee's grip as well, leaking through his fingers as the magic exhausted it.

The ranger stood, facing the people nearest him. "Did anyone understand what he said?"

Everyone shook their head. Many of them returned to helping friends and family who'd been wounded in the battle.

"He was giving thanks."

Baylee glanced at Aymric. His friend stood between Serellia and a young boy, not yet able to support his own weight. His tunic flapped where it had been cut away to expose the wound. All that remained of the injury was a long, scab-covered line. Patches of red-inflamed flesh still carrying some infection surrounded the scabbing on either side.

"You understood him?" Baylee asked.

Aymric nodded. "Some of what he said. It was a very old dialect."

"An elven tongue?"

"Yes."

"From where?"

Aymric wearily shook his head. "You should know our history better than any human, Baylee. Once the elven races dominated Toril, then we massed at Myth Drannor, and eventually retreated to Evermeet. That tongue is still spoken in some areas. But you have to know also what time that poor soul came from."

"You saw his clothing."

"Yes."

"And the sword."

"As you held it, yes." Aymric nodded. "To find that tongue spoken now, I'd wager you'd have to go to Evermeet to hear it. But to hear it spoken then—" He shrugged painfully. "It could have been from a number of places."

"He was a wild elf," Baylee stated, feeling certain about his conjecture. "You saw that the armor he wore was scant. Wild elves don't wear much armor." He touched his face along his jaw. "And there is the matter of the tattooing, which again indicates his heritage."

"Sy-Tel'Quessir," Aymric said. "And the god he cried out to was Solonor Thelandira, who watches over those attempting to survive in the wilderness. I did not understand everything, but the parts I did understand were quotes from *Hunter's Blessing*. That's the closest it translates to the human tongue."

"I've heard of it," Baylee said. "It's supposed to be one of the most ancient texts of Solonor Thelandira. From a discourse from a much longer work that has been lost to the Tel'Quessir."

Aymric nodded. "Some of the words he spoke may have been some of the missing stanzas. I will remember them and submit them to the proper authorities." He gave a weak grin. "Mayhap we've already uncovered part of the treasure you seek."

* * * * *

You failed!

The lich's voice thundered inside Krystarn Fellhammer's head as she returned to the hallway she had left only moments ago. "There was not much margin for anything but failure," she responded. "Your spell put us down in the center of the forgathering. There were dozens of them, perhaps even scores."

Baylee Arnvold yet lives.

"Would it have been better had we all died killing him?" Krystarn demanded. "Even the skeleton warriors were turned against us at the end." She strode angrily down the hallway toward the wall, thinking the way might be open to her.

Instead, only a blank wall greeted her. Folgrim Shallowsoul refused to even have a proper audience with her.

Krystarn wanted to cry out with rage. Her need for vengeance soared. She had been so careful in her life never to walk into a situation she could not control, yet the lich insisted on shoving her down on her knees and placing the blade of an opponent at her throat.

Then he expected her to vanquish that foe. Black spots swam in her vision as she turned back to face the hallway. She looked back at the drow warriors as Sergeant Rr't'frn reached into the bag of holding lying in the middle of the floor and pulled men out of it.

"How many dead?" she asked the sergeant.

"Seven," Rr't'frn replied.

Krystarn cursed. Nearly a third of her men had been sacrificed in the attempt. She had counted six dead, two of them men she had killed herself with the hand crossbow. Captain V'nk'itn's death was regrettable, but necessary. With the curse put on the circlets of the skeleton warriors she had known there was the possibility of someone using the undead as a means of tracking them down if they were unable to recover them. That was why she had commanded the one she controlled to leave itself defenseless. When the axe had shattered the skeleton warrior's skull, a sharp pain had razored through Krystarn's mind, sending her back to her own body.

She watched the bloodied and battered drow warriors stagger to their feet, two of them feathered with arrows. Seven warriors dead in one night—in a matter of minutes—and she had lost less than that in four years of searching through the catacombs.

I wouldn't have forgiven you even in death, Shallowsoul assured her. *The men who became the skeleton warriors you used tonight died a second death unforgiven.*

"I acted as you wished," Krystarn said. "It was your plan. Had I a voice in such matters, I would have recommended we act in another way."

Treacherously? Shallowsoul laughed.

"As any true Drow would have," Krystarn returned. "What matters is winning, not the how of it."

You say "drow" as if you are so proud of your heritage, as if what others think of it does not matter.

"It doesn't. And if you had not wanted a drow as a partner—"

Not a partner, Krystarn Fellhammer. Never make that assumption, or that mistake again in my presence.

Krystarn fell silent.

Excellent, Shallowsoul said. *You're very attentive . . . a good vassal . . . when you wish to be.*

A short prayer to Lloth filled Krystarn's mind, asking for the ability to conceal her true emotions from the lich at that moment.

See to your men, Shallowsoul ordered. *While I try to find another means to slay this Baylee Arnvold. . . .*

Krystarn felt the lich's thoughts fade from her mind. Before she could move, a bag suddenly appeared in the hallway. Glass vials spilled out of it, each containing a pinkish fluid with a syrupy texture.

"Malla?" Rr't'frn looked at her expectantly.

Krystarn approached the spilled vials, knowing Shallowsoul had sent them but not knowing for sure what they were. She took one up and unstoppered it. Crossing to the nearest wounded drow warrior, she grabbed the fletched shaft protruding from his leg and roughly snapped it off. Reaching behind the wounded leg, she pulled the other half of the arrow through the limb, ignoring the sudden spurt of blood.

The warrior only groaned in a muffled voice and did not try to pull his leg away.

Krystarn poured the syrupy pink liquid over the wound. Almost instantly, the bleeding stopped and the flesh started to heal.

"Those are healing potions." Krystarn handed the vial to the wounded man. "Use them well, *Captain* Rr't'frn."

The drow warrior looked at her, understanding full well he'd been promoted. He bowed his head. "I will serve you well, Malla."

"I will expect no less," Krystarn replied, "upon certainty of death. Take care of your men."

"Yes, Malla."

Krystarn left them there, walking through the hallway and returning to her rooms. Shallowsoul had never told her how Fannt Golsway had found out about the library, but she felt the threat now as keenly as the lich did. After seeing Baylee Arnvold in action tonight, after seeing the anger in his green eyes—something that she as a drow could clearly understand—she knew the ranger would not easily be put off the track.

Killing him was the only way. Only the opportunity remained to be found.

* * * * *

". . . may the Lady keep you all in her sight . . ."

Baylee knelt on bended knee in the group of rangers and other forgathering attendees. His wrists crossed over his raised knee. He kept his head bowed, but his eyes open. After the attack last night, no one felt safe in the clearing. The morning sunlight fell down across his back, muted by the tree branches, and stretched long, early shadows across the hills of chopped sod where they'd laid their friends and family to their final rest.

". . . and may she know you fought bravely and well here," the priest went on. He stood at the front of the group, a thin old man with a white beard and a tall staff bearing the whirl of stars in an artificed hoop that were Mystra's newest symbol.

No one had gotten any sleep after last night's attack. Baylee's back, shoulders, and arms ached from all the digging. Seventeen rangers had fallen in the battle, as well as three druids, and a priest in the service of Mystra.

Baylee had known them all. The youngest had hardly been more than a boy, fourteen summers old. Baylee felt the ache in the back of his throat as he watched the boy's parents consoling each other. The boy's animal follower, a shaggy gray wolf showing scars from past battles, lay atop the boy's grave. As the priest finished his prayer, the wolf loosed a loud howl of mourning that echoed throughout the forest.

The ranger looked over the carnage. Twenty-nine people still occupied tents, too wounded to attend the service. Bandages draped others as they knelt in the clearing. Myriad other prayers to as many other gods followed on the heels of the priest's invocation.

Baylee kept his head bowed as he surveyed the graves. There would come an accounting, Mielikki willing. He touched the white star and green leaf over his heart.

* * * * *

"You were the eye at the center of this particular storm."

Baylee listened to the steady words of Civva Cthulad, a justifier. *Through no fault of his own,* Xuxa said in Baylee's defense.

Veteran of dozens of campaigns spread out virtually across all of Toril, Cthulad stood ramrod straight. His chain mail armor, still not removed from the fight during the evening, held dark spots of dried blood. His face carried lines as well as scars. His hair was gray and the dirty yellow color of old bone. Blue eyes rested on either side of the hawk's nose. A fierce mustache ran down either side of his mouth. "Nor was such intent implied," Cthulad said. "I like this boy."

"I'm no boy," Baylee corrected, feeling defensive. The night without sleep on top of the fierce battle had left him feeling unbalanced.

"My apologies," Cthulad amended. "I meant no disrespect."

"None taken," Baylee said. He took a deep breath and let it out. "I'm not myself this morning. That's why I came out here to be alone." Soon after the morning service for the dead was over, he'd slipped away from the forgathering, getting away from friends as well as the watchful eye of the Waterdhavian watch lieutenant. But even here, in the midst of the forest, he did not feel any better.

"None of us are ourselves this morning," Cthulad said. "I had no wish to intrude on your thoughts."

Unable to feel comfortable saying anything, Baylee turned to the old ranger and asked, "What exactly is it that brought you out here?"

"I'd heard you'd lost Golsway," Cthulad said. "I was greatly sorrowed to hear that."

"Thank you."

"I trust you are going to search for the people who did this."

"Of that," Baylee said, "let there be no doubt."

The old ranger nodded in approval. "Spoken as I was sure you would. There are many among us who think we should provision a band and send them in search of the drow female who led the attack last night, tracking her even to the Underdark should it be necessary."

"I think that would be a mistake," Baylee replied.

"As do I. I said as much to the people who came to talk to me."

Baylee wasn't surprised that the justifier had been consulted. Of them all, Cthulad was one of the most seasoned in battle. "A large group can be tracked more easily than a small one."

"Agreed," Cthulad said. "Which is how I was able to convince them that they should allow me alone to go in their stead."

Baylee shook his head. "No disrespect intended, but this is mine to do."

"I understand your feelings. My mentor was killed when I wasn't much younger than you are now. Hector Glayne was a brave, fierce man. As a warrior, I'd seen him clear rooms, just him and that axe he carried everywhere he went. He was attacked and killed from behind by two men he considered to be friendly to his cause, if not friends indeed. It took me three years to find them and bring them to justice for his murder."

Baylee looked at the man.

"Those people that lost loved ones and friends," Cthulad said, "need that same release you're hoping to achieve by finding that drow female. I've undertaken the job of representing their interests. That way they can get back on with their lives, trusting me to help them lay this to rest."

"I could lose you in the forest," Baylee said, "just as I could lose those Waterdhavian watch members."

"Maybe," Cthulad grudgingly admitted, "but I've been hunting and fighting men longer than you've got years . . ." He cleared his throat. "You are very good at what you do, Baylee, but exploring isn't the same as handling military engagements. It may well be that you could use someone with my experience."

Baylee thought about the offer.

"There are things you haven't considered," Cthulad said.

"Such as?"

"Calebaan, Lieutenant Cordyan's partner, has been keeping wards up against any who would scry on this area. Have you any protection against that?"

"No," Baylee had to admit.

"You're aligned, for whatever dark purpose we ultimately discover, against foes who have vast resources at their command." Cthulad regarded him quietly. "I'm asking you to let me help you."

Baylee, Xuxa said. *He's right.*

I know. But Baylee's own independent nature warred against accepting anyone he couldn't control into his sphere of operations. He looked back through the trees, at the fresh graves that littered the hill behind them. *If I fail, I've no right to deny these people the chance to right the wrong that has been committed here. Tell him.*

Baylee turned to the old ranger and offered his hand. "I'd be glad to accept your help."

"You won't regret this, Baylee Arnvold."

Baylee gave him an ironic smile. "Let's just hope *you* won't."

15

"What is that book that you work in so diligently?"

Baylee looked up at the question and saw Cordyan Tsald watching him. He closed the leather-covered book and marked his place with a finger. He held a quill in his other hand. "A book."

The watch lieutenant stood before him, dust covered her riding leathers as it covered them. A handkerchief hung around her neck, her lower face white against the dirt-encrusted upper part. "I've watched you work in it for the last three days of this trip," she said. "In my line of work, curiosity is generally considered a boon, but to have to carry it around inside you when you cannot guess at the answer is hard."

In spite of the dark mood that had hung around him since leaving the forgathering three days ago, Baylee smiled. And when the effort felt so good, he couldn't be totally antisocial. "I know the hazards of curiosity."

"I'm sure you do." She made no move to come any closer, standing a few paces from where Baylee sat in the fork of a tree above her head.

The forest was quiet around them, filled with the bright, quick movements of colorful birds. Nearly a hundred paces away, a mountain lion paced them, working out her own curiosity. The big cat had followed them for the last two hours. Baylee judged she would soon stop, coming to the edge of the territory she claimed as hers.

In the distance, Civva Cthulad, Calebaan, and the watch members sat around the remains of the midday feast they'd just shared. Cthulad enjoyed his tea, and had laid in a goodly supply, finding a kindred spirit in the watch wizard. It was an humble table the members of the watch sat with the rangers, mostly journey cakes, sweetmeats, and jerked meat they had been supplied with from the forgathering. Baylee had added to it with berries and nuts he'd gathered before the others had gotten up.

You should not be so stand-offish, Xuxa chided from higher up in the tree.

Baylee looked up to where the bat hung upside down, regarding him with those white, pupil-less eyes. *You should stay out of things.* Over the last three days of hard travel, the azmyth bat had taken time to point out that the watch lieutenant was also a good looking woman, and to make the occasional disparaging remark about Jaeleen. He knew that most of the conversation of that ilk was meant to distract him rather than to offer any real attempt at encouragement.

It wouldn't hurt to talk to her, Xuxa insisted.

"She talks to you?" Cordyan asked.

"She," Baylee growled in irritation, "won't shut up. She's worse than the mother I never had."

"You had a mother," the watch lieutenant said, shaking her head.

Knowing the woman didn't understand, Baylee said, "I'm sure I was born to a woman, but Fannt Golsway was the only parent I ever knew."

"I didn't know. I'm sorry."

"They didn't tell you everything about me?"

She shook her head. "I saw the likeness of you that Golsway had in his rooms."

Baylee was taken by surprise. "I wasn't aware that he had a likeness of me." He'd never sat for a painting, and the old mage had never mentioned getting one of him. "Are you sure it was me?"

"Yes," she replied. "It was a very good likeness." She wrinkled her brow, perplexed. "It was signed by someone named 'Vi.' "

"That's not a name," Baylee said. With the understanding came a return to the sharp hurt he'd first experienced when he'd heard of Golsway's death, but it was also a bit of a balm. "Those are Golsway's notations, not a signature. He drew the picture."

"Golsway drew that picture?" Cordyan seemed genuinely surprised. "He could have been a very well paid artist if he'd wanted."

"He was a man of many parts," Baylee admitted. "But the only things he ever drew were things he wanted to—" He stopped short, his voice suddenly thick with emotion.

"Only things he wanted to what?"

"Only the ones he wanted to remember," Baylee finished.

"I see. I'm surprised you didn't see this picture. It held a place of prominence in his private rooms."

"I've not been—" Baylee stumbled over the word *home*. "I've not been back in some time."

"The housekeeper told us there had been some discordance between yourself and Golsway."

"Back to work, lieutenant?"

Cordyan smiled. She poured water from her waterskin onto the handkerchief and rubbed the back of her neck. "I never stray far from it."

"There were some problems," Baylee admitted. "I think we were on the verge of working them out."

"What problems?"

Baylee gazed down at her. "And if I choose not to answer?"

She shrugged. "Then I have more to wonder about when we resume our travels."

"You had parents, I assume," Baylee said.

"Of course."

See? Xuxa put in. *Already you're finding common ground.*

Baylee ignored her. "Did you ever rebel against your parents?"

"Perhaps, at times."

"And how do you get along with them now?"

"They're dead," Cordyan replied.

The answer caught Baylee off guard. He hesitated, forgetting about the argument he'd been building toward. "I'm sorry."

"It happened some time ago," Cordyan said. "An accident."

Baylee searched her face for any signs of lingering pain, but read nothing. Over the last three days he'd noted that the watch lieutenant could keep her own counsel. "My disagreement with Golsway was much simpler than either one of us would allow it to be. I thought I was grown, and he didn't agree."

"So you left?"

"According to the Lady's teachings, each of us must find our own path. The reward of that path of independence is in how much closer you can be to those whose lives have touched yours."

"Where need and want are one."

164

Baylee nodded. "You follow the teachings of Mystra?"

"I am an interested observer, but not a passionate worshiper. Not yet. I take it you are."

"To be a worshiper is so simple," he said. "All you have to do is look around you. When you are taught where to look, you will see the Lady's work everywhere. Just as I see Mielikki's." Despite his first allegiance to the Lady of the Forests, he also owed a great deal to the teachings of Mystra.

"As yet, I do not share your confidence." She looked back at the group. "I'll leave you to your book." She turned to go.

Baylee watched her. Over the last three days, he'd maintained his own company. Xuxa kept him in conversation all during the day, and watched over him at night when his thoughts busied themselves while he stared up at the stars. But it wasn't the same as talking to someone who didn't know him, someone who didn't try to guess his every thought.

"Wait," he called. He capped the inkwell and replaced it in his pack.

She turned, looking up at him.

Baylee dropped easily out of the tree, brushing journeycake crumbs off his breeches. "This is a journal. I was just making notes."

"About what?"

"The things I can remember from the last few days," Baylee explained. "Conversations I can remember having with Golsway in the days before I left his house."

"May I see it?"

Baylee gave it willingly. The journal was thick with parchment, most of the pages filled with his writing. Each entry was dated.

Cordyan looked at the last page in the book that he'd been working on. Drawings covered the page on the right, while script covered the facing page. "This is the woman you saw that night?" she asked.

"As well as I can remember," Baylee agreed. He studied the drawings. He'd kept most of them simple, drawing the drow female's face from a number of angles, front, and profile.

"These are very good."

"I'm a poor artist," Baylee said, feeling uncomfortable. It was one thing for someone to compliment him on his researching skills or on his ability to recover a particularly fragmented vase even though he'd never seen it whole before.

"How can you say that?" Cordyan flipped back through the pages, finding the renderings he'd done of the circlets that had imprisoned the skeleton warriors. There were even renderings of the skeleton warrior kneeling as it had with its face turned toward the sky. The tattoo had been exploded in another view, and the whole of it drawn in as best as Baylee could imagine.

"Golsway taught me," Baylee said. "It is not so incredible. But when you've uncovered some of the masterpieces we discovered during our journeys, the way some of those artists were able to work in the mediums, whatever modest talent I may have pales by comparison."

Cordyan ran a finger along his pages of script. "Your handwriting is beautiful as well."

"Golsway never accepted anything less than my best," Baylee said. "He always told me that an explorer wasn't worth his salt if he made records no one could read."

"So what do you write in here?"

"Anything," Baylee replied. "What I think, what I hear, what I see. Any conjectures on my part. Sometimes information I can copy down from reference books."

Cordyan flipped the journal open to the first page. "You write a lot." She flipped through the pages, opening to maps of areas Baylee had walked through, seeing faces of people Baylee had seen, seeing a handful of pictures here and there rendered in ink and sometimes chalks of picturesque areas where the ranger had camped.

"It's a big world."

The watch lieutenant stopped at a page that had a drawing of the pirate ship that had attacked a merchanter Baylee had traveled aboard. "You've only been working in this journal for the last three months."

Baylee glanced at the notation on the front of the journal and saw that she was right. "Yes."

"You travel a lot," Cordyan said.

Watching the woman, Baylee tried to figure out what she was after. He'd questioned people himself in his own line of work, and he could tell she was closing in on a thread she pursued. "Yes."

She glanced at him, handing the book back. She appeared threatening in no way, merely interested in his journalizing. "You must fill up a lot of books like these."

"Three or four a year," Baylee admitted. "Sometimes more. It depends. When I worked some of the sites Golsway and I discovered, we sometimes filled up a half-dozen such journals each."

"What do you do with them when you fill one?" she asked. "I notice you keep a light pack."

Then Baylee realized what she was after. Evidently no one had found journals like his in Golsway's house. "I have a place that keeps them for me."

"What place?"

"Candlekeep. Perhaps you've heard of it."

"I've heard of it," Cordyan said. "You've been there?"

"Yes."

"I'm told the price of admission is quite high," the watch lieutenant said. "Usually a book of some sort, and worth no less than ten thousand gold pieces. If your journals are kept there, they must be highly regarded."

"I have a friend there," Baylee said. "Brother Qinzl, who claims to entertain a certain vicarious thrill of exploration when he reads one of my journals."

"I thought you would have kept your journals with Golsway's."

"No," Baylee said. "Not since Golsway deemed that my writing was strong enough to stand on its own."

"When was that?"

"When I was fourteen," Baylee answered.

"You've written journals at fourteen that are in *Candlekeep?*" She seemed amazed.

Baylee shook his head. "You have to think about the time period. During those years, Golsway was much more active than he has been of late. That was one of the things we argued over. I was still willing to go rushing after the vaguest whisper, while he was more content these days to look for a big strike. When he was younger, they were all big strikes, some just bigger than others. Those early journals detailed what members of the Explorer's Society deemed important finds."

"But they were still good enough to stand on their own?"

Baylee looked into the woman's copper eyes. "If you're asking if Golsway's journals are there, the answer is no."

"Why?"

"Because Golsway didn't want to chance a loss of the information we've discovered. If Candlekeep burned down, which won't happen because the magic wards within it prevent paper catching fire within their walls, then both sets of our works wouldn't be lost."

"Where did Golsway keep his journals?"

Baylee shook his head. "I don't know."

Her copper hued gaze remained on him, weighing the answer she'd received.

"Wherever they are," Baylee said, "you can be assured that it's a matter of record."

"Why wouldn't Golsway have told you?"

"It wasn't a matter of him not telling me," Baylee said. "I never asked. At that time, I knew everything he did. He had no secret considerations about things we'd found that he didn't share with me."

"It sounds like the two of you were very close," Cordyan said.

"Maybe too close," Baylee agreed. "If there had been space allowed somewhere along the way, maybe I would have been there when he needed me."

If Golsway could not take care of himself at the time, Xuxa interposed, *you would only have died with him.*

"Do you know what he was working on?" Cordyan asked.

"No. Did anyone find a journal like this one?"

Cordyan shook her head. "Not yet. A team was still investigating the premises when I was told to find you. Maybe they've found it in my absence."

Behind her, Cthulad and Calebaan broke up the conversation after the meal. The members of the Waterdhavian watch group gathered their traveling packs once again.

"Looks like we're about to get back onto the path," Baylee said.

Cordyan nodded. "I'm sorry to have interrupted your work time."

"No need," Baylee replied. "It was an enjoyable talk. I look forward to another."

The watch lieutenant walked away.

Baylee watched her, admiring the sleek roll of hips beneath the tunic's edge. She didn't walk like someone deliberately drawing attention to herself. The swaying gait was a natural part of the woman.

She turned abruptly. "Where did Golsway keep his journal at his home?"

The question almost caught Baylee off guard. He never let his features change. "There's a desk in his study. Did anyone check there?"

"I'll ask when we get back."

Baylee watched her go again. *She's good,* he told Xuxa. *We'll have to be careful around her.*

She'll only find out about Golsway's hidden precaution if you let it slip. Xuxa paused. *You don't have to worry about that because I won't allow it to happen.*

16

"Do you trust him?"

Cordyan Tsald glanced at Piergeiron, who stood in the wreckage of Fannt Golsway's house beside her. She had seen the Commander of the Watch on a number of occasions, and talked with him at times as well, but he still made her feel like a green recruit.

"No," she replied. "Baylee Arnvold holds to his own agenda of things." She shifted her gaze back up the stairs to the men under her command who were shifting debris again, taking out things Baylee said meant nothing to their investigation. "I would stake my life that he had nothing to do with his mentor's death. However, he will tell us only what he wants us to know."

Piergeiron shook his head. "That is all Golsway's doing. The old mage had a certain way of looking at social responsibility."

"Such as waiting until he was finished thinking over whatever he wanted to think over, then deciding what the best course of action was? For everyone involved."

"Exactly. Golsway was never one to be an oarsman, unless he was pulling his own boat." Piergeiron shifted irritably, anxious to be on with other things.

Cordyan didn't want to mention to her commander that she could handle things at the house quite easily. She covered a yawn with one hand. The last week had been spent nearly nonstop traveling to the warded area in the Dragonspine Mountains where they had used the gateway there to make the jump back to Waterdeep. The gateway was a closely guarded secret of Piergeiron's, and the command word they had been given only worked once each way to cut down on the months of travel that would have otherwise been necessary.

"What do you think he knows?" Piergeiron asked.

"He knows where Golsway's journal is," Cordyan replied.

"You're certain?"

"I know what I believe," she answered. "But what I can prove is entirely another matter. What have you found out about Civva Cthulad?"

"The man has an excellent reputation," the Commander of the Watch replied. "From all accounts, you have nothing to fear where he is concerned."

"I was worried about him when he volunteered to come with us."

"Cthulad is the type of man who would volunteer immediately after such an event." Piergeiron glanced at the man that appeared in the doorway. "I've got to go to another meeting. If there's anything I need to know, get word to me immediately."

"Yes, Lord Piergeiron." Cordyan bowed her head. She was conscious of the big man leaving, but her eyes were on Baylee Arnvold.

The ranger worked in the drawing room where Thonsyl Keraqt had been burned alive. Although a number of watch investigators had been through the room with all five senses and divination spells, they'd found nothing. Baylee's attention seemed to be concentrated primarily on shattered models that lay broken and scattered across the floor. The azmyth bat hung from the ceiling above him, its wings wrapped around itself as it slept.

"What is he working on?" Calebaan walked up behind the watch lieutenant without warning. He offered her some of the cinnamon bread he'd brought in for his breakfast.

Cordyan accepted the bread, as well as the small crock of honeycomb. She knew the wizard was talking about Baylee. "I don't know," she replied.

Baylee continued working carefully, dragging up some pieces of colored papier mâché and discarding others. He had brushed debris out of the center of the area where a number of tables had been.

"What was there?" Calebaan asked.

"According to the housekeeper, there were a number of tables that held models of dig sites that Golsway had been to."

"Dig sites?" The wizard studied her shrewdly, then turned his attention back to the ranger. With calm and purpose, Baylee continued putting hunks of papier mâché together, seeming to get more confidence as each piece fit together. "You mean excavation points? Caves in the ground?"

"And buildings." Cordyan nodded. "They were memories, according to the housekeeper. Sometimes Golsway would invite a promising student over to study an interesting facet of the archeological find. But that was not often."

Calebaan scratched his chin thoughtfully. "Curious, isn't it?"

Cordyan lifted an eyebrow and smiled. "The possibility that Golsway left the find he was working on out in plain sight?"

"Yes."

"I find it frustrating that the old mage would have thought of something like this. Yet, it is very believable."

"You have to wonder, though, how Baylee thought of it."

"The answer to that is simple enough," Cordyan answered. "He had to know what Golsway was working on."

"Even though he told you he did not?"

"Either he was lying, or seeing this room and those models brought a perception to him that he didn't know would be made. He went through the house with me on his heels for six hours this morning." That was one of the biggest reasons Cordyan was so tired now. When *Copert's Conquest*, the ship they had taken from the other end of the dimensional gate, had tied up at the docks just after midnight last night, Baylee had insisted on coming to the house instead of taking a room at an inn and sleeping.

"I'm glad I got the sleep I did," Calebaan commented. "Have you been to bed yet?"

"No."

"You should think about it."

"I do," Cordyan admitted ruefully, "and those thoughts make keeping my eyes open even harder."

"I can take over here," the watch wizard offered.

"No." Cordyan blinked her eyes with effort again, feeling the grains of sleep moving around in them. She knew Calebaan wouldn't take the decline of his offer personally. They had worked together long enough for him to realize that she was thorough and liked to do things her way. "If Baylee can do without the sleep, then so can I."

The ranger looked up abruptly. He sat cross-legged on the floor, his forefingers steepled together and supporting his chin. He hadn't shaved his facial hair in the last few days, and a dark shadow covered his jaw line. "Can you get something to eat brought here?"

Cordyan studied the man. It was the first time he'd asked for anything, almost the first words he'd spoken independently without being prompted with a question since entering the home. "Of course," she answered. "What would you like?"

"There's a tavern down along the wharf in the dock ward," Baylee said, "called the Emerald Lantern. If he still works there, a cook named Tau Grimsby will set a plate showcasing the best from the sea and from the fields, along with an assortment of steamed vegetables and sautéed mushrooms, for only a few silvers. Maybe you could send someone for it." He offered a purse that held the clink of coins.

"Of course."

"Thanks." Baylee tossed the coin purse over to her, then turned his attention back to the model he was reassembling. "Feel free to have them get you anything you'd like as well. But I recommend this plate."

Cordyan sent for a watch officer and bade him go to the Emerald Lantern. Hardly had he gone when Baylee called for her.

"I think I have it," the ranger said.

"Have what?" Cordyan crossed the room, stepping over loose debris and blackened boards.

"Where Golsway's interests lay," Baylee said, "if not exactly what he was searching for."

Cordyan studied the mound of grass-green papier mâché piled on the floor in front of Baylee. "And what do you think it is?"

"*Where* it is," Baylee reiterated. "You've heard of the Greycloak Hills?"

"Of course." Cordyan was intrigued. The Greycloak Hills were a known destination for adventuring bands.

"In years past," Baylee said, making a final adjustment to some of the papier mâché pieces he'd fit together, "the Greycloak Hills were called the Tomb Hills. Tombs from the Fallen Kingdom were spread throughout those hills. Many valuable artifacts were found there. Golsway and I went on three major expeditions to the area. Never did we return empty-handed."

Cordyan surveyed the model he'd assembled. "How do you know this wasn't an old representation of one of those excavation sites?"

"Because we never found anything in the Greycloak Hills that Golsway would have put on exhibition," Baylee answered.

"And this is new?" she asked.

"I've never seen it here."

"You believe that Golsway was interested in a new dig site in the Greycloak Hills?" Calebaan asked.

"No." The ranger pointed out identifying landmarks. "This is a very old one, one of the very first. More than a hundred years back, the exact year is open to some conjecture, an adventuring party under the leadership of Bulwgar Helmm journeyed there and discovered enough in treasure to help open the floodgates of tomb raiders that slipped into the area."

"You believe that Golsway discovered something that had been missed in the earlier excavation?" Cordyan asked.

"That fits this scenario." Baylee shifted, trying to find a place that fit him more comfortably.

Cordyan understood his motivation. She was tired of staying inside the house, wearied from standing so much in one spot. And she'd not been hunkered over the little pieces of models for hours.

"Those early excavations were purely cursory," Baylee said. "Groups charged into the area and took what they could find. A number of hidden areas were missed."

"You didn't find Golsway's journal, did you?"

Baylee shook his head. "You've been with me the whole time. Did you see me find it?"

"No." Cordyan stared at the model, willing it to make sense. Only it sat there. "I need to be better convinced of the authenticity of your claim."

"All right. In the north ward, you'll find a mapmaker," Baylee said. "His name is Yassit Daggle. For a price, you can persuade him to come here with his topographical maps and confirm what I'm showing you. This section of the Greycloak Hills is quite distinctive to someone who's been there."

Cordyan glanced at Calebaan, silently seeking his advice.

"I know of Daggle," the watch wizard said.

"If his fee is a consideration," Baylee put in, "I'll gladly pay it myself."

"No," Cordyan replied. "The coffers of Waterdeep and the Watch are not so shallow that they cannot cover a mapmaker's expense."

"Good. I'll need him here, and whatever latest maps of the area he might have to make a better guess about what Golsway was after."

"The elves from Evereska have taken over the lands of the Greycloak Hills of late," Calebaan said. "There is much speculation that they have discovered sources of magic, and perhaps even treasures, that have not yet been found."

"Everyone connected with this has displayed a vast resource of magic," Baylee said quietly.

Cordyan held her own counsel. The conclusions the ranger offered fit the circumstances. She looked into Baylee's jade green gaze. "It will take time to find the truth."

"Maybe more than you realize," Calebaan said. "The elves dwelling in the Greycloak Hills these days are very territorial."

The watch officer who had been sent to the Emerald Lantern returned carrying a large basket and a wine flask. He placed the food and wine on a nearby table. "The cook wishes for you to enjoy your repast," the man said. "And wishes for you to drop in on him as time presents itself."

Baylee crossed the room to the table. When he lifted the lid on the basket, Cordyan smelled the aroma of the food. "Would the two of you care to join me?" the ranger asked. "Enough was sent."

Cordyan shook her head, trying to keep distance between herself and the ranger. Over the last days of travel, keeping that distance had been hard. Baylee was a friendly man, and despite the present situation, generally of good humor. And his travels around all of Faerûn made him an interesting conversationalist.

"If you really don't mind," Calebaan said, "I might nibble on a few things."

"Please help yourself." Baylee pulled the wine flask up and turned it so he could read the label. He smiled in appreciation. "Tau must have been in a generous mood today." He showed Calebaan the label.

"A very good year," the watch wizard agreed.

Baylee held out his hands, showing the dirt and the grime from reassembling the model pieces. "I'm going to wash up and come right back." He left the room, going up the stairs.

Calebaan rummaged in the basket, bringing out a large buttered shrimp. He bit into it, then made a growl of approval. "You should really try this."

Cordyan felt irritated at her friend, which let her know exactly how tired she was. "No, thank you." She stared hard at the model. "Do you believe him? About the Greycloak Hills?"

"I can find no reason not to." Calebaan searched in the basket still further and emerged triumphant with a cube of beef that still showed a little pink. "Why? What do you think?"

"What I think," Cordyan said, "is that Baylee Arnvold would make an excellent card player." She rubbed the back of her neck, wishing her eyelids did not feel so heavy. As she rotated her neck, she noticed the azmyth bat no longer clung to the ceiling. "Where is Xuxa?"

"Who?"

Cordyan gazed around the room, noting the open window leading out to the balcony. "The bat," she explained. Where she had spent time with Baylee, Calebaan had spent most of his time with Civva Cthulad.

Calebaan put the beef into his mouth as he glanced at the ceiling. "It was there."

"Not any more." With a sinking feeling in the pit of her stomach, Cordyan ran up the stairs to the privy there. The door was locked from the inside when she arrived. She pounded on the door. "Baylee."

The other watch officers clearing debris looked at her as if she'd lost her mind.

But there was no answer from the other side of the door.

Cordyan drew her foot back and smashed it against the jamb. The door popped open at once. When she stepped inside, she spotted the open window on the other side of the room. She crossed over to it and looked out. Even though Fannt Golsway's house was sequestered to an extent, many streets ran by it.

She didn't see Baylee Arnvold on any of them.

* * * * *

Your departure from the house isn't going to be appreciated, Xuxa said.

Baylee ran through the streets of the Sea Ward. It felt good to be out, back in the town where he'd been raised. There was a scent blowing in from the Sea of Swords that he'd missed these last months.

I couldn't stay there, and you know that. He slowed his pace as he neared the more populated sections of the city.

Whether Golsway left a message for you or not, Xuxa pointed out, *your credibility with the watch is going to be invalidated.*

Anger flashed through Baylee, but he knew it wasn't really directed at Xuxa. She was stating the things he needed to be thinking about while he pursued his goal.

If I had told the watch about the message drop Golsway had shown me those years ago, the whole of Waterdeep would have known by nightfall. Golsway gave his life for this secret, whatever it is. I'm not going to be responsible for it getting out.

I know. But what if you are wrong and Golsway left no message for you?

Baylee was quiet for a time, still using a long-legged stride. Only two more streets in front of him, he spotted Hakamme's blacksmith shop. Hakamme also had horses and a full kit, for a price.

I don't know, Baylee finally answered. *First, I need to know if there is a note.*

* * * * *

Cordyan got her men organized quickly, splitting them up into groups. Luckily, some of the men had horses nearby. She heard about the purchase Baylee Arnvold had made at Hakamme's only moments after it happened. The blacksmith was reluctant to give the information, but when he found out he was speaking to a lieutenant of the watch, he gave the answers quickly enough.

Seated on her borrowed mount, Cordyan wheeled about. All the blacksmith had was the general direction Baylee had taken: further into the heart of Waterdeep.

"He has a destination," Calebaan said. "Does Golsway have any other holdings in Waterdeep?"

Cordyan shook her head. "None that we've found."

"What about the law-reader Golsway used?"

"Senior Civilar Closl has already talked to him. There was nothing he could tell us."

"Could or would? Mayhap he's only awaiting Baylee's arrival to turn over whatever properties he was charged with handling for the old mage after his death."

Cordyan conceded that it was a good point. She called to one of the other riders and sent him spurring his mount away. She was angry with herself. She should have known not to trust the ranger.

But to further complicate matters, Civva Cthulad had also disappeared from the house.

* * * * *

Baylee tied his newly acquired horse in front of Nalkie's Ale and Bitters. He spoke a few soothing words to the gray dappled gelding, easing its mind. He could tell from the way it moved under him that it had picked up on his anxiety.

Nalkie's was down in the dock ward, and fully half of the building hung out over Waterdeep Harbor. With space around the dock area being at a premium, old Nalkie had been offered several times what the building and the business were worth over the years, but had repeatedly declined to sell. Part of it was because he enjoyed the men his establishment brought in, usually sea-faring men and adventurers.

The other part was because men like Fannt Golsway chipped in with an annual stipend to make running the business more worthwhile. Men who were going to get things done without being in the public eye needed a place where they could meet men who dwelt in shadows. No one knew exactly how much Nalkie brought in on an average year. To hear Nalkie tell it, though, every year he'd just missed ending up in the Lords' Court for not paying his taxes.

Baylee kept Xuxa hidden under his cloak, feeling her body pressed against his. The road in front of the tavern was narrow and treacherous. Stores fronted each other in a horseshoe bend. A pocket of trees separated Nalkie's from a clothier's next to it, and the trees reached all the way down the hillside to the ocean. The tide had worn the rocks smooth over the years, creating distinct borders within the stone.

A fountain occupied the center of the horseshoe space. Baylee knew none of the original work orders for the fountain remained; nothing that would tie Fannt Golsway's name to the building of the fountain.

Huge and round, it depended on pressured aqueducts from the groundwater from the heart of Waterdeep to keep the merry splashes dancing in the sunlight. The statue of a zaratan filled the center of the fountain amid the spraying water. On a much smaller scale than the giant turtle, the statue still held an island on its back, the peaks of the mountains reaching up.

Baylee sat near the head of the zaratan. No one else was about, although most of the shops held customers.

You'll never have a better opportunity, Xuxa coaxed.

With a feeling of trepidation, Baylee counted three stones down from the lip of the fountain. The one he selected didn't look any different than any of the others. He pressed inward, but the stone didn't move. For a moment, he thought that he'd been wrong, that Golsway had sealed the hiding spot and that the last words he'd remember with the old mage would be ones spoken in anger.

Then the stone sunk in a few inches with a smooth click like bones rubbing against each other.

Placing his fingers against the surface, Baylee pressed and twisted, and the stone slid even further back. He reached down into the hollow and brought up a small metal flask that had an ornate stopper. The flask was almost circular in shape, slightly smaller than his closed fist, covered with intricate runes.

He drew his hand out, then pressed against the stone twice. The stone clicked into place.

Holding the flask, he ran his finger against the surface. There was no dust. It had been placed there recently. He smiled, surrounded by the city he'd grown up in, the city he probably would have died in without Golsway's help, and the city he surely would never have seen the extent of if it hadn't been for the old mage.

"One last toast," he said. Then he walked across to Nalkie's.

17

"A table in the back?"

"Yes," Baylee said. "And I don't want to be disturbed."

"Of course." The waiter, a young man with a foppish attitude but a well-worn dagger hilt, walked toward the rear of Nalkie's.

Baylee followed, noting with surprise that it seemed nothing had changed in the time that he'd been gone. But then, remembering, he didn't think anything had changed at all since the time Golsway first brought him into the tavern.

Wood dominated the decor, but none of it was fancy or showed an artful hand. The floor fit together neatly, but did not have a shine. The tables held carved initials as well as burn marks from pipes. Lanterns hung over the table, but they were brass functionals with stubby candles instead of oil.

In spite of Nalkie's spendthrift ways, the larder was well provisioned and all of his cooks knew their way around the kitchen.

Baylee took the booth in the back. The sides concealed him from any other tavern patrons. For the moment only a handful were in the front section of the building. He gave his order to the waiter, ordering a glass of water for the moment.

He gazed out at the view over Waterdeep Harbor. White sails cleaved the green sea and the blue sky on both sides of the breakwater. Sitting there, in the booth he'd shared so many times with Golsway and the people they'd talked with over the years, the ache of the old mage's passing filled the ranger. He said a quiet prayer to Mielikki that he never forget the love he had for the old man no matter how rough the times had gotten.

Xuxa struggled against Baylee's arm, pushing to get out from under his cloak. Freed, she crawled under the table and clung upside down. No one saw her.

The waiter returned with the water and a recitation of the menu.

Baylee ordered an entree of swordfish and vegetables because he knew he needed something to eat. He wished he'd dared show up at the Emerald Lantern and get another plate from Tau Grimsby, but he guessed that the tavern would be one of the first places Lieutenant of the Watch Cordyan Tsald would check for him.

She is a very intelligent woman, Xuxa put in, *as I've told you over these last few days.*

Do we have to talk about this now? Baylee asked as the waiter walked away. He felt the resistance in the azmyth bat's mind and readied himself for it.

No.

Good. Baylee sipped the water, tasting the clean bite of it. Then he took the silver flask from his pocket. His fingers only shook slightly as he unstoppered it. In his hands, he felt the antiquity of the flask. Then he spoke the command word he and Golsway had agreed upon years ago, the name of the foul-mannered donkey Baylee had had to ride down into the valley in the Storm Horn Mountains when the ranger had been only twelve.

Instantly, Fannt Golsway sat across the table from him. The old mage had a pipe in his mouth. From the posing going on, Baylee knew Golsway had conducted the spell in front of a mirror, getting himself set. Pipe smoke wreathed his head.

"Well, my boy," Golsway said, "I'm here and you're there, which means I'm dead and you're not."

The words, spoken in the no-nonsense way Golsway preferred in his dealings, brought a lump to Baylee's throat. He wanted to speak to Golsway, let the old mage know everything that had been in his heart and in his head last few days. But he couldn't. The nature of the spell, however, required that he could interact only in a limited fashion. The vision dancing in Baylee's head also was not visible to anyone else, even if they walked up on him. The exchange of thoughts went on rapidly, much faster than real time.

Golsway smoked on his pipe again. "I can't say that I can quite imagine what it must be like to be dead. Curious, I suppose, because there may be limitless possibilities to explore. And in the afterlife, maybe all the mysteries of what has gone on before will finally be explored to my satisfaction. I doubt that, but one can hope."

Baylee laughed, but tears warmed the sides of his eyes.

"Baylee," Golsway said, "you don't know how many times I've filled up this bottle of thought for you over the years. So I'm not going to wax eloquent on whatever I may think of the afterlife. I just hope it's not boring."

"A good wish," Baylee said. "I hope it's true for you."

"Before I get into the why and wherefore of my death, at least as I can reconstruct it while sitting here and it hasn't happened yet, I want to talk of something else." The old mage's face soft-ened. "We've been estranged of late, dear boy, and I wish that had not happened between us."

"Nor I," Baylee said.

"However, that would be as foolish as wishing geese didn't fly south in the winter." Golsway's memory held a coal to his pipe, sucking the pipeweed into renewed life. "You grew up, and you wanted your own life. There's no fault in that. I wanted to hang onto you. There's no fault in that. Know that wherever you went, Baylee, my thoughts were with you."

Remember his words, Xuxa encouraged. *Knowing Golsway as you did, you know those weren't easy words for him. He hated admit-ting he wanted anyone around.*

"Getting back to the murder at hand, so to speak," the old mage said. "If I've come to a questionable end, then I must point you in a direction. Assuming that I didn't get killed by some stripling in a tavern when I was deep in my cups. Or simply passed away from old age, the Lady forbid."

Baylee waited, amazed at how healthy the old mage looked. Crawling through the burned remains of the house, the images that had filled his mind were terrible, twisted and blackened.

"I'm sure that this all goes back to a new expedition I've been planning," Golsway went on. "I've been awaiting a few more pieces to come into my hands. I've already prepared some messages to go out for you to call you home—if you are willing. Mayhap one of them has already reached you and that's why you are in Water-deep now." The old mage's thought-induced image paused. The familiar twinkle fired in his eyes. "This could well be the big one, Baylee. The one I've been waiting all my life on."

Baylee felt all the old excitement that Golsway's tales and stories could make rise in him fill him to the brim. "Myth Drannor!" he whispered.

"This all begins near the fall of Myth Drannor," Golsway said. "You're aware of my interest in the area. But it has been so hunted over, so infested with beasts and creatures so deadly to man that I consider it foolishness to simply wander in and hope for the best." He shrugged. "Still, in my younger days, I'd journeyed there a few times. I found nothing that wasn't picked over or nearly worthless."

Baylee waited, captivated.

"Back in those days, even before the Army of Darkness descended on the City of Songs and the final battles were fought, some of the elves had started arranging for the flight of the elves to Evermeet."

Anxiety chafed at Baylee, but he knew Golsway would only tell the story the way he wanted to.

"One of these men was a wood elf named Faimcir Glitterwing. He was one of those who reluctantly went along with Coronal Eltargrim's decision to open the gates of Myth Drannor to the humans and dwarves, and others. Glitterwing was related to the Irithyl family, but was in no way close for the contention of being Coronal. He had been a hero in the Crown against Scepter Wars, and fell in one of them. But during that time, Glitterwing built a huge library, a library that rivaled even the greatest of libraries ever assembled by the elves. A library, by all accounts that I have seen, that rivaled what is maintained at Candlekeep."

Baylee tried to imagine what such a library would hold. Magic, for certain, because the elves always had an interest in the arcane. But the histories, the geographies, the biographies and hopefully autobiographies, the stories of lands now dead and barely remembered, all those would be in there as well.

And more. By the Lady of the Forest, how much more could there possibly be?

"When it became apparent," Golsway's image said, "that Myth Drannor was doomed to fall and the mythal could not keep the hordes of evil out, Glitterwing's heirs sought to move the library to Evermeet. The task fell to Gyynyth Skyreach, Glitterwing's granddaughter. Both of Faimcir's sons had been killed in the Crown against Scepter Wars. Skyreach was every bit her grandfather's blood and temperament, according to the records I've read. But to move all the library at once would have taken a huge fleet."

Baylee's imagination fired at once, seeing the elves cutting across the Trackless Sea, the ships heavily laden with the library. But knowing about the library wouldn't do him any good. Nor would it have gotten Golsway excited. The library would have been out of reach in Evermeet.

"Skyreach had only started moving the library when the Army of Darkness swarmed over Myth Drannor, beating the City of Songs down to her knees. Skyreach herself was aboard a ship, leading a fleet toward Evermeet. She didn't reach her destination."

Baylee waited with his breath held. A ship or ships had washed up on the shores somewhere around the Moonshaes and hadn't been discovered in hundreds of years. The possibility was staggering.

"I've researched this particular piece of information for decades," Golsway said. "A piece of gossip here, a thread of a tale there. But nothing seemed to add up. Nothing, at least, until a pictograph detailing Glitterwing's family's part in the Flight of the Elves was recovered. Uziraff Fireblade found the pictograph and sent it to me. I paid him a small fortune for it because he knew some of its worth, but not all. I'd planned on dealing with him myself because I know he and you don't get along very well." The old mage sighed. "Well, evidently that's not going to happen. So you'll have to make new plans."

Baylee's mind was already working.

* * * * *

"You're sure this is him?"

Tweent looked at the man sitting at the far end of Nalkie's. "There is no mistake," he said.

Zyzll, his cousin, looked at him and shook his head. They sat in a booth across the room and at the other end. "There can be no mistakes," Zyzll said. "The drow woman who hired us for this thing said she would have our heads if we failed. I believe she means it."

Tweent glanced at his cousin with disdain. "I can't believe you think of failure at a time when one of our greatest successes lies within our hands."

"Don't look at me that way," Zyzll complained.

Tweent touched his features, running his fingers along them and wondering what look his cousin referred to. The face was only hours old, and the newly absorbed memories danced around in his head like live things. "It's hard to look at you any other way."

They were dopplegangers, young by their standards, but still used to killing others to use for their identities. The faces they wore now belonged to two sailors they'd found late last night while stumbling back to their ship after a trip down the Street of Red Lanterns. Both wore dock clothing and carried a multitude of daggers. Zyzll carried a cutlass and Tweent carried a boat hook.

"The female drow paid us half the agreed upon price in gold coins," Tweent said. "When we meet her again tonight, wearing this man's face, she'll pay us the balance."

Zyzll frowned. "I don't trust her."

"She's a drow," Tweent said. "Don't trust her. She won't be offended. In fact, she may feel quite honored." He smiled. Trying out a new face's emotional range was one of the greatest things about having a new body.

"Suppose we kill him here and now," Zyzll asked, "and we go to meet the drow tonight but she doesn't show?"

"Don't forget," Tweent said. "Once we kill this man, we'll know most of what he knows. It could be we'll know enough to find her and make her pay."

"Perhaps." Zyzll cut his eyes toward the human in the booth. "There is something else, though."

Tweent raised his eyebrows. It was a favorite thing of his no matter what face he wore. "What?"

"We've not yet decided who gets to become this man."

Producing one of the shiny new gold coins paid them by the drow, Tweent spun it high into the air. "Call it then, cousin."

* * * * *

"Baylee, if you breathe a word of this to anyone, you're going to be buried in would-be adventurers seeking a quick fortune."

The ranger knew the thought-specter of his old mentor was exactly right.

"You will find Uziraff Fireblade at one of his usual haunts in the Moonshaes," Golsway said. "He knows nothing of the elven ships that went down in the ocean somewhere near where the pictograph was found. He did not give me the location or the circumstance of how it was recovered. I did not want to tip my hand too early. But when you show up on his doorstep, he's going to know."

I have never liked that man, Xuxa said, making an unpleasant clucking noise. She had tapped into the thought bottle's contents through her telepathic link to Baylee's own mind.

Baylee only half-listened to the azmyth bat. In his mind he was already planning his meeting with Fireblade. He had no love for the man either, and was surprised that Golsway had even had anything to do with him. Uziraff Fireblade was a full-time pirate and part-time archeologist, learning just enough to let him know when he could demand extra money for the return of an object he "found." Golsway had worked with the man in the past, but had never enjoyed the experience. Fireblade was a braggart, but he was an excellent swordsman with the twin cutlasses he carried.

"The trail won't end there if you follow it carefully enough," Golsway said. "But if it does, I'm sure what you can recover from the wreck will more than pay for itself. My only hope is that some of the books will survive in some form after all these years of being on the ocean floor."

Baylee hoped so too. The thought of it almost made him too excited to sit there.

"And now," Golsway said, "it is time for me to go. But before I do, I wish you Mystra's favors in this endeavor or in any other that you choose to undertake. Take care, my son, and know that if I can, I shall watch over you."

Golsway's final words echoed in Baylee's ears as the old mage faded from his view. He sat back in the booth, gazing at the silver flask in his hand.

The waiter brought his meal to the table, and he ate with more appetite than he expected. The pain over the loss of Golsway warred in him with the excitement of the elven ship sitting on the ocean floor awaiting his arrival.

The first thing we're going to need to do, Baylee told Xuxa, *is find a ship heading for the Moonshaes.*

In these waters, the azmyth bat responded, *that will be easy enough. Trade ships go back and forth all the time. Money and supplies are another matter.*

Baylee finished his plate and pushed it away. He nursed the single glass of wine he'd taken with the big meal. *I'll go see Madonld, Golsway's law-reader. If Golsway intended for me to make this expedition, he'd have left money for me.* He gazed out at the green sea, wondering if he could book passage on a ship sailing this afternoon. He didn't relish the idea of getting back out on the ocean. Even the short trip up the Sword Coast had tested his compatibility with sitting inert on a ship.

He left money on the table for the meal and the wine, including a large tip that would mark him as one of the men who frequented Nalkie's. The tip would ensure that no one would remember seeing him in the establishment later, in case Cordyan Tsald and her men from the watch came looking. He took Xuxa back under his cloak.

Outside in the noon air, with a breeze coming in from the sea, everything smelled crisper, cleaner. He felt good, ready to be adventuring. Then he heard boot leather scrape on the road behind him.

We've been followed. Xuxa leapt from under Baylee's cloak, taking wing and darting around him.

Baylee said nothing as he turned to confront the two sailors that stepped down from Nalkie's porch behind him. He thought at first that he'd been mistaken, too paranoid for his own good. Then he spotted the weapons in their hands.

18

Enter.

Krystarn Fellhammer stepped through the wall and into the library. The fifteen drow left in her command stood in rank behind her, dropping out of view as the dimensional door spell eclipsed.

She felt tense as she went through the library stacks on either side of her, drawn by Folgrim Shallowsoul's voice in her head. The stacks towered over her head in this wing of the great library, the spines and jackets crafted in fine woods and showing great artistry. She badly wanted to take one down, imagining how fine the wood grain must feel, only guessing at what it might contain.

"Two of the agents you recruited in Waterdeep have found Baylee Arnvold." The lich's physical voice sounded gravely and happy.

Krystarn's stress did not alleviate. She knew the lich hadn't called her into the library for a celebration. She took the next turn to the left, then walked up the circular stairs to the next floor landing.

Shallowsoul stood in a cul-de-sac of walls and windows that overlooked the section of the library Krystarn had just walked through. "There is a problem, however." He gestured to the crystal ball on the short, narrow table before him where a book lay open atop a half dozen other books. The open one possessed a striking amethyst cover that looked cut from a huge, flawless stone. All of the pages appeared to have been cut from the same stone, sliced extremely thin. The writing was engraved on each page, complete with pictures.

"That's good." Krystarn ignored the small figures in the crystal ball on the table, concentrating on the loose stack of books, drawn into the puzzle of what the lich might be researching.

"No," Shallowsoul snapped, "it isn't." He closed the amethyst book, then draped his robes over the collection of books.

Krystarn shifted her gaze to the crystal ball. "Why?"

"I need him alive."

"Until now, you've needed him dead." Krystarn met the lich's gaze more bravely than she had in the past. Since the battle with the skeleton warriors, Shallowsoul had only seen her once. And then only to take from her the personal items she'd stolen from each of the agents she had hired in Waterdeep to look out for Baylee Arnvold.

"Things have changed." The lich waved to the crystal ball. "The spell I had placed upon this ball's tracking abilities let me know as soon as one of your lackeys had found the ranger."

Krystarn had not known such a spell was possible. Scrying usually only entailed looking for, or at, a subject by the viewer, not having the ball do the work. Even more astounding was Shallowsoul's claim that the ball could track more than one subject. She had employed nearly two dozen spies to search for Baylee Arnvold.

"When I knew they had found him," the lich went on, "I watched them. He had with him a silver flask which I believe to be a bottle of thought."

Krystarn was familiar with the magical item. "Who's?"

"I don't know. But this ranger has no one else with him, so I assume it's from someone who knows about the library."

"Fannt Golsway."

"Yes," Shallowsoul answered. "It would make sense that he would leave a message for his protégé."

Krystarn peered more deeply into the crystal ball. "What would you have me do?" She did not recognize the two men closing in on Baylee Arnvold, having to take for granted that they were indeed men she'd employed.

"Speak to the doppleganger filth you have tracking the ranger. Tell them he is to be left alive."

"How?" The fact that they were dopplegangers limited the names to a list of six.

"They will hear you." Shallowsoul touched the ball with a talon.

An amber glow clouded the glass, but didn't dim the clarity of the image.

The lich's instruction let Krystarn know the crystal ball was evidently one of Moredlin's, able to transmit sound from the viewed location to the scryer, and from the scryer to the viewed location. She leaned forward, her breath fogging the amber-tinted crystal.

* * * * *

Xuxa took to wing at once and swooped toward one of the approaching sailors. The man's cutlass whistled by only inches from the azmyth bat.

Baylee dodged a blow from the viciously twisted boat hook the other man held. The ranger stepped to the side, looking for a means of escape.

The sailor with the boat hook reset himself and came again. His movements were precise and measured. Evidently he was a skilled fighter and no neophyte to actual battle. Baylee blocked the blow, slapping the back of his wrist against the man's weapon forearm and using his strength and leverage to keep the arm from descending. The ranger threw a bunched fist into the sailor's face, snapping his head back.

For a moment, the sailor's face seemed to wobble, and the ears grew longer. He staggered back, his free hand across his nose and eyes.

Baylee recognized the long ears and twisted features for what they were. He had fought dopplegangers before. *Xuxa.*

I have seen, the azmyth bat replied. *They are all foul, cowardly creatures.*

But in nowise less dangerous, Baylee pointed out. He gave ground before the doppleganger as it came at him again. Xuxa tried to keep the second one occupied, and to get close enough to use her own unique powers to end that part of the battle. But her attacks took glide time to maneuver. As soon as she broke off, the second doppleganger joined the first in attacking Baylee.

Without warning, a feminine voice spoke from the very air

around them. "Keep the ranger alive," she said, "or you'll know my wrath."

"Alive?" the one with the cutlass argued. "But that was not the bargain."

"The bargain has changed. Surely you, of anyone, would understand change."

Baylee believed he recognized the voice as belonging to the drow woman. They had tracked him. The pursuit had not ended.

"It is all right, Zyzll," the other doppleganger with the boat hook said. "She only needs him alive. Not of a whole piece. We'll still take his arms and legs. And if need be," he held up the cruel boat hook, "we can take his eyes as well."

Seizing the moment, Baylee turned and fled. His action caught the dopplegangers by surprise, and he gained three good strides on them before they took up pursuit. The ranger headed for his mount tied up in front of Nalkie's. He came up from behind it at a dead run, used his hands on its rump to vault up, then landed with his feet on the saddle. He took one step as the horse shifted in surprise, and leaped onto the solid wood awning over the tavern, hoping that it would hold his weight. He ran the length of it, away from the sea and deeper into the shops.

A glance over his shoulder showed him that Xuxa winged toward him. The two dopplegangers raced after him as well. One of them rippled, the arms and legs stretching as it grew two feet taller than it had been. At its new height, it easily grabbed the edge of the eaves over Nalkie's and hauled itself up.

The eaves vibrated beneath Baylee's feet as the creature dropped onto the awning. The doppleganger with the boat hook followed along on the street below.

Baylee ran, quickly as he could, leaping over the open gaps between the awnings. A handful of shopkeepers and their patrons came out to watch, not daring to get too close. But Baylee knew the watch would be called, and with them would be Cordyan Tsald.

The line of buildings ended only a short distance ahead, leaving only the street or the alley behind the buildings. Baylee vaulted the low roof overhang of a leatherworker's business and ran for the back of the building.

At the end of the roof, he took one glance down and spotted the trash heap behind the seamstress's shop. He dropped into discarded fabric, breaking his fall, then clawed his way out. The footsteps on the roof above crashed, sounding close. With its greater stride, the doppleganger pursuing him across the rooftops gained ground.

Further down the alley, a young man swabbed out the back of a butcher's shop, the door wide open behind him. He looked up as Baylee approached, freezing into place.

The ranger eyed the handle of the mop. It looked good and strong, the grain showing that the cut had been made with it instead of against it. A thud sounded behind Baylee, and he guessed that the eight-foot tall doppleganger had dropped down.

The youth mopping out the butcher's shop stared past Baylee with wide eyes. The ranger reached out for the mop, snatching it from the youth's hand. "Excuse me. I need this." He turned to face his pursuer.

The doppleganger was almost on top of him. He couldn't have outrun it any longer. The creature's borrowed face split in a huge grin. "You're going to fight me with a *mop?*"

"If you're not too cowardly," Baylee replied, holding the mop defensively before him. "After all, we are alone. Your kind generally prefers to outnumber an opponent. And I am a fair hand with a mop." He breathed fast, trying to keep his breath regular after the exertion. Even fighting for his life as he was, part of his mind was occupied with what might be on the elven ship.

The doppleganger waved the cutlass with certain menace. With its enhanced height, the heavy-bladed weapon looked small.

Baylee shoved the youth back into the butcher's shop, out of the way of the confrontation. He ducked under the doppleganger's first slash. Instead of striking back as he stood and moved back from his taller foe, he put the wet end of the mop on the ground, then stomped the handle just behind it. The oak handle broke in a jagged arc. He side-stepped the next thrust.

The other one is coming, Xuxa warned.

I know. Baylee took another step back, giving ground, getting the feel of the changed weight of the mop handle. It was too short to be a true staff, but in his hands it was a dangerous weapon.

The doppleganger swung another cut at him, stepping forward in anticipation of Baylee moving back again.

Baylee deflected the blow, stopping enough of the sword before deflecting it to ensure the doppleganger's hand would ache from the impact. Caught off guard, the creature was unprepared for Baylee's reversal of the mop handle, or the swing that connected with his face.

The doppleganger roared with rage and pain, struggling to get the cutlass up.

Baylee ducked to the side, reversing the mop handle again and striking the doppleganger on the side of the knee with a meaty smack. The leg trembled and almost went out from under the creature.

Trying to recover, the doppleganger aimed a backhanded blow at the ranger. Baylee parried the cut and came across the top of the cutlass, ramming the rounded end of the mop into the creature's forehead hard enough to jerk its head back.

The doppleganger stumbled back, a worm of blood already threading down its face. The creature howled with rage and threw itself at its opponent.

Baylee whirled away, catching sight of movement behind the first doppleganger. Xuxa tried to intercept the second doppleganger, but managed only to narrowly escape the boat hook. Keeping his attention on his first foe, the ranger slid the handle through his hands and swung it hard.

The heavy oak caught the doppleganger on the foot, breaking bone. The creature hobbled, trying to stay upright on its injured foot.

Swinging again, Baylee connected with the doppleganger's head, knocking it to the ground. Before it could rise, he ran the sharp end of the handle into its throat, up into the brain. The doppleganger ceased its struggles, shivered convulsively, and died.

Baylee turned, the handle in his hands, and watched as the second doppleganger came to a halt only a short distance away.

The creature's eyes widened in fear, but anger shaped the features. "You killed Zyzll." The doppleganger raised the boat hook.

"Choose well," Baylee said, "your next move. It could well be your last."

"Take him," the drow woman's voice spoke from thin air. "I know you, Tweent. If he doesn't kill you, know that I will."

The doppleganger screamed and came at Baylee with the upraised boat hook.

Baylee blocked the hook and avoided his foe's charge. Stepping to the side, he slipped the handle under the other doppleganger's cutlass and flipped it into the air, making it come back toward him. With a skill that would have caused a carnival knife artist envy, the ranger caught the cutlass by the haft. As the doppleganger tried coming back around to get at him again, Baylee swung the cutlass at the juncture of head and neck.

The cutlass's keen edge separated tissue, muscle, and bone in an explosion of power. The doppleganger's head leaped from its shoulders.

Baylee looked down at the creature, feeling a little remorse. There had been too much death already in the pursuit of whatever prize Golsway had learned of. Talking to Golsway's pseudo-shade had brought all that home to him.

"He was fairly warned and fairly fought," a deep voice thundered. "There's no need for reconsideration here."

Baylee looked up, spotting Civva Cthulad ahorse at the other end of the alley.

The justifier slid his own sword back into its scabbard. His horse shifted under him, its hooves ringing against the flagstones. "I'm sure the watch has been called. Do you want them to catch up to you?"

Baylee tossed the cutlass away. Xuxa landed on a support strut beside the ranger and hung upside down, folding her wings around herself. "What are you doing here?" the ranger asked.

"Following you, of course."

"I never saw you back there," Baylee said. *How did you miss him?*

I don't know, Xuxa answered honestly, sounding surprised

herself. *But then, a bat flying through Waterdeep in midday has to keep a low profile herself in order not to attract a lot of attention. Or become a cat's dinner.*

"You were never intended to see me." Cthulad urged his mount forward. "I've been at your heels since you left your mentor's home. I should imagine Junior Civilar Tsald is vexed at both of us."

"They have no place in this," Baylee said. "The people that are responsible for Golsway's death aren't from Waterdeep. The answers to their identities aren't even in Waterdeep."

"You talk as though you've found out some things."

"Yes."

"Perhaps you'd care to elaborate," Cthulad suggested.

Baylee shook his head. "Not now. We're being scried upon at this moment."

A small smiled twisted the corners of the warrior's face. "Then I suggest we attend to that first. I have a friend who can expedite matters."

"So do I," Baylee replied. "And he can be trusted to keep his mouth shut." He paused, studying the justifier. "If you were so close to me, why were you so far away when these dopplegangers attacked?"

"I saw you take the flask from the fountain," Cthulad said. "I guessed that it might be from your mentor. While you were in Nalkie's, I thought it would be better if you had some time to yourself to sort things out. By the time I saw what was going on, it was over."

Baylee nodded, satisfied with the answer. From start to finish, the battle with the dopplegangers had lasted hardly any time at all.

"I have to tell you," Cthulad said. "I don't mind cutting the Waterdhavian watch out of our operation, but I feel a bit rancorous about being cut out myself. As I told you, I represent the families and friends of those slain at the forgathering. I shall not shirk that duty."

"I represent them as well," Baylee said.

"No, my young friend. You represent your own interests. Not

to say that you are in nowise selfish, but you are closely involved in these matters. A clearer head will prevail. If you allow me, I can be of service."

"Perhaps."

Cthulad laughed. "You against the world? Baylee, that's only your youth talking. Your mentor left you a clue to the next part of this quest you are upon, or I'll eat my horse. Do not foolishly assume you can defeat a power that took his life. By all accounts, Fannt Golsway knew his way around a spell or two. The foes you may be facing could be formidable indeed."

Baylee remained silent.

"I should like an answer," Cthulad said. "Your word that I shall be included in this endeavor. Or we can part here and I'll dog your tracks anyway." After a moment, he offered a hand, reaching down from his saddle.

"You've got my word," Baylee said, taking the other man's hand.

"Good. Then let's get your horse and see about removing those scrying eyes."

* * * * *

Folgrim Shallowsoul waved a hand over the crystal ball. The amber tint faded from the crystal, but the figures of Baylee Arnvold and Civva Cthulad remained. The lich turned his hollow-eyed gaze on Krystarn Fellhammer. *He knows where the wreck is.*

Krystarn met the lich's gaze straight on, wondering how best to play the bit of information she'd just received. "What wreck?"

Shallowsoul ignored the question. *Do you have a means of getting in touch with the other agents you have in Waterdeep?*

"Only by teleporting there and contacting them. As you know, I can't do that until after dark." Krystarn almost shuddered at the idea that the lich might ask her to journey to Waterdeep for such an undertaking anyway.

"By then you will be too late," Shallowsoul said, and Krystarn jumped at the sound of his spoken words. "I don't think they'll remain in the city much longer. He turned away from the crystal ball.

Krystarn stared into the crystal ball's depths, watching as Baylee returned for his mount at the front of the tavern. Together, he and Cthulad rode along the docks, going north.

"After all these years," Shallowsoul said, "the library will once more come closer to being complete. How I have longed for this day. And to have it threatened by this Baylee Arnvold, who is not much more than a mere boy, is insufferable."

For the first time, Krystarn heard the madness in the lich's words. She had always heard such creatures were quite mad, but she'd seen no real example of it. The weakness gave her hope. As a drow, she'd been trained from birth how to exploit the weaknesses of others.

"Perhaps," she said, "you could send me to this shipwreck and I could prevent the ranger from arriving there."

The lich turned to her, its grotesque face tweaked into angry mirth. "Do you take me for a fool, Krystarn Fellhammer?"

"No," she answered quickly.

"Good. Because I don't take you for a fool either. Were I you and had a chance at the things that you might find in that wreck, I would take what I could and run. Studying those things alone would take several lifetimes, even for a drow." The lich shook his head. "No, it would be better if you were not subjected to such temptation. I would be loathe to kill you while you are still of use to me."

Krystarn waited quietly, watching Shallowsoul open the amethyst book and read. In the crystal ball, Baylee and his companion arrived at a small shop in Waterdeep. A few moments later, the image in the crystal ball silently closed like a giant eye. It did not reopen.

"Baylee is gone from us now," the lich said. "Use the crystal ball to reach your other contacts within the city. I want to know how he leaves Waterdeep. The crystal is already attuned to all of those you gave me information about."

Krystarn sat and began her work. When she was finished, Shallowsoul dismissed her like a child. She mastered her anger and didn't say anything. She felt his hollow-eyed gaze on her all the way back to the dimensional door. But her mind was busy thinking up ways to make Baylee's diversion pay off for her.

* * * * *

"I'm afraid I wasn't able to get you much," Madonld said apologetically. He was short and wiry, silver-haired with a neatly cropped beard. Despite wearing the robes of a law-reader, he also wore the worn sword at his hip with authority.

Baylee looked at Golsway's old friend. The ranger hadn't often talked with the law-reader over the years, but there had been a few occasions when the old mage had invited the man to their table for eveningfeast and conversation afterwards. Those conversations always turned to the stories and twice-told tales they all shared as new speculations had arisen and been debunked all in the same hour.

"I did not expect miracles," Baylee said. They sat in the back of a pipeweed shop near the dock area. A few silver pieces had purchased the room for an hour. A number of shops fronting the wharf area had the same business practices. A number of "trade" agreements had to be reviewed, as well as any bribes paid that needed paying. The room was small, having only a circular table and three spindly chairs. Candles in wall sconces lit the room and filled the air with the odor of burning wax.

Madonld passed over the money belt from a bag of holding he carried. "I think you'll find you're well provided for there, Baylee, but Fannt left you much more. It's just at the moment, all those belongings and moneys are being scrutinized. I've already had an officer of the watch banging on my door less than an hour ago."

"Cordyan Tsald?" Baylee asked, buckling the money belt around his waist.

"That's her." Madonld gazed at him carefully, glancing back at Civva Cthulad, who stood by the door. "Are you in some kind of trouble? Maybe it's something I could help with."

No trouble that you could help with, Xuxa put in.

"Maybe I should be the judge of that," Madonld said.

Law-reader Madonld, if there was anything you could do besides what you're doing here and now, don't you think I'd be the first to know?

"Xuxa's right," Baylee said. "She would tell me to talk to you.

And she wouldn't take 'no' for an answer." He checked through the pockets of the money belt, surprised at the amount of gold coins he found.

"You'll find that you've been quite well provided for," Madonld said to Baylee. "Fannt wanted you provisioned for whatever expedition he's set up for you, and he wanted you looked after so that you may 'charge with the winds, wherever your curiosity and sense of adventure,' as he put it, takes you."

"I never expected this," Baylee said in a strained voice. "He was someone—" His voice finally broke. "You just thought he would live forever."

Madonld put his hand on the back of Baylee's neck. "I know." The law-reader's voice was husky. "I'm going to miss him too. So you be sure you get this matter cleared up and get back to me. I don't want to see you lost as well."

After a moment, Baylee stood. "I haven't been to Golsway's crypt to say my good-byes. I can't go now because the watch will probably have it surrounded."

"There will be time later. A more proper time."

"Would you do me a favor?"

"Yes."

"Would you send someone to take a flower blanket to put over his crypt? Wild red roses, with the thorns left on, and some dark purple orchids if you can. He never said so, but I knew they were his favorites."

"Of course."

Baylee shook the man's hand and left the room, Cthulad at his heels. He had money enough, now. All he had to do was find a ship.

19

"It's not much, is it?" Baylee looked around at the ship's cabin he'd been assigned with Civva Cthulad.

"I've bivouacked in worse," the justifier said. He struck flint to a lantern on a wall sconce, then blew gently on the wick to get it going. When he was satisfied, he lowered the glass again and adjusted the flame.

The yellow glow splashed against walls that needed a good scrubbing to get rid of the black-green mildew. Scars decorated the wood, as well as names, curse words, and pieces of prayer that had been carved into the surfaces. The ceiling wasn't tall enough for Baylee to comfortably stand in. He dropped his duffel on the floor beside one of the two cots suspended above the floor. All the bedding looked worn and moth-eaten.

"With the accommodations looking like this," Baylee said, "you have to wonder what the food is going to be like."

"Pray that you're hungry enough to eat it anyway," Cthulad said good-naturedly.

Xuxa hung from the struts coming from the center of the ship. The azmyth bat hadn't made any complaints yet, but the ranger knew they would come along soon enough.

"And I don't think the fare will be all that bad," Cthulad said. "I've got a food pouch that will give us an additional meal a day each of nuts, grains, and dried fruits. We won't starve, and we won't have to worry about scurvy on the trip."

"And I've got a few packages of jerked beef that will last for a time." Baylee lay on the cot. "We've got an hour or so before we sail out of the harbor. I don't think it would be a good thing for me to be seen above deck." He put his arms behind his head. "I'm going to take a nap. If there's anything I need to know, wake me."

* * * * *

"When did the ship sail?" Cordyan Tsald asked the watch officer giving her the report. She stood at the dock and gazed out at the Sea of Swords. A number of sailing vessels floated in the large anchorage behind the breakwater. The pinging of sail cloth cables ringing against the masts created an undercurrent of sound almost as loud as the waves breaking under the docks.

"Perhaps as much as two hours ago," the watch officer replied.

Cordyan cursed silently. They had managed to track Baylee to Nalkie's. Although none of the staff at the tavern readily admitted to seeing the ranger there, patrons and shopkeepers across the street had volunteered information that led her to believe Baylee had been the man they'd seen. The two dead dopplegangers in the alley cinched it.

"He has gotten away," Calebaan said, gazing out to sea with her.

"For the moment only," Cordyan said. "What was the name of the ship?"

"*Kerrijan's Hammer*," the watch officer replied.

"And where is she bound?"

"The maritime office here in Waterdeep says she's a regular traveler between Waterdeep and the Moonshae Isles. She's a cargo ship with contracts between businesses on both sides of the sea."

"What is her usual anchorage in the Moonshaes?"

"At Caer Callidyrr."

Cordyan dismissed the watch officer, leaving herself alone with Calebaan. "Why do you suppose Baylee travels there?"

"The obvious answer would be that he has received some kind of communication from Fannt Golsway," the watch wizard said.

"So he takes off on his own to go up against an opponent strong enough to kill Golsway in his own home? That's foolish." Despite her harsh summation of the situation, Cordyan felt fearful for the young ranger. In their days together on the journey back to Waterdeep, she had seen much to like about him.

Calebaan turned to her, his face only slightly amused because worry showed in there as well. "And what do you propose to do?"

"With Piergeiron's blessing," Cordyan said, "I'll sail after him."

"Why?"

"Because what he knows could offer a threat to Waterdeep," she said stubbornly.

"It has been nearly two tendays since Golsway was killed here in Waterdeep. There have been no further evidences of any threat to this city at all."

"Just because you don't see it, don't think it's not there."

"I suppose that is the stance you're going to take with Piergeiron and Senior Civilar Closl."

"Yes." Cordyan glanced up at her friend. "Do you think it will work?"

The watch wizard nodded. "Maybe. But I don't know whether to be wishful for you that it does, or wishful for you that it doesn't. Baylee Arnvold is not sailing a safe course at the moment. Those two dopplegangers back there are mute testimony to that. Someone wants him dead."

"I know, Calebaan, and I should hate to hear of that happening." Cordyan walked back to the hitching post where they'd left their mounts.

"You like this young man, don't you?" the watch wizard asked.

Cordyan felt her face color and she didn't dare look at her friend. "He is a brave, good man from what I have seen."

"That's not what I asked."

"That's the only answer that I'll give you, Calebaan. Anything else is for my thoughts only."

"Then you should not wear them so apparently on your sleeve."

"You think you know so much, then tell me where Baylee is right now and what it is that he seeks."

Calebaan only laughed, which infuriated Cordyan even more.

* * * * *

"You missed dinner last night."

Baylee took his plate from the mess hall and crossed the deck to sit with Civva Cthulad near the middle of the cargo vessel. The morning had brought rough seas, and eating in the galley hadn't seemed a good idea. Xuxa hadn't liked the idea at all.

The justifier sat on the rise of deck just above the cargo hold, his plate held before him. Sailcloth cracked and popped overhead. Sailors scurried through the rigging, dropping and adding sheets as orders were carried out.

"I didn't know I would sleep through the whole night." Baylee dropped into a cross-legged position in front of the old ranger. He balanced his plate on his knees, piled high with wheat cakes, bacon and breakfast steak, fried potatoes, and two oranges. He'd had to pay the cook a few silver pieces above his boarding passage for the extra fruit.

"Evidently you needed it. I know you didn't sleep well on the journey from the forgathering."

Xuxa flew to a net of ship's rigging over Baylee's head and remained within reach. She waited politely as he peeled the first orange and sectioned it out. He broke the first wedge in half and offered it up.

Thank you, she said as she took the offered bit of fruit. She chuckled contentedly as she began to eat.

"I offered her dinner last night," Cthulad said, "but she deigned not to eat, chancing instead to await you."

Little did I know you were going to sleep away your life last night, Xuxa chided.

Sorry. Silverware appeared to be something of a luxury aboard *Kerrijan's Hammer.* Baylee rolled up the first wheat cake, all smothered with butter and honey, and ate it. The wheat cake, after spending the night without food, seemed as good as any he'd ever had. "She meant no offense."

"Oh, none was taken. She explained how she felt and I graciously accepted her decision." Cthulad smiled at the bat. "I sat with her and kept her company. She is quite eloquent."

"There are times," Baylee admitted, "when you can't get her to shut up." He took a strip of bacon in his fingers, broke off a tiny piece, and offered it to Xuxa.

The azmyth bat lapped at it with her tongue. She wouldn't eat the meat out of preference, but she did like the taste of the grease.

"She seems quite concerned about your relationship with a young woman named Jaeleen," Cthulad said.

Baylee dropped his hand away from Xuxa. She made a frantic grab and managed to snatch the bacon morsel from his fingertips. "That has no bearing on our present course," Baylee pointed out.

"True." Cthulad finished the last bite of his wheat cakes. "Tell me about Uziraff Fireblade, the man we are going to the Moonshaes to meet."

"He considers himself an explorer." Baylee made a grimace of disgust. "But he is little more than a freebooter who sometimes strikes the skull and crossbones to do a little trading with those who wish to purchase certain discoveries he's been fortunate enough to discover."

"I wouldn't think a man of Fannt Golsway's reputation would deal with such a man."

"When it comes to antiquities," Baylee said, "those are the people an honest explorer deals with most of the time. Grave robbers. Tomb raiders. Body snatchers. Thieves. And killers. You run the gamut of the bottom of all Faerûn when you seek to uncover the past. And you have to deal with them all."

"Why?"

Baylee sopped up more honey with another wheat cake and popped it into his mouth. "Because those are the people who generally get into areas that you haven't been able to get into yourself. Some of the regions they make discoveries in are sanctioned, and explorers are viewed only as interlopers. They take things that are better left to museums and true collectors."

"For a price?"

"Yes. If you have a collector with a deep purse, those grave robbers know they can get a lot of gold pieces from someone who really wants a particular piece."

"I've heard some say that the work of an explorer is only one step removed from a grave robber," Cthulad said.

Baylee started to take offense.

He is only asking, Xuxa said, *seeking to better understand how you see yourself.*

Forcing himself to relax, Baylee said, "In some respects, I suppose the comparisons are inevitable. We operate from the same deep purses. The grave robbers demand the money after they've made the discovery. Explorers ask benefactors to put the money up ahead of time, wheedling and pleading, and showing as much of the information as they dare so that it is not stolen and used by someone else. In the end, all the items that are worthwhile and are recovered end up in the same museums and collectors' hands. Only the prices differ. A thief won't care about the history that goes with a particular piece, but an explorer will learn from it first before passing it along. In fact, many of an explorer's discoveries will be of things that are not of gold or silver. Codices to a forgotten language, for example."

"So it wasn't unusual for Golsway to deal with someone like Uziraff?"

"No. In fact, most of the business we did involved dealings with people like him. And much worse." Baylee handed another section of orange to Xuxa. "There are some who lure a willing buyer into a remote location to close the sale, then kill him and seek out yet another buyer."

"When we see Uziraff, will we be able to trust him?"

"If we don't let him out of our sight."

"He has a crew and a ship?"

"Yes."

Cthulad made a sighing noise. "Have you considered the fact that there are only two of us—"

Three, Xuxa added.

"Three," Cthulad corrected himself, "of us who are walking into this pirate's den to strike a deal with him?"

"There is no one else to deal with," Baylee stated simply.

"It will be hard to hold him accountable to any bargain we may strike. Unless you know something I don't."

"If we try to hold him accountable by force," Baylee said, "he'll know he has something worth a great deal. It would make him even harder to bargain with."

Cthulad gazed out over the open sea for a time. "I'd feel better if we had a small group of battle-hardened men."

"If that were the case," Baylee said, "we wouldn't even find Uziraff."

"What is it Uziraff has?"

"The location to a shipwreck that happened during the Flight of the Elves from Myth Drannor," Baylee explained. Then he embellished the story, bringing in all the details of Faimcir Glitterwing that Golsway had told him.

When he finished, Cthulad said, "Evidently the library is guarded by someone with a lot of power. Even if you are able to divine the library's location from something in the shipwreck, there remains that to consider."

"I know," Baylee said. "But I'm working on this expedition only one miracle at a time."

"Perhaps it would be better to ask for help from Waterdeep. They have shown an interest. And I've some knowledge of Lord Piergeiron."

"You know him?"

"We've met."

Suspicions filled Baylee's head. *Xuxa?*

His thoughts are unreadable to me, the azmyth bat responded. *But everything I can sense about him and his reasons for joining us are nothing but good and honorable.*

"Lord Piergeiron would undoubtedly be interested in your mission," the old ranger went on.

"I prefer to chart my own course for the time," Baylee stated evenly. "Gifted as Lord Piergeiron may be in other matters, this is my field of experience."

"I understand perfectly," Cthulad replied. "I only sought to offer an alternative that may be more palatable at a later date."

"We'll consider it then," Baylee said. "Until such time, I still have to find Uziraff."

* * * * *

"Shouldn't we have overtaken *Kerrijan's Hammer* by now?" Cordyan Tsald asked, shading her eyes as she peered out over the Sea of Swords.

"Thirteen hours to be precise," Westalfe Sternrudder replied. The dwarf captain stood beside Cordyan on the specially built box in the prow of his ship that gave him a higher perspective than his short size would normally have provided. He was thick-bodied and able, with a square-cut black beard and a weathered, pinched face. "And we lay fallow for two days early on in this venture, as I'm sure you recall, while waiting for the winds to become more favorable. There was every chance that *Kerrijan's Hammer* wasn't so encumbered by fate." He patted the railing of the ship with genuine affection. "*Tsunami Dancer* is a proud ship. She'll do fine by you in the end. You'll see."

Cordyan gave up staring across the blue-green expanse of sea. She hated traveling by ship. The only way to truly see the world was from the saddle of a horse. "How far out from Caer Callidyrr are we?"

"Another two or three days," the dwarf captain answered, "should see us in the anchorage. Even if *Kerrijan's Hammer* wasn't mired in the windless sea as we were, we should arrive within a few hours of her. One way or the other."

Cordyan excused herself and walked back amidships.

"Troubled?" Calebaan asked. He sat in the shade of the main mast, reading a tome of magic that was written in a language Cordyan had no comprehension of.

"No," she answered irritably.

Calebaan closed the book, using a cloth ribbon to mark his place. "You received this ship when you asked Lord Piergeiron."

"Somewhat reluctantly, it seemed to me."

"Yet here you are." The watch wizard paused. "There are times in your life, Cordyan, when you just have to trust to the gods."

"I would," the watch lieutenant agreed, "except that I know there are those among the gods themselves who would only see evil wrought. Cyric casts a long shadow these days."

"So you see Cyric's hand in this?" Calebaan seemed slightly amused.

"Stuck aboard this ship this past tenday, especially with the two days of lackluster sails," Cordyan snapped, "I've had time to see this pursuit from all sides."

"Don't give up on your ranger," the watch wizard counseled. "From the time I knew him, and from the stories Civva Cthulad knew of him, Baylee Arnvold is quite a resourceful man."

Cordyan silently hoped it was true. But then, she knew the enemies the ranger had were also quite resourceful.

* * * * *

Krystarn Fellhammer's eyes ached from constant staring at the crystal ball Shallowsoul had charged her with. She had used her contacts among the docks of Waterdeep to find out all the ships that had left within a few hours of Baylee Arnvold's disappearance from the city. It had been twelve days, and she still could not believe so many had left at that time, nor that she had been through them all, yet hadn't found the ranger.

Still, he was one man among a whole crew. It would have been easier searching for a party rather than an individual.

She silently damned his soul once more, and leaned back from the crystal ball. She stood and crossed the room to the wine flask in the corner, pouring herself a small drink.

Shallowsoul had allowed her to bring the crystal ball to her rooms within the subterranean complex, convincing Krystarn that the lich was indeed concerned about the ranger's actions. She couldn't understand why. The Moonshaes were a long distance from the depths beneath Myth Drannor.

The crystal ball, though, was a blessing. When she had brought the device through the dimensional door leading to the library, she had felt within the crystal ball the resonance that opened the door. After working on it for a time, she felt certain she might be able to open the door with a spell of her own, triggering the release of the magic Shallowsoul already had in place.

But a more proper time awaited. She was beginning to think it might be in her best interests to see that Baylee Arnvold did in fact arrive at Myth Drannor, providing a diversion for the lich.

The twisted path of her plan delighted her. It was the first of any sort that she'd found with any hope of achieving her own goals. Mother Lloth willing, she could soon act like a true drow for the first time in over four years.

She returned to the crystal ball and peered into the glass. It was still tracking the latest ship she searched. She waved a hand over it, thinking of Chomack, Taker of Dragon's Teeth and Chief of the Sumalich Tribe.

The crystal ball clouded for a moment, then opened again to an image within the vast caverns outside the library area. The hobgoblin chieftain was locked in battle with another hobgoblin.

Krystarn watched in growing fascination as the hobgoblin chieftain cracked his whip across his opponent's face, wrapping the strands about the other hobgoblin's head. Then he lunged in with his short sword, knocking aside his opponent's axe and burying the blade in the hobgoblin's heart.

With a shudder, the other hobgoblin dropped to the cavern floor.

Chomack stepped back, holding his bloody sword aloft in victory.

Opening her perspective of the view offered, Krystarn saw that the hobgoblin chieftain was surrounded by nearly four times as many hobgoblins as the day she'd found him. Evidently the one-on-one fight had been for the control of the tribe recently encountered.

"Chomack," Krystarn said into the crystal ball.

The hobgoblin chieftain stared up, searching. "What do you want?"

The other hobgoblins drew their weapons and stepped back. Some of them yelled for Chomack to take cover.

"I look in on you today," Krystarn said, "only to offer my congratulations. Your tribe has grown."

"Because I am strong enough to take them," the chieftain roared back.

A ragged cheer broke from the ranks of the hobgoblins. Many of them beat their swords against their shields.

"I also remind you of your promise to me," Krystarn said.

"I will keep it," the hobgoblin growled. "As long as you keep your end of the bargain."

"Chomack," Krystarn said, thinking of the gold and silver that must be secreted away in the library, "I shall give you even more than I promised." She waved over the crystal ball and picked the next ship on her list. Its name was *Tsunami Dancer*. She had scried it twice before, feeling an empathy within it when she'd searched for Baylee Arnvold.

20

"Uziraff Fireblade is in the back, but I wouldn't go in there if I was you."

Baylee looked at the whiskered barkeep behind the scarred counter of the Fickle Mermaid. The place was one the ranger vaguely remembered from a time when he and Golsway had been through the area to talk to Uziraff before. The decor was bawdy, featuring a few dozen carved mermaid statues in various forms of debauchery with mermen, humans, and even unicorns. All of the statues had been glued to whatever surface they sat on to keep the tavern's patrons from walking off with them.

"And why not?" Baylee asked.

"He's talking business with someone."

From behind the door to the barkeep's left came the sound of blows being struck, leaving no illusions about what was going on.

"Talking?" Baylee asked. "Or listening?"

The barkeep gave an evil grin. "Uziraff owns the Fickle Mermaid. I don't think anyone could make him listen in here."

Baylee walked around the end of the bar as someone groaned in pain.

The barkeep reached for a belaying pin he kept under the counter. He fisted it and came at Baylee. "I told you stay out of this."

Before the man knew it, Civva Cthulad had his long sword at the end of the man's nose. "Unless," the old ranger said in a calm voice, "you wish to learn to start breathing through your ears, step away."

The barkeep went cross-eyed looking at the unwavering sword tip. Conversation across the rest of the bar died as heads turned to the counter. A few men got up, their hands going to their hilts.

"Gentlemen," Cthulad said, addressing the crowd, "I assure you taking part in this would be your greatest mistake. I will kill the first man to interfere with us just to let the ones who follow have no surprise what their fates may be."

"This isn't exactly the quiet kind of entrance I had in mind when we came here," Baylee said in a low voice.

"You dealt the play when you threw the dice," the old ranger replied. "You could have waited till Uziraff was finished with his business."

But Baylee couldn't have, because he thought he knew what kind of business it was that Uziraff was conducting. He watched as the men in the bar stood their ground, wary of Cthulad's sword. Baylee placed his hand on the doorknob and found it locked. He knelt and used a set of lock picks he carried with him, then passed through.

The room on the other side of the door looked nothing like the rest of the bar. A few books lined one wall, a hodgepodge of subjects, titles, and authors. Baylee doubted that Uziraff had read any of them. Niches held other vases and objects d'art, none of them worth much, actually on display in the room for their visual impact. Twisted creatures held men in their grip, sometimes even whole ships. A model of a treant held two humans in its branches while fire surrounded its base.

Generous in floor space, the room held a large desk, two couches, and a half dozen chairs in front of the desk. The first time Baylee had seen the office, he thought it hadn't fit the pirate's reputation.

But today, seeing Uziraff with his knee in the chest of a young man sprawled across that desk, a lead-filled cestus covering one hand, Baylee thought that it looked more representative of the pirate.

"Who dares interrupt me?" Uziraff roared, turning to look over his shoulder at the door. He was a little more than six feet tall, bronzed from the sea and the wind, and his dirty blond hair was pulled back out of his face. Wide gold hoops dangled from his ears. His beard was full, but kept short, following the angles of his face. He wore a red silk shirt and black, heavy-weight breeches that tucked into roll-top boots.

The boy's one eye that wasn't swelled shut stared in rounded terror. Blood covered his bruised and battered face, and ran down his neck. Two men held his arms spread out at his sides.

"You know me," Baylee said. He gestured for Xuxa. The azmyth bat leaped from behind him.

Uziraff didn't move from his victim. The pirate's face twisted in a grimace. "Fannt Golsway's whelp. I've heard the old mage finally got himself killed."

Xuxa landed under one of the supports across the ceiling, hanging upside down. She kept her wings open for immediate movement if necessary. *Be careful,* she advised.

"Get off that boy," Baylee ordered.

Uziraff didn't move. "This boy stole from me. I was only teaching him a lesson, and deciding whether I should take a hand for my trouble as well."

"And this is the man you're going to deal with?" Cthulad asked quietly, pulling the door closed to the main bar.

"I'll not trouble to tell you again," Baylee said in a cold voice.

"You dare to come here and tell me how to run my affairs?" Uziraff laughed, joined by his men, who started to close in, drawing their weapons.

As quick as thought itself, Cthulad stepped forward. His long sword swept out before him in a series of strokes. Three men lost their weapons, drawing back bleeding hands.

Uziraff abandoned his victim, reaching for the cutlass in the red sash at his waist. "I'll suffer no such treatment of my authority under my roof, old man."

Cthulad turned to face the freebooter. "The boy here wants you left alive. I'll humor him as long as I am able." His long sword rose to an *en garde* position. "Though, by nature, I am not a fanciful man, I must warn you."

"Who are you, old man, to come to me in such a threatening manner?" Uziraff demanded.

"I am Civva Cthulad, justifier, a known warrior and general of armies. I was raised on combat, schooled in warfare, and have kept a sword as my constant companion for as long as I can remember."

"I have heard of you, Justifier, but usually you are with an army in one nation or the other of the Dalelands. Here you are just one man. Perhaps only a breath short of dying."

"And perhaps even further than that," Cthulad challenged.

Xuxa spread her wings and shrieked, startling several of the pirates into dodging back. *Do not forget about me, Uziraff Fireblade. No one will touch Baylee without paying full measure.*

"Let the boy go," Baylee commanded.

"You're not even armed," Uziraff protested.

"That can change. There happen to be a number of swords laying here on the ground. I'm proficient with any style of them."

"What do you want?" Uziraff asked. "I know you didn't come here to save this miserable wretch." He nodded at the boy.

"I came here about the pictograph you found and took to Golsway."

Uziraff's interest showed on his face. "I thought there might be more than Golsway let on." He gestured to the two men holding the boy across his desk.

The men released the boy, who stumbled out of the room. He shot Baylee a look of thanks.

Uziraff took a bar towel from a nearby chair and wiped the blood from the desk. "Sit down and we'll talk."

Baylee took a chair and sat in front of the desk. "I want to find the area where the pictograph came from."

"That can be costly," Uziraff said.

"If it's too costly," Baylee said, "then I'll go elsewhere."

Uziraff leaned across the desk and put a thumb to his chest. "I sent that pictograph to Golsway. How many other men do you think knows where it was even found?"

"I don't know," Baylee said, "but I can start by checking to see who disappeared or turned up dead around that time. It could be that I'll discover that person was the first to find the pictograph. And it could be that the pictograph was offered to other buyers before you ended up with it."

"Golsway trained you well," Uziraff said.

"Yes." Baylee returned the pirate's level gaze. *Can you read any part of his thoughts?*

As always, Xuxa replied, *Uziraff's mind is closed to me. But I do sense some of the emotion connected to the pictograph. He possesses a lot of excitement about it. And he is knows more than he is telling. I do sense some anxiety as well.*

"What can you pay?" the pirate asked.

"Five hundred gold pieces," Baylee said.

Uziraff broke into a loud booming laugh. "For a trip such as that, I'd require nothing less than ten *thousand* gold pieces."

"For that, if I had ten thousand gold pieces," Baylee said, "I could buy a brand new cog just like yours." He stood up from the chair.

"I'm not just selling the boat ride," Uziraff said. "That you could get anywhere. You're also buying the information as to where that pictograph was found."

"Mayhap," Baylee said, "I'll be able to find them both, for considerably less than you offer." He walked to the door. *Tell me, Xuxa, is there any weakening to his resolve?*

Uziraff is curious and anxious, the azmyth bat answered.

Then there must be another source that could give us the location of the shipwreck.

Yes.

"Wait," Uziraff said.

Baylee turned back toward the pirate.

Uziraff spread his hands. "Surely you can offer me a better deal than five hundred gold."

Baylee waited, staring at the man. "Eight hundred gold, and our passage is included so that we get our meals. You're leaving me precious little to get back to Waterdeep on."

"Both of you are going? Then the price is—"

"The price is more than fair," Cthulad said.

For a moment Uziraff bridled at the harsh bite of the other man's tone. Then he sat back in the chair and grumbled, "As you wish."

Xuxa? Baylee asked.

His curiosity is showing most, the azmyth bat answered. *Nothing duplicitous.*

"How soon can you be ready to leave?" Baylee asked.

"Now it's a rush job as well?" Uziraff laughed and shook his head. "Really, Baylee, you're well on your way to being as insufferable as Golsway himself."

"How soon?"

"Two hours."

"Fine," Baylee said. "We'll meet you at *Windchaser*." He headed for the door.

"Don't try to beat out my price, Baylee Arnvold," the pirate called. "We have a deal."

"I'll be there."

"And bring my gold with you."

* * * * *

"He's not a man to trust."

Baylee glanced at Cthulad. "Not if we had another choice. But it could be that finding anyone who knows anything of the pictograph here in Caer Callidyrr will be near to impossible. The people in this circle don't like to give away their information, and they hate to admit they know less than you. Just the act of asking questions will set other hounds loose on us." He peered toward the docks fronting the mouth of the natural harbor.

Broken rock littered the coastline, some of them in the distance drawing white water. In the winter, the winds whipped over the harbor brutally, shutting down most avenues of trade except for the most desperate. The smell of brine was thick in the cool air.

Baylee led the way through the uneven line of porches fronting the shops around the harbor area. It felt good to be moving, not cloistered away aboard the cargo ship anymore. The encounter with Uziraff had left a bad taste in his mouth.

We are being followed, Xuxa said.

I know, Baylee replied. *I picked them up as we left the Fickle Mermaid. Keep an eye on them to make sure they don't get too close.*

"We have company," Cthulad said.

Baylee nodded. "They'll be with us till we show up at *Windchaser*. Until then, we'll take a stop here, then find a good lunch. You won't have such a thing when we're aboard *Windchaser*."

The building was a narrow expanse between a leather-working

shop and a jewelry shop. Hand-lettering across the glass read Vlayn's Potions and Potables.

"What do we need here?" Cthulad said.

"The wreck is under water somewhere," Baylee said. "We're going to need a way to get down to it."

"So you're going to buy a potion of water breathing?"

"It does seem advisable."

Cthulad nodded. "Don't forget to pick up a few healing potions. With Uziraff along, I think we'll need them."

Baylee halted inside the door to the apothecary. "Where will you be?"

"I spotted a weapons shop a little further down," the old ranger said. "While you haggle over the potions, I'll see if there's anything there we might need. You still don't have a sword. I thought I might find a present for you."

"I don't usually like to carry a weapon," Baylee said. "There are ways to deal with problems rather than violence."

"These are not usual times," Cthulad said. "And we are dealing with Uziraff and his sense of greed. Just the—the *three* of us."

Listen to him, Baylee, Xuxa urged.

"Yes," Cthulad added. "I am an expert in these matters. Uziraff will not be satisfied until blood has been spilled at this point."

Baylee nodded.

"What would you prefer?"

"A composite long bow," Baylee said after a moment. "Tilmentus, the weaponsmith there, makes a good, collapsible bow that stores in a quiver of arrows. Tell him its for me and he'll know the draw of the arrows and the pull adjustment. Also tell him that I want sheaf arrows, three dozen in a side-by-side back quiver, with a half dozen of those already set up as incendiaries. A bag of caltrops. A spring-bladed parrying dagger. A good combat knife. And a long sword. And a brace of throwing knives."

Cthulad raised his eyebrows slightly. "Is there anything else?"

Baylee regarded him. "Only if you think there is anything I've forgotten."

"No, that should be quite sufficient. I'll return as quickly as I can."

"Our splitting up is going to worry the people tailing us somewhat, so try to stay in sight."

Cthulad tossed him a quick salute and walked toward the weapon shop.

Baylee entered the shop. It was dark and mysterious, smelling of arcane flowers and herbs. Most people who entered it would have been intimidated by the four skeleton displays hanging from hooks on the walls. They would have felt even more menaced if they knew Vlayn could have called them forth to defend him if he needed it.

"Baylee!" the heavyset apothecary called out from behind the counter. "It has seemed like forever since I have seen you last, my friend."

"And it's felt twice as long," Baylee responded. Then he settled in to haggle over the potions. Vlayn was a friendly merchant, but he always drove a hard bargain.

* * * * *

"You are Junior Civilar Cordyan Tsald?"

Cordyan studied the old sailor who stood before her. He was a shriveled brown nut of a man, his iron-gray hair in disarray. She had barely arrived at Caer Callidyrr when she'd been accosted. Her hand rested on her sword hilt. Her men had only begun disembarking. "Who are you, and how is it you know my name?"

"I am Floon, Junior Civilar, merely a day laborer hoping to earn an honest day's wages. I was charged with awaiting your arrival and getting a message to you." The old sailor seemed uncomfortable as members of the watch surrounded him.

"Who charged you with such a task?"

"An old man. A warrior by the look of him. One who's been in a number of battles. He said to tell you Civva Cthulad, but I don't know for sure that he gave me a true name."

Cordyan swapped looks with Calebaan. She looked back at the old sailor. "What was the message?"

"That the person you're looking for is aboard *Windchaser*."

"A ship?"

"Aye, lady, and a bad one at that. She's under the command of Uziraff Fireblade. And a worse pirate there's never been."

"Where might I find this ship?" Cordyan asked. She felt some constriction at the back of her throat. Why had Baylee turned to someone like Uziraff Fireblade?

"*Windchaser's* already left," the sailor answered.

"Where?"

"Sailing north," the man answered. "I talked to some of her crew before she left as the old warrior suggested, helping them load the supplies for a few silver pieces. They talked of going to Mintarn."

"What's in Mintarn?"

"Lady, I could not say."

"Thank you." Cordyan reached into her purse for a few coins.

Floon held up his hands. "I could not. The old warrior, he more than adequately paid me for my time."

"You would know *Windchaser*, though, wouldn't you?"

The man nodded.

"And you're familiar with the sea in this area, and Mintarn?"

"Aye, lady."

"Then perhaps I could hire you to guide us. Our captain is not overly familiar with these waters."

The man smiled and nodded. "It's been many a day since I was out for a real sail, lady. I'd appreciate the opportunity to be of service."

"Then you're hired, Floon." Cordyan turned to her sergeant. "Hammal."

The sergeant turned to face her.

"Get the supplies loaded quickly. We need to cast off again at once."

The man gave her a crisp salute. Then he turned and started shouting orders to the other members of the watch.

"How long ago did *Windchaser* leave?" Cordyan asked.

"She set sail three hours ago, lady."

"Have we a chance of catching her?"

The man hesitated, then shook his head. "She's a cog, lady, much like your own. But Uziraff has her set up to sail in these islands. She is as fleet as they come."

"Then we'll do the best we can. I'll have you taken to the captain. Tell him I want you to take a look over the provisions. If there is anything we need to purchase that we don't have, let him know to buy it." She called for a nearby guard and sent the old sailor off with the man. She turned to Calebaan, who was regarding the sea with amusement. "Why would Cthulad tip us off as to where they were going and who they were going with?"

"There is the possibility he lied," Calebaan pointed out.

"Do you think that's probable? You spent more time with him than I did."

"No. I said that in jest. With Civva Cthulad's real name being used, you know the message was given by him. And he is not a man prone to lying to escape trouble."

"He might, if he thought we were offering him or Baylee any harm, yet did not want to harm us either."

Calebaan regarded her. "You've been given too much time to think. What do your instincts tell you?"

Cordyan took a deep breath and let it out. "Only that Cthulad realized Baylee was getting them in over their heads and he guessed that we might be following."

"So he's using what he has available to manage the situation as best as he can." Calebaan nodded. "Now that sounds more like the man I talked with."

"Then let us hope this three hour lead *Windchaser* has doesn't get us there too late to help them," Cordyan said.

21

"The pictograph came up in a lizard man's net," Uziraff Fire-blade yelled over the whip and crack of the sailcloth. "He didn't understand what he'd found, but he took it to a man I do business with in Mintarn. The lizard man got a couple gold pieces and was very happy. The man I do business with got a hundred gold for his time, and considered himself fortunate. I, on the other hand, got a few thousand from Golsway. And now I'm starting to think I was made a fool of too."

Baylee stared down into the murky green depths, ignoring Uziraff's complaints, thinking about the long dive that awaited him. Dusk was already starting to drink down the sun. It would be full dark by the time he dropped into the ocean. But that didn't matter much, because at the depth he thought he might be diving, it wouldn't be light anyway. He'd come prepared for that, however.

"You've heard of nothing else ever being found in this spot before?" he asked.

"I've never heard of anything being found out here." The pirate captain said. He was backlighted by the lanterns hanging from the masts and rigging above the wide pots of sand placed there in case the lanterns fell. "Have you?"

"No," Baylee answered honestly.

Xuxa hung from the rigging above Baylee's head, and Civva Cthulad stood to one side by the railing, alone.

"The one discovery sparked an intense search by someone," Uziraff said. "Had there been another, I'm sure it would have done the same. That pictograph had been down there for a long time. No one has been looking."

Baylee silently concurred. "Why are you so sure this is the spot from the lizard man's description?"

"Because I can see what you can't." Uziraff took a tube from

221

inside his jacket and uncapped it. He handled the sheaf of parchment inside tenderly, carefully unrolling it. He displayed it to the two rangers. The parchment was completely blank. "What do you see?"

"Nothing," Baylee replied. Cthulad agreed.

"But I do," Uziraff said. "This map possesses great magic. It only has a limited number of uses, so I don't use it often. I didn't use it when the lizard man brought me out here, but now that you're here, following up the trail Golsway gave you before he died, I felt it was well worth the investment. And it was. The ship you're seeking lies just beneath us, two hundred feet down."

"I've never heard of such a map," Cthulad said.

Baylee had, though he knew that they were very rare. On the sea, it could automatically map a circle sixty miles across, even though the ship had not been there. And it would include avian creatures over twenty-five feet long, and sea creatures over twenty feet long. On land, that distance was cut to forty miles.

Only the map's user could activate the magic inherent in the map.

"The ship is down there?" Baylee asked.

"*A* ship is," Uziraff agreed. "I can think of no others that would be. From what I have seen in the map, the shipwreck is broken into a number of pieces."

Baylee's sudden enthusiasm outweighed even his wariness of the pirate captain. "Then it's time we found out." He reached into his bag of holding and found one of the vials he'd gotten from the apothecary.

I must admit, Xuxa said, *this is the one part of your plan that disturbs me most. I don't like the idea of being separated from you. And you will be out of range of my call should you need me.*

There's no help for it. Baylee unstoppered the vial and drank deeply. The liquid burned the back of his throat going down, and filled him with a lightness of being that felt almost euphoric.

"You'll be careful down there, lad," Cthulad said quietly.

"I think you're the one who has the more dangerous part," Baylee replied.

"A yard of good steel makes a warrior a mighty good neighbor," the old ranger said. "These baying dogs won't dare attack me without feeling they have the upper hand. And Xuxa is waiting in the wings, so to speak, to tilt the scales."

"Get a net over the side," Uziraff bellowed.

A half-dozen sailors ran to do his bidding, heaving a mass of weighted nets over the side.

Baylee looked at the pirate captain.

"I claim rights of salvage," Uziraff said. "You paid me to bring you here, not to transport anything back for you."

"I expected no less from you," Baylee replied. "All I want is a look."

Uziraff looked somewhat troubled by the way the ranger took the announcement.

Does he have a clue? Baylee asked Xuxa.

That you are lying to him? the azmyth bat asked. *No. From his surface thoughts that I have access to, he clearly believes he has the upper hand.*

Then let him continue thinking that. Baylee stepped to the ship's railing. "But don't expect me to load it for you."

"I don't." Uziraff took a vial one of his men handed him. He drank it down deeply, then accepted the backpack another gave him. "I'm coming with you. Didn't you think I wouldn't have had you followed to the apothecary's to find out what you'd purchased from him?"

Instead of answering, Baylee threw himself over the side of the cog. The potion filled him with its magic. He drew in a deep breath, taking oxygen from the water around him as easily as his regular breathing. Also, he found his movements not impeded by the water in any way. The potion counter-acted those effects also.

The potion worked just as Vlayn said it would. Moving rapidly, Baylee swam straight down. As well as the potion worked, it would only last an hour, but with the other part of the magic allowing him normal movement even beneath the water, traveling two hundred feet below the ocean's surface was a matter of minutes.

Three other splashes sounded in his ears. Normally much of

his hearing would have been distorted by the water and the pressure. With the potion active in his system, the sounds were almost normal.

He glanced up, spotting Uziraff and two of his men swimming after him. Evidently they'd drank vials of the potion as well. At two thousand gold pieces a potion, the pirate had evidently invested heavily in the expedition.

The depth took the light away, turning the water darker. Baylee reached into his bag of holding and took out the other article he'd purchased before leaving Caer Callidyrr. The lantern was small, almost on every corner of the city, but at three hundred gold pieces each, not everyone was going to have them.

He opened it, knowing it would be protected by the same magic from the potion as the rest of his gear. The lantern contained magic that filled it with light. He opened the shutter, unleashing a cone of light that shot down through the darkness. He followed it.

* * * * *

A few moments later, so far from the ship above that everything looked black overhead except for the three pirates following him, Baylee spotted the first coral-covered planks of the shipwreck sticking up from the silt of the ocean floor.

Fish moved away from him, curious at first, then afraid. Luckily, none of them were big enough to consider themselves predators.

Baylee turned and landed in the silt on his feet. He held the lantern up high, trying to get his bearings. The bulk of the fishing net thrown *Windchaser*'s side was behind him.

Uziraff and his companions touched down not far from the ranger's position. Together, they had enough light to penetrate the gloom and illuminate the first few feet of the large ship that protruded from the ocean floor.

"Gods," Uziraff said, "I've never seen the like. That's an elven ship, isn't it, Baylee?"

The thrill of the discovery dulled the fear and wariness in the ranger. He felt the siren call of the ship. "Yes," he replied. "Yes it is." He walked across the uneven plain of the ocean floor.

"What was her name?" Uziraff asked.

"She was called *Chalice of the Crowns*."

"What happened to her?"

The ranger shook his head. "I don't know."

"By the gods, she's old. Look at the coral covering her."

"I know." Baylee kept going forward, less than fifty paces from the shipwreck now.

She had broken into two main pieces. Planks and spars, masses of rigging, and sailcloth lay strewn across the ocean floor. The chill at this depth, negated by the potion Baylee had drank, had preserved what was left of her. Parts of the ship had drifted away with the currents, torn free as the ocean had claimed her.

"Was she from Myth Drannor?" Uziraff asked.

"I believe her to be." Baylee answered to the excitement that he heard in the pirate captain's voice. He couldn't believe he had only Uziraff to celebrate the moment with. Golsway should have been here at his side. Thoughts of the books that would have been in the shipment from the library swirled in his head.

"Gold!" one of the other pirates yelled. He crouched down, letting go of his lantern as he reached for the gold vase that thrust up from the silt.

No longer in contact with his body, and out of the reach of the potion's magic, the lantern extinguished immediately, then collapsed in on itself as the pressure crushed it.

The display was a grim reminder to them all.

"You fool!" Uziraff snarled at the man holding the urn. "Now we've got one less light down here to work with." He continued berating the man, using up even more time. Finally he ordered them to bring the net and start filling it.

Baylee walked onto the broken hull of the ship, making his way across the clusters of coral. He went carefully, knowing that one small tear across his skin could release enough blood into the water to draw predatory sharks—or worse—from miles away.

"Baylee!" Uziraff yelled. "Do not think you'll get away with anything! Everything we can load into this net is mine! Don't make me kill you for trying to hide any of it!"

The ranger ignored the threat. Gold and silver and gems littered the ocean floor. If Uziraff and his men were limited to the hour the potion gave them, they would feel the pressure of time passing and would be more inclined to pick up everything that was easy.

"Baylee!" Uziraff bellowed. "Where are you going? Come back here and help us load these things up! You'll at least get to see them that way. Baylee!"

The last glimpse the ranger had of the pirate, Uziraff was digging something from the ocean floor and pointing to another object embedded in the silt only a few feet away.

Baylee knew the ocean floor was probably littered with artifacts from the ship for a ways back to the east. *Chalice of the Crowns* hadn't gone down all at once. Her dive had evidently been steep, judging from the pressure marks on the broken planks, but time had passed before she'd finally settled. There would be a line of non-perishables along the path she'd taken.

Uziraff still bellowed in the background, his voice sounding garbled now coming through all the water separating him from Baylee.

In the center of the ship, Baylee found the true horror. Books and manuscripts, all precious vessels of knowledge, of learning, of history, lay scattered across the ocean floor. There were no bodies of the crew. Those would have been taken care of by the nature of the sea, dissolved back into the dust they'd first come from.

And some of the books had been dealt with as harshly. They held no pages, but the covers—of precious metals and other hard materials—remained behind.

Baylee stood on the side of the overturned vessel and played the beam of his magic lantern over the wreckage. So much was lost, possibly forever. The disappointment hit him like a physical blow.

Fish swam by lazily, watching him.

Then, glancing below, he spotted a stone tablet laying against the deck, partially shielded by the broken main mast. He made his way down carefully, swimming to the tablet.

Slipping his knife out, he pushed the blade against the side of the tablet. When it didn't fragment or crack, he put the knife away and risked picking it up. Some cultures had been written on stone tablets with a heavy sand content. Baylee had watched inexperienced site diggers reduce hundreds of years of records to dirt in seconds.

The stone weighed his arm down. He held the lantern to shine the light over the tablet. The language looked familiar. It wasn't the true elven tongue; it was something older than Myth Drannor, but it was human. Perhaps even something from Netheril, the civilization of human mages that had lived on floating islands in the sky.

He wiped at the built up silt and coral, but couldn't clear the face of the tablet. He knelt and opened his bag of holding, taking out yet another bag. This one he hadn't told Cordyan about when they'd talked about his journals. He shoved the stone tablet inside, then closed it. When he opened it again, the tablet was gone.

He smiled at his good fortune. He hadn't known if the bag would work under water. Looking at the debris left of the books broke his heart. So much was so lost.

Still, he made himself continue the search. Most of the vases made of precious metals—as long as they didn't have inscriptions or sigils—and other items he tossed onto a pile on the ocean floor. Items he found of interest went into the bag only to disappear a moment later. The bag stayed empty.

Scouring the ocean floor, he managed to find seven books that appeared to be fairly complete. Two of them had to do with the divination of ground water for the building of early cities. A quick glance through the slate sheets with runes carved on them let him know that spells were on the pages as well. All of the books went into the bag.

He was freeing a large display case of early arrowheads and gemstones from the sand when Uziraff and his two companions swam over the top of *Chalice of the Crowns*. They dragged another net with them, this one empty.

Spotting the pile of gold and silver on the ocean floor, Uziraff waved his men over to the pile. He grinned at Baylee as he landed on the ocean floor and took a look around. "If you keep this up, I may have to give you a cut."

"You told me I'd have a chance to catalog them," Baylee replied.

The pirate captain nodded, his attention drawn to the booty spread out around him.

Knowing he couldn't gather anything else up into the bag without Uziraff seeing him, Baylee abandoned the search outside the ship. He chose the front half of the vessel, walking around it till he found a narrow gap under coral studded planking and the sea bed.

Baylee crawled down and pulled himself through the gap. The silt flowed around him, spilling into the interior of the ship as he went through.

The first part of the ship consisted of what remained of the hold. Baylee found three more books intact but didn't take the time to try to decipher the language in them. He put them into the bag at once. He tracked through the silt, searching through the rooms. A jewel encrusted sword hilt lay in the center of one of the rooms, the blade eaten away by time and the brine.

The fifth door he tried was locked. He stepped back and rammed a foot against the jamb, splintering the wood and shoving it inside.

Moving silently, bleached white bone against the murky depths of the sea, four men boiled out of the room and came at him. They resembled corpses, bloated and discolored flesh padding out their frames, faces holding only empty eye sockets. Tatters of clothing clung to them, whipped about by the ocean currents.

Baylee gave ground at once, hoping that the potion would allow him to escape them. He recognized them as drowned ones, men who had died at sea and been granted a vengeful unlife. He experienced a momentary bout with nausea, but it passed quickly.

The ranger moved faster than they did, but he knew they would never allow him to simply escape.

He hung the lantern on a stub of a broken spar, knowing the magic within it would keep it from being crushed or extinguished by the water, then drew the long sword and parrying dagger Cthulad had purchased for him in Caer Callidyrr. He dropped into a fighter's crouch and met the first drowned one's sword thrust.

* * * * *

"Shallowsoul!" Krystarn Fellhammer stood at the wall and waited for the dimensional door to open.

What is it? the lich asked irritably, his voice echoing inside her head.

"I have found the ranger. And I have found the ship."

The wall wavered at once.

Krystarn stepped through, met immediately by the lich. The part of the library she appeared in held two stone benches sitting in a magical arboretum where flowered plants wended up through stacks of books for over forty feet. This wing of the library carried an atmosphere unlike any she'd ever been in before. Where the others had primarily been closed in and reverential, this one seemed somehow gay and open. The area above the arboretum even looked like an open sky, even though the drow knew that couldn't be so.

Where are they? The lich took the crystal ball from her grip, peering into the device's depths with its hollow-eyed gaze.

"North and east of Mintarn," Krystarn answered. The image trapped in the glass clearly showed Baylee Arnvold in the ship-wreck's hold, battling animated corpses. For days she had been following the Waterdhavian contingent of watch officers under Junior Civilar Cordyan Tsald. At first, the drow had believed Baylee to be aboard the watch's ship, but it had taken two days before she realized that, in truth, the ranger had eluded them too. Watching the Waterdhavians had taken precious time away from her.

They have found it, the lich said. *And now, so have I.* The creature reached beneath his jacket and took out a pouch. Placing the crystal ball in the air, he left it levitating there at eye level. He poured the contents from the bag into one bony hand.

Krystarn got only a glimpse of the figurines there. The one the lich chose was a carving of a whale.

Shallowsoul spoke aloud old words in the elvish tongue that Krystarn did not understand. Some of them seemed familiar, but she couldn't be sure. She felt the magic weighted in them, causing sporadic backlashes in the shield she kept in place against the lich.

When he was finished, Shallowsoul closed his hand over the whale figurine. "Now," the lich said in a quiet voice, "now it will be finished."

Krystarn watched the floating crystal ball, seeing Baylee Arnvold fighting for his life. She waited to see what form the lich's magic would take, an uncontrollable shiver racing through her.

* * * * *

Baylee pressed the release on the parrying dagger, unleashing the two side blades and making a proper claw out of it. He turned the first drowned one's blade with the dagger, then slashed with the long sword, caving in the drowned one's head.

The animated corpse went slack, floating away on the ocean currents circulating through the hulk.

Baylee dodged the next attack, moving to his right for greater freedom of movement. He slashed at the next drowned one's leg, shearing it at the knee. It flopped feebly, trying to get at the ranger. Baylee crushed its skull with the dagger hilt.

The other two drowned ones met similar fates at the end of his long sword. Cautiously, he closed the spring blades of the parrying dagger and sheathed it. He took up the lantern again and walked into the cabin the drowned ones had guarded.

He searched the cabin, finding an overturned trunk with an iron lock that had rusted closed. Using the long sword's hilt, he shattered the lock. It took a moment longer for him to pry the lid open.

The trunk was filled nearly to the brim with gems and gold pieces. It was a king's treasure, perhaps the treasure of several kings.

But on top of it all was a book.

Picking the book up, Baylee full well expected it to start falling apart. The tome was put together of parchment, but there must have been magic in it because the pages turned easily and showed no signs of distress from either time or brine.

He ran his hand across the embossed surface, feeling as well as reading the name in the lower right-hand corner. Gyynyth Skyreach.

* * * * *

The leader of the whales heard the old call in his head. The knowledge of the call had been passed down from generation to generation, as well as the story of the debt that they owed the one who called.

The whale leader sounded his mournful cry and heard it echo through the nearby waters. His pod came to him, falling into line in his wake immediately.

"A way will be made," the voice inside the whale leader's head said. "You are very far from your goal. But if you trust me, I will get you there."

The whale leader trumpeted in agreement. A moment later, the water rippled in front of him. He swam through without hesitation. The debt his people owed the one who called was immense.

And he felt the dimensions shift around him, just as the Elders had described in their stories.

* * * * *

A light nimbus approaching from the hallway outside warned Baylee that he was no longer alone inside the ship. He opened the bag and shoved the book through. He closed the bag and looked inside a moment later. The book was gone. He was relieved, because he'd never tried to shove through so many things at one time.

He bent down and grabbed the corner of the trunk, barely able to get it started moving.

Uziraff came around the corner. "I saw the drowned ones," the pirate captain said. "I thought perhaps something had happened to you."

"Thought, or hoped?" Baylee asked. He waited for Uziraff to grab the other end of the chest. Together, they managed to stagger through the doorway with the chest.

"Have you found anything else of interest in here?" Uziraff asked.

"This chest," Baylee answered. "But I've not gotten the chance to search much further. Most of the cargo appears to have been lost."

"We've picked up a lot of it outside." Uziraff grinned in the lantern light.

Baylee kept silent, struggling to get through the gap and bringing the chest with them. They had nearly made it to the waiting net when one of the two pirates pointed and screamed.

Turning, Baylee looked back in the direction they'd come from. The lantern lights were barely bright enough to illuminate the huge gray bodies as they swam into view. The alien eyes, bigger than the ranger himself, stared at him.

Then the whales swam into the wreckage of *Chalice of the Crowns*, smashing it into even smaller bits than it had been. The turbulence created by their passing shoved Baylee from his feet. For a moment, he was tangled in the net with the treasure Uziraff and his two men had gathered. Then he was free, the lantern in hand as he swam for a rocky outcropping.

Uziraff joined him a moment later. "Where in the nine hells did *they* come from?" the pirate captain demanded.

"I don't know," Baylee said. "But I'm glad they didn't arrive while we were still inside."

Both major parts of *Chalice of the Crowns* crumbled to pieces under the giant whales' assault. In the gathered darkness, Baylee wasn't sure how many of the creatures there were.

On their next pass through the area, they opened their mouths and shoveled in the broken pieces of the ship, swallowing them whole. More whales glided through the water and raked the silt in the nearby areas, dredging up huge tracts of the ocean floor.

Miraculously, they did not see the two nets Uziraff had been using.

A moment later, they were gone. Baylee pushed himself away from the rocky outcropping, staring at the long ditches where *Chalice of the Crowns* had lain for hundreds of years.

22

"I'll want a boat before I let you strand us out here," Baylee said. They were back aboard *Windchaser*, his clothes still dripping cold brine. The whales had completely left the area and, according to the pirate crew, never even broke the surface.

Uziraff stood at the prow of the cog, lanterns throwing light over him. The boom arm creaked threateningly as it lifted the second of the nets free of the ocean floor while the crew yelled in triumph. The pirate captain turned his attention from the glittering gold and silver pieces in the dripping nets to Baylee. "Who are you to make demands at this point? I could have all of you killed, cut up into chum for the sharks, and thrown overboard."

Baylee was aware of Civva Cthulad shifting beside him. The old warrior's hands were already on his weapons. "That would be a misadventure on your part," Baylee said.

"How can you stand there and say that?" Uziraff demanded. "You're outnumbered almost nine to one!"

"Think about it," Baylee said in a neutral voice. "How often have you seen me go armed?"

Uziraff leaned on the railing, gazing down at the ranger.

Baylee knew what he was saying was true, and it gave the pirate captain pause.

I promise, Xuxa said, opening her thoughts to Uziraff, *that I will kill you if Baylee falls.*

"They're only two men," one of the nearby pirates shouted out. "I say kill 'em and be d—" His voice froze in his throat, blocked by the quivering throwing knife that suddenly took shape there. The pirate gurgled, finally managing to yank the throwing knife free of his throat. But it was too late, his life was already spent.

"Anyone else want to venture an opinion?" Baylee asked. He fanned three throwing knives out in front of him, then made them disappear with the grace of a fan dancer. "If you try to attack me, I have nothing to lose."

None of the other pirates said a word.

"I await your answer," Baylee said.

Uziraff hesitated only a moment, then gestured to his men. "Give them a lifeboat. We've got the treasure. They can't take that away from us."

"Well, lad," Civva Cthulad said in a whisper as they faced the pirate crew, "I must admit I didn't expect you to kill that man outright so quickly. You seem to be rather laid back for that kind of thing."

"He would have talked them into killing us," Baylee replied. "And we would have killed more of them than the one whose life I took."

"Agreed. But we will be vulnerable to attack while we descend to the lifeboat."

Not entirely, Xuxa put in. *I can watch.*

The lifeboat was lowered over the side. "Go first," Cthulad invited.

"In a moment." Baylee drew the snap-together composite bow from its waterproof quiver and assembled it smoothly, locking the sections into place. He took up four of the heavy flight arrows, nocking one of them into place while he held the other three in his fist, and stepped over the side. The lifeboat was less than eight feet below and maybe three feet out. He landed in it, crouching to regain his balance, and managed to remain standing. The bow stayed at the ready. "Come on down."

Cthulad turned and clambered over the side, stepping down quickly into the lifeboat.

One of the pirates heaved an oil lantern toward the lifeboat, hoping the drench the occupants with flaming liquid.

Baylee loosed the shaft he held in his fingers, punching the heavy war arrow through the man's chest. Another man started raking at his face, coming away bloodied. Xuxa was a leathery whisper of movement just above him a moment later.

The oil from the lantern spread across the ocean's surface and caught fire. The flames twisted and licked at the lifeboat. Cthulad grabbed the oars and started rowing them away from the cog as well as the flames.

Only two other attacks were made on the lifeboat. Baylee put a shaft through the eye of an archer, and Xuxa ripped the face of another. Then Uziraff's voice split the night air, calling the pirates into order. *Windchaser's* sails filled and she pulled away.

Baylee took the bow apart and put it back into the waterproof quiver. He knelt down and checked the stores under the bench seat in the prow. The dive into the ocean, despite the potion, had taxed his reserves. With wet clothing draping his body, he felt the chill of the night air.

"You're quite good with the bow," Cthulad said, putting the oars to rest.

"When I have to be," Baylee agreed. He found a water flask as well as a wine flask, and a pouch with foodstuffs. For the moment he ignored the food, offering the wine to the old ranger. "I've found fighting gets in the way of discovering."

"But sometimes you can't have one without the other." Cthulad hoisted the wine flask in a salute. "To the times of exploration without fighting."

Baylee drank to that. In spite of the situation, he couldn't help grinning.

"Why are you so amused?" Cthulad asked.

Because, Xuxa said, *he found the ship.*

"Yet we're stranded out to sea, Tyr alone knows how far from any coast."

"No more than seven or eight miles, actually," Baylee replied. "The ship was only two hundred feet or so down. I studied nautical charts on the trip out here. The coastal plains don't drop off sharply into the ocean bed for another three miles or so. We need to head west and south to get to shore. *Chalice of the Crowns* would not have sailed to the south of Mintarn to reach Evermeet; they would have gone north." He gestured toward the sky. "We have a clear night, so it should be no problem to steer in the right direction."

Baylee freed the small mast laying in the bottom of the lifeboat and pushed it into the locks designed for it. When it snapped into place, he pulled the mast rigging into place with Cthulad's help.

"We're lucky they didn't kill us," the old ranger declared. "Or did you think that Uziraff would play fairly with you?"

"Never once," Baylee said.

"Then why deal with him at all?"

"Because he had the location of the wreck."

"And you knew he had that magical map," Cthulad said.

Baylee moved the sail into position, then dropped the small tiller into the water. "I had heard about it, and I saw it once. I was sure it was what it turned out to be."

"So he used you to verify the veracity of the ship," the old ranger said.

"And I used him and his mystical map to locate the shipwreck much more quickly than dredging the ocean bottom for miles. There have been others who were looking for that ship." In terse sentences, Baylee revealed what had happened below the ocean's surface, leaving out the books he'd salvaged. "If I had not used Uziraff to confirm the shipwreck's existence in this area so quickly, the people who killed Golsway might have already claimed the prize. There could have been nothing down there to find."

"Well, it was a masterful plan, lad," Cthulad said, relaxing against the thwart. "But Uziraff has taken off with the treasure."

"Only for a while," Baylee said, adjusting the sail and looking up at Xuxa hanging upside down from the rigging. "How long do you think it will be before Cordyan Tsald and the Waterdhavian Watch unit arrives?"

Cthulad's sharp eyes regarded Baylee in a new light. "You knew about that as well?"

"While you were at the weaponsmith's in Caer Callidyrr?" Baylee nodded. "We had plenty of time to get the things I needed from the apothecary and visit the weaponsmith. Security dictated that we remain together. That would have been one of the firmest principles you would operate by. Yet you split us up. That left the only reason for that behavior as your need to be alone. And why else would you need to be alone?"

"To bring along the manpower we needed to see this through," Cthulad said agreeably.

"I left word back in Waterdeep that would have set them on our trail," Baylee admitted. "And I asked the apothecary to get word to them as well as whomever you charged with that."

Understanding dawned in Cthulad's eyes. "You wanted them to draw attention away from you," Cthulad said.

Baylee grinned. "If someone with the ability to scry far distances was searching for me, for this shipwreck, it only made sense to give them a more logical target to search. Would you spend your time searching for a merchant ship, or for a contingent of Waterdhavian Watch?"

"So you never intended to find the shipwreck on your own?"

"Oh, I fully intended to find the shipwreck on my own. And I planned on Uziraff double-crossing us. By the way, how well do you think Uziraff would have gone along with us if Junior Civilar Tsald and Calebaan had been there?"

"By having just the two of us—"

Three, Xuxa put in. *Yes, by having only the* three *of us, Baylee allowed Uziraff to feel confident enough that he was thinking about greed and not survival. That way, he brought us to the site of the shipwreck.*

"A masterful plan," Cthulad said in obvious delight. "Though it irks me that I played a part without knowing it."

"If you had known," Baylee pointed out, "you would have done the same thing. Only perhaps not as convincingly." He hung the lighted lantern he'd used below the ocean from a piece of rope, then ran it to the top of the ten-foot mast. Yellow light belled out around it.

"It appears that you planned for everything."

"Not everything," Baylee disagreed. "The whales. I never planned for the whales."

* * * * *

Krystarn followed Shallowsoul at a dead run. The lich ignored her, fleeing through the library stacks. After a time, he came to a door set in a wall black as anthracite. He waved an intricate gesture at it and said a word of power. A lock clicked.

He stepped through the entrance and Krystarn trailed him, catching the door before it could close.

The room on the other side of the door was a huge cavern with fiery pink walls that met in the rounded shape of a horseshoe nearly ninety feet in height. A huge pool of water three times that height in length eddied in the center of the room.

Shallowsoul stood at the water's edge and made gestures too quickly for the drow to follow. A moment later, a giant whale surfaced in the pool. At least, it partially surfaced, because it easily exceeded the nearly three hundred feet of space left open in the pool. Water spumed from its blowhole.

Then it opened its mouth, disgorging bits of broken ship in the shallows and on the bank. When it was finished, it sank into the pool again and another took its place.

Krystarn counted eight whales all together. The piles in the shallows grew, containing silt and broken bits of ship, rotted sailcloth, rigging, and the unmistakable gleam of gold and silver.

Shallowsoul gestured toward the pile. Immediately, objects pulled themselves free of the mud and floated in the air. "Leave now," the lich commanded her.

The drow barely had time to acknowledge the dimensional door that opened beside her, then she was shoved through by a strong gust of wind. She landed in a heap on the stone floor on the other side of the wall in the hallway.

As she pushed herself to her feet, she cursed what little remained of the lich's soul. She glanced up at the drow warriors awaiting her and found that none of them looked at her. It was good that they chose to not see her ignominious arrival because she could not have spared any more of them. However, Chomack's hobgoblin army remained available once she found a way to open the dimensional door.

She returned to her quarters without a word, followed by the drow warriors. Inside her room, she took out the crystal ball Shallowsoul had forgotten about. She held it in her palm and concentrated on the lich.

The image in the crystal came slowly, but finally opened on the lich. Shallowsoul was still in the huge pink cavern. Objects danced before him, inscribing abbreviated orbits before aligning themselves.

Krystarn wished she dared to watch the lich longer, but the crystal ball had to remain her trump card. Evidently it was only a tool to Shallowsoul, not a prized possession. And now the lich apparently had what he wanted.

It remained to the drow elf to achieve her own just deserts. She turned her thoughts to the ranger, Baylee Arnvold, and sought to find him.

* * * * *

"There!"

Baylee stood in the lifeboat and gazed in the direction Cthulad pointed. In the distance, sailing through the shimmering fog that lifted from the Sea of Swords, a cog swelled into view. "At least it's someone," the ranger said.

I can fly on ahead to find out, Xuxa offered.

Yes, Baylee agreed. *But be careful.*

The azmyth bat dropped from the rigging, then flew low over the smooth sea.

Baylee watched her go with some trepidation. He guessed that Uziraff wouldn't hesitate about leaving the area, but there was a possibility the pirate captain might have decided to return to kill them.

It was an hour or so before dawn, the sky just beginning to lighten in the east, slate gray clouds speared through by pink threads of the rising sun. The northern wind brought a warmer breeze that fought the chill of the sea that soaked up into them.

"The flag at the back," Cthulad said, peering through a collapsible spyglass he retrieved from his kit, "is Waterdhavian."

Baylee's heart lifted at that. He and Cthulad had shared watch during the night, both of them wisely taking what sleep they could against the morning's activities. But he was anxious to get back on the trail again.

It is Cordyan Tsald, Xuxa announced when she returned.

Sitting back in the bow, Baylee altered his course for the cog. A few minutes later, he and Cthulad scrambled up the rope ladder sailors above cast down.

Cordyan met Baylee at the top of the railing. "You and I," she stated clearly and distinctly, "are going to have a long talk. And you're going to have to be very convincing to keep me from throwing you into chains." Her anger was unquestionable.

Unable to contain his excitement once he had a ship under his feet again, Baylee said, "We need to go talk to the captain."

"Why?" Cordyan demanded. His behavior evidently caught her off guard, because she was a half-step late in catching up to him as he started for the steering section.

"To set a new course," Baylee replied. He ran up the steps leading to the steering section.

"What new course?"

"An attempt to overtake Uziraff," Baylee answered.

* * * * *

Baylee told the story over a plentiful morningfeast from the ship's galley. Fresh fruits and cooked meats that hadn't yet had to be heavily salted festooned the plates. The ranger took his meal at a table set up on the prow deck of the ship. *Tsunami Dancer* cleaved the water cleanly, racing for Mintarn.

Cthulad and Xuxa also chimed in. The watch lieutenant and wizard sat in silence, absorbing as much of the story as they could.

"This was an elven ship from Myth Drannor?" Calebaan asked in disbelief at one point. "You can prove this?"

"She was called *Chalice of the Crowns*," Baylee answered. "Charged with transporting one of the great libraries near Myth Drannor to Evermeet."

"I've never heard of such a ship," Calebaan said, "and I've studied much of Myth Drannor."

"She was headed up by Gyynyth Skyreach," Baylee went on.

Calebaan shook his head. "Another name I've not heard of."

"Skyreach was the granddaughter of Faimcir Glitterwing."

Calebaan leaned forward, obviously interested. "Ah, now that name I've heard of. She was in charge of this vessel?"

"I found her logbook."

"Intact?"

Baylee nodded. He intended to tell them everything before it was over. But not at the moment. At the moment, he wanted to find Uziraff.

*   *   *   *   *

Four hours later, they found what remained of *Windchaser*. The boat was a battered hulk listing in the water. Her sails and rigging rose and fell lifelessly on the ocean surface.

Baylee recognized the stress fractures running through the cog's mast and sides. The whales had returned to finish what they had started.

The captain of *Tsunami Dancer* put the ship to anchor cautiously, and had men up in the crow's nest to keep lookout. They organized a search for any survivors, but only found dead men in the swirled tangle of broken planking.

Baylee used the second potion he'd bought from the apothecary to search the ocean floor one hundred sixty feet below. He only found three dead men caught in the knotted length of the anchor line.

None of the treasure remained.

"What do we do now?" Cordyan asked as he climbed back aboard *Tsunami Dancer*. "The trail apparently ends here."

Baylee shook the water out of his eyes. "It doesn't," he said. "We'll pick it up again in Candlekeep."

"How do you figure that?" Calebaan asked.

Baylee took out the special bag from his bag of holding. "Uziraff didn't know about this," he said grimly. He took out a piece of paper from his journal and scribbled a hasty note on it. He put the note into the bag, then closed it. When he opened it, the bag was empty.

"Where did it go?" Cordyan asked.

"Candlekeep?" Calebaan asked.

Baylee nodded. "I've got a friend at Candlekeep. Innesdav, an acolyte there, gave me this bag when I was still a teen traveling with Golsway. He took the time during one of my visits there to read some of the journals Golsway had instructed me to fill at certain sites I'd had interests in. Innesdav liked my writing, told me I had a keen eye for putting information down on paper in a way that allowed people to sense it for themselves. He said the bag was a gift, and that I should use it to send him my journals as I filled them, or special papers that I wanted him to see." He looked out at the stricken ship. "Uziraff didn't know about the logbook."

"And now the logbook's at Candlekeep?" Cthulad asked.

Baylee nodded. "Unless something went very wrong."

"Do you know what's in it?" Calebaan asked.

"Maps," the ranger replied. "It looked like Skyreach had written down the location of the lost library of Faimcir Glitterwing in her notes, but I didn't have time to study it further."

"Then your treasure chase is still on," Cordyan said.

Baylee nodded. "As soon as I get to Candlekeep. I'm not going to let it slip away. Golsway gave his life to get this far."

23

"Awe-inspiring, isn't it?" Baylee asked. He stood in the prow of *Tsunami Dancer* days later, looking up at the rocky volcanic crag where the citadel sat. Candlekeep boasted many towers that stabbed straight up at the blue sky.

"Yes," Cordyan answered. "I've only heard stories about it. I've never actually seen it before."

"Well, today you'll get a closer view of it," Baylee said, "than most everyone on Faerûn. Provided Innesdav got my note." He peered at the dock at the bottom of the crag. The rock was volcanic and black, reaching down into the green of the Sea of Swords. It made it harder to see the group of acolytes gathered near the small docks in their black robes.

Calebaan came up beside them, clinging to the rigging as the ship sailed through the choppy water of the tiny harbor. "I've only been here once myself, and it was an experience I'll never forget."

Xuxa dropped from the rigging above and took wing, speeding across the water. *Innesdav is there,* she cried joyfully.

Minutes later, *Tsunami Dancer* put into the harbor. The black robed acolytes tied the ship to the mooring anchors while the sailors unlimbered the boarding platform. It thumped solidly onto the dock.

"Baylee," one of the acolytes yelled from the crowd, "it is good to see you again."

The ranger's heart sped up as he spotted his old friend. He bounded down the boarding platform and seized the man by the upper arms. Innesdav returned the grip, the old man's strength still surprisingly strong. "And it is good to see you again, old friend," Baylee said.

"I thought perhaps you would be here yesterday."

"Blame the wind," the ranger said, feeling of higher spirits than he had since finding out about Golsway's death.

243

Innesdav was a half-head taller than Baylee, but thin as a post, almost looking like a scarecrow instead of a man. He pushed his cowl back, a smile on his wrinkled face. "It has been so long, young warrior."

"The years pass so fleetingly," Baylee agreed. Besides Golsway, Innesdav was the other important figure in the ranger's life. Where the old mage had been a stern disciplinarian, Innesdav had been the doting uncle, always there with a gift or a piece of candy when Golsway wasn't looking. And in those years when Golsway was most active at Candlekeep, Innesdav had provided a vast tutelage of his own, bringing to Baylee's attention fantastic stories told just for the sheer wonder and amazement of it.

"You have sent me a very interesting, if abbreviated library, my boy."

"They arrived?" Baylee asked as the acolyte dropped his arm across the back of the ranger's shoulders and guided him up the carved stone stairway that curled up around the uneven face of the crag to the citadel that waited on top.

"Oh yes, they arrived." Innesdav laughed. "I must admit to some frantic consternation when gallons of seawater seemed to be pouring into that old closet we set up to receive your journals. For the first few moments, I thought you'd been drowned somewhere and this was going to be the first notice I received of it."

"I'm sorry," Baylee said. "I couldn't tell if any water was going through with the books."

"Yes, and plenty of it. I mopped for hours. After I looked at those books, of course." Innesdav held up a hand and Xuxa flew down and grabbed the little finger of his hand. "Ah, Xuxa, and how have you been?"

Running for our lives, up against foes that we have not yet named, the azmyth bat replied, *pursued and harried by the Waterdhavian Watch, and chasing after what could potentially be one of the greatest finds ever made.*

"That," Innesdav said, "sounds almost like the accounting you gave me the last time you came here."

Xuxa chirped in amused agreement

Baylee reflected on that event, trying to place the time in his mind. "That was when we found Tchazzar's scroll, which outlined how the smaller kingdoms of Chessenta united and what the trade agreements were supposed to be."

"Exactly," Innesdav nodded. "That scroll was supposed to have been writ in the blood of the men who agreed to it. And the man who could produce it would have controlled the lineage of those kingdoms and possibly been able to step into a ready-made country ripe for the taking. If the person seizing the scroll was a good enough mage."

Baylee nodded. The story had been told for decades since the fall of unified Chessenta. But Golsway had uncovered new knowledge that had led them on a merry chase to the scroll they recovered. It now resided in Candlekeep for security reasons. There were some who said that the ghosts of the men who'd signed the document could be summoned back from the beyond to wreak vengeance on the men who'd sundered the realm they'd put together.

"Did you ever discover if the scroll Golsway and I found was truly the Tchazzar Scroll?" the ranger asked.

"We checked as much as we were able. It certainly looks like it. But there is only one sure way to tell, and no one here is going to allow that to happen."

* * * * *

They met in one of the many outbuildings that were as close to Candlekeep as any outsider was ever allowed. A terraced rock garden surrounded the building, dotted with numerous trees and stone benches. Natural springs ran through the rocks and across the landscaped areas.

Baylee felt at home there, relaxed in spite of the last few days and what still lay ahead, almost at peace because of the security he felt there. He sat across from Innesdav and beside Cordyan, too aware of her and too aware also that she was female.

Calebaan and Cthulad sat on another bench, the latter puffing contentedly on a pipe.

You should have been thinking more along those lines on the voyage to Candlekeep, Xuxa said.

Quiet, Baylee admonished. The junior civilar shifted beside him, and he wondered if the azmyth bat had included Cordyan in their silent communication.

"You were right about the logbook," Innesdav said. "It does contain maps of Glitterwing's library."

Baylee's attention centered immediately on the acolyte's words. "In Myth Drannor?"

"Not in Myth Drannor proper," Innesdav went on. "In a forest north of Mistledale. You are familiar with Mistledale?"

"That is a big forest," Baylee said.

"It is actually nearer the Standing Stone than it is Mistledale, I believe."

Baylee shook his head, thinking through the logistics of such an expedition. "If the library is underground, it could take years to find it. Surely there's a way to cut the search down. Have you read the logbook?"

"We're working on it," Innesdav said. "We believe the written language Skyreach chose was deliberately obscure. You have to remember, her grandfather schooled her."

"I didn't know," Baylee said. "I know very little of her."

"Well," the acolyte went on, "let me say that in the matter of his granddaughter, the apple fell not far from the tree. She was every bit as bright, every bit as driven, as her grandfather."

"What language is it?" Calebaan asked. "I'm quite good at languages myself."

"This one is long dead," Innesdav replied. "And to make matters even more complicated, Skyreach evidently created a code all her own as well with it."

Calebaan nodded. "Then I shall wish your people well with it."

"There is something else," Innesdav went on. "Here in Candlekeep, we have the means to open a dimensional door to the woods near Mistledale where you can find the library." He focused his gaze on Baylee. "I have talked to Ulraunt about the possibility of sending you there. But it would be on the behest of Candlekeep, and anything you may find would become the property of Candlekeep."

Baylee thought about the offer. He'd known when sending the

books through to Innesdav that Ulraunt, the Keeper of the Tomes, would demand an entrance to the bounty that might be forthcoming. "Would I be given an opportunity to study whatever we find at a later time?"

Innesdav spread his hand. "Of course. Since I've known you, you've had an eternal invitation to this place. Should you succeed in finding this lost library, you could stay here the rest of your life studying if you chose."

Most people, Baylee knew, didn't get to stay at Candlekeep for more than ten days.

"It is a generous offer," Innesdav said.

And more than that, Xuxa said. *If you found this library and it is as big as you say it is, where else would be better to keep it than here?*

"Wait," Cordyan said, letting Baylee know the azmyth bat had projected her thoughts to everyone there, "what of Waterdeep? I represent some strong interests in these issues."

"The Lords of Waterdeep, you mean?" Innesdav asked. His quiet voice seemed barely louder than the bubbling of the streams.

"I mean Lord Piergeiron in particular," the civilar said. "He personally funded the ship and the men who have chased after Baylee Arnvold. If it had not been for us—"

"Young Baylee had already sent the book to us," the acolyte pointed out. "And I don't think you can truthfully say you saved his life in the Sea of Swords. It seems to me he'd already saved himself."

"The monk does have a point," Calebaan said.

"I can take this group of men with him," Cordyan said. "Lord Piergeiron granted me leave to do as I saw fit. If you send Baylee into that library area without adequate manpower, you may very well never see him again."

Innesdav regarded her with a twisted smile that Baylee remembered all too well. "Child, every time Baylee leaves these towers, I know that could be true. Yet, could I protect him from all the wonders he would seek out in Faerûn?"

"You're talking of sending him straight into the arms of this one," Cordyan said.

Baylee felt agitated as the two discussed him as if he wasn't there. "Wait a minute. This is my decision to make. If I want to go, I'll go, and it'll be on my own terms." He faced Innesdav. "Tell Ulraunt that his terms are acceptable."

Cordyan turned to face him. "You'd stupidly throw your life away? Just like that?"

Baylee didn't know what to say. He wanted to be angry at her, but at the same time he was afraid to be too angry because it would make things between them even more strained.

"If that's true, Baylee Arnvold, you are not half the man I thought you were." Cordyan turned from him.

Confusion ran rampant in the ranger. He wanted to fight, to change her opinion, but he wasn't really sure where to begin, or that it would even make a difference.

"Actually," Innesdav said, "we were hoping you might offer assistance, Junior Civilar Cordyan. In return, we would be willing to grant Lord Piergeiron certain liberties within the towers of Candlekeep as well."

Baylee wheeled on the old monk. "What does she know about archeological digs? If you send her on this trip, she and her men could well destroy much of what you seek to save."

"Dear boy," the old acolyte said, "that is the chance we must take. There are many risks here. Even more than you might imagine." He stood. "Come, let us take our eveningfeast inside and talk further."

* * * * *

Baylee picked at his food despite the fact that the monks of Candlekeep set a good table. And they had excellent silverware. He sat in his chair and barely managed to restrain himself from pacing. He thought better when he moved.

They sat in one of the many dining rooms in an outbuilding maintained around the towers where guests from outside Candlekeep were allowed. Monks waited on them, bringing great trays of food to feed the armed men and sailors. The men of the watch and the crew of *Tsunami Dancer* hadn't been allowed into the libraries, but the monks wouldn't turn them away from the tables.

Xuxa's shadows as she hung from the candelabra above the table fluttered in all directions. *She has men who can help,* the azmyth bat said, continuing the argument they'd been having for the past hour.

Amateurs.

Not when it comes to fighting. Lord Piergeiron wouldn't send green warriors after you knowing how fierce the opponents were that you faced.

Baylee gazed into the great fireplace on the wall behind him. He wished he didn't feel so confused about the issue of Cordyan's involvement. But during the voyage to Candlekeep from Mintarn, he'd enjoyed her company, enjoyed the sound of her laughter.

The silence in his head when Xuxa didn't jump in with a comment was deafening.

A monk came to Innesdav and whispered in his ear. The old man smiled and tapped his water glass with his spoon, drawing the attention of everyone at the table. "It has just been confirmed. Lord Piergeiron has agreed to our terms. In the morning, we will send all of you through to begin your journey."

The men of the watch cheered.

Baylee figured they were only excited by the prospect of the odd gold coin tumbling into their pockets when no one was looking. They wouldn't even understand the intrinsic historical significance of the coins. They would be spent for ale that wouldn't stay in their bladders till morning.

The thought was almost enough to turn Baylee's stomach.

* * * * *

"I know you don't fully appreciate everything that's going on here."

Baylee looked at Innesdav as the old monk guided him through the labyrinthine hallways of the Candlekeep outbuilding. "They're an army, not a trained, expedition-ready staff."

"And an expedition party isn't equipped mentally or physically to do battle the way these people are," Innesdav said. He held a lantern ahead of them, chipping away at the shadows that filled the hallway. "What you trade off of one, you more than gain on another." He found Baylee's room and shoved the door open.

The room was a small square, nearly filled by the bed and the reading table near the window overlooking one of the inner courtyards. Xuxa leaped from the staff that Innesdav carried the lantern on and flew ahead into the room.

"But you could send me first," Baylee protested. "After I've had a look, if necessary, the Waterdhavian Watch unit could be sent through."

"Had not Golsway himself been killed by whatever forces guard the library, I would have recommended just that," Innesdav said. "But the fact remains that I lost a dear and true friend. I do not want to lose two such friends."

"There is no arguing?" Baylee persisted. "I could be sent through tonight, perhaps even be back before morning."

Innesdav shook his head. Then he swept an arm toward the interior of the room. "I have laid aside some of your favorite books, and a selection of ones that I thought you might find interesting." The old monk indicated the pile of books on the reading table. He touched the lantern to the candles on the table, lighting them. Wards protected Candlekeep from ever burning down despite the torches, lanterns, and candles that seemed to burn in every room.

"Thank you," Baylee said.

"But those are intended only if you find you can't sleep," Innesdav warned. "Sleeping tonight is probably the best thing you can do."

Baylee ignored the advice. His senses thrummed inside him, threatening to explode out of his skin. He walked to the open window and peered out. The full moon hung high in the sable night.

Glancing down and to the right, he saw Cordyan Tsald walk past a window. He only caught a glimpse of a diaphanous nightgown over smooth, curved flesh. Then the shade was pulled, leaving only an interesting shadow limned against the material.

"If there is anything else you require?" Innesdav asked.

"No." Baylee turned around and faced his old friend. "No, thank you. You've been more than generous, as always."

Innesdav stood there in the doorway, the lantern hanging from the end of his staff. "I care about you, Baylee, and I don't want to see that love of adventure and exploration that Golsway instilled in you get you killed. You rush in where most others would hesitate. That courage has served you in the past, but don't be drawn to this prize only to find that the only thing you've discovered is your own doom."

"I've not found anything yet that I couldn't walk away from."

Innesdav was silent for a time. "Success, young warrior, that's one thing you've never walked away from. And it is hard for most men."

"Why would you want to?" Baylee asked.

"The answer to that," the monk said, "lies within yourself."

"Is that a quote?"

"No," Innesdav said in a quiet voice, "that is a fact of life. I bid you good night."

Baylee said good night as well, then went back to staring out the window, waiting for the morning.

Innesdav was right, Xuxa said. *You should sleep.*

I can't.

You're more disciplined than that, Baylee.

This is it, Xuxa. Can't you feel that?

Yes. But it makes me afraid at the same time. The azmyth bat dropped from her perch and flapped over to the ranger. She landed heavily on his shoulders, then stretched out a wing to touch his cheek lightly.

Everything is going to be all right, he told her. And he hoped it was true.

24

"Wait till after my signal, then begin riding through."

Baylee sat astride a horse lent to him from the stable of Candlekeep. The rest of the unit was similarly equipped. He wore a chain mail shirt in deference to the danger they could possibly face in a short time, hating it for its restriction on his movements and its likelihood of making more noise than he wanted to.

Civva Cthulad wore a full suit of elven chain mail that burned bright in the morning sun. He carried his helm under his arm for the moment.

Cordyan Tsald and her men of the watch wore chain mail armor as well, but their tabards carried the Waterdhavian crests. They looked like an army, forty men strong, counting the recruits they'd picked up from among the crew of *Tsunami Dancer*. Some of the sailors wanted to try their hands at finding the library as well.

The monks of Candlekeep lined up on either side of the adventuring party. The robes ranged from mauve to black, and the faces betrayed their own excitement.

Baylee shifted his attention back to the Candlekeep wizard at the head of the party. The man walked carefully among the inscribed designs on the flagstones along the outer edge of the cliff overhanging the harbor letting out to the Sea of Swords. He inspected each drawing, apparently satisfied with them all.

Innesdav stood beside Baylee, one hand on the ranger's knee. "If you have any concerns," the old monk said, "now would be the time to voice them. Brother Darhakk's dimensional door will not settle properly over land."

"As long as it'll get us where we're going," Baylee said, "what more could we ask for?"

Brother Darhakk finished the last of his inspection and turned to face the assembled riders. "If the necessary alignments for such a long portage were more favorable, I could place the dimensional door wherever I wanted. This morning, at this time, the door you see before you is the only one that is possible to get you where you are going. Even so, I will not be able to keep it open long."

Cordyan shifted in her saddle, turning back to face all of the assembled men. "If there are any of you who do not want to ride over this cliff into that dimensional door, bow out gracefully now. For if you don't, and your cowardice later causes the death of anyone else, rest assured that I will hold you accountable."

No one moved.

"You have my talisman?" Innesdav asked.

Baylee touched the obsidian triangle on the leather thong around his neck.

"Good," the monk said. "With the scrying crystal I have access to, I should be able to see you at least part of the way of your journey." He reached up and clasped hands with the ranger.

Baylee felt the back of his throat grow tight. But the excitement kept the fires blazing in his stomach, feeding off the nervous energy filling his mount. "Keep a stew pot on, old friend. I'll be back before you know it."

Brother Darhakk called for their attention. Innesdav stepped away. Darhakk began chanting in a loud voice.

Attuned to the magic assembling around them, Baylee felt the strength of the spell as it built. Then the sky over the edge of the cliff turned a virulent shade of green.

"Ride!" Darhakk yelled.

Baylee put his heels to his horse, urging it for the cliff side. Xuxa released her hold on a nearby branch and swooped past the ranger, winging toward the dimensional door. Baylee concentrated on her, wondering if she would pass through the door entirely and end up flying over the sea where he would fall, or if she would just end up being rendered discorporate by the magic.

Xuxa disappeared.

At the last moment, as the cliff ended before Baylee, the horse tried to fight him. He pulled hard on the reins, guiding it through the ten-foot square. He heard the final click of the horse's hooves leaving the stone. Then there was a moment of free fall, a vision of *Tsunami Dancer* berthed in the harbor below—and he fell.

In the next instant, Baylee grew aware of the thick forest spread all around him. He tugged on the horse's reins to maneuver it from a collision with a towering, old-growth tree. *Xuxa?*

I am here.

Baylee swung around to gaze in all directions. Sunlight shafted through the trees, a muted yellow that lit up emerald green leaves and grasses. He was back in the Dalelands; he could smell the difference. *Are we alone?*

Except for the local flora and fauna, the azmyth bat replied, *yes.*

The ranger swung the horse around, his hand still resting on the hilt of the long sword at his side. Hoof beats sounded behind him. He turned and watched Cthulad come through the dimensional gate, followed swiftly by Cordyan, Calebaan, and the other riders.

In minutes, all of them were gathered in the forest. Cordyan took charge at once, ordering the men into position.

Baylee reached under his tunic and took out the map Innesdav had given him. He looked around the forest, reading the game signs he saw. Nothing human or shod had been through the area. He started north, knowing if the dimensional door hadn't worked right and they'd ended up in an altogether different part of the forest, they'd be days in sorting out the map.

"Baylee." Innesdav's voice came as a strained whisper to the ranger's ear.

"I am here, old friend."

"And of a piece?"

Baylee grinned recklessly. "And of a piece," he said.

* * * * *

Baylee quickly found that all of the trails marked on the map were different now than they had been six hundred years ago. However, the topography was the same.

After a few hours' travel, they found a stream that flowed in the direction they wanted to go. Riding alongside it, the way got easier. They had their noonday meal while walking the horses, giving them a break from carrying all the weight.

The ranger made an effort at staying away from Cordyan, but in doing so, he took more notice of her than he wanted. Xuxa flitted through the trees, staying close to Baylee.

She is a beautiful woman, the azmyth bat stated.

She doesn't listen.

She's merely independent minded. And she's brave.

Getting yourself in over your head doesn't necessarily constitute bravery.

She's smart enough to know the difference, Xuxa replied.

Baylee continued the argument, but after awhile, he found he was arguing with himself as well as with the azmyth bat.

* * * * *

"How much longer do you think it will take us to reach the city?"

Baylee glanced over his shoulder as Cordyan rode up beside him. "Another hour or so. Perhaps a little longer."

The forest continued on unabated though the stream had played out four miles or so back. The horses' hooves thudded almost soundlessly against the loose loam. Birds flew from tree to tree, letting Baylee know no predators had been through the area lately.

The thing that concerned him, though, was the accumulation of rain clouds building up from the north. Dark and ugly, they skated across the gray sky, showing signs of intermittent lightning in their depths.

"What is it you don't like about me?" she asked.

The question was so unexpected, that Baylee didn't have an answer at first. "I never said I didn't like you," he said finally.

"You've given me the distinct impression you don't approve of my being here."

Baylee regarded her. "Your being here has nothing to do with how I feel about you."

"You couldn't do this by yourself," she said.

"I guess," Baylee said harshly, "we'll never know, will we?" He kicked his horse, putting distance between himself and the civilar.

She was only trying to talk, Xuxa protested.

I'm not stopping her, Baylee said. *There are plenty of others for her to talk to.*

* * * * *

They came upon the remnants of the city unexpectedly. Baylee rode point and halted the line as soon as he came to the crest of the hill overlooking the area where the city had been. According to the map Innesdav had reconstituted from Skyreach's logbook, the city had once been called Rainydale, known as Selarrynm in the elven tongue, and had been one of the larger trading posts outside of Myth Drannor proper.

The Army of Darkness that had crushed Myth Drannor had rolled over Rainydale. Little of the city remained except for a few foundations that poked up through the tangle of underbrush and trees.

Baylee leaned across the saddle pommel to stretch his cramped back muscles. He wasn't accustomed to long hours of riding.

"Rainydale?" Civva Cthulad reined in his horse next to Baylee.

The ranger nodded. The old excitement at discovering the unseen and unfound filled him, vibrating inside him like a tuning fork. "From here, we need to find the temple of Corellon Larethian, and the well that is attached to it. There should be a passage at the bottom of it."

"The temple shouldn't be hard to find," the old ranger said. "Corellon is chief god among the elves. His temple will have been one of the larger structures."

Baylee nodded in agreement. "Ask Junior Civilar Tsald to spread her men out while keeping the perimeter security intact."

Cthulad nodded, without stating the obvious and telling Baylee he could have done that himself.

Baylee guided his mount down into the ruins of the city. He visualized the streets in his mind, building them from the map Innesdav had provided. Less than an hour after he began, he located the well.

Precious little remained of the temple of the elven god. And an immense stone slab covered the well itself. He used rope from the gear they'd brought to rig a crude block and tackle through the nearby trees. Even then, it took a team of horses to lift the slab away.

The well possessed a mouth six feet across. The lip above the ground showed only broken and smashed rock. Brackish water filled the bottom of the well, and the stench gave evidence that it had been salted when the city had been razed.

Calebaan joined Cordyan, Cthulad, and Baylee at the well. "Now it begins in earnest," the watch wizard said, peering into the well's depths.

And Baylee couldn't wait. He pointed up. "Rig another rope from that tree," he said. "I'll need it for support to make the descent. Those who follow me will need it as well."

Cordyan ordered the men into motion.

Retreating from the group, Baylee found a wall of brush to keep his modesty intact. He stripped off the chain mail armor and clothing.

"What are you doing?" Cordyan asked.

"Getting ready to make the descent."

"Unarmored?" The watch civilar stood on the other side of the brush, watching doubtfully.

"Chain mail is great if you're going into battle," Baylee said. "But not for getting around ruins." He opened his bag of holding and pulled out the leather armor inside. It was a full set of gnomish workman's leather armor, complete with a hood that fit snugly over his head. But this set of gnomish workman's leather armor had been built to fit Baylee precisely, allowing him access to the dozens of pockets and secret areas inside the armor. When he'd traveled with Golsway and found out about the armor that came complete with multitudinous pockets, he'd wanted a set. It had taken nearly a year for him to build a friendship with a party of gnomes who followed the explorer's way themselves. In the end, they'd made him the suit in return for help he'd given them.

He ran his hands over the pockets, knowing the positions of all the lock picks, hammers, chisels, brushes, and other implements he'd found of service while crawling through excavation sites. As he'd donned the armor, his trepidation about descending into the well had waned. He pulled his boots on again, then pulled the leggings of the armor tight. Each device in his pockets was placed carefully enough that it didn't clink or make a sound when he moved.

Finished, he started for the well.

"Baylee, I hope your pride and your overconfidence don't get you killed down there," Cordyan said.

"It's not going to," the ranger said. "I'm better than that. This—this is what I live for, Cordyan. And what Golsway lived for, too." But he couldn't deny the seed of fear twisting in his stomach. He started to walk away, feeling Xuxa's eyes on him as she hung from a tree branch.

Then he turned on his heel and approached Cordyan directly, feeling more afraid of what he was about to do than any thought of descending into the well gave him. Before she could pull away, he put his hand to the back of her head and pulled her to him, kissing her fiercely. He was surprised at how she kissed back. Behind him, men shouted out ribald encouragement.

Then he stepped away and she slapped him. Not as hard, Baylee knew, as she was capable of. But the ribald encouragement became faked groans of sympathy and laughter.

"What was that for?" he asked.

"For making me worry about you," she replied. "And for even daring to *think* you could do that, much less act on it."

"But you kissed me back."

"I did no such thing. And if you don't mind to keep a civil tongue in your head when you address a civilar of the Waterdhavian Watch, I'll have the tongue from your head."

Even more confused, Baylee approached the well. *I thought you said she liked me,* he accused Xuxa.

Liking you and putting up with improprieties are a totally different matter, the azmyth bat said. *You should have asked.*

She would probably have said no. And it was just kind of a good luck token.

I get the strong feeling that Cordyan Tsald would never allow herself to be anyone's 'token.' And if that kiss was for you alone because you're scared, then that was very selfish of you.

Guilt stung Baylee. He hadn't wanted to descend into the waiting darkness without reaching out to someone. It was a weakness he hadn't expected at the moment and didn't like to admit. He hesitated on the lip of the well to secure the lantern of continual light to his belt, then turned to look at Cordyan. "I'm sorry," he said. He dropped over the side of the well, the rope sliding through his gloved hands as he dropped rapidly.

Xuxa dropped with him, flitting to a rest on his shoulder.

The lantern spewed out yellow light, striking harsh reflections from the murky water below. Baylee wondered how deep it might be, working his jaw to finish easing out the sting of Cordyan's slap.

A jutting section of stone caught his attention almost at the water's level. He squeezed his hands together and halted his downward flight. Removing a twist of horsehair from his leather armor, he secured it to the rope, making a stirrup for himself further down. He stood in the stirrup and leaned toward the wall, adjusting the light to play over the jutting stone.

Sections of letters showed through the stone. They held curlicues of elven script, a recent language Baylee knew. Evidently whoever had hidden the secret door hadn't used the dead language Skyreach had used in her logbook.

Maybe Glitterwing wanted the library found, Xuxa proposed. *In case they couldn't get it out in time.*

Baylee knew it was possible. Glitterwing wouldn't have wanted the library kept away from his heirs. He took a brush from the armor and carefully cleaned out the letters. Luckily, the water table hadn't been high lately, so he dealt with dirt rather than mud. The letters cleaned easily, and with every one that became visible, his confusion went away and the excitement took over.

"What's going on down there?" Cthulad called.

"I've found what has to be the hidden door," Baylee said. "But there's writing on it." Finished cleaning the letters, he raised the lantern and translated aloud. " 'For he who would seek the knowledge contained beyond this portal, let him first acknowledge his right to such passage with the trinity of truth.' "

"Is there anything else?"

Baylee examined the wall beside the stone. "A series of gems inset in the stone. They have pictographs above them. Religious symbols. I recognize them all." His finger traced the crescent moon. "Corellon Larethian." Next came a bird silhouetted on a cloud. "Aerdrie Faenya." Followed by a star with asymmetric rays. "Erevan Ilesere." And a heart. "Hanali Celanil." And a setting sun. "Labelas Enoreth." A great oak. "Rillifane Rallathil." And, finally, a silver arrow. "And Solonor Thelandira."

"All gods of the elves," Calebaan said.

"Yes." Baylee studied them, remembering their mythologies easily.

"And you are supposed to pick three of the seven present, I assume?"

"That's my best guess," Baylee answered. He shifted, taking a length of rope from one of the gnomish workman's leathers and tying a harness around himself. When he had it finished, he turned to place his feet against the side of the well.

He brushed along the lines of mortar, finding small holes in the material along the big stone. He figured he was right about it being a door. It looked like it slid back once the locking maneuvers were completed. But the space also left room for some rather nasty surprises.

"Which three?" Cthulad asked.

Baylee shifted, reaching out to touch the gem with the crescent moon. "Corellon Larethian, of course, because all the elves set him above the others."

"Wait!" Cordyan said. "What if you have to pick them in a certain order?"

Baylee hesitated, his finger above the inset gem. "I've already figured on that. That's why Larethian has to be the first." He slid his finger across the gem's surface, tensing as he heard grinding on the other side of the wall. A moment later, it stopped. "So far, so good." He surveyed the other choices.

Labelas Enoreth has to be the second choice. Xuxa hung on the well wall nearby, her wings wrapped around herself. *He was considered to be the teacher of the elves. The philosopher, as well as the ideal of elven thought and superiority over other races.*

Agreed. Baylee let out a tight breath and touched the gem beneath the pictograph of the setting sun.

The grinding repeated itself, lasting longer this time. Then it faded away, echoing to the top of the well.

"The second was Enoreth?" Calebaan asked.

"Yes." Baylee wished the wizard would be silent and let him think.

"Hanali Celanil would probably be the third," the watch wizard yelled down. "She was the goddess of elven beauty. Remembering the vases and other things you say Glitterwing collected, it would be a logical choice."

"You can't be logical in this business," Baylee called back, remembering words Golsway had spoken, "not and survive. You're generally dealing with madmen and zealous protectors who wanted to die and take their treasures with them."

What would make Celanil important to Glitterwing? Xuxa asked.

Nothing, Baylee answered. Glitterwing wouldn't have been interested in beauty. Everything the ranger had read of the man suggested an iron-edged pragmatism.

What about the one that doesn't fit? Xuxa asked. *Erevan Ilesere is the elven god of change and of rogues. Maybe Glitterwing intended it as a protest against what was being done by letting the humans and dwarves into Myth Drannor.*

In a way, it made sense. *Rillifane Rallathil is god of the wild elves. Glitterwing was a wild elf.*

An acceptable answer, Xuxa said. *However, there remains only one way to find out.*

Wishing the Lady's blessing on his efforts, Baylee touched the gem beneath the oak tree pictograph.

Steel shafts plunged out of the mortar at Baylee. He let go the harness and plummeted down into the well a couple feet before stopping himself. The trident-trap set into the wall missed ripping into his flesh by less than a finger's breadth.

He stopped his fall by squeezing on the harness ropes and held his position as the trident retracted into the wall.

"Baylee!" Cordyan yelled from above.

"I'm fine," he called back. With shaking arms and legs, he

climbed back up to the pictographs. When the trap had retracted, it had also reset the gems. *Well, we know the first two are right.*

That only leaves four more possibilities, Xuxa replied. *Do you think you can dodge them all?*

A memory flooded into Baylee's mind as he touched the first two gems. *Remember when we were attacked by the skeleton warriors? One of them got down on his knees and prayed.* He gazed at the fletched arrow pictograph. *And it was to Solonor Thelandira, not Rillifane.*

You're assuming those skeleton warriors once knew Glitterwing, and that they shared religious beliefs.

They were also elves, someone who Glitterwing could have forced into servitude as skeleton warriors. If he was desperate, maybe he would have used his own people.

A slim case, at best.

I can't build one for any of the others, Baylee responded. His finger caressed the gem. When the grinding started again, he was already dropping, hoping to avoid the trident trap yet again.

But this time, the door in the side of the well opened into a yawning blackness.

25

"It's open," Baylee called out. He scrambled up the rope in the well, drawn by the mysteries waiting within the door. Hanging even with it, and no trident in sight, he held up the lantern.

A straight shaft, carefully mortised in to make smooth surfaces along the sides, led back. It was a crawl space only, not large enough for him even to squat and walk through.

Xuxa fluttered in front of him, a smaller target and fully able to see in the dark with her infravision.

Baylee pulled himself through after her. Behind him, Cordyan was ordering men down into the well. The ranger crawled perhaps thirty feet before the tunnel suddenly ended and opened up onto a large cavern. He walked forward, looking at the crush of houses and buildings that had been flattened beneath the surface of the ruins. The ground had grown soft over the years, drawing the remains of the structures deep into the tunnels below.

The tunnels looked dwarven in nature, and Baylee thought the elves might have built Rainydale over an old dwarven mining city to use the underground storage areas for their fruits and vegetables. And, as a military man, Glitterwing would have wanted it as a more defensible position.

He consulted the map as Xuxa clung to the wall nearby. The cavern was shown on the map, but it held a different shape than it did now. He had the lay of the land figured out by the time Cordyan had all of her men organized.

When looked at properly, the trail could be seen snaking through the fissures to the right. With the long sword naked in his fist, Baylee trotted forward.

The intense earthquake caught him off-balance. Out in the open area of the cavern, rocks crumbled and fell, and stalactites dropped from the curve of earth overhead.

"What was that?" Cthulad demanded.

Baylee got to his feet, watching the choking dust rise from the tunnel floor. The dust shortened his visibility. "I don't know. But it couldn't have been good." He continued along the trail, knowing the library lay somewhere up ahead.

* * * * *

Krystarn Fellhammer shoved herself back to her feet, yelling at the drow warriors around her to get back into position. Mild tremors followed the large quake.

She gazed around the caverns, wondering what had set the earthquake in motion. There were still a few echoing quivers every so often, reminders that the land had been cruelly torn in the battle with the Army of Darkness.

"He seeks now to destroy us all," a voice whispered behind the drow.

Krystarn turned, spotting Nevft Scoontiphp behind her.

The baelnorn didn't look at her, staring instead at the new fissures that had opened up in the walls of the cavern.

"You're saying Shallowsoul did that?" Krystarn asked in disbelief.

"He failed to stop them," the baelnorn said. "He never intended for the map Skyreach had among her things to reach humankind. He was supposed to hold the library here until a suitable heir could be found."

"An heir?"

The baelnorn nodded. "In his mortal life, he was the caretaker of the library, hand-picked by Glitterwing himself, and transformed into the lich by Glitterwing as well. Haven't you learned anything in these years you've been among us?"

"There is no heir." Krystarn ignored the creature and started her men moving down the trail again. "And the way through the well will be blocked once we kill all the humans who have invaded these caverns. I can't believe Shallowsoul hadn't already blocked the way."

"He was charged not to. And after awhile, I'm sure he forgot it was even there. His mind is not what it once was."

Krystarn fell into the group of drow warriors, her morning star naked in her fist. Shallowsoul had alerted her only moments ago of the breach made by the group of humans. She'd even watched Baylee Arnvold lead the way through the hidden door.

"The humans have near to fifty warriors," Scoontiphp stated.

"We are drow," Krystarn said. "For us, it is but more who will die by our hand."

The baelnorn smiled. "Thinking of that as your epitaph?"

Before Krystarn could reply, Scoontiphp disappeared, leaving only his mocking laughter twisting in the echoing emptiness behind the line of advancing drow warriors.

She pushed the baelnorn's words out of her mind. She had her own agenda to pursue, and the hobgoblin army under Chomack was awaiting her word, still totally unknown to Shallowsoul. It was a comforting thought, one totally drow in nature.

* * * * *

Baylee felt the pull of a trip cord before he saw it. "Get down!" he roared over the creak of a spring loosing. A huge stone block pulled free of the nearby wall and slammed against the wall on the other side of the trail. It burst into a shower of rock, leaving only the thick pole that it had been tied to.

Pushing himself to his feet, the ranger regained his lantern from the ground and took stock of the situation behind him. Cordyan was next in line, shaken but still grimly in control of the watch unit.

The trail continued to wind down deeper into the earth. At times it picked up even older tunnels than the ones they had traveled through from the well, telling Baylee that Glitterwing's library had been laid where much of the work had already been done.

From the tailings he'd found in several of the areas, he now knew the system of underground caverns had been a mining operation for metals. In a few places, he'd even found iron railings where mine carts had been. A few of the mine carts were even in the corners of some caverns.

Another quake hit the caverns, this one stronger even than the last.

"This is not a natural occurrence," Civva Cthulad said. "Someone is causing this."

"Or some*thing*," one of the Waterdhavian Watch members muttered further back in the line.

"How much farther?" Cordyan asked Baylee.

The ranger shrugged as he turned a corner ahead. "We're more than halfway according to the map, that's all I can say. Distances are not recorded." Sweat poured down him. The gnomish workman's leather armor was hot in the underground environment. He tightened the cinches on his gloves.

As he rounded the next corner on the narrow trail, a feeling of vertigo assailed him. Ahead, the land suddenly sheared away, racing down to a black emptiness so far below Baylee really doubted there might be a bottom at all. The trail continued against one wall, barely three feet wide.

"Tighten up your men," the ranger said to Cordyan, "and get me some rope."

"What are you going to do?" the watch officer asked. She reached into the backpack of the nearest man and took out a coil of rope.

"I'm going to run a line to the other side," Baylee answered, taking the rope she offered. "If another quake hits while we're scattered across the middle of that, I don't want to risk losing any of the men."

"You didn't even want them along," Cordyan said.

"Yes, and this is one of the reasons why," Baylee said. "I could have come alone or with Cthulad and mapped these areas, then set up a proper expedition. I didn't get to do that, but I'm not going to allow those men's lives to be thrown away."

"You make this sound like I had a choice in the matter," Cordyan said. "Don't you think anyone else can feel as deeply driven to do their duty as you obviously feel you are to do yours?"

"That's not the point at all."

"That's *exactly* the point as I see it."

Baylee blew out his breath and finished tying the extra rope around his waist. "This is hardly the place for such a discussion."

Xuxa telepathically agreed, then chirped in angry frustration. *Now is not the time to get caught up in other thinking,* the azmyth bat counseled.

Tell her that, Baylee said.

I believe I just told you both.

The ranger ignored the retort and started out on the narrow trail. He kept his long sword unsheathed in his hand. He guessed the distance to be something over forty feet.

At the other end, he selected a stone that appeared strong enough to take the weight if any of the Watch members fell over the side. He cupped his hands and shouted back at Cordyan. "Have the men tie on, then start them across. Ten feet apart."

The watch lieutenant was staring at her sword. In the dimness, even across the distance, Baylee saw a circular glow in the sword hilt.

The ranger sensed rather than heard the movement behind him. But he was too late to do more than avoid the bulk of the blow. He saw the grinning drow face, followed by two others as they filled the open mouth of the next cavern. Knocked off-balance, Baylee fell over the side into the chasm. In the long shadows below, it looked like nothing was beneath him.

* * * * *

"Baylee!" Cordyan screamed the young ranger's name as she watched him plummet. The Shandaularan coin glowed brightly in her sword's hilt. At the same moment that she spotted the drow warriors on the opposite side of the open chasm, she heard men behind her yelling.

"Hook horrors! Hook horrors!"

Cordyan glanced back, watching the shambling figures closing rapidly from behind. The creatures stood nine feet tall. A thick, mottled gray exoskeleton covered them, tough enough to turn most sword blows and glancing arrow shots. Their front limbs ended in foot-long hooks capable of slicing through leather armor easily. Their back legs held huge feet with three splayed and clawed toes. A vulture's wedged-shaped head sat atop the shoulders, possessing a hideously curved beak and multifaceted eyes.

Cordyan tapped two men closest to her. "Hold the trail."

They nodded and settled into place with their swords.

"Calebaan, can you do something about those beasts?" Cordyan asked. She peered through the gloom and watched the wizard as he stepped forward to confront the first of the insect-like creatures. The chittering and clacking of the hook horrors punctuated the anxious conversation between the men. Cthulad took up a stance slightly in front of the wizard and bared his sword.

A moment later, a shimmer left Calebaan's fingertips. Then a solid wall of stone formed, cutting off the trail from that direction, running straight into the walls surrounding the cavern. In the next heartbeat, the first heavy blows of the hook horrors started pounding against the wall.

Cordyan turned back to look for Baylee, but did not see him in the darkness. A crossbow quarrel slammed into the rock near her. She fell into hiding beside the rock.

"The wall's not going to hold," Calebaan called up. "The hook horrors are starting to break through!"

* * * * *

Krystarn Fellhammer pulled her *piwafwi* about her and tugged up the hood. With the cloak's magic, she disappeared from the rear guard of the drow warriors.

Shallowsoul had sent her to intercept the humans and kill them, but she doubted he would be watching her. Without warning, the caverns quaked again. Huge chunks of the ceiling fell, bouncing all around her. She had to dive forward to avoid being flattened by a boulder the size of a firbolg.

No doubts remained in her mind that Shallowsoul was at the root of the earth shudders. She couldn't imagine what the lich was doing, but she thought she had a way to find out.

Standing beside a wall after the earthquake subsided, she took the crystal ball from her cloak. Activating it, she peered into the library.

The lich stood in front of a maze of whirling gems that floated in the air before him. She listened to him chant, not recognizing any of the words. The gems—sapphires, rubies, emeralds, and diamonds—all swirled faster, gaining speed. Then they smacked together. Instantly the earth shook around Krystarn.

And for a moment, the library shivered and disappeared.

Fear seized Krystarn's greed in its cold, greasy grip, shrinking it as the certainty filled her. Shallowsoul had discovered a way to take the library from the prime material plane where Faerûn was located to another plane of existence. Either that, or he'd had a way all along, but didn't want to use it till after he recovered the shipwreck—or until humans had found the location of the library.

She waved a hand over the crystal ball, changing the focus and filling her head with thoughts of Chomack.

A moment later, the image cleared, showing the hobgoblin chieftain and his tribe. They numbered almost a hundred now. Chomack had continued to win converts or beat joiners into submission. He'd also managed to kill three human and elf adventuring parties and seize some of the weapons they had, further adding to his power.

At the moment, Chomack and his tribe hid in a cavern not far from the hallway where Krystarn kept her quarters. "Chomack, Taker of Dragon's Teeth," she said softly.

The hobgoblin chieftain looked up, not quite finding her gaze with his own. "What?"

"And are you ready?"

"By Maglubiyet's good graces, yes."

"I will join you in minutes. There will not be much time after that." Krystarn ran through the twisting tunnels before her. Lloth willing, Shallowsoul would be too involved with his own machinations to discover hers.

She thought nothing at all of leaving her drow warriors there to die if need be.

* * * * *

Baylee watched the light eclipse as the chasm closed overhead.

He released his lantern, not fearing losing it because it was secured to his arm by a strap. Working from memory, he pulled a thin rope from the gnomish workman's leather armor. He shook it out, watching it move on its own.

Baylee! Xuxa called, winging after him.

The ranger ignored the azmyth bat as he flicked the rope at the chasm. He said the command word that activated the magic in the rope, watching as it jerked and suddenly fastened itself to a projection on the wall.

He hung on as he reached the end of the rope. The braid slipped through his hand at first, then he clamped on tighter after the immediate descent had been slowed. Coming to a full stop, it still felt like his arm was being yanked from its sockets. He held on to the long sword with the other, barely able to keep it in his fingertips.

He slammed against the chasm wall opposite the side with the trail on it. His breath whooshed out of his lungs, and he lost another few inches on the rope. When he had his breath back, he sheathed the long sword and climbed the rope to the chasm top.

The drow didn't notice him from their position, concentrating their crossbow fire on the humans they had pinned down.

Baylee slipped his quiver over his shoulder and opened it. He assembled the long bow and strung it quickly, gathering up a fistful of arrows. He pulled the first one back smoothly, letting the fletching touch his ear as he lined up his shot. Then he released.

The heavy flight arrow smashed into the drow's chest, penetrating the chain mail shirt the warrior wore. He crumpled without a sound. By that time, Baylee had two other arrows in the air.

One of them took the drow behind the first through the neck. The second missed its target as the drow warrior ducked back to safety.

Baylee reached into his quiver and chose one of the incendiary arrows, knowing it from the way the fletching was put together. He broke the glass-vialed tip, then ignited the end with a flint and steel striker. The flames caught at once, twisting into a ball of flames at the end of the arrow.

Putting all thoughts of conventional and civilized warfare from his mind, the ranger loosed the arrow into the body of the first drow he'd killed. It was the only source of flammable materials he had at his disposal.

The arrow sailed across the intervening space like a comet, then thudded into the corpse with a meaty smack. The flames spread out in fiery bits, catching the dead man's clothes on fire at once.

The other drow drew back, handicapped by the bright light that dimmed their sensitive vision.

Baylee stood and threw the coils of rope across the chasm, commanding it to take hold again. He tied the lantern to his chest on one of the many straps the armor had. Once the enchanted rope had secured itself to the other side, he tied the other end to a stalagmite. Slipping his bow across the rope, he held on to both sides, then slid across the rope, landing on the trail in a crouch. He dropped the bow at his feet, drawing the long sword. A blur of movement warned him of the quarrel's flight as it sped toward him. He spun, bringing the sword up and hoping. He didn't catch the quarrel squarely, but the swing did move him from in front of it.

Xuxa swooped in without mercy, raking her claws and tail across the drow's face.

Baylee surged ahead, drawing the parrying dagger and opening the spring-trigger. The two side blades sprang out at once. He engaged the drow who had fired the crossbow bolt, catching the man in the midst of reloading. He struck the hand crossbow aside with the parrying dagger, then buried his sword in the man's chest.

Another drow swung at him with a short sword.

Baylee blocked the cut with the parrying dagger, put a foot on the dead drow he'd run through, and yanked his sword free. Xuxa swooped across the drow, raking away his eyes.

The dark elf fell back, screaming in pain.

"Down, lad," Civva Cthulad called from behind Baylee.

The ranger ducked at once, watching as the justifier thrust his military pick deep into the drow's chest. The drow struggled to get free, but Cthulad leaned into the weapon, giving his weight to it. The length gave him comfortable room to work with even from behind Baylee.

"Now," Cthulad said, withdrawing his weapon. The dead warrior dropped.

Baylee stood, aware that Cthulad was going to await any openings that might present themselves. Baylee cut and thrust, beating the swords of the next opponent down. The flames of the dead man's burning clothes continued to burn bright enough to cause the drow warriors problems.

"We can't stay out here in the open long, lad," Cthulad said, thrusting again. "We'll have to break the drow before the hook horrors get through Calebaan. Otherwise, a lot of those men behind us will die."

Baylee dodged another sword thrust, sliding quickly to the side. In a roll of motion, he thrust the parrying dagger on the ground, then reached for the extended arm of the drow, grabbed the man's elbow, and threw him over the edge of the chasm. The drow screamed the whole way down, then quieted abruptly. Long before then, Baylee had the parrying dagger in his hand again.

Cthulad lashed out with the pick again, driving another drow back. Baylee surged into the gap left by the retreating drow and the one he'd dragged over the side of the chasm. He used the long sword to hammer through the circle of steel the drow warriors tried to put up to block him. He swiped the parrying dagger across a man's arm, rendering it useless in a spray of crimson. The blood splashed across Baylee's face but stayed out of his eyes.

A drow behind the wounded man thrust out with a spear, driving it toward the ranger's face.

"Watch it, lad," Cthulad warned.

Moving with fluid grace, Baylee caught the spear thrust in the grip of the parrying dagger and turned it toward the left to the stone wall of the tunnel. The steel head grazed sparks from the rock, then came to an abrupt halt. Before the drow could draw his spear back, Baylee chopped it in half with the long sword. He brought the backstroke around as the man tumbled off-balance, opening up his midsection.

The drow went down trying to hold himself together. Baylee kept himself distant from the horror of the dying man. The watch party couldn't be allowed to be caught out on the ledge. He stepped over the drow warrior and felt the man grab for him. Bloody hands slid slickly over the ranger's leg, unable to get a grip.

Cthulad ended the drow's struggle with the pick.

Shadows wrapped around the tunnel in front of Baylee. He was uncertain of the placement of his opponents. He depended on his other senses, trained in the woodlands and honed by Golsway's attention, to make up the difference.

He felt Xuxa's leathery wing brush across his cheek, then he caught a glimpse of her as she hooked her claws into the drow's face just ahead of him. The man screamed in pain as the bat bit deeply, then reached for her.

Baylee thrust his sword, burying it almost to the hilt in the man's throat. The lantern swept across the scene, providing only brief glimpses of the drow warrior. Xuxa leaped into the air again.

Use the body as a shield, Xuxa advised.

Despite the fact that the dead man had bled profusely, Baylee stepped in close and sheathed the parrying dagger. He knotted a fist in the man's tunic, supporting the dead weight by bringing it close to him. He freed his long sword, then shoved himself forward. One of the drow behind the dead man tried to shove a sword blade through the corpse, but the blade halted only inches through the dead man's stomach, barely putting any pressure on Baylee's armor.

A moment later, Baylee listened to the whip of leathery wings, then heard a man scream in agony. "My eyes, *my eyes!*"

The tunnel dipped down suddenly, throwing Baylee off-balance. He released the corpse as the tunnel opened up into another chamber. Shadows moved before him, but he had trouble discerning targets. Light from his lantern glinted across a sword blade swinging at his head. He blocked it, then instinctively followed the line of the slash and found the flesh and blood body in the shadows at the end of it. Before his opponent could draw back, the ranger thrust again. The man was dead before he hit the ground.

Light filled the chamber without warning. Baylee was careful to keep it at his back, letting it play over the handful of drow warriors in front of him. "You have a chance at living," he told them. "Take it and run. We're coming through."

The drow seemed uncertain, looking among their ranks for someone who could provide an answer. Then two of them went down with throwing darts embedded in their foreheads. The remaining ones broke and ran.

From the exhibition he'd heard about at the forgathering, Baylee knew who'd thrown the darts. He turned toward Cordyan. "They didn't have to die."

"I disagree," she said coolly as she stepped forward with her lantern. She put her foot on the faces of the dead men and tugged her darts free. "These are drow. If I could have, I'd have killed them all. Now we have to worry about the survivors getting confident enough to try sneaking up on us in the dark and killing whomever they can." She wiped the darts and put them away in her clothing again.

Calebaan brought Baylee his bow. "She is right," the wizard said. "You can't trust even a drow's cowardice. There may be something he lies about that he is even more afraid of."

Listen to the truth, Baylee, Xuxa said.

The ranger settled the strung bow over his shoulder, tying it to the gnomish work leather. He took up his lantern in his empty hand, keeping the long sword naked in his fist. He kept his thoughts to himself about the matter, but he felt there was usually some other alternative to outright killing if an opponent wasn't directly menacing.

"What about the drow woman?" Baylee played his lantern over the dead scattered in the tunnel.

"We haven't seen her," Cordyan answered.

"She's part of this."

"Well, she's not here now."

"Her path may yet lie ahead of us," Cthulad said.

The ground shook again, more forcibly this time, knocking them all from their feet. The duration of the tremors lasted longer this time as well. Rocks and debris rained down from overhead, banging painfully into Baylee.

"The hook horrors have broken through the wall!" someone shouted from behind.

"Lead or get out of my way," Cordyan yelled. Lantern light played across her blood-stained face.

"A moment," Baylee responded. He played the lantern over the dead drow again. "They're not carrying packs, nor any extra rations."

"They're from somewhere near," Cthulad agreed. "The question is, though, are these all of them?"

Baylee shook his head. "The female wasn't with them. There's something else afoot in these twisted tunnels." He went forward, charging into the darkness. Behind him, he could hear the chittering and clacking of the hook horrors.

* * * * *

Krystarn felt a stab of fear as she rounded the final corner and came face to face with the hobgoblin horde. Despite the fear she had put into Chomack, she knew there was the possibility that the hobgoblin chieftain could have figured to put her powers to the test. In a way, it was humorous, her gifting Chomack with the same skill at duplicity as she was currently employing against Shallowsoul.

The hobgoblins showed her only fear and deference. They were a ragged, motley bunch, covered with dust from the swirling debris that ran through the caverns. Chomack strode out of the waiting shadows.

"Sorceress," the hobgoblin chieftain acknowledged.

Krystarn nodded at him. "Are your warriors ready, Chieftain Chomack?"

"Aye."

The drow elf took the lead, guiding the large party through the labyrinthine mazes of tunnels that led up to the partially collapsed structure where she kept her rooms. In minutes, they were at the wall where Shallowsoul had always opened the dimensional door.

No lights burned in the hallway. If it hadn't been for Krystarn's own infravision and that of the hobgoblins, she knew she wouldn't have been able to see a thing. Broken rock from the ceiling over-head covered the floor. She made her way through it carefully.

Halting at the dead end, she brought out the crystal ball. She chanted, summoning up her spell energy, and praying to Lloth as she focused the forces she used through the crystal ball. The crystal ball was already in tune with the magic the lich was using. She knew how to cast a dimension door, but casting one into the library was much harder. For one, she didn't know exactly where it was in the physical world even though she'd been through it a number of times. And for another, she felt the actual distance it was from the dead-end wall was much further than she could transfer herself using her own spell.

The hobgoblins fell into line behind her at Chomack's order. Their bared weapons clinked against their armor.

Perspiration covered Krystarn's face as she locked into the exchange of energies. A headache throbbed at her temples. She pushed herself past the pain, thinking of the library only, of all the power that would be within her grasp in the next few minutes.

Through her slitted eyelashes, she saw the wall start to glow. At first it was a patch no bigger than the end of her finger, but quickly spread until she couldn't cover it with both hands. And it kept growing as the dimensional door swung open wider.

26

The trail came to an end in a crypt.

Be careful, Xuxa warned as she fluttered to a wall and perched upside down from the rough, craggy surface.

Baylee played his lantern over the crypt, lighting tumbled stone caskets thrown across the interior of the smashed building. The roof was long gone, but the cavern above had sunk to within a few feet, giving it the appearance that a roof still existed. Pieces of half a dozen skeletons lay strewn across the floor, but none of them tried to reassemble themselves or grab for weapons, as Baylee more than half expected.

"Which way?" Civva Cthulad asked from behind him.

"The map shows that the trail runs west," Baylee responded. "But this crypt wasn't shown."

"It sank from above," Cordyan said.

"Yes," Baylee replied. The lantern light broke against the cracked back wall. Going through it would still have constituted something of an engineering miracle.

"The drow must not have come this way," Cthulad said.

Baylee aimed the lantern at the plain of smooth dust and dirt in front of the crypt. "If they did, any footprints they might have left have been erased or covered over."

"Perhaps there's a way around," Calebaan said.

Baylee pulled back out of the crypt and went around to the left of the building. A narrow space between the building and the one next to it loomed in a slice of darkness. He shoved the lantern forward, playing it over the jumble of rock waiting ahead of him. The incline went down, deeper into the series of underground caverns. Beneath the rubble, he spotted the set of stone-carved steps that had been depicted on the map. They sat in the narrow mouth of a tunnel that continued west.

"Here," he said.

"Get a man on that crypt door," Cordyan ordered one of her guardsmen. "If anything moves behind us, I want to know about it."

The hook horrors had given up the chase a few minutes before, after one of them had been doused in oil and set afire. And one of the tunnels the party had traveled through had been too narrow for the large creatures to get through. However, the hook horrors had managed to locate one of the drow warriors trying to follow the Waterdhavian unit.

Baylee let his long sword guide the way, holding the lantern up. He started down the stone steps, then the next series of quakes shook the ground. Blocks of stone tumbled from overhead.

"Shields up!" Cordyan screamed. She extended her shield over Baylee and herself as the debris poured down.

Baylee stayed under the proffered shelter as the stone battered against the shield. He held his left arm up and Xuxa fluttered down to hang from it. The quake this time lasted longer than the other times.

"They're getting worse," Cthulad said. Rock pounded against his upraised shield with deafening thuds.

Gradually, the deluge stopped. Baylee pushed himself out from under Cordyan's shield and went forward. Other buildings lay in a tumbled-down mess before him. He held the lantern high and went quickly. Being between the buildings when the next quake hit was going to be dangerous. Any of them looked capable of crumbling down and doing serious harm to anyone under them.

Baylee found the end of the steps and paused on the last one.

"What are you stopping for?" Cordyan asked.

The ranger took a brush from the gnomish work armor. He worked at the bottom stone step. "There's supposed to be a trip switch here somewhere."

"A trip switch for what?" Cordyan knelt and helped him look along the step.

"A doorway of some kind." Baylee cleaned the front of the step with the brush, below the top surface.

"The trail goes on beyond," the civilar pointed out.

"But it doesn't go where we want to go." Baylee moved his

lantern, directing the light over the stone step. He barely made out the crevice that ran along the front of the step, halfway down. "Please hold this."

Cordyan took the lantern and kept the light on the step.

Baylee released his long sword, keeping it beside him, and took a miniature pry bar from one of the pockets in the gnomish leathers. He slipped the end into the crevice and started adding pressure. The crevice was artificed so carefully, he didn't know if he would have seen it without all the damage the quakes had done. After a moment, a thin sheeting of stone that ran the length of the step came loose in his hand. More dust had filtered through, covering the surface beneath. He put the pry bar away and used the brush again to reveal eight symbols inscribed in the stone, covering squares of stone that Baylee believed to be attached to counterweights.

Beside the symbols was an inscription. Baylee translated, guiding the lantern in Cordyan's hand. " 'If you've a love of lore and a love of culture, you'll know of Schyck Raveneyes.' "

"Raveneyes?" Cordyan asked. "Who was Schyck Raveneyes?"

Calebaan crowded closer, bringing his light to bear as well. "Raveneyes was one of the lesser known elven heroes of myth and legend. Not much was written about him." He paused. "I don't know what those symbols represent."

Baylee forced himself to think. His mind raced and his heart hammered inside his chest. He touched the symbols, hoping the contact would give him a clue. They were representations of Raveneyes. He felt frantic as his mind repeatedly reached into his memory and couldn't quite grasp what he needed.

Be at ease, Baylee, Xuxa offered.

I can't. What I need is right there. Baylee traced the symbols again, trying to fathom these. They were of a ship, an arrow, a dragon, a cloud, a morkoth, a child, a river, and an altar.

"If it's the story of Raveneyes," Cordyan said, "then maybe you're supposed to press them in order."

"Of course you're supposed to press them in order," Baylee snapped. He felt guilt over his behavior and turned to face the civilar. "I'm sorry. It's just that I can barely remember this story."

"What story, lad?" Cthulad asked.

"The story of Schyck Raveneyes." Baylee looked at the symbols again. "He was given eight tasks to do by Solonor Thelandira. Evidently these are supposed to be pressed in order."

"Then the picture of the child must be the first," Cordyan said.

"No," Baylee replied. "That has to represent the firstborn child of Coronal Fhastey, who got some of the early families of the wild elves to agree to trading camps and fairs. Fhastey's son was kidnapped by a gang of rogues seeking to break some of the trade agreements. Raveneyes found the coronal's son and brought him back safely. But that was among the later stories." Sluggishly his mind turned to the stories he remembered.

"If you remember that, you should be able to remember the rest of it," the civilar said.

"There are eight of them," Baylee said, "and the stories of Raveneyes were an interest a long time ago. He left nothing behind except these legends."

"Evidently Glitterwing liked him," Calebaan said.

Baylee blinked perspiration out of his eyes. "Raveneyes fought the Cloud of Kellagg first. He was fifteen years old. The cloud gathered in the cemetery of Notts Docks, a trading post on the River Ashaba even before Myth Drannor existed. It brought the dead up out of the ground, fulfilling an ancient curse."

"Raveneyes found the Gem of Despair and shattered it, ending the threat as I recall," Calebaan said.

Baylee nodded. "Fragments of that gem are supposed to still exist, giving limited control over those recently killed by violent means. Families, they say, can purchase the use of the gem and allow the dead to rise and avenge themselves."

"Press the symbol," Cordyan said.

Hesitantly, Baylee pressed the symbol. It sank in, then clicked and stayed inset. "Then came the threat of the goblin pirates along the river." He pressed the river stone, getting more tense when it locked into place rather than relaxing. He couldn't help wondering what would happen if he guessed wrong.

The arrow designating the hunt for the unicorn burial ground, there to find components necessary to make a potion to save

Raveneyes's own daughter, came next. It was followed by the altar which represented the drow pocket of civilization Raveneyes had destroyed when those dark elves encroached too far into the forest. Thinking about the story, Baylee realized the drow could have come through these very caverns back then, and Glitterwing's own research into the legends could have helped him found Rainydale.

The ship followed after, representing Raveneyes's journey to the Moonshaes while seeking to find a scroll for a wizard who was favored of Solonor. He was left with the dragon, the child, and the morkoth. Why couldn't he remember the end of the stories? His breathing sounded ragged in his ears.

Baylee, youre doing fine, Xuxa said.

No! I can't remember! Mielikki take me for a fool, I can't remember! I know the child pictograph comes in the middle, but which is next? He stared at the dragon and the morkoth, amazed that he could forget. His mind filled with facts, half-remembered stories, and things he was sure he'd never thought of before. The story of Raveneyes seemed even further away.

"The child," Calebaan said. "There was something about Raveneyes's rescue of the boy."

Baylee struggled to remember, then it came to him. "The shield!" He glanced at the wizard, seeking agreement.

Calebaan nodded. "The shield he had made from the scales of the red dragon, Ysolim."

Feeling more excited, Baylee hit the last three stones in succession, waiting for each click before going on to the next. At the last stone, the sound of gears grinding came from the wall on the right side of the tunnel. A huge stone block that conformed to the outer appearance sank back into the wall along smooth tracks carved into the floor.

When it stopped, it perfectly blocked the new tunnel eight feet back.

"It's not clear," Cordyan said. "The tunnel is still blocked."

Another quake hit, rolling the underground like a giant shrugging its shoulders. Baylee rode out the movement easily. Being in the tunnel away from the majority of the debris that came tumbling down helped. Huge rocks rolled across the caves in the distance, creating thunderous echoes.

"Is there another riddle?" Calebaan demanded.

Baylee shone his lantern into the recessed area. For an unexplained reason, most of it failed to reach the end of the tunnel. He picked up a rock and threw it. The rock never hit the other end of the tunnel.

"It's a dimensional door," Cthulad said. "But where does it go?"

Baylee was on the verge of suggesting there was only one way to find out, when a spectral voice came from behind the party.

"To the library, of course. Where else would it go?"

Baylee swung the lantern to the left, lighting the figure standing there.

The lantern's glow robbed the cloak of its shadows, revealing the features of the being wrapped within. He was tall and striking, and probably would have been thought of as handsome in his days when life was still within him. Seeing the shriveled skin and glowing white eyes, Baylee had no doubt that the man before him was dead. Pointed elven ears stood out at the sides of his head.

"Who are you?" the ranger asked, bringing his long sword to the ready.

"I am Nevft Scoontiphp, a baelnorn charged with protecting the crypts of my family. Those crypts are now endangered by the lich you seek." The creature regarded Baylee with its colorless gaze.

"What *lich?*" Baylee was aware that Cordyan had spread her men out behind him, their weapons at the ready.

"The library caretaker," Scoontiphp replied in his eerie voice. "He calls himself Folgrim Shallowsoul these days. His mortal name is long forgotten, even by himself, I believe."

Xuxa? Baylee prompted.

His intentions are honorable, the azmyth bat replied.

Baylee knew about baelnorns from his studies of old elven legends, but he'd never met one. Nor had he met anyone who had. "Why do you show yourself to us?" he asked. He'd always heard they were solitary creatures who didn't like anyone outside of the family they protected to see them.

"Because there is no one else who will rise up against Shallow-soul." A cold smile twisted the dead lips. "I even entertained ideas of supporting the drow woman's bid for power over the lich, but she wouldn't have me."

"What drow woman?" Baylee asked.

"Krystarn Fellhammer. She believes that her goddess, Lloth, Queen of Spiders, led her to Shallowsoul and placed her in his control so that she might learn from the great library Glitterwing had assembled." The baelnorn turned his head toward the tunnel with the dimensional door. "She pursues the lich now as well. Shallowsoul has been so intent on killing first Fannt Golsway, then yourself, that he has missed much of what she is doing. She's assembled an army of hobgoblins here in these caverns and is now breaking into the library."

"How do you know this?" Cthulad demanded.

The baelnorn flicked his dead gaze over to the old ranger. "Because I am there as well."

Baylee remembered then that a baelnorn possessed the power to project an image across a distance. But that story had never been confirmed. Until now.

"Why should we trust you?" Cordyan asked.

"You shouldn't," Scoontiphp replied. "Because I seek to serve my own ends."

"Here as well as with the drow?" Cthulad asked.

The baelnorn nodded. "Else why would I be in either place? I would gladly not suffer humans set foot in these caverns. I've killed dozens over the years who would not heed my warnings when they neared the crypts of my family. And I've killed other manner of men and near-men."

"Then why are you here?" Baylee asked.

"Because Shallowsoul must be stopped," Scoontiphp answered. "If that is possible. Even now, it may already be too late. He seeks to move the library, to shift from this plane into the astral plane itself. There, amid the floating rocks and bodies of dead gods, he feels he will be safe from any more interlopers. And there will be less chance of anyone coming to take the library. If he succeeds, the vacuum left by the library's absence will be horrendous. Perhaps all of the underground will be destroyed. The library is very big."

What do you want from us? Xuxa asked.

"In another part of these caverns," Scoontiphp said, "I am helping Krystarn Fellhammer gain entrance to the library. She will attempt to steal as many books as she can, and in doing so, she will set off a number of alarms the lich has in place in the library. That will provide a diversion for you for a time. Maybe even enough time to succeed."

"Succeed at what?" Cordyan asked.

The baelnorn fixed her with his dead gaze. "Weren't you listening? Shallowsoul is a lich. As such, he will have a phylactery."

"I don't know what that is," the civilar replied.

"It's a container," Baylee said automatically. "When a lich is created, it also creates a phylactery to hold its life essence. That way if the body is destroyed, it can be reborn in some manner."

"Exactly," the baelnorn replied. "I'm glad you understand the situation. You'll also understand that we do not have much time. Krystarn Fellhammer and her hobgoblin army will be through the dimensional door she's been using to get into the library in the next few minutes. If you wait for very much longer, your chances of success are virtually non-existent."

"Maybe they'll be *more* non-existent if we go with you," Cordyan said.

"That's for you to decide. In truth, you are all humans, and I could care less if you all die in this endeavor. Myth Drannor and its environs should never have had to suffer the presence of humans, dwarves, or any of the other barbarian species that came into the City of Songs and drew her down." The baelnorn turned to the dimensional door at the end of the tunnel. "But I'm going. The only chance I see that you have is in finding the phylactery while Shallowsoul is engaged in keeping the library from being plundered by Krystarn's hobgoblin horde." Without another word, Scoontiphp ran into the dimensional door and promptly disappeared.

Baylee held up the lantern, making sure the baelnorn was gone. He took a fresh grip on the long sword and started forward.

"Wait," Cordyan said. "You aren't just going to walk through that after him, are you?"

Baylee looked at her, not believing she didn't feel the same excitement he did at venturing into the library. "Walking is safer than running, and I feel like running." He turned and kept going.

"Right behind you, lad," Cthulad said.

Calebaan came as well.

Baylee stepped into the dimensional door, watching how his leg abruptly truncated as it moved on into the next plane ahead of him. Still, he could feel it. And the air in the next room felt colder than even the breezes cycling through the caverns. He heard Cordyan naming men to guard the tunnel while they were gone.

Then he passed through the dimensional door, and for a time, he knew nothing.

* * * * *

In front of Krystarn Fellhammer, the dimensional door continued to flutter and spark, not quite opening and staying open. She grew aware of a presence at her side. Her attention strayed from the crystal ball she focused through, angry at the interruption.

"You'll never get through that on your own," Nevft Scoontiphp said as he stepped through the nearby wall.

"Did you come to gloat, ghost?" Krystarn asked sarcastically. "If so, perhaps we should see how much pain you can endure before you turn and run." She held up the morning star.

"I came to help you."

Krystarn studied the baelnorn's milk-white features, as fine-boned as her own face but with wrinkled skin instead of the smooth flesh she carried. "In what way?"

"To help you open that dimensional door."

"And what do you get out of it?"

Another earthquake shivered through the hallway like a snake dying of a broken back. Scoontiphp stood in the hallway, totally unmoved by the action though Krystarn was thrown from her feet along with the hobgoblin warriors standing in lines behind her.

"If Shallowsoul is not stopped," Scoontiphp replied, "he's going to bring all of the caverns down on us when he takes the library to the astral plane." He pinned her with his gaze. "Now, do you want help or not?"

"You can get us through this door?" Krystarn asked, regaining her feet.

"By helping you through the crystal ball? Yes. It won't be easy, but it can be done. I would ask one thing, though."

"And what is that?"

"Only your promise that—should you survive your encounter with Shallowsoul—you won't bother the crypts that are under my protection."

Krystarn wanted to laugh at the presumption of the baelnorn. "Foolish creature, what could you have that would be worth anything near as much as what I will find in the library?"

"Nothing," the baelnorn agreed readily. "But in your greed, you might not remember that at some future point. Though we can be allies through this, you will find I can be one of the worst enemies you've ever made, if need be."

"Agreed," the drow said. "I'll not touch your precious crypts." But the quick way he'd confirmed there was nothing there for her served only to whet her curiosity about the crypt area. Once she had the knowledge at her fingertips that was contained in the library, she knew the baelnorn could not stand against her.

Scoontiphp leaned forward and touched a fingertip to the crystal ball. "Now, employ your spell," he invited.

Krystarn focused on Lloth, willing that the dark goddess grant her success. Then she chanted the spell. In moments, the dimensional door spread, becoming more and more solid.

Then it locked into place with a hissing snap. Krystarn maintained it almost effortlessly. She peered through the opening, thinking the baelnorn might have tried to trick her in some manner into jumping somewhere she wasn't supposed to be.

Instead, she saw the library.

"Chomack," she said in a hoarse, strained voice.

"Aye, sorceress."

"Follow me." Krystarn tightened her grip on her morning star and strode through.

27

Stacks of books swarmed into Baylee's view at the other end of the dimensional door. For a moment, he couldn't do anything but turn slowly around and try to take it in. Shelves extended up into the shadows that clung to the ceiling far overhead, until they finally vanished. But he knew the books didn't end there.

Half a dozen stairs ran up in spirals twisting along the walls. From the way they were laid out, he felt certain that all of them lead to other areas, not simply higher up. He sheathed the sword, walking over to the nearest shelves. He could barely make out a title in one of the written languages known to him: *The Creation of Dragons*. Other books on the same shelf seemed to deal with dragons as their topic as well. So did the books above and below.

He reached for a book bound in maple, the red and white striped wood as polished and finished as any piece of furniture he'd ever seen. An ornate mist dragon, more noticeable because of the small ears and wedge-shaped head outfitted with a trailing mustache, glowed silver-blue on the book cover. Beside it was a book that looked like it had been bound in plates carved from running water. He could even hear the sound of water rushing by.

"Don't," Scoontiphp warned in a harsh voice.

Hold, Xuxa echoed.

Baylee stayed his hand with difficulty.

"If you touch any of those books," the baelnorn went on, "you'll bring Shallowsoul down on us immediately. Once you have the phylactery and have defeated him, if possible, then you can search through these books to your heart's content."

Reluctantly, Baylee took his hand back. He noticed Calebaan standing next to him, the same hungry look in his eyes that Baylee was certain was in his own.

"You're wasting time we don't have," the baelnorn called from the bottom of a flight of stairs.

Darkness filled the library, beaten back only by the lanterns the party carried. Baylee thought he spotted things crawling and twisting in the shadows. Using both hands, he secured the lantern to his chest with straps from the gnomish leather.

"How far to the phylactery?" the ranger asked. Ahead of him, Xuxa flew around the curve of the spiral staircase and disappeared.

"I don't know," Scoontiphp answered. "But we're getting closer. I can sense it,"

Baylee let his free hand trail along the edge of the stairway. He glanced down, seeing the floor they'd just left disappear into the darkness again. Reaching into one of his pockets, he took out a piece of chalk that glowed yellow in the darkness. He sketched a quick arrow pointing back the way they'd come. The library was huge by any account, and he didn't want to get lost in case they had to hurry back.

"Will the dimensional door be there when we get back?" the ranger asked.

"It should be," the baelnorn answered.

Long minutes later, they reached the top of the stairs. Baylee's heart beat rapidly, and he breathed hard from the exertion. The drow blood had dried on him, making the skin across his face pull tight.

Two stone columns occupied space to either side of the stairwell. Scoontiphp seemed to scent the air like a hound, though Baylee doubted that was possible because the baelnorn—from all accounts—didn't breathe.

Then, in the distance, came the sound of men fighting, the crash of steel and the hoarse yells of agony. For a moment, Baylee thought the battle was coming toward the party, then he realized it was only the beginning sounds of the fight overtaking them from the right.

Scoontiphp turned and headed to the left. "Come on. Shallowsoul can only be minutes away."

* * * * *

Krystarn Fellhammer watched the dead rise from the floor of the library. She held a bag of holding, stuffing one tome after another into the cloth. "Chomack!"

The hobgoblin chieftain tore himself free of the group he was leading in their plundering. He hefted a battle-axe he'd evidently acquired during his underground reaving, and charged the first of the undead.

She was a wiry woman who wielded a curved scimitar in flashing swipes. She hadn't quite made it out of the hole in the stone floor that had evidently served as her final resting place when Chomack brought the battle-axe down in a two-handed stroke that almost cleaved her in half. She dropped at once.

Another man erupted from the floor in front of Krystarn. She finished shoving the book into her bag, then blocked the poorly aimed dagger blow with the small buckler on her wrist. Backhanding the morning star and putting as much of her weight into the blow as she could, she almost took the dead man's face from his head. He stumbled backward into two more rising corpses and knocked them to the ground in a flail of limbs.

The hobgoblins attacked en masse, outnumbering their already dead opponents. But the risen dead accounted for a number of the hobgoblins. The corpses refused to die by most killing strokes, requiring a blow that crushed the skull.

"You would steal from me, Krystarn Fellhammer?"

The drow elf glanced up at a high balcony overhead.

Shallowsoul leaned on the railing, peering down at her. He gestured, and Krystarn saw the ripple of magic energy leave his hand. She turned and fled, dodging through a pair of the walking dead.

Something crawled across the back of Krystarn's neck. She slapped at it with her free hand, crushing something with a crunch just as teeth bit into her flesh. Harsh groans of pain and anger from the hobgoblins echoed behind her as she raced for the library stack in front of her. She vaulted up onto the shelves, placed her empty hand on top, and leaped over to come crashing down on the other side.

A dead youth with sightless eyes reached up for her, mouth open to show rotted teeth. Krystarn quelled her revulsion as she landed on the dead boy. The corpse tried to wrap its arms around her. The drow lashed out with her morning star, breaking one of the arms with a brittle snap. Then she smashed the corpse's face and head.

Wheeling as she got to her feet, Krystarn ran to the end of the bookcase. She looked up on the balcony again and spotted Shallowsoul urging his undead minions on. She gathered her mystical energies, summoning her spell, unfolding it clearly in her head, then she threw it at the lich. Lightning bolts danced from her fingertips, streaking for Shallowsoul.

As expected, the lich blocked the brunt of the attack. The lightning bolts pealed thunder as they slid off Shallowsoul's shield and touched the stacks of books beside him. The paper of the books immediately caught fire, blazing high. It bothered Krystarn to see the damage being done to the books, possibly irreplaceable knowledge being destroyed once and for all, but not nearly as much as it caused consternation in the lich.

Shallowsoul screamed loud and long, and turned his attention to the burning books.

Krystarn looked about the library, seeing the hobgoblins still warring with the risen dead. Slowly and steadily, the hobgoblin army was being decimated.

"Sorceress," Chomack rumbled. "We are dying."

Krystarn faced the chieftain, seeing blood painted across his terrible features. "You'll raise another army, Taker of Dragon's Teeth. After this battle, you'll be known far and wide. Hobgoblins seeking a leader to help them wrest their fortunes from others will flock to you."

Chomack didn't appear content with her announcement, but he didn't attack either.

"Gather your men," Krystarn said. "We're going to go up further into the library."

"We should escape."

Krystarn pointed back the way they had come. "The dimensional door we used to get here has been wiped away. I can't open another that way. We'll have to kill the lich if we can, and find another way out if we can't."

"Where's the white elf?" the hobgoblin chieftain demanded. "He helped you open the door the first time. He can help you open it again."

"If you find him, let me know."

Chomack growled, then turned and neatly sliced the head from the shoulders of a dead woman approaching him from behind. "He's run off then?"

"I don't know." Krystarn looked back the way she'd come when Shallowsoul had launched his magical attack. Beetles swarmed the hobgoblins and the undead in the area. The hobgoblins fared the best, suffering only from the bites while the undead became feasting grounds for the beetles.

"He's nowhere to be found. He set you up."

Krystarn believed that was the truth as well. She glanced up at the lich, who was hastily casting spells and summoning some of the undead to control the fires. Three of the undead seeking to beat out the flames with their bare hands caught fire themselves, becoming walking torches that spread the threat of loss.

"Get your men," Krystarn repeated. "Now!"

Chomack called to his trumpeters, who blew the rally call. The battles broke off as the hobgoblin forces sank back toward their chieftain.

Krystarn summoned another spell, then hit the advancing line of undead with the mystic energy. A sheet of fire twenty feet tall formed between the uneven line of hobgoblins and undead. Controlled by their master's wishes, the undead kept coming forward, immolating themselves on the fire barrier. They twisted and turned away, burning bright.

"You're going to die a horrible death, drow!" Shallowsoul promised over the roar of the blaze.

"After you," Krystarn shot back as she raced out of the room. A narrow flight of stairs took them up scarcely three feet, but it opened onto another room. This room was squat and oval in shape. Light from the flaming corpses and burning books threw garish shadows into the room. Smoke rushed into the empty space in great, gray clouds.

Krystarn looked through the three passages open to her, trying to choose the path that would be more valuable for looting. And hoping that there was a way of escape. She cursed the baelnorn for running out on them.

Light flickered from a balcony above her. At first, the drow believed it was a reflection from the fires behind her. Then she saw the light overhead move smoothly along and disappear.

"We are not alone in the library," Chomack said.

"No." Krystarn searched the twisting spiral staircases until she spotted the one that took her up to the level where she saw the light. The baelnorn had helped her enter the library, possibly he had done the same for Baylee Arnvold. He could have made a deal with the human ranger. Of anyone in the caverns, Scoontiphp would most know what secrets the library held. She changed her course to the spiral stairway. "Follow me."

Chomack and his warriors pounded after her. She no longer feared their loyalty. None of them could get out of the library without her.

* * * * *

"Something's burning." Cthulad drew in a deep breath.

Baylee silently agreed, and the thought sent a chill through him. All the priceless works of art and knowledge in the library could be at risk. He hesitated at the next staircase the baelnorn plunged up.

No, Xuxa advised. *Whatever threat there is to the library, the lich will act against. Including us. And he will be better equipped to handle those threats than you are.*

Overcoming his urge to return and trace the smell of smoke, Baylee closed the distance between himself and Scoontiphp. He heard men praying to their gods behind him, and realized that even he had been repeating the prayer for the Mielikki's grace.

"How much further?" Baylee asked.

"Not far," the baelnorn answered.

"Have you been here before?"

"No. Never to this part of the library."

"You've been in the library before?"

"Of course. Shallowsoul has always been a threat. And he has been trying to recover the items that went down on *Chalice of the Crowns*. Not all of them would have been destroyed by the brine and the long years. You found that for him, which was something he hadn't counted on. It was the last tie holding him to this plane."

Baylee swung his head, taking in the rooms they passed as they ran down one of the stone hallways. The library honeycombed the underground, deeply entrenched in the bedrock. He caught tantalizing glimpses of displays of the past: vases, pottery, clothing, and armor. And more books than he thought he'd ever see in his life, even more volumes than were gathered in Candlekeep.

He followed Scoontiphp to the right and ran into a large room. Grabbing the lantern hanging from his armor, he flashed it around the room. The ceiling was forty or fifty feet over his head, reached by spiral stairs that whirled around the room. Everywhere he looked were more shelves.

In the center of the room, the lantern light flashed from the swirl of gems caught up in an invisible maelstrom. Baylee walked toward the whirlwind of sapphires, emeralds, rubies, and diamonds, almost hypnotized by their beauty and motion. They moved incredibly fast, their orbits changing constantly.

"This is it," the baelnorn said. "The center of the spell Shallowsoul has woven to take him from this plane to the next."

"Are you sure he can take all of this?" Baylee gestured toward the shelves and the rooms. "He can't possibly—"

"He's more powerful than you could ever imagine," Scoontiphp said.

"But if he's killed," Calebaan said, coming up to join them, his eyes captured by the swirl of gems, "all of this will remain behind."

The baelnorn faced the wizard. "If it can be managed."

"Getting the phylactery will give us an upper hand," Cordyan said.

"It's not that easy." The baelnorn moved closer to the bejeweled whirlwind.

"Where is it?" Baylee asked.

Before the baelnorn could answer, some of the watch members shouted out an alarm.

The drow, Xuxa warned from somewhere overhead.

"Form up ranks!" Cordyan bawled lustily, the coin in her sword's hilt shining. The members of the watch scattered across the room, seeking shelter behind the free standing shelves of books.

Baylee sheathed his long sword and ripped his bow loose. He grabbed a fistful of arrows from his quiver and nocked one back. He loosed it at the first hobgoblin he saw. An instant later, the fletchings quivered against the hobgoblin's chest. The creature slowed its all-out rush into the room and dropped to its knees, staring, perplexed, at the shaft buried in its chest.

The darkness hampered the Waterdhavian group, but they rallied quickly, meeting the hobgoblins near the center of the floor. They were outnumbered, but they were trained by Watch practice to work in closed quarters.

The line of hobgoblins broke against the shields of the watch guard. The watch members used the shelves as a skirmish line, striking from behind them.

Baylee leaped to the top of the nearest bookcase , crouching to keep himself as small a target as possible. He pulled another arrow back and put it through a hobgoblin's throat. Two more arrows sent hobgoblins down with arrows through thigh and arm.

Cthulad was at the epicenter of a mass of razor steel strokes. He moved among his enemies, taking advantage of their own pedestrian training with their weapons to use them against each other.

Calebaan stayed behind a shelf and used the magic he had available to him. When hobgoblins came too close, he whipped the iron-shod staff with grim and deadly efficiency. At least five members of the watch went down under the hobgoblins' swords, though. Their infravision versus the humans' normal sight couldn't help but be a telling factor in the battle.

Baylee moved along the top of the bookshelf, walking easily. A thrown hand axe bit deeply into the wood only inches from his feet. The ranger pulled another handful of arrows from the quiver and took aim at the hobgoblin who'd thrown the axe at him. The line of hobgoblins were almost upon them now, rendering the bow almost useless. Still, he loosed his shafts deliberately, making them count.

A hobgoblin charged the bookcase, aiming himself at Baylee. The ranger kicked the creature in the face, breaking its nose in a wild spatter of blood. Baylee dropped the bow and abandoned the high ground. He ripped his long sword free of its sheath.

Two hobgoblins rushed at him, screaming foul obscenities as they raised their swords. Baylee met their charge with a lightning fast display of sword play. One of the hobgoblins went down almost immediately, its throat sliced open by the long sword. The other hobgoblin fell back for a moment, long enough to draw a hand axe and bring it arcing toward Baylee's head.

Baylee reached up with his free hand and swatted the axe away. Using the movement and speed he'd already invested, he whipped around in a full turn, bringing the long sword in a short, powerful blow that cut halfway through the hobgoblin's chest. The ranger wrenched his sword free of the corpse.

He scouted the terrain, trying to find Cordyan and the baelnorn. Instead, he found Cthulad ringed by hobgoblins only a short distance away. The old ranger's skill kept his attackers respectful of his sword, but he was still presenting his back to his enemies as he turned about in their midst.

Baylee filled his free hand with throwing knives and threw them with deadly accuracy. Two hobgoblins died before they could turn around, and three others were out of the fight with grievous wounds. Another hobgoblin turned on him, a sword in each hand.

"Now you die, human!" the hobgoblin declared. It swung its swords in a double-attack, well seasoned in two-handed fighting.

Baylee gave ground, batting the blades aside as he reached for the parrying knife. He flipped the spring release loose and caught one of the hobgoblin's swords in the dagger. He twisted, but was unable to pry the sword from the hobgoblin's grip. He blocked the other sword, then stepped forward and kicked the hobgoblin in the crotch. The swords came loose then.

Reversing his long sword in his hand and grabbing it by the hilt again, Baylee drove the point through the hobgoblin's throat and twisted, leaving the creature dying behind him. He glanced over at Cthulad, who was finishing up the last hobgoblin before him.

"For a man who would rather talk than fight, lad," the old ranger said with a grin, "you're a remarkable warrior."

Baylee brushed his shirt sleeve across his face, removing the fresh blood that covered it. "I never said I couldn't fight, just that I like to figure a way around it where I can. There's no way for that here."

"Agreed." Cthulad took a glance around the large room.

Only a few feet away, a hobgoblin rushed a member of the watch, knocking them both back into the mad whirl of gemstones. They flew off their feet, twisting into the invisible vortex, still wrapped in a death embrace as each sought to kill the other with their daggers. Before the struggle could last more than a few heart-beats, they were sucked into the center of the whirlwind. The gems moved with such speed and force that they penetrated the bodies of man and hobgoblin and left only corpses twisting in the storm winds.

Nevft Scoontiphp stood near the swirl of gems. He thrust his hands out to his sides, his robes snapping and cracking with the pull of the wind. His bone-white hair fluttered around his face. Without warning, lightning jumped from his hands.

A tongue of wild lightning climbed to the top of the room and ignited into a ball of white fire that illuminated the impromptu battlefield. It stayed there, lighting the whole, cavernous room. The rest of the lightning gathered around the whirl of wind and gems that were the lich's planar spell.

"You have no time, Baylee Arnvold," the baelnorn shouted grimly. "If we are to succeed here, you have to get the phylactery and destroy it. Hurry."

"Where is it?" Baylee beat back an attack by a hobgoblin, suc-ceeding in striking a deep wound in the creature's arm. It fell away, screaming in pain.

"At the top of the stairs," Scoontiphp answered. "A room is there with a selection of vases. Shallowsoul's phylactery is an emerald drum the size of a man's head."

Baylee stepped aside as another hobgoblin rushed at him with a hand axe raised. He kicked the creature's shins as it streaked past, tripping the hobgoblin. The creature had only a moment to scream, then it slipped into the spell zone. The hobgoblin's head exploded when a large diamond slammed through it.

"The drow!" Scoontiphp said. "She overheard about the phylactery!"

Baylee crossed swords with two hobgoblins in his way. Sparks flew from the steel as he blocked and riposted. One of the creatures died in a handful of seconds. He side-stepped the next, gazing up at the circular stairs.

Krystarn Fellhammer ran to the stairs. At first, Baylee thought the drow was going to climb over the railing and start running up. Then he saw her lay a hand against the railing, pause for just a moment to kick her boots off, then start scurrying up the railing levels like a giant spider. Her hands and feet stuck to the stairway railing easily, moving rhythmically from one to the next.

Xuxa! Baylee called.

I'm coming, Baylee! the azmyth bat responded.

The ranger fought his way across the room. The hobgoblins and watch members were totally mixed, separated into pockets of battles. Behind them, Baylee spotted a couple dozen undead in various stages of decomposition.

Blocked by the battles spread out across the room, Baylee vaulted to the top of the nearest bookcase, then pulled himself up and ran across, leaping the gaps.

Xuxa flapped into view beside him. *What is going on?* she asked.

Baylee pointed at the drow, already nearly halfway up the fifty-foot expanse to the top of the room. *She knows where the phylactery is too.*

It is up there?

According to Scoontiphp, yes. The bookcase in front of Baylee had been knocked out of line. He wheeled and turned to the left, barely able to make the longer leap. The bookshelf teetered uncertainly under his feet for a moment, then slid over into a slow topple. By that time, the ranger had reached the end of it and made the leap to the next. He glanced over his shoulder, groaning in dismay as the books went tumbling, spines cracking as they slid across the floor and across the corpses.

When he turned back around, one of the biggest hobgoblins he'd ever seen was climbing up the end of the bookshelf coming at him. Baylee stopped, bringing the long sword up in front of him.

The hobgoblin raised his battle axe in both hands, the haft spanning his chest. "I am Chomack, Taker of Dragon's Teeth, Chieftain of the Sumalich. You will die by my hand."

Baylee didn't even think about an introduction. He stepped immediately forward, bringing the long sword over in a skull-splitting sweep.

The hobgoblin chieftain raised his axe, taking the blow on the haft. Sparks leaped from the steel haft. Handling his weapon as if it weighed nothing, the hobgoblin struck back, uncoiling his arm in a backhanded slash.

Baylee narrowly avoided the blow. The axe head raked across the gnomish leathers, slicing them open across the midriff. A flap folded down, exposing his skin beneath as well as the thin line of the cut the blade had done. Parrying another axe blow, Baylee was barely able to get out of the way of it even with the parrying dagger slipping the heavy head slightly.

Moving quickly, Baylee leaped from the bookcase he was on to another free-standing stack, taking care to push at the one he left with his feet. The stack slipped sideways, falling away from him. He'd hoped the hobgoblin would go down with it, that the eight-foot fall would be disabling.

He hadn't counted on the hobgoblin actually beating him to the next bookcase. He only had one foot down when the hobgoblin swung the battle-axe from side to side. He managed to leap again, feeling the axe slice across the top of his leg.

He had to stretch out to make a landing on the next bookcase. He landed on both feet and his left hand, the handle of the parrying dagger thumping hard against the wooden top. He pushed himself up, tripping the spring blades on the parrying dagger to close them, then sheathing the weapon.

Chomack dived at him.

Baylee turned and fled to the left. Pound for pound, he didn't want to go against the hobgoblin. He didn't fight to see who was the better sword. He fought to win, and the hobgoblin had size and strength on his side. Landing on the next bookcase, only three more shelves away from the stair railing where Krystarn Fellhammer was still climbing toward the top of the room, he reached into one of the pockets of the gnomish leather. He brought out a handful of caltrops and scattered them across the top of the bookcase in front of him.

Chomack obviously didn't see the move. The hobgoblin landed heavily on top of the bookcase, then immediately roared out in pain, trying to find a way of standing that didn't cause agony. He drew up a boot that held four caltrops sticking out of the sole. Blood already seeped from the wounds.

Baylee unleashed a blow at once, slashing the hobgoblin across the chest. The force of the contact drove the big humanoid back, sending him roaring onto three of his fellows battling a pair of watch members below. All four hobgoblins crashed to the ground.

Chomack's battle-axe dropped to the top of the library shelves. Curious about the make and design, Baylee lifted it by the haft, finding it far lighter than any he'd ever hefted. A slight tingling raced through his arm. A hobgoblin reached up for him, wrapping its fingers around one of the ranger's ankles. Instinctively, Baylee chopped with the battle-axe, amazed at how easily it parted flesh, muscle, and bone. The amputated arm dropped away as the hobgoblin roared in pain.

Using some of the ties on the gnomish armor, he secured the battle-axe, then draped it across his shoulders. The weight was negligible and it held to his back easily.

Turning his attention to the drow, Baylee raced across the remaining bookcases. The dark elf was past the halfway mark on the stairs.

28

Baylee sheathed the long sword and took out the enchanted rope again. Throwing it upward, he said the command word. The magic in the rope caused it to slither up at once. It attached to the tallest staircase railing. With another word, Baylee commanded the rope to knot itself.

Once the knots were in place, the sixty-foot rope shortened to fifty feet, but it was long enough to reach him. He gripped it tightly, then swarmed up the rope. Perspiration soaked the gnomish leathers, and his muscles ached as he pulled.

The unnatural grace Krystarn Fellhammer exhibited unnerved him somewhat. He hadn't gone over ten feet before the rope beneath him quivered, letting him know someone else had grabbed it. He reached for one of the small throwing knives hidden in the gnomish leather workman's armor, ready to sacrifice the rope if he had to.

"It's me," Cordyan yelled up.

"What do you think you're doing?"

"Helping. Or do you think you're going to be able to take that drow on all by yourself?"

Shut up and save your breath for climbing, Xuxa ordered.

Baylee turned his attention back overhead. Krystarn Fellhammer had reached the uppermost railing, twenty feet above him. He pulled harder as he watched the drow disappear from view further back on the ledge.

A sudden explosion of fire and light came from below. A heartbeat later, a wave of concussive force slammed against him, bruising his chest against the railing in front of him. He held his position, looking back over his shoulder.

Scoontiphp remained by the whirling maelstrom in the center of the room. His clothing shifted, torn by the winds. The lightning dancing from the palms of his hands. Calebaan stood nearby, defending the baelnorn from any hobgoblins who crept around the net of steel Cthulad and the Waterdhavian watch had put up.

The sphere of whirling winds detonated again, scattering sparks from the baelnorn's lightning. The gems seemed to slow, and the residual tremors that had been part of the underground since the earlier earthquakes appeared to fade.

Then a shadow sailed out into the room. With the continual light spell Scoontiphp had in effect overhead, Baylee guessed that the new arrival had to be Folgrim Shallowsoul, the lich who kept the library.

Shallowsoul stood in the middle of a carpet that flew effortlessly through the air. The carpet hovered only a few feet from the sphere and stopped.

Baylee yelled down a warning, wondering if the baelnorn knew the lich was there. Then it became a moot point because the lich gestured toward Scoontiphp. An invisible wall of force slammed into the baelnorn, knocking him from his feet and into a set of bookshelves behind him. The force was so great that the baelnorn didn't stop there, knocking down two other sets of shelves behind him.

"Climb!" Cordyan yelled up.

Baylee reached up and grabbed his next handhold. More blasts of light and bursts of incredible noise rose from below. He gained the top and swung a leg over. Only his finely tuned senses warned him of the morning star streaking for his head.

He ducked and rolled to one side as the weapon smashed splinters from the stairway railing. He came up standing, but had to shift again as Krystarn Fellhammer fired her hand crossbow at him. The shaft ripped through the sleeve of his left arm, and he felt an immediate numbness that told him at least part of the poison had entered his system. He fought against it, barely able to keep his mind clear.

"You made a mistake in coming here, human," the drow hissed.

"I don't think so," said the ranger, shaking the double images of the drow from his sight.

"Why?" she taunted. "I killed your old mentor, trapped him like a rat in his own home, then snapped his neck like a rat. What makes you think I'll have any trouble with his whelp?"

Baylee focused on her words, backing away as she came at him. Thick support columns ran down from the ceiling overhead. They provided cover from her spellwork. Another crossbow quarrel chipped away stone only inches from his face.

Rooms opened up off of the runway the stairs led up on. Baylee glanced through them hurriedly, hoping to see some sign of the emerald drum Scoontiphp had spoken of.

Get ready, Baylee, Xuxa said, *I am on my way.*

No! Baylee responded. *She's too quick, too dangerous.*

And you're wounded.

Frantically, Baylee searched the open area above the room below. Even with all the pyrotechnics coming from the battle raging below, he couldn't spot the azmyth bat. But with his blurring vision, he didn't know if it would have been possible anyway.

Xuxa swept in like an arrow, her wings wrapped tight against her body. She hit the drow sorceress from the side, not hesitating. Her claws dragged across Krystarn Fellhammer's cheek, ripping the flesh open and sizzling electricity at the same time.

Stay ready, Xuxa cried as the drow spun in her direction.

Baylee tried to remain steady, but the poison in his system counteracted his reflexes. He staggered slightly but managed to keep the long sword up in front of him.

Before the drow could attack Xuxa, she twisted in pain, turning back to the rope Baylee had just quit. As she turned, the ranger saw the trio of darts sticking out of her back, driven deep between the links of her mail shirt.

Krystarn Fellhammer lifted a hand and began a series of intricate manipulations with her fingers as Cordyan pulled herself over the railing twenty feet and more back.

Baylee ripped a throwing knife free of the gnomish workman's armor and flung it at the drow. It sank deeply between her shoulder blades. He felt less than honorable attacking her from behind, but he couldn't stand by and let Cordyan be killed.

Move to the attack, Baylee, Xuxa said. *For the moment, you are soundless. The drow can't hear you.* The azmyth bat had the ability to magically create silence in the area near her once a day. He moved swiftly behind the drow, getting a good grip on the long sword.

As the drow turned back around, he took her head off cleanly with the long sword. Blood sprayed an arc of bright color against the wall behind her as her headless body dropped to its knees and toppled forward.

Exhausted by his efforts, Baylee slumped to the floor when the latest earthquake hit. He tried to remain on his feet, tried to maintain his hold on the long sword, but the poison surged through his system unchecked.

"Baylee," Cordyan said, approaching him with her sword before her.

He tried to speak, but nothing came out.

He was poisoned, Xuxa said. She fluttered to the wall in front of Baylee, gazing at him worriedly.

Cordyan rummaged in the pouch at her side, coming out with a vial. She unstoppered it, then poured the contents into Baylee's mouth. He felt a warm lassitude spread through him, the sharp ache of the poison suddenly dulled. His limbs still felt heavy, but his breathing already felt less labored.

The watch lieutenant gave him another sip of the heal potion. "Drink it down."

Baylee's mind cleared, followed shortly by his vision. He forced himself to his feet with Cordyan's help. "The phylactery?" he asked.

The light from downstairs started to fade gradually. Another quake rocked the great library, letting him know who was gaining the upper hand in the battle of spells going on below.

"I don't know," the civilar answered.

I found it, Xuxa announced.

Where? Baylee stared through the gloom and found the azmyth bat as she released the wall she'd clung to.

Xuxa flapped her wings and headed into the room to Baylee's left.

The ranger stumbled in pursuit, his reflexes starting to feel more normal. The room he entered was filled as was all the others, with volumes and volumes of books. A tall desk occupied one end of the room. A carved stone chair with a high back sat behind it.

No one was in the room.

All of the walls held items scattered amid the books. Skulls, some from real creatures and others carved from precious metals, glinted in the lantern light. Dozens of crystal balls occupied unique mounts, including the skeletal hands of men and creatures. Vases numbered the most among the items scattered along the shelves.

Where? Baylee played the lantern light over the shelves. A flicker of green caught his attention on the left.

Xuxa winged to the shelves in the center of the lantern's beam and hung upside down over a statue that must have been three feet tall. *Here.*

Baylee moved forward, targeting the statue of a woman with two faces, the second one occupying the space where the back of her skull should have been. She was naked, revealing twisted and broken limbs clothed in loose flesh. She held the emerald drum above her head. Her features, both sets of them, held only horror.

He moved closer, hypnotized by the beauty of the emerald drum. He didn't know how much it would be worth to a jeweler or a collector, but the burnished surface captured the light from his lantern like a fire had started deep within the emerald. He reached for the drum.

Before his hand touched the drum, a strident voice rang out behind him.

"Stay away from that!"

Baylee turned, bringing the long sword up.

Folgrim Shallowsoul floated through the door on the flying carpet. His clothing still held sparks that burned bright orange. He gestured toward the ranger.

A wall of incredible force slammed into Baylee. He flew backward, flailing to regain his balance. He rolled across the broad floor but came up on his feet.

"You're in league with that foul baelnorn," Shallowsoul said as he drifted into place behind the stone desk. The carpet landed gently beside the desk. "But you're too late to stop me from shifting this library to the astral plane where you and your kind will never find it."

Cordyan rushed for the phylactery. Before she reached it, a gust of wind blew her aside.

Baylee slipped a throwing knife from the gnomish leather. He flung it from the side, trying to mask the movement till the last possible moment. The knife flew like a dart.

The lich raised his hand and caught the knife in his skeletal fingers. He walked behind the desk without concern. "The baelnorn has killed you all," he declared as he took the seat behind the desk. Tossing the knife away, he waved his hand over the desktop. "I've kept this library safe for hundreds of years. How can you think I'd shirk my duties now?"

Without preamble, an earthquake tremor shivered through the room. Baylee braced himself, amazed at how the books didn't fall from the shelves.

A cloud of smoke erupted from the top of the desk, taking the shape of a huge, naked humanoid. The smoke kept coiling and climbing. In less than a moment, the desk was gone, reshaped into a stone golem that stepped ponderously toward Baylee.

The golem stood nine and a half feet tall and was as broad as any two men. The stone flesh marbled, turning white under the ranger's lantern light. It opened its mouth in a soundless scream.

"In moments, this library will shift to the astral plane," the lich said. "There's nothing you can do to stop it. And once we get there, you won't escape this labyrinth alive!"

Moving much faster than the stone golem, Baylee swung his long sword at the creature's arm, hoping to sever the limb or at least render it useless. Instead, the sword shattered against the stone skin, falling in gleaming shards. It swung its hand at the ranger.

Baylee barely managed to duck under the blow. The huge hand slammed into the nearby bookshelves, toppling them over.

"No!" Shallowsoul screamed, sitting upright in his chair. "Don't hurt the books!"

The golem hesitated for just a moment, giving Baylee time to discard the useless sword hilt. He unfastened the straps holding the battle-axe he'd taken from the hobgoblin, bringing it around swiftly in his hands. The ranger gave ground, using the time to his advantage. He ran for the emerald drum.

Xuxa, Baylee called.

I am here, the azmyth bat replied. *I know the lich controls the golem. When I have a proper opening, I shall try to distract him.*

Be careful. Baylee placed a hand on the emerald drum in the twisted statue's hands. A tingling sensation, like that he received from the haft of the battle-axe, ran through his palm. The magic in the emerald drum was a physical presence.

"Destroy him!" Shallowsoul ordered.

The golem lumbered to do the lich's bidding.

Another tremor ripped through the library. Baylee barely maintained his balance. He tried to pry the emerald drum from the statue's hands, but failed. Grabbing the battle-axe up, he brought it smashing down hard against the emerald drum. Bright green sparks jumped from the keen edge, but there was not even a crack to mark the blow he'd struck.

"You're going to need more magic than that pathetic axe has to destroy my phylactery," the lich said.

Switching his grip on the battle-axe, Baylee smashed the heavy warblade into the statue's upraised hands. The wrists shattered, but the stone hands still clung to the emerald drum. However, it was enough. Baylee grinned, knowing his success was only seconds away from being taken from him as the stone golem bore down on him.

He reached down and seized one of the broken stone hands holding onto the drum. The phylactery was heavier than it looked, but he managed it easily enough.

Baylee Arnvold. The ranger recognized the baelnorn's voice in his head, sounding weak and agonized. *Bring the phylactery to me. I am downstairs with the astral shift spell. I can help.*

Baylee ducked under the golem's arm. The huge stone hand thundered against the wall, knocking books from the shelves and breaking a dozen vases or more. He looked up and spotted Cordyan slipping behind the golem. She swung her blade with force and using all of her body weight. The sword bit into the golem's back, sending fracture marks through the stone.

The golem turned ponderously, as if unwilling to shift too much and put strain on the wounded area.

"Get back," Baylee said.

The civilar slipped out of the way of the golem's fist. Then the creature turned completely, trying to trap her between its out-spread arms.

Unbelievably, Cordyan froze where she was.

Baylee's stomach turned over at the thought of what those terrible stone hands would do to her. "Move!" he shouted, already on his way to the door.

Cordyan didn't flinch at all as the golem reached for her.

Looking past the civilar, Baylee saw the lich holding a hand toward her. He guessed that Shallowsoul had enspelled her. *Xuxa, take him.* The ranger rolled the emerald drum toward the door, then took up the battle-axe in both hands. "Cordyan, when you're free, get the drum." He launched himself at the golem, pulling into position, then bringing the axe into the creature's knee joint.

The axe head buried deep in the stone flesh, sending fissures running through the injured leg. Stunned and hurting, the golem turned back to Baylee, its face a mask of inarticulate rage.

Baylee ducked under the outstretched hands. He caught a brief glimpse of Xuxa streaking across the intervening space in front of the lich. Then the azmyth bat raked her claws across the back of Shallowsoul's hand. The lich drew his hand back, breaking the spell.

"Get the drum," Baylee said. "We've got to get it downstairs to the baelnorn." He drew back the axe and chopped at the golem's leg again. Fist-sized chunks flew from the creature's limb this time.

Cordyan broke free and streaked for the drum. She caught it up in one hand and ran for the door.

"No!" the lich screamed behind her.

Baylee drew back from the golem, luring it into position so that it blocked the lich behind it and served as a shield from any spells Shallowsoul might cast. He turned and ran after Cordyan, vaulting over the headless corpse of Krystarn Fellhammer.

A concussive wave overtook him, buffeting his body. He glanced over his shoulder and saw the stone golem suddenly blown toward him, coming at him impossibly fast. Ripped from the floor, the creature flailed soundlessly in the wind blast.

"Get down!" Baylee yelled in warning, diving to the ground beside the door.

The stone golem blew by overhead, rolling and turning as it shot out over the railing. But one of its flailing hands caught Cordyan a glancing blow, knocking her over the side. She almost caught herself, one hand wrapping around the railing.

Baylee pushed himself up, aware of the emerald drum balanced precariously on the edge of the railing, one of the broken stone hands still holding onto it, somehow wedging against the railing. He dropped the battle-axe.

He ran forward, telling himself there was time to save both, to save the woman and the phylactery. Both had managed to find a grip on the railing. The phylactery would have to come first, of course. After all, it was more precariously perched. Cordyan could at least hold on.

He took another step, his mind racing with everything he needed to do, then the step after that. Getting to the woman and the drum was going to be easy.

Then a tremor shivered throughout the library again, one of the worst ones so far.

Baylee lost his footing and went to the floor. He heard Cordyan scream in renewed fear. "No!" he shouted as he watched the drum's balance point shift over the side of the railing. It slid over the side, starting a slow tumble.

By the gods, it wasn't fair! Baylee pushed himself to his feet. He breathed a quick prayer to Mielikki, begging the Lady of the Forest's indulgence in asking for so selfish a prize. He could catch the drum before it hit the ground, there was time.

There had to be. Losing it meant losing the library, and losing the library meant losing an incalculable amount of knowledge. All the dreams he had ever had, all the questions that he could ever hope to have answers for, the drum contained them all. The loss couldn't be allowed.

"Baylee!" Cordyan shrilled.

The ranger shifted his gaze, watching as the woman's hand slipped and she fell. He grabbed the enchanted rope from the gnomish leather and vaulted over the side. Fifty feet of free fall opened up below him. On one side was the woman; and on the other was the phylactery.

And he only had time to save one of them. And that one only at the risk of his own life.

Saying the command word while in free fall himself, Baylee threw one end of the rope toward the cavern roof. The rope slithered around a projecting bit of rock and tied itself.

Letting the rope burn through his gloved hand, the ranger made his choice. Cordyan looked up at him, her face tense, barely keeping the fear at bay. Reaching for her, he caught her free hand. "Hang on!" He wrapped his arm in the rope and tightened his grip.

When they hit the apex of their drop, he felt her hand sliding out of his. The pain in his shoulders was incredible as he took the strain. "Don't let go!"

Cordyan gripped his hand.

Baylee knew what she was thinking because he was thinking the same thing. Once the phylactery hit the ground, it would shatter. Whatever control they might have been able to exercise over the lich would be gone. The library would be lost.

The drum hurtled down, spinning over and over as it fell toward the whirlwind of gemstones in the center of the room. Baylee was vaguely aware of the pockets of battle between the watch and the hobgoblins and the undead that were going on.

The stone golem hit the ground first and shattered, sending debris in all directions.

The civilar grabbed Baylee's leg, then managed to grab the rope as well. The ranger hung on with grim determination as their swing arced them out high over the center of the room. Cordyan shifted, taking her weight from Baylee to the rope. The ranger felt the load lighten immediately.

He glanced back over his shoulder, watching as Calebaan and Cthulad ran to intercept the falling phylactery. The rope swung back, and Baylee twisted with it, losing the view for a moment.

When he turned back around, he spotted Folgrim Shallowsoul swooping in on the flying carpet.

The lich snatched the phylactery from the air and glided around the spinning field of gemstones. Nevft Scoontiphp gestured toward the lich, but Shallowsoul held out a hand.

Whatever spell the baelnorn had employed failed. A moment later, Scoontiphp was covered in fire. His screams echoed throughout the caverns.

Get down, Xuxa warned.

Cordyan slid down the rope, working her way across the knots. Baylee was only a heartbeat behind her. The rope just managed to reach the floor.

"Now, human," Shallowsoul said as he flew toward Baylee, "now you're going to pay full measure for your part in this."

Baylee reached into a pocket and took out a handful of caltrops. He flung them backhanded as hard as he could. The caltrops spun through the air, blackest black against the shadows. The lich was less than fifteen feet distant. The sharp pronged caltrops embedded in his face and upper chest.

Screaming in pain, obviously weakened from all the spellcasting he was doing, the lich fell backward from the flying carpet and landed in the swirl of gemstones. He disappeared at once, but it took longer for his screams to die away.

Baylee touched down on the ground just as a quake ripped through the ground. Chunks of earth pushed up through the floor while other sections of the floor dropped away.

Incredibly, Scoontiphp pushed himself up from the ground, beating at the flames that couldn't quite devour his flesh.

Baylee crossed the trembling floor, leaping across the broken areas of flooring. "What happened?" he asked the baelnorn.

"We failed," Scoontiphp answered. "The lich's spell is still in effect."

Baylee watched the prismatic rainbow of gems as it swelled to start filling the room. "But Shallowsoul is dead."

"Maybe not." The baelnorn remained erect with effort. His clothing held burn marks.

The prismatic bubble that had been the swirl of gems grew at a fantastic rate, driving the men and hobgoblins before it. Books and whole shelves leaped across the intervening distance, caught up in the cyclone winds being generated by the growing prismatic bubble. A hobgoblin, unable to find shelter quickly enough, was swept up in the bubble. The humanoid's body didn't penetrate its surface. Instead, it exploded against it, with not even enough time to yell.

Baylee scooped up a few books from a nearby shelf just as they were starting to lift up. He tried to hang onto them, but they were pulled too strongly, threatening to drag him into the bubble as well. He had no choice but to let them go. They flew into the embrace of the whirling winds and vanished.

"This way!" Cthulad yelled, twisting into a corridor off the big room. The members of the watch followed the old warrior immediately.

"Look at it," Calebaan said as he passed Baylee. "So much knowledge, and it's all being taken away from us."

Baylee watched in silent frustration. He called Xuxa to him, then tucked her inside the crook of his arm so the winds wouldn't harm her. Books and vases and skulls and display cases whirled madly, sucked one after another into the prismatic bubble. He felt a hand on his shoulder.

"Come on, Baylee," Cordyan said, urging him to follow the others, "there's nothing else to be done."

The vacuum increased so much that even boulders and stalactites were pulled against the bubble. They shattered at once, blasting out against the surrounding walls hard enough to leave scarring. The bubble continued to increase in size.

It can't fill all of the library, can it? Baylee asked Xuxa as he stepped into the corridor.

I don't know, the azmyth bat said. She squirmed against his arm.

The next room held another prismatic bubble that was already starting to spread to fill the room, trapping the party in the corridor.

Nevft Scoontiphp knelt and traced lines of green fire on the floor with his forefinger. A shimmering filled the air at that end of the corridor. "I can get us to safety," the baelnorn said. "But we have to hurry."

Without hesitation Cthulad led the way into the shimmering area, promptly disappearing. The party filed quickly through the magical gateway. In a moment, only Baylee and the baelnorn remained.

"I can't hold the way much longer," Scoontiphp warned.

Go, Xuxa ordered.

The library, he replied.

For now, Baylee, it's gone, disappeared somewhere into the astral plane. It will be harder to get to, true, but not completely unattainable. The next discovery you make may lead you straight to it. A spell, a legend, something will put a little more knowledge into your hands. If you keep looking.

Baylee said nothing, watching the mad swirl of prismatic lights engulf the room.

Baylee, you have to go. Now.

I know. But he couldn't. It was too much to walk away from.

The library's gone, Xuxa said, *but it hasn't gotten away. Not as long as you are alive to pursue it.*

Without any other course of action open to him, Baylee turned and went through the shimmering portal. He felt a moment of lightness, then he was gone.

Epilogue

Crouched in the bottom of the well after hours of labor to remove all the rock that had fallen into it from the earthquakes, Baylee shined his lantern into the hidden shaft that had first taken them into the underground lair under Rainydale.

It's covered over, Xuxa said.

Baylee silently agreed. From where he stood on the mound of debris that had filled the well, only a jumbled mass of rock was visible, and there was no telling how much remained of the caverns themselves. Baylee covered the lantern and secured it to his gnomish armor. He climbed back up the rope trailing over the lip of the well. Topside again, he breathed in the clean, fresh air of the evening. The sun was already sinking in the west.

"The way?" Cordyan asked, sitting nearby. Her face was grimed and scratched from digging in the well.

Scoontiphp's spell had taken them back to the hills not far from the well. The watch members who'd been left there had managed to keep the horses together, so they wouldn't have to walk out of the woods. Of the baelnorn, though, there had been no sign. Baylee knew Scoontiphp had entered the shimmering area after him, but he had no way to known where the baelnorn had gone.

"Totally blocked," Baylee announced. "It would take a team of dwarves who were both skilled and patient to get back into those caverns."

"Even then," Calebaan said, sitting under a tree only a few yards away, "I don't think there would be much of the library for them to find."

"No." With exhaustion sinking into him, Baylee collapsed beside the well. Xuxa fluttered to hang from a nearby tree. Despite his fatigue, the ranger rummaged in his pockets and turned up a small journeycake made of nuts and berries. He unfolded the cheesecloth it was stored in and pinched off a bite for Xuxa.

The azmyth bat chirped in appreciation.

Baylee took some of the journeycake for himself, savoring the flavor. Even the land on top of the underground caverns had changed. Uprooted trees lay scattered across the countryside. Cracks broke through the ground, but none of them that Baylee had investigated led down into any caverns. Still, in a matter of weeks, the forest would reclaim the land, making it look no different than any place around them.

After a look from Cordyan, Calebaan excused himself and left them by themselves. Cthulad was already shouting orders at the men, organizing them into the party they'd need to begin the long trip back to Waterdeep.

"I want to thank you for saving me back there," Cordyan said. She wiped at her face with a rag she soaked with her waterskin, and ran her fingers through her hair.

"We were both lucky," Baylee replied. "But you're welcome."

"So where do you go now?" she asked.

"I don't know," Baylee said. "I've got some leads that I want to follow up in my journal. And there are those books I sent to Candlekeep from the shipwreck. Maybe they'll offer a direction."

She was quiet for a time. "There remain things to be taken care of in Waterdeep. Fannt Golsway's will, among others. Lord Piergeiron would probably appreciate the chance to talk with you."

She is right, Xuxa put in from her branch. She held the journeycake in her front claws.

For some reason, the memory of Cordyan's soft lips against his returned to Baylee with an intensity he couldn't remember ever experiencing. He shot a look at the azmyth bat, wondering if Xuxa was deliberately triggering the experience.

The bat contentedly ate her journeycake and responded with not a thought.

"But if you chose to go on from here," Cordyan said quickly into the silence that followed, "as a member of the Waterdhavian Watch, I no longer have reason to ask you to accompany me back."

Baylee nodded. "I think going back would be a good idea. There are some things I need to have put in order."

"Golsway's home in its present condition may not be a proper place to stay while you're there. Do you have anywhere else?"

"There are some acquaintances," Baylee admitted.

"I see."

"Unless you have somewhere else in mind?"

The civilar looked flustered. She glanced away again, running her fingers through her hair. "I was going to suggest the rooming house where I stay. The food is good, the beds are decent, and the rent is reasonable."

"That sounds good."

"We'll talk about it on the way back." Still acting self-conscious, Cordyan pushed herself to her feet and walked toward the group of watch members.

As he watched her walk away, Baylee felt the disappointment of losing the library after such a hard chase lift slightly. A few days in Waterdeep to settle affairs, and dinners with old companions to remember Golsway were in order. The thought warmed him. And he had lost the library *after* finding it. Finding something, as Golsway had always pointed out, was half the joy of the hunt.

He said a quick prayer for his mentor, asking Mielikki's blessing for the old mage, then pushed himself to his feet and trotted after the watch lieutenant. "Hey."

Cordyan turned to face him and Baylee fell into step beside her. "Well, getting back to our discussion about the rooming house. . . ."

She waited, not making it easy for him.

"You mentioned the beds and the meals," Baylee said, "but you said nothing at all about the company."

She held her features straight for a moment, then let a smile curl her lips. "Actually, the company can be quite charming. When properly inspired, of course."

And Baylee smiled back at her, thinking of the future instead of the past for the first time in a long, long time. It was a good feeling.

Explore the

From the distant past of the Arcane Age® . . .

The Netheril Trilogy
Sword Play
Dangerous Games
Mortal Consequences

The barbarian Sunbright's destiny becomes entwined with the decadent archwizards of the Empire of Netheril and the course of the history of Faerûn is changed forever!
by Clayton Emery
Available now!

. . . to the climax of the FORGOTTEN REALM'S longest running series . . .

The Harpers #16
Thornhold

An order of paladins is about to fall at the hands of the Zhentarim, and the young Harper agent sent by Khelben to stop it comes face-to-face with her own past. A birthright that may mean the end of the Harpers!
by Elaine Cunningham
Available August 1998!

. . . and the continued exploration of the . . .

Lost Empires Book Two
Faces of Deception

Atreus, a young nobleman, driven from his home, is hidden with a disfiguring spell that has kept him alive, but made his face a twisted mockery of human. Only in the faraway realms of the Utter East can Atreus find the secret to reversing the spell. But what more will he find there?
by Troy Denning
Available November 1998!